THE MANCHESTER WHEELERS

A NORTHERN QUADROPHENIA

Dave

For authenticity, certain places and names are mentioned and included to accurately give the story the feeling and character of the Soul Mod subculture of Manchester in the mid to late nineteen sixties. However any resemblance to persons living or dead are coincidental, and the circumstances and events described within this novel are entirely fictionalised.

Lyrics quoted are acknowledged as:

©   What Is Soul – Ben E. King - ATCO Records

©   Bits And Pieces - Dave Clark - Decca Record

©   Boogie Chillun' - John Lee Hooker - Chess Records

©   The Birds and The Bees - Jewel Akens - London Recordings

©   I Like It Like That - Smokey Robinson - Tamla Motown Records

©   Never Could You Be – Curtis Mayfield - ABC Paramount Records

Manning Joke © Saint Bernard of Manchester Humour

© Any inaccuracies or copyright notifications will be acknowledged and corrected in future editions.

Copyright © 2009 DAVE
Revised FIRST EDITION
All rights reserved.

All rights reserved. Permission is granted to copy or reprint portions for any non-commercial use, and for reviews etc; limited to reasonable quotations. Quotes and portions may not be posted online without acknowledging the source.

Order Copies from:
SOULPUBLICATIONS Website: http://www.soulpublications.co.uk/

Cover design and book layout: Sarah Butterworth

* * *

LONDON
AMERICAN RECORDINGS

MADE IN ENGLAND
THE DECCA RECORD CO LTD

45 R.P.M

℗ 1965

Recorded by
CHARGER,
Hollywood
Cross M. Ltd.

HL
9953

THE "IN" CROWD
(Page)

DOBIE GRAY

It's deep within us, it doesn't show,
A soul is somethin' that comes from deep inside,
But a soul is a somethin' that you can't hide.

'What Is Soul' – Ben E. King

CONTENTS

CHAPTER ONE
Meeting at the Wimpy — 1

CHAPTER TWO
DeWalt in The Wheel — 31

CHAPTER THREE
That Sunday Morning Feeling — 47

CHAPTER FOUR
The First Time I Met the Blues — 59

CHAPTER FIVE
The Manchester Mods — 69

CHAPTER SIX
The Boneyard and Rubber Souled — 81

CHAPTER SEVEN
Meeting in the Jiggy — 91

CHAPTER EIGHT
Going to a Go Go — 99

CHAPTER NINE
Otis Plays and Plays — 109

CHAPTER TEN
The Blue Note and Stax — 115

CHAPTER ELEVEN
Torquay: Hi Ho Silver Lining — 129

CHAPTER TWELVE
On The Buses and a Little Spastic Girl — 143

CHAPTER THIRTEEN
Night Train, Night Train ... 149

CHAPTER FOURTEEN
The Lost Stash ... 183

CHAPTER FIFTEEN
Another Monday ... 191

CHAPTER SIXTEEN
Blackpool ... 207

CHAPTER SEVENTEEN
Tales from the Wheelers ... 215

CHAPTER EIGHTEEN
English Bands at the Club ... 239

CHAPTER NINETEEN
Sid Nicks the Records ... 245

CHAPTER TWENTY
Last Night ... 249

CHAPTER TWENTY ONE
A Time to Love, A Time to Cry ... 255

CHAPTER TWENTY TWO
Last Fight at the Blue Note ... 275

Author's Notes ... 291

THE

MANCHESTER

WHEELERS

Once upon a time, in Manchester…

THE TWISTED WHEEL CLUB
6 WHITWORTH STREET, MANCHESTER 1

Late Night Rhythm & Blues
SATURDAY, 14th OCTOBER, 1967

Junior Walker & THE ALL STARS
From 11 p.m.

MEMBERS ONLY 25/-   MEMBERSHIP CARDS MUST BE PRODUCED WITH THIS TICKET

CHAPTER ONE

Meeting at the Wimpy

Saturday night in Manchester, 1967: the Soul Mods needed to take their Amphetamines – the 'Gear'– and gather at the Wimpy bar before going to the Twisted Wheel All-nighter. Pill pushers needed to have their supplies ready. The story is narrated by Dave. There were numerous Daves who were Soul Mods in the city;

'You ain't been nowhere till you've been in with the In Crowd' - Dobie Gray

Manchester's buildings were black, everywhere you looked, all the buildings on every street - black. When it rained, it would come tippling down. Consequently the rain provided an additional tone and turned the buildings into a mixture of wet-look blacks and greys of all shades. If you looked closely, a dirty black mist floated on the water outlined with an inner greyness, a wet sliding paisley pattern with disgorged black sooty edges moving like amoeba riding on the water's surface and sliding down the walls. Drizzling rain collected, then poured out of high roof gutters and down the black bricks, making the walls shine; rivers that flowed vertically down, eventually to sharply change direction and pour across the street. Wide, flat, single-dimension rivers that rushed over the blackened grey pavements, running around white chewing gum islands and onwards into the black tarmac road, where the rain turned into rivulets, racing off to find a tumbling gutter of rushing dirty water with floating dog ends, all gushing into a swollen grid.

I doubted anyone noticed these things because it was simply the way things were. Things we see often fade into our unconscious; being so obvious they get downgraded to an almost

The Manchester Wheelers

invisible background to our daily lives. I was noticing these things, and acutely so, because I had slipped into a different mode of consciousness brought about by consumption of a handful of pills. They adjusted my perception; I was becoming more awake than wide-awake. It was one of the first noticeable signs of their effect.

Manchester was black due to the years of the industrial revolution; decade upon decade of soot had coated all the bricks and stonework. As a result the walls of the buildings, if you bothered to look, were black sooty velvet when dry and a wet-look black leather effect in the rain. Hundreds of mill chimneys joined thousands upon thousands of rooftop chimneys from row upon row of terraced houses all belching out black, white and grey smoke.

The opening titles of the TV Soap Opera from Manchester had got it right: 'Coronation Street'. It was a black and white film set. Films were made about the North, some set in Manchester. Films like 'Billy Liar', where Julie Christie looked like she was walking across Piccadilly Gardens, but it was actually Bradford. 'A Taste of Honey' with Rita Tushingham and Dora Bryan on the bus passing blackened statues in Albert Square, St Ann's Square and Piccadilly. Later there was 'Charlie Bubbles', although this was in colour; it showed the demolition of row after row of the old Manchester terraced housing, with swinging balls of steel hung from cranes crashing into the walls, the entire scene becoming enveloped in dust.

A common sight was half the street in ruins, while the other half was perfectly intact and being cared for; painted red, brick by brick; here and there a red Geranium in a pot and all the steps yellow donkey-stoned. Mums running, hanging the washing out to dry after the dust had cleared, from around the last demolished house opposite: clearing and emerging like a ghostly apparition from the smog generated by the collapsed house it now became possible to see lady's hanging out their washing on the once obscured back street. Manchester Mums with their hair in rollers inside a turban scarf – they would wear their patterned pinafore overalls, and keep up their standards in the midst of the intermittent grey dust storms set off by demolition and dampened down by the rain showers Manchester was famous for.

The Manchester Wheelers

It seemed depressing; it looked like it was 'Grim Up North', but it was far from that. The soul of the city was the underground Mod Soul scene, ironically with its black American music. Soul was black – well, mainly black; our city was black, and so was the music that the clubs blared out in dark underground cellars. However, the music and 'our' scene gave us a set of colourful, bright and enthusiastic reasons for Mod Mancunians to get excited about their city.

After riding down town and parking my scooter outside the Wimpy Bar near Piccadilly, I walked through the drizzling rain just to stretch my legs. And as I walked, I remembered other days and times past.

Tuesday and Thursday nights we would go training and racing on the Fallowfield Cycling track; it was a velodrome, known to us as the Toast Rack due to the shape of the roof profile on an adjacent building. Reg Harris was still racing, but that night he just gave the prizes out. I was no prize-winner – I'd crashed out, falling through the bunch on the highest part of the track.

A few Blueys sorted out the pain and after the prize ceremony we planned to go dancing at the Twisted Wheel. Our cycling club, the Prestwich Olympic, was joined by our mates from the Manchester Domino, and others from the Manchester Wheelers. In the end about fifty of us went down to the club in Brazennose Street just off Albert Square where the majestic Town Hall towered above us in all its blackened Gothic glory.

We chained all our bikes together outside the double white doors and went dancing in the club. This was the Twisted Wheel, it was 1963, and it was known as a Beat club. We streamed downstairs to dance in our cotton racing vest tops and cut-off padded gloves. Our frayed-end bell-bottom denim jeans had been recently released from our metal cycling clips, and we were clinking about in our cycling shoes with the metal pedal grips underneath. If you could have heard the metal plates under our shoes tapping the concrete floor it would have been like a tap dance, but no one could; the speakers had drowned it out with

Howlin' Wolf's 'Smokestack Lightning'. That had been when the Wheel was in its early music mixture stage of Beat, Pop, Folk music, Jazz and Blues, especially Blues, with Alexis Korner soon to become the resident band.

That was only a few years before at the 'old Wheel', but since then everything had changed. Cycling had faded as a core activity on my agenda of things I was really driven to do, replaced with the fervent All-nighter scene that had developed rapidly. The drugs would fit with cycling, but there wasn't much time left to train at the level of commitment it required, and the 'new Wheel' scene at Whitworth Street was, incredibly, perhaps even better than that fantastic last year of 1965, at Brazennose Street – well, almost.

Although the Mod scene probably finished in London by the middle of 1964, it continued in Manchester, and in '66 fashions had stabilised on smart suits with everything. The American Army Parkas we wore when riding scooters only hid this fact. Smart was the dress code, and the way you did the smallest of things – like how your handkerchief was folded and placed in your suit jacket top pocket. The fact that you only fastened the top button of your Mohair threads denoted who you were, but only to those that knew the code. To the rest you became invisible – but *smart* invisible.

I looked around outside the Wimpy to see who was around, who was going, as the memory of those old cycling days faded. The rain was washing my scooter; it glinted with the reflection of passing bus headlights, traffic lights and the multicoloured wet-look neon signs mirrored from the surrounding buildings. The mirrors on my scooter reflected back the same multicoloured signs inside the raindrops as they hit, then they drizzled down and streaked the side panels with wet coloured streamers of rainwater. The chrome side panels held off most of the rain, almost pushing it away as if by some anti-magnetic force. I let such thoughts fade – it was just the Brasso polish I had 'Duraglited' onto them before coming down here from Blackley.

Today was Saturday 14th of October, 1967. It was a special event tonight at the All-nighter, the biggest night there since the 'Original' Drifters had appeared at the end of April. The year had begun in a fantastic way for Manchester Soul Mods, with The Spellbinders on at our favourite All-nighter club, soon followed by Otis, and the Stax Tour at the Palace Theatre on Oxford Road. To celebrate the appearance tonight of De Walt (better known as Junior Walker), lots of us had promised to dig out our scooters for the occasion. By the end of 1966 scooters and the Mod scene had faded out in London, but not so much in Manchester where we had our own private Soul thing going.

The growling, unmistakable sound of high powered scooters ended in a slowing down, *put-put-put-put* noise as two immaculate GT 200s pulled up alongside my 250cc Durkopf. The guys got off, brushing water from their full-length leather overcoats. One leather was green, the other guy's was dark purple, and double breasted. Only one Mod in Manchester had a purple coat like that; Sid from Langley. Sid was a tough guy. He was a scaffolder and bricklayer by day, a pill pusher by night.

No one was inside the Wimpy; at least none of our lot. Others were irrelevant. We knew who we were and we could recognise each other at a glance. Mods had a certain look. If you were one, you knew it but you never let on. You never claimed to be a Mod. To say you were a Mod would immediately bring ridicule, and quick as you might have said it you'd be 'out'. Such a status was earned and never openly claimed.

We rarely went inside the Wimpy; if we did it was for a coffee or a coke. No one in their right mind would have a hamburger before an All-nighter at the Wheel, unless you wanted to throw up on the dance floor. Some people threw up anyway, but as a result of all the dancing mixing their stomach bile with a concoction of pills and stomach acid. Bennys, Green and Clears, Black Bombers, Blueys and Dexys, and the saliva from constantly chewing Wrigley's gum, all shaken and stirred by continuous dancing; it was a mix that could easily make you sick enough to vomit.

I was already partly 'blocked' or 'coming up'; that was the descriptive phrase everyone used. Shivers like energy waves were going all through my body, especially up and down my spine. I wanted to move, to dance, to talk. Dancing or talking incessantly was what these pills did to you, and you could do it all night. You became 'blocked' after taking your 'gear', and after around twenty minutes had passed by, all of a sudden your perception changed; it was like coming up in a lift, but the lift was in your head. Adrenalin energy would pulse out from your stomach, all body aches and pains would just vanish. You felt a compulsion to move about, to dance, to speak. You couldn't keep still, often moving in jerks, uncontrollable repetitive movements - things did speed up! Thoughts were rapid, speech too – and Speed appeared to affect the blokes more than the girls, with certain almost unmentionable side effects.

"Hiyyyaaa Dave, have you seen Angelo?" said Sid, looking sternly into my eyes as he unbuttoned his full-length leather, revealing his grey shiny Mohair suit below. "Are you going?"

"Definitely," I answered, "it's Junior Walker!"

"Get me a hot chocolate," shouted Terry as he struggled to pull back his white GT 200 onto its stand. Terry was Sid's sidekick; he was always in his shadow.

"Wimp," breathed Sid under his breath, and he wasn't referring to the hamburger bar. Then Sid gave Terry's scooter a push from the front to get it on its stand.

Sid and I entered the Wimpy, with steam rising from our coats; mine was a parka with my grandma's fox stole sewn across the shoulders. Long dead glass eyes stared out from my right shoulder.

We sat down and waited for the waitress; Terry then joined us. "Have you seen Angelo?" he said frantically as he sat down. "He's got a load of our gear, and we need it for tonight."

"Calm down," said Sid, "he's probably hiding it in a stash somewhere. He will be along, soon." He turned, and mumbled into my ear: "He better be..."

I could see Terry was exhibiting the far away paranoid look that some members of our fraternity exhibited; it was due to being too many days in a row on amphetamines. His lips were sore, very red and with a black outline highlighting them, tracing a sharp dark silhouette all around them, and his eyes were large like a 'bush baby's' staring vacantly, unfocussed, around the room as he spoke:

"The bastard better had, he was at the match today. Georgie was fantastic with three goals, and that shitty Man City were total crap; Francis Lee, Colin Bell - what a set of twats! and Summerbee! *Summerbee, Summerbeeeee; who the fucking hell is he?*" he sang, churning out the current anti-City theme that everyone sang in the Stretford End.

"Did you go, Dave?" Sid asked me.

"Yeah," I said, "fuckin' brilliant! We should win the league again this year."

"Fantastic. Fan-bloody-tastic! You know Best is great, the greatest, but he needs Denis. Without Denis the entire team would be shit. If he doesn't score, he's the one who passes it to George for him to hit the back of the net." Sid made this statement glassy eyed, adoringly.

We all sat silently then, reviewing the match; our eyes were open with blank stares as the rain ran down the outside of the windows. As we stared through them, we were seeing the footie earlier that day at Old Trafford superimposed on them, mentally lost in the visions of the game. We were brought back to the present moment with another raging outburst from Terry.

"Where the fuck is that twatting bastard with our gear?" he said, just as the waitress arrived at our table. She up picked the round imitation-tomato plastic ketchup 'bottle' and gave it a wipe, ignoring the abrasive swearing.

"Two coffees and one hot chocolate please," we said in a chorus. Terry pretended to spray her with machine gun bullets from an imaginary Elliot Ness-style machine gun and shouted, "*Al Capone's Guns Don't HHHArgue…..*" trying to imitate Prince

Buster. Then he started singing *"Dum Dum Dum Dum Da Da Da Da,"* clicking his fingers, swinging around on his seat.

"The fucker's totally blocked," said Sid.

Terry shouted, "Joke," and proceeded to tell it without pausing: "A Chinese couple get divorced. She goes back to Peking... he goes back to WAN - KING... do you get it?"

Sid ignored Terry's antics, and began to give me an explanation about their missing gear:

"We got 400 Green and Clears from your friend Angelo," he said, putting a menacing tone on the word 'friend', then after slightly stuttering a bit, he carried on. "And we swapped them for cash in the bogs at the back of the Stretford end. He's training to be the shop manager in a pharmacists. It's great gear, and straight out the bottle, so to speak."

After a pause, he frowned. "Funny name that, 'Angelo'. He comes from Middleton, from a long line of Italian Ice-cream makers. There's an Ice cream shop there in the woods, Alkrington Woods. Dave, you know him don't you? Wasn't he one of your cycling mates from years back?"

"Maybe," I said, "Does he wear a green Tonic Mohair with a 23-inch centre vent?" I was purposely forgetting to tell them that I went to school with Angelo.

"That's him," retorted Sid, with a look that I took to mean he wasn't having any of my vague reply.

"So why are you saying he's got your stash?" I asked.

This seemed to upset Sid no end and he answered with an increased stutter: "B-b-b-because.... because, because...fucking because, we gave him most of it back again for safe keeping, to bring it here tonight. So right now at this very moment in time he has our gear and, and, and our cash."

He stuttered again and then went on in a tirade. "That bastard Sergeant, what's his fucking name? ...Oh yeah, fucking Plummer – he's after us, he frisks us on sight these days... so we took what we needed at the match. Then gave him, Angelo, back the rest and, and," – Sid began stuttering once more – "a-a-a-and our fucking cash, for safe keeping! He said he would meet us here half an hour ago, fucking bastarding rain. It took ages to get here and now we're soaked and fucking frozen."

"And late," said Terry, stating the obvious.

"Why did you give him back the money?" I asked.

"Because, Sergeant drugs-'el-supremo'-what's-his-face would have something on us if he pulled us and nabbed us with just too much cash for a Saturday night out." Sid spat out the words in disgust.

"Right," I said, nodding.

"He stops and searches us every time he sees us," Sid said repeating himself angrily.

Back with us after staring vacantly all around the other tables, Terry then changed the subject completely, as is the way of the blocked.

"I'm going to get some skin-tight leather gloves," he said. "You know the type with all them little holes in them, driving gloves they're called." Terry then opened up his hands spreading out the fingers wide. "Look at my hands. You can almost see through my knuckles, they're so fucking white."

"Shut up," Sid growled at Terry, "Just shut the fuck up. You're always rambling on about shit."

"So have you seen the fucker?" Sid asked again, turning to me.

"Who?" I replied.

Sid was getting fierce. His neck was turning red, the blue veins bulging: "FUCKING Angelo, you cunt," he shouted over the table, attempting to put his face straight into mine.

A menacing atmosphere was generated. I rapidly decided on submitting no further methods of diversion.

"No, I only just got here, just before you came," I said.

"Maybe he's in the Shakespeare or the Town Hall or some other fuckin' pub," Terry interjected. "Maybe we need agent Double O Soul, that Spy from the F B I, or Secret fucking agents on the case," he smirked, "or let's send out an SOS…" Terry went rambling on… blocked uptight. "I bet he came on time and now he's gone in the Dive Bar at the other end of the Street." His eyes brightened a bit. "Let's go down there," he said.

"Don't be fucking stupid, that's where all those fucking City bastards beat the shit out of us…. And twice! I'm not going over there tonight," said Sid, turning from me to face Terry, glaring at him, their noses almost touching.

I asked what had happened, and my question seemed to break the air of conflict.

"It was two weeks ago – we'd sold out all our gear in the Shakespeare. Then after, we legged it to the Town Hall Tavern and stayed for a half, some City cunts started on us. So we left and went down the Dive Bar, and the bastards showed up there later! We ended up being dragged out of the place, punched and kicked."

"We got away and ran all the way back through the streets with the bastards trailing us to the Town Hall Tavern. We went past and hid in a doorway - in the doorway of the Old Cona. You remember the Cona Café – first time we saw you and your pal the other Dave? It was in there." Disjointed sentences were the hallmark of Amphetemised speech.

His remark triggered a forgotten memory: I remembered Saturday afternoons drinking cappuccinos listening to Roger Eagle telling us about his latest imports and all of us admitting to liking Bob Dylan's 'Times They are a Changing' as it came on the Juke Box in the Cona Café on Tib Lane.

Sid ended his tale saying, "Thank Christ the bastards went back into the pub so we could get away."

"If the City mob have taken over the Dive Bar then Angelo will be somewhere else; maybe he's in Tommy Ducks," I said.

"Look at my fucking new brogues," said Terry.

And we all did, even the waitress; she had arrived with our drinks.

We all got out some change from our pockets and individually paid her.

"Yeah, they are shitty," I agreed with Sid, and told him to wipe them on the hand towel roller in the bogs. Moments later, off he went.

"He's becoming an arsehole," said Sid. "He's getting blocked up all week, not just weekends, how he keeps going at work, working as a hod carrier is beyond me: the feeble twat doesn't look like he could climb a ladder holding on with both hands, never mind with a hod of bricks. It must be the fucking 'gear' that's fuelling the bastard up there!"

We laughed.

"So you *are* going then?" I drawled with my speech slurring as another shuddering jolt from the pills ran through me.

"Yeah," Sid replied. "I'm buzzin!" He followed on and asked the obvious: "You?"

I replied automatically, initially saying, "Yeah." Then as I fully realised the momentous event ahead I became more animated; "Without a doubt… I only go for the music, and the birds and the dancing and tonight… Junior Walker!"

"The Music that's gooooood," Sid said, gazing into his drink – he was on his way up.

We both were 'coming up' and feeling that feeling.
"And the deals… I love the deals; that helps the income. We're on bastarding piece work, and if that twat falls behind…" He pointed at the toilet door that Terry had just disappeared through, to clean his shoes.

Sid continued after being distracted for a moment with a 'coming up rush' and said "On the bricks we lose out; we're a team… but then there's the supplementary income…"

"Shoplifting!" shouted Terry as he returned.

"No – dealing, you cunt," Sid shouted at Terry. He then continued:

"And there'll be none of that tonight if that twat Angelo doesn't show up." Sid was now shouting and all signs of his previous stammer had disappeared.

The sinister atmosphere was returning. Silence interrupted us, and again we all looked out of the window where outside about twenty or so Mods had materialised. We hadn't noticed them until now due to being engrossed in our conversation.

"So how did you get your stuff for tonight?" I asked them as it was obvious they were under the influence.

"We took a few at the match," replied Sid, "and then we stopped in Cannon Street, just as Monica from Langley was getting off the 121. She gave us enough to get us up."

"For now," interrupted Terry, indicating he was anticipating a fuller recharge sometime soon.

"Angelo - what a fuckin' stupid name," said Sid, bringing the conversation back to where I wished it wasn't.

"Poof name," said Terry.

"Yeah, poof bastard," agreed Sid.

I thought it wise not to mention that I knew Angelo and that he was no 'poof'. His name was Italian, and lots of Italians went to our school. It was due to Angelo that I had become a cycling fan; it was he who told me all the stories about his cycling hero Fausto Coppi. Our school was Roman Catholic, so all the Italians from North Manchester sent their kids there.

We both hero-worshipped Jacques Anquetil the French cyclist, and had haircuts that matched his; cut short all over, very short at the front and longer towards the back, the sides the same - all combed backwards for streamlining on a bike! Later this style was developed longer and longer with a back-combed elevated top; it became very popular, influenced by the Small Faces.

It was a good practice to take your stuff before going into the Wheel, as the plain clothes drug squad sometimes raided the toilets in the club. I usually took my gear on the bus; I didn't even need a drink. I could easily swallow twenty pills without a drink – practice makes perfect.

This time I took the pills on the scooter, opening my mouth and drinking in the rain to wash them down. One of the effects of taking the pills, or the 'Gear' as we affectionately called them, was that they made everyone very, very friendly. Well, they were prescribed as anti-depressants, but they could sometimes do the opposite with certain types, and Terry and Sid's bemoaning of Angelo was exhibiting this type of paranoia. I could see that hanging around with these two could be dangerous, so I swigged at my drink, told them I just saw my girlfriend outside, said 'Tarrah' and hopped it.

* * *

Mod girls all tried to look like Dusty Springfield, or Mary Quant, or Julie Driscoll. Twiggy, Patti Boyd, Rita Tushingham, or even Amanda Barrie. A full set of such almost 'look-a-likes' or 'Dolly Birds' were now gathered outside the Wimpy, sheltering from the rain underneath the concrete overhang. And so was Doreen. I was in love with Doreen – she was a Julie Driscoll type.

Outside the Wimpy a large crowd of people who were all getting together to go down to the All-nighter had formed. The Wimpy was a well known Saturday night gathering place for us to meet up.

As I walked over towards Doreen, a soaking wet Mod said, "Hiya, I'm Pete from Blackpool, have you seen Fred from Stockport? I've got this record for him, it's 'Sixty Minutes Of Your Love' by Homer Banks; Fucking rare, man, on the Minit label."

But before I could respond, Dave Leyton came up and danced around me singing, *"Get on up… Da Da Darrrr Da Dat Da… Hey… You over there… Get on up now… We're gonna dance, dance, dance, and boogaloo… AND BOOGALOO…!"*

Spinning round on the last note of the song by the Esquires, he ended up with his face right next to mine, his wide-eyed dilated pupils fixed on me.

"Hiya," he said his face all flushed red and beaming, holding his fixed stare through his glasses right into my eyes.

"And that reminds me," he said, "Please – I'm saying it nicely – have you got my record that you nicked on Thursday in the Blue Note?"

"What?" I said, looking towards Doreen, who was talking with two guys I hadn't seen before.

"You know what," Said Dave 'L'.

Dave 'L' or 'DL' was his nickname. There were just too many Daves around, so he'd acquired a nickname to distinguish him from other less, notable Daves. In fact his full nickname was Dave 'Rubber Legs' Leyton. He was indeed an accomplished dancer and had just demonstrated his talent out here in the street.

"Yes, *my* 'Boogaloo Party' by the Flamingos," he said, emphasising the 'my' as he went on: "It's mine, it's rare, it's on the Philips Fontana label, the Blue Label, number BF 1786. It's got my DL sticker on it inside a little white circle. It's in a white picture sleeve with Flamingos on the front and you or your pal Angelo nicked it." His delivery was faultless and pedantically accurate.

It had been nicked but it wasn't me – it was Angelo who'd done the evil deed. DL had come into the Blue Note during the week and raved about his latest find, 'The Boogaloo Party'. He'd pulled it out of his airline bag to show it, when someone grabbed it for a laugh and passed it overhead to the next person. Soon it had gone from hand to hand overhead, over the tables, then traversing the dance floor a couple of times with everyone laughing. It was all light hearted until it was snatched by Angelo, where it disappeared down the front of his trousers. Angelo was an accomplished record shoplifter. DL must have blinked as Angelo stuffed the 45 away at lighting speed, leaving him bemused and hopeful of its return, which had never happened.

Just then I was rescued by someone who had met DL at last Saturday's All-nighter and couldn't remember Dave's name. He addressed DL and said, "Aren't you Dave… thingy, err…?"

I laughed and said, "Its Dave 'L' or 'DL' to you."

I was glad to change the track of DL's conversation with me.

"L, what is that for?" said the bloke.

"Legs, rubber legs. Dave Legs; Rubber Legs Leyton," I spurted out, laughing.

I was struggling to change DL's intention to corner me about the 'Boogaloo Party', so I adopted a somewhat stupefied change of course to the conversation.

"Anyway did you know that Mr what's his name... another 'L'... what's his fucking name... you know... oh fuck, what's his name? Something like... 'L' you know him, he did pictures, paintings: matchstick men and women... outside mills, and chimneys..." I chuntered on hoping to divert DL's attention.

"And cats and fucking dogs," said DL. He was sharp, and homing in on my nonsense.

"So what?" he said, as I saw that he had put the name to my blocked-up brain's search for it.

I got the name just as he did. I said with a puzzled frown, "Oh yeah... Lowry."

"Well, what about the fucker?" chorused the wet Mod from Blackpool and DL.

"Well, he used to be my grandmother's Rent Collector, Mr Lowry. He does pictures of Manchester, some of them in the fucking rain!" I told them. I was hoping that my changing the subject would throw him off the scent of his 'Boogaloo Party'.

Often the pills we took would make you struggle for a word or a name. Many times you heard people trying to remember something or other, often giving up and the conversation heading off at a complete tangent.

"So what's that got to do with *my* 'Boogaloo Party'?" DL shouted as we began to wander together up and down and around the gathering crowd.

"Nothing, nothing, nothing at all," I said. I was going to tell him that my grandmother had been offered one of Lowry's drawings and that she had given it back to the man with advice about making his figures look a bit more realistic, and that he should try harder. However just as soon as this memory popped into my head, I dismissed it. Instead I clicked the fingers on both hands and continued:

"It's Junior Walker. I hope he does 'Cleo's Mood', it's my most favourite track of his, it's great, it's moody... it's fucking moody and fucking great. Imagine that thundering out live in the Wheel!"

At this break in the conversation the Mod from Blackpool waved around his Homer Banks single asking if anyone had seen Fred, but he got no answer. At the same time, the gathering realised it was 11:30 and like a flock of spooked starlings without any one starting it off, all at once everyone moved off together. The rain had eased up and those at the front of the troupe began to sing, *"Let's go, Let's go..."*

At the front it was 'Lets Go (Pony)' by the Routers that they were chanting, whilst us at the back turned it around into 'Lets Go Baby Where The action Is' (the 'B' side of Barefootin' by Robert Parker). We all took off through Piccadilly, down London Road, past the army and Navy and then Mazell's second hand record shop, past the Indian restaurant down the hill to the Wheel; The New Wheel on Whitworth street. We called it the New Wheel in deference to the one before, the first Wheel that was on the corner of an alley with Brazennose Street, just off Albert Square.

We began to skip and dance, we were all: 'Dancing in the Street'. Our 'gang' used to do this often, clicking fingers, jumping up and swinging around lampposts, just like the Jets and the Sharks in West Side Story; except we were Manchester Soul Mods – cooler, smarter, hipper, switched on to black music and 'blocked up'!

One of the Impressions LP covers showed three very smartly dressed guys, in silver shining lightweight Tonic Mohair suits. This was certainly an influence upon the Northern Mod scene. Shiny Tonic Mohair suits with 13", then 15", and then 17" side vents. Then came centre vents, and even, in one period, centre pleats. '*Who is the coolest guy…..*' sang Charlie Rich….. It was Mohair Sam and we wore the Tonic Mohair: we were the Kings, we were the Cool Jerks, we were the Soul addicted Mods.

Top pockets had handkerchiefs, and only silk ones made the grade. Ticket pockets were an essential feature of our suits. Searches for military and paisley patterned ties took hours, but they had to be found otherwise you could be 'out'. Silk ties, even flat bottom knitted ties, silk handkerchiefs, tight fitting leather driving gloves had to be obtained, even if it meant shoplifting them; we had to be in with the 'in' crowd.

Patent leather dance shoes: flat ones for blokes, and red four-inch high heels for girls. Long leather coats were always 'in' probably because of the cost. Winter in the North dictated that long warm overcoats were needed, and so a new fashion started for Crombies, and for hats and long, long, university scarves epitomised by Rod the Mod, the Scottish singer in the Steam Packet.

DL danced around me; had he been black he would have been a dead ringer for David Ruffin of the Temptations, and they both wore exactly the same specs. This was no accident on DL's part, as he idolised the Temptations. He even said he could never forgive Otis for doing a version of 'My Girl'.

I managed to get away from him, but he was approaching once again. 'Bollocks,' I thought as he went on and on about his missing record, but then as his fifteen or so Green and Clears fully kicked in, his mind went onto a different track.

"I got 'Secret agents', an import on Mirwood 5513 by the Olympics, it's great, it's fantastic; it's just fucking brilliant." He started to sing it – "*Honey West and old I Spy are working together for the FBI… But I'm missing my 'Boogaloo Party'.*" And all sung by him to the exact rhythm of 'Secret Agents'. You couldn't help but smile at him.

DL was one of those guys who knew every record, its catalogue number, the 'B' side, the producer, the USA originating record label, etc. He would buy or shoplift Tamla Motown records and their previous Stateside label releases to get them all in numeric and release date order, searching for them all over the place. His intention was to have them all and to store them sequential. He was always asking for early Oriel, Fontana and Stateside and Motown singles, often by number, not by artist or record title. He learned to do this as it helped when requesting 45's in record shops, and it impressed the proprietors. Sometimes they thought he was the company Sales Rep! Well, he did dress far smarter than they did. He was a walking card index system, invaluable as a resource to DJs who were seeking to find rare tracks.

A guy from Warrington joined us and immediately burst out with comments from his last visit to the Wheel. "Did you see Graham Bond last week, the other week or whenever it was? My fuckin' memory is packing up man, I'm sure he did a few Ike and Tina Turner songs? Or was it the DJ that played 'A Fool In Love', and a great version of that Darrel Banks track 'Somebody Somewhere Needs You', dead good songs they are."

On hearing this DL began singing, '*He's such a good man but he treats you like a fool...*' The lyrics echoed inside my head as I watched the same two blokes from outside the Wimpy walking along in front with Doreen.

The lyrics seemed to fit my changing mood and I sang them out with venom in a duet with DL: '*Fool in love... When he treats you like a fool when he's such a good man...*' The track was from the Ike and Tina Turner Review. People passing by on the pavement would shake their heads and mutter "Nutters", as they pulled up their coat collars and scurried past.

DL picked up on my jealous mood, realising I was singing whilst watching Doreen in front. Probably motivated by his frustration with my avoidance about his missing 45, he started sticking the knife in, singing: "*You're her puppet, you're her puppet.*" He was singing contrary words to the song by James and Bobby Purify, and acting out being a puppet with arms outstretched, wobbling along like Pinocchio.

We could remember most of the lyrics to our favourite Soul songs; they were drummed into us on a weekly basis. Music would replay over and over continuously inside your mind when you were blocked. Sometimes the entire repertoire of an All-nighter would play back in the hours of the following days inside your head. It wasn't too bad during the day, but would almost drive you crazy at night when attempting to get some sleep.

Sometimes I would think how strange it was that I had no power to stop this continuous replay. Many times I would command it to stop, but after several intense efforts it just moved on to the next track, like a Dansette record player on auto. When the songs eventually died out I just lay there trying to sleep, every noise irritating beyond belief, every twitch generating a reciprocal itch at some other body location, like acupuncture gone mad. Then just as warm cosy sleep arrived, the alarm would ring for work.

Doreen stopped in front, turned around and waiting for me to catch up. The two guys carried on. She began dancing... skipping... *"I'll always love you... Baby... I'll always love you..."* She was singing the track by the Detroit Spinners... and she was spinning around me, then she just danced away. She left a strange after-image inside my mind's eye of her Mary Quant hair gliding past in slow motion. This after-image was left together with a dim brooding feeling – Would she? Always? Who are those two blokes? Love sickness had got a hold on me!

We joined the back of the queue; it was strung out around the block, around the White Heart pub and up London Road. People tended to be in groups – they came from all over Manchester and the surrounding towns, and many from far off exotic places like Huddersfield. In fact they came from all over the UK; there were groups from Connah's Quay North Wales, from Scotland, even London.

I noticed Doreen had been 'let in' the queue further up the line by those same two blokes. Anger was growing.

The people in front of us were from Oldham, and those in front of them were from Sheffield. They shouted back to us that they went to the Mojo Club. DL told them to "fuck off" and said to them that "it must be crap or else you'd be there" and that "this was the Wheel the one and only." We both said this in a jovial friendly manner; everyone was really everyone's friend at an All-nighter. However, joking aside, we were sort of serious about the remark. To us, only the Wheel was worthwhile. The Wheel was the greatest, and the only other place that was great for music, but not for All-nighters, was the Blue Note. It was the music that mattered to us the most.

A group joined behind us from Blackpool; they were singing, all of them singing, and really soulfully: *'People Get Ready..... for the train to Jordan.'* They were clicking fingers, chewing gum, (we called it 'Spoggy') twirling around, just dancing and blocked up in the queue, singing that great Impressions' song. As we got closer we could hear the dull thumping sound from below, inside the club.... *'Neighbour, neighbour... Don't worry how I treat my wife...'* sung by Jimmy Hughes. Then it changed to 'Determination' by the Contours. Louder, louder and LOUDER as we got nearer. Looking at the Fire Station across the street, someone was shouting *'Fire, Fire'*, like *'Liar, Liar, Town crier...'* putting their own lyrics to the Castaways' tune.

With excitement mounting we reached the door. The Adabi Brothers, the owners of the Wheel were both at the door, looking at our round Wheel membership cards and taking our twenty five shilling pre-paid tickets; we often came down mid-week to get them. We passed the door anticipating going down the steps, down into the Wheel. We had one hand holding the other elbow moving our arms from side to side, the thumb in our mouths, playing a dummy Saxophone, imitating Junior Walker. Daft we were. Blocked we were. Pill Heads we were, exactly as Roger Eagle the original Wheel DJ described us.

Ivor on the door rolled his eyes at us impatiently as we constantly and agitatedly moved from leg to leg sideways, swinging our shoulders dancing on the spot, waiting for his new-style ticket scrutiny. Anyway, these were real tickets not like the fakes we had used for the Drifters several months or so ago. It was our mate Roland who did the printing of the fakes. He did it to get some extra funds, but did some free extras for us too. Everyone helped each other out, we were all the best of pals. Manchester Soul Mods stuck together.

Through the sound system Jimmy Smith was mumbling away trying to get his 'Mojo Working' as I was putting my cloakroom ticket in my top pocket behind my showy pink silk handkerchief. After queuing in the cloakroom line inside the club for around half an hour, it was then that I remembered with shock and shouted out loud:

"Shit, my Scooter! I left it outside the fucking Wimpy!"

Outside Again

They gave me a pass out on the door, an ink marker stamped on the wrist from a rubber pad. I explained that I left my scooter in an insecure place. "It could get nicked," I told Ivor at the door. I'd also got my Parka back from the cloakroom, but then I realised outside that I didn't need it as the rain had eased off. I raced up London Road back to the Wimpy, passing lots of the 'crowd' heading for the Wheel.

It was still there. Well I didn't really believe anyone would nick it, it was a wreck. It was there alright, and so too were Terry and Sid.

Amazingly, my 'BOAC airline' bag was also there, where I'd left it on the central running board of the scooter over the foot pedal controls. It contained my change of clothing for the morning: jeans, shoes, toothpaste, towel, soap, and my 'aqua de Selva' after-shave. 'How stupid, how fucking stupid, how could I have such a stupid lapse of memory?' I chastised myself inwardly; but also told myself no one would have nicked my scooter. It was a beat up crap Kraut crate.

Terry was proudly cruising his scooter along the pavement to the annoyance of several old ladies trying to walk by. Then he came to an almost dead stop standing up with feet on the running boards and revving the throttle but sliding the clutch just to make a loud noise. The front wheel was beginning to jerk forwards, the back wheel was hopping jerkily forwards bit by bit and white smoke was pouring from his back tyre; his scooter was like a mad mechanical kangaroo. Sid stood there watching, repeatedly punching one fisted hand into the other.

I got on my German machine, forgetting to wipe off the rain. "Bollocks," I said to myself. My arse was soaked. Shit – that meant the razor sharp creases I had soap ironed into my strides had just collapsed, as well.

Then roaring along and rounding the corner came about twelve scooters, all with Parka-hooded riders. It was the Bolton mob with their 'leader' Molly. He had this name in a transfer stuck on both sides of his front wheel mudguard, and there was Angelo with them.

"Thank fuck," said Sid and shouted to Terry: "Oi, Terry! Stop pissing about and get our gear off that twat."

Sid's real underlying concern was probably the risk that Angelo could have been rolled. Not by any of the Mod types – we all had a code of honour and never nicked each other's gear or cash, just maybe the odd record. Sid knew for certain that Angelo would never really cheat on a deal. It was the Jamaicans, and especially the half-castes, that would target one of us for rolling like that.

The group of scooters pulled up alongside mine outside the Wimpy, further embarrassing me. They all had bright shining chromed machines with loads of mirrors, whilst mine was a poor German imitation, more like a red painted motorbike.

Angelo gave Terry the stuff in a large plastic container, and their wad of pound notes in a roll up with a rubber band around, pulled from his Parka pocket. He had nicked the plastic container from his mum's Tupperware collection.

He nodded in my direction. He was a school friend of mine and was now a trainee chemist shop manager at a Boots branch in Salford. I knew he only robbed his employers for correct reasons: to pay off his scooter, and to buy himself respect and esteem from the ranks of cooler risk-takers with more bottle, the ones who would sell the stuff outside the Wimpy, or overpriced inside the bogs in the Wheel. He only charged us, his mates, half price.

Many times he had to work overtime without pay when the pharmacists were off. He had to do the stocktaking! It was a sort of joke. It would be on a Saturday and Sunday afternoon, usually when United had a home game, which pained him – so he made up for it with his joke. He would say, "It's only stocktaking, it's just a little bit of shoplifting."
"Fuck 'em. Fuck Boots the chemists." It was becoming his catch phrase. His other statement was "Do they pay us enough? Do they 'eckers like!" as he'd stuff his pockets with hundreds of Amphetamines and Benzedrine's, Black Bombers and the like, he'd chant his mantra: "Stuff them! Fuck 'em, fuck Boots the fucking chemists!" He always did the deed before closing up the shop, locking it up securely – "So no other bastard can steal from us!" It was yet another of his repetitive statements.

He was my source of supply. We had endured school together. It was a bonding process that overcame the Catholic indoctrination we had thrust on us there. He was paying off 'on the drip' for his Cento Italian scooter and had already planned to buy a GT 200 with the money he got for nicking pills from his employers. We took off side by side on our machines, at first with our feet gymnastically outstretched in front and below each side of the handlebars, then moving to a standing position as we did a Wimpy fly past. Soul Mods had to show a certain stylish mode of riding.

I asked him why he was selling pills to Sid; it was dangerous to cross him, didn't he think it was somewhat dodgy to be dealing with him? Sid had a reputation for rolling people. But Angelo didn't seem to care. He was blocked to the gills in any case. He said Sid was paying him a little extra for a 'safe supply'. Sid and Terry 'did chemists' the hard way, and Angelo was hatching a plan to fake a break in at Boots; in fact at several branches. He had Sid as his 'fence'. It meant Sid didn't have to actually break in, which was his current method. Angelo thought the risk was worth it, so long as he could figure out how not to be fingered by any other staff. He was planning fake break-ins so that larger amounts of drugs, instead of our regular handfuls, could disappear.

Angelo was in a buoyant mood and sang out: "*I've got a secret plan... Break-ins could be happening soon at Boots, Just say I'm 'Clare Voyent'... Like that woman on the Golden Mile at Blackpool... I can see the future!*"

We headed down London Road to Piccadilly Station car park. Angelo was shouting to me as we weaved through the traffic; he said his plan was now changed. He was forgetting about buying a GT 200 – he laughed and shouted over; "You get pissed-wet through on the fuckers anyway." He was going to have enough cash from his fake break-in plans for a Mini. Minis were 'in' in London in a big way, and consequently scooters would be 'out' here soon.

He passed a handful of pills to me; more Green and Clears. I downed them in one gulp.

To get extra cash he also had a job as a waiter during the week at The Cabaret Club above the News Theatre Cinema on Oxford Road. It was a late night drinking, gambling and eating joint imitating the Las Vegas Sands Casino where they had Frank Sinatra, Sammy Davis, Dean Martin and Jazz records playing – but Vegas it wasn't. It could never be so cool. For one thing, it had English comedians appearing like Ancoats-born Bernard Manning, and others like Al Showman, Norman Collier and Freddy 'Parrot Face' Davis, and it also had pie and peas on the menu, which everyone called 'meat growlers and mush'.

Piccadilly station had a car park at the side, and it was the safest place to leave your scooter overnight. There was no overnight charge, as the man on the barrier had left long ago and would not be back till early Monday morning. It was here that we met Frank, parking his 'mobster vehicle' - a purple painted Austin

Wolsey with gangster style side running boards.

We called him Frank 'Nitty' after the 'caretaker' for the Al Capone mob we had seen in the TV series 'The Untouchables'. It was one of our favourite programmes. Not so long ago a lot of the 'Wheel Soul Mods' had taken to dressing like gangsters with sideburns, wide lapels on pinstripe suits and very wide trouser bottoms with turn-ups, held up with wide braces. Everyone tried to find a pair of white spats to fit over their Brogue shoes, but only one stylish guy succeeded.

We walked down the dripping, water-flushed steps from the station to the underpass below. Few people knew these back street tunnels called snickett's and ginnel's: secret routes that ran through some parts of Manchester. We did because we were from Manchester, born and bred, and that fact made us walk taller than the out of town Soul Mods. They only turned up at weekends – this was our city seven days a week.

We joined the queue just as Sid, Terry and the Bolton Mob arrived into Whitworth Street, where they parked all along the opposite side of the road, joining some LI 150s already parked there. Others were parading up and down the street outside the club, revving up their machines. They drove along the road back and forth, then onto the pavement, running along the brown ceramic tiled wall of the fire station and ironically the 'cop shop' too! It was always a joke with us that 'Mr Plod and his drug squad' were right there just over the road from the Wheel. Another derogatory name for them was 'Sergeant Plummer and the Woodentops', after the kids' TV programme, meaning they have wooden brains.

Then everyone began revving up even louder and in unison. Above them, the fire brigade had eventually had enough of all the noise. All at once about a dozen of the windows high above opened in concert, and twenty or so buckets of water poured down, obliterating the puny intermittent drizzling raindrops and joining with them into a river, a torrent, a waterfall pouring all over the Soul Mods and their scooters below.

Cries of "Fucking fireman!" and "Piss off, Mr fucking fireman!" came up from the mob of now-soaked Soul Mods below as the windows closed, each with a grinning-faced fireman behind.

On the door entrance to the Wheel I could see Ivor smiling too, he had tried repeatedly to tell everyone to be quiet out there, and was very concerned about complaints.

I showed my pass out to Ivor. He was distracted and obviously pissed off with the noise outside, and I was let in immediately. He remembered my predicament – I told him I got my scooter parked OK now, whilst Frank and Angelo's tickets were scrutinised more than usual. I heard Ivor Adabi moaning to my pals about being on guard for fake tickets as I swiftly walked on.

The Drifters fake tickets had been printed by one of my mates. It was Roland, and I didn't want to get remotely involved, as that was the method I and all of our gang had used to get in for free on that occasion. The Abadi brothers were of course Jewish, and had certain racial characteristics like hiking up the entrance fee to a quid for the Drifters, as they'd expected to get an extra windfall. They did alright on the first appearance back in March, but a large group of us had gone for a 'barny' in Blackpool as it was Easter Weekend. The club-owning brothers guessed an extra large crowd who missed the Drifters first time around would come for their return All-nighter, but they got stung by the fakes, and were consequently on double guard whenever a huge Stateside act was appearing.

I left the entrance behind me with Ivor's words about fake tickets echoing through my thoughts. He was particularly pissed off as the fire brigade had complained recently about the number of people packed into the club. 'Were the rear exit doors adequate enough in case of a fire?' 'Did the fire escape ladder work?' 'Had it been tested?' These were the gormless questions they had posed. He had mentioned some of it to my friends last week, and was repeating it at the entrance now to Angelo.

"Annoying the firemen is going to cause me more trouble – they're already complaining about the fire risk in here," said Ivor.

"Fuck that," said Angelo rapidly, "What the fuck can catch fire down there; the dance floor? The fucking walls? Its all concrete and bricks." I heard Angelo's words floating alongside an Impressions track – 'I Can't Satisfy' – coming up from below.

I knew Ivor was worried. It was the fire brigade, and not the council that had forced the closure of the 'Old Wheel' – there'd been no fire escape there, only one way in and out and, just to make it worse, it was up several flights of stairs. He was paranoid they were out to get him again. But they did have a point, and that's why they had to move from the old Wheel to the new one. He also got it in the neck about people becoming ill due to drugs. He wasn't to blame, but every other week or so someone was taken out of the club to hospital for a stomach pump, and parents often came around looking for their lost daughters. It was hardly ever sons.

The Wheel's reputation for noise and drug taking were making the council look at ways to close it down. The chief constable had waged war on late night drinking in the city. He was a religious man, so god only knows what his thoughts might be about a drug-fuelled den of dancing and inequity like the Wheel! But then, like any outsider, he probably wouldn't notice the underlying drug element because the revellers were all smartly dressed and well mannered. To an outsider it probably all looked like a bunch of normal, very smartly dressed young people enjoying themselves – and without any alcohol on the premises, where's the harm?

At the Drifters All-nighter the place had been fully packed, and blocked up, so to speak, with around a hundred extra people due to Roland's forgeries. The place was chocked. It was more difficult to move around than normal. If you went anywhere – the toilets, or the stage room, or the café upstairs – you got stuck and maybe didn't get back to your original point for half an hour due to the extra-tight crush.

Roland was a printer, but still an apprentice. He'd studied a real Drifters ticket. He had in fact bought a legitimate one. It was printed on yellow antique gold card. It was a simple matter for him to requisition some similar card from the stores at his print-works and set about duplicating the printing. It resulted in tickets that were slightly better printed than the originals. We joked that he should have asked for a future contract with the Adabi's, and give them a lower cost, they were Jewish after all!

The reason he did it was due to a crash with his scooter at the lights on Ancoats Street. He'd crashed into another Mod and somehow ripped his suit in the process. It turned out to be Molly, the leader of the Bolton pack, one of the smartest Mod guys around, and with a pack of mates to back up any threats he made. Normally he was a real OK bloke, but having his new suit ripped by catching it on Roland's brake lever made him angry. He'd threatened Roland, who promised to pay him enough for a new suit – and a two-ounce Tonic Mohair cost around twenty eight quid!

So that's why he forged the tickets. Funny thing was that when Roland gave him the money, he sold him a Drifters ticket too at half price. Consequently they became great mates. He also made quite a packet from the printing, especially as their face value was a pound. But in spite of all our pleading, he never risked it for a second time.

* * *

The Manchester Wheelers

CHAPTER TWO

DeWalt in the Wheel

"Tonight we should dance all the time and not talk all night, like last fuckin' week. We spent all night on the fire escape rabbiting on about everything under the sun and missed Ben E. King."

- Overheard conversation at the Wheel.

Back Inside

The first thing I noticed was the heat. It hit me like walking into a wall. It wasn't unpleasant even though it was body heat generated from the dancers and the packed crowd; they were all scrupulously washed, clean, smartly dressed. The blokes full of deodorants and aftershave, and the girls perfectly perfumed. Everyone either chewed Wrigley's gum or ate several packets of Polo Mints. Everyone's breath was sanitised, along with their deodorised bodies. This heat was dynamic, energised and it generated an atmosphere of togetherness as you became engulfed within it.

Licking my lips feverishly, I rubbed eyes that were becoming acutely alive and awake, due to the extra Green and Clears Angelo had given me as a top up. I was again into the unmistakable signs: I was coming up again, higher and higher. It was a good description: 'coming up'. Something from somewhere deep inside started to switch on your levels of awareness and there was a distinct feeling of coming upwards, of rising and awakening, of really 'being there' right behind your eyes. Then waves of golden shivers flowed outwards from the stomach region; adrenalin. These shivers rippled up from the bottom of the spine, moving into the back of the head, then changing direction and flowing in waves across the head to the back of the eyes.

Coming up was an accurate term. Another was blocked. People were blasted, or blocked up; blocked out of their heads. It meant you'd taken a load of gear and had come up to the next state: totally blocked. The very next level after this meant that you were 'out of it' and your memory of anything later on would be wiped out. That's why many All-nighter goers could hardly remember who had been the live act just the week before. It all slid into a huge memory blob without any sequential remembrance of events or time.

Right then there were golden shivers rippling up my spine, waves flowing inside my back. I couldn't keep still, wanted to dance... had to move... couldn't be still... twitching about... tense and then loose... hopping from left to right leg. Jerking about. I was packed with energy.

I had downed a load of Green & Clears by this time; around 25 with Angelo's top up, and these were best because of the slow time-release mini balls inside the capsules. As their name suggested, one side of the capsule was green, the other clear and see through; a plastic window onto the tiny little balls inside. Each had a coating that broke down in the stomach over a twenty four hour period, so the effects were up and down in feverish sequences – and then hours or sometimes days later, you could be blasted again for a while.

I was waylaid upstairs for ages, can't remember who I was talking with; time could pass you by without you really noticing... and then it was 2 am.

A saxophone was lamenting with a Hammond organ doing a slow staccato rhythm. It was coming from downstairs. It was a very slow version of 'Hip-Hug-Her', originally by Booker T. & the MGs, but Junior was now playing this and adding unique saxophone notes.

Shit – they had started. I realised I'd been distracted, talking and holding onto my Parka for ages, so I once again exchanged it for a 'raffle' coat ticket from the girl in the cloakroom. I then jumped down several steps at a time to the lower cellar; the dance floors and the stage were down there.

Midway down, I entered a strange state – I became self aware and felt distant from my body. I was moving quickly but my mind observed in slow motion; down the stairs, down the steps I saw each one in acute detail. I watched my shoes as they glided over each step. I went down the stairs, down. I went down there, wide-awake into to the throbbing labyrinth below. I was merging into a pulsating mass. It was like everyone was joined magnetically or telepathically together; we had the same thing going, the right clothes, and the right music. This was the right club and we were all blocked together into a single mass, we were a tribe. This was our time and our place, and the place was packed tight, a 'blocked up' amorphous dancing mass.

It was going to be difficult to push on through to see Junior.

Eventually, by pushing and squeezing and upsetting a lot of people, I got to the back of the crowd watching in the far stage room, just as Junior Walker and the All Stars played 'Shake and Fingerpop'. I had missed them starting up with a great live version of 'Tune Up', and they'd moved seamlessly from a slow 'Hip-Hug-Her', which they used as an interval tune between their planned set. This was the start of probably the best live act I had ever remembered seeing at the Wheel. They were so polished, so professional and sounding exactly like their records. There was Junior: large as life on the Wheel stage! I had found out from DL that his real name was Autry DeWalt! He was there with a huge saxophone and three guys – The All Stars - with him on keyboard, guitar and drums. Junior was wildly energetic swinging around that sax and all of the group were dressed alike with grey black and white suite style jackets.

Droplets of condensation from all the sweat of the crowd were coalescing on the black ceiling above, dropping on my head and then running down my neck. It was refreshing as I was hot and packed in tight. I couldn't maneuver out of the path of the droplets. But what the heck, this was warm rain, and far more acceptable than the stuff I had been dodging outside.

Each droplet seemed to hit with each changing rhythm; Mr DeWalt was doing a great job with 'Shake and Fingerpop'. The rhythmic drops changed then to match the beat of 'Roadrunner'… 'Shotgun'…'Shoot Your Shot'… 'Cleo's Mood'… drop, drop, drop accompanied Junior's sax, and each track was interspersed with a slow 'Hip Hug-Her', and sure enough the droplets became slow, very slow drops when the tempo changed.

On and on in a timeless bubble went Junior's saxophone. I was chewing gum till my mouth blistered, my lips stuck together. I clicked my fingers so much they started blistering too. I could feel my eyes, wild and sticking out like stalks, my eyelids rolled back and forth to the saxophone rhythms. Junior too, he was in a sort of dream, becoming exhausted, playing his sax like that; pumping up his cheeks so much they became balloons that I thought would burst open. He was visibly forcing air into his saxophone, then swinging his sax around behind him, spinning back around and shouting into the microphone. I watched transfixed as several streams of cigarette smoke from the standing front row audience were curling up and around Junior – his breath then sucked the smoke into the sax and blew it out. Fantastic. Fucking fantastic, and the most fantastic of all was when he almost blew the roof off doing the intro to 'Do The Boomerang'.

I was trying to remember things, fighting to recover my own memory; but trying to get things exactly right when blocked was hard. Time seemed to merge into one single event, and then the memory track I was grappling for connected. It was Booker T. & the MGs; whom I'd seen a few months earlier on the Otis-Stax Tour in Manchester at the Palace Theatre. They'd been playing a Junior Walker track, 'Cleo's Mood', as an interval between their sets; it was fantastically well done and a great tribute to Junior Walker. Amazing coincidence that right now Junior was doing the same with the Booker T. track 'Hip-Hug-Her'. My crazed mind was running on several tracks at once, and my body was running on auto-pilot.

Then it was over.

Clapping, shouting, whistling, the applause went on and on. Then came distant music, with lesser quality than the live sounds of Junior, then the almost extinguished sound system eventually burst forth with The Formations' 'at The Top Of The Stairs', an MGM USA import. Funny that, as I had to go there – back up the stairs to the bogs.

When the Wheel was crowded and in full swing, going anywhere was difficult. I was still tightly blocked, and the feeling had subsided from a tingling high to a similar feeling like being euphorically but strangely drunk. Faces peered into my vision, leered at me and disappeared. Ahead of me was a tunnel of turning heads looking at me, each saying hello as I proceeded slowly, determinably, onwards, heading for the stairs, up to the bogs.

I re-entered the strange self-awareness state that had happened before. I was observing what condition my condition was in – I was two people in the same head. I became nauseous and felt as though I was spinning around, it was like that awful feeling you can get when thoroughly pissed, like lying on a bed as the room turns around you. If you close your eyes it's even worse, and it was just like that. I thought I was going to collapse.

"Hiyaaa, I'm Dave, where you from?" shouted out a bloke with very long sideburns over the sound of the Impressions wailing out 'You've Been Cheating'.

"I'm John from Stoke." a hand was outstretched for a vigorous handshake. My response was automatic but limp and vacant.

"Hey, I'm from Blackburn, and this pal of mine is from Stockport, he's Dave."

"Hi man," said Dave, nodding, "and this is my mate Jimmy Riddle from our street."

"We're from Stockport," Jimmy proudly shouted in my ear as I passed by.

"Hello," shouted a girl into my other ear, "I'm just going to put my handbag in the middle. I'm Jeanette from Middleton. This is Jean from Failsworth. Have you got a scooter?"

Her friend looked over and said: "Forget scooters, it's Minis – Mini Coopers are 'in' now."

I began to think I'd never get to the stairs. My spinning feeling passed after I leaned on the wall for support for a while. All the guys in front of me were in a circle dancing together, and ignoring the girls nearby. The Impressions faded out and immediately Little Anthony kicked in with 'Gonna Fix You Good'. Feeling the sound, the beat, the Soul, my body moved automatically without my intervention – my mind had separated from it. The intoxication of music and the charge of amphetamine time capsules bursting in my stomach was sending signals coursing up my spine – rivers of glowing shivers that began to move like a wave and push at me. I dissolved. Then I returned, changed.

I was watching without being within it all and it was all viewed in cinemascope. I flipped from being 'in myself' then 'out of myself', becoming increasingly self-conscious and in this strange state; having a feeling of being intensely 'me'. I can only express the feeling as being really there, slap bang behind my eyes and in this acute state I had to traverse around the ring of blokes dancing together in front. It was like learning to walk. I sensed I had to consciously make an effort to move.

I passed that group, then I found myself in the centre of another dancing ring, this time a mixed gender dancing group; Dave from Stockport asked Paul from Stretford if he knew Alex from London? Alex from London asked if anyone had been to the 100 Club. But even he - a genuine old London Mod - said the Wheel was the best.

Anytime anything was said it had to be shouted into an ear, over the sound of the blasting Soul music. Sometimes two people were shouting at both sides of my head at once. I moved on, I was really out of it. I reached the stairs. I staggered, almost falling up the steps. All the way up, hands were shaking mine as people moved down. Everyone was so pleased to meet everyone else, it was some kind of result of the mixture of the place, the event, the atmosphere, the anti-depressant drugs and the feeling of arriving within a place where you really did belong – that all these people were *our* people, and this was *our* music. It was a real physical presence of belonging. At some deep level the drug had affected our minds and linked us all in this, our togetherness. Eventually my weird feelings passed and I went to the toilet for a pee, just as Sid and Terry were leaving after selling all their gear. It was a risky business to bring stuff into the club as it got raided often, and the drug squad always headed for the toilets.

Sid and Terry made a point of mentioning to me in a menacing way, that due to Angelo they couldn't 'get rid' earlier because he was so late, and they'd been forced to sell in the toilets like amateur gear vendors. Sid was proud of his professionalism, and it was belittling his pride to push his gear in the bogs. He gave me an evil angry look. 'Heaven Must Have Sent You' by the Elgins was ringing out of the wall speakers.

The toilets were often packed for the first couple of hours with the pill sellers; the amateur types as Sid had classified them. They did their business in there due to the security facilities, the theory being they could flush the gear down the bogs if the cops arrived. Often the pushers missed the live acts. They had a watchman in the café area ready to send an alert to the toilets and if Mr Plod a.k.a. Sergeant Plummer did arrive, there were always a few volunteers to swallow the stuff at no extra charge rather than flushing them away.

The rest of the time it was full of people talking; just gassing on and on in the only place you could, apart from hanging out on the fire escape ladder where it was also quiet enough for a conversation. Sometimes these talks were quite interesting: politics, Vietnam, the Second World War, record collecting, Motown versus Stax, all sorts of stuff. It was the pills that made everyone talk. It was the pills that drove the dance floor. It was the pills that gave the energy to stay awake all night. The bogs were the place if anyone needed a top up as frequently the amount that did the job last time was not quite enough for the next week. We called it pill creep. You always needed more to regain that evasive last time rush.

Sometimes you could get drawn into a conversation and be caught up in the toilets for hours. I was convinced some people just got trapped there all night! Speed made you lose track of time, and also made it so that changing or doing something else required a great mental effort; it was as though your mind had locked into a state of apathy. If you talked, you talked maybe for all of the night, and if you danced you did so till you almost dropped. It became a major effort to change the rut of current behaviour, to make a decision to do something else. If we weren't addicts, we certainly had slavish addictive behaviour.

One bloke in the toilets commented that we were wasting lots of gear just by pissing it away, and suggested we get a glass and drink it. Another was explaining that Purple Hearts in the 'old days' really were purple-blue and heart shaped, but these days just looked like ordinary blue pills, hence the name 'Blueys'.

At last, after a long discussion about whether or not Minis were becoming further 'in' as Mod icons than scooters, the conversation moved onto films, and I escaped to the dance floor to find Doreen; The Jarmels were singing 'A Little Bit of Soap'.

* * *

This was October 1967. In Manchester the Mods were still going, even though in London where it all began it had probably finished in mid 65 at the latest. Oh well, maybe we were just Northern hicks from the sticks, clinging to an outdated regime – but still, all things Mod and Soul were preferable to becoming a Hippie.

We still felt like Mods even though the new trends were

moving towards the Hippie phase. We, however, never changed our smart methods. Our dress code was our own possessive smart code of honour. I guess we thought of ourselves as Soul Mods – now a differentiated branch, a schism wholly centred here in Manchester.

The fashions and subtle trends still applied at the Wheel, but at the start of the Mod scene fashion and style had changed weekly and frantically – like going from 'see through' plastic Macs and bell-bottom jeans, to ice cream van salesman's jackets dyed ice-blue with button down shirts and paisley ties, almost in a blink of an eye. These things changed rapidly in 64 and 65. Then it became more classical. The size of your suit vents, your top handkerchief positioning, or the way you buttoned your suit, these things would show to those who knew if you were really in or out. It was a secret code. If you were a 'King' and a 'Cool Jerk' you knew it, but it was of course sacrilegious to claim to be so cool yourself.

Coincidence? Maybe, but it was strange that 'Stop Her On Sight' was going strong when I found Doreen and her pals dancing around their handbags, which were piled up in the middle of their dance circle. I joined. This was the DJ room, and they had stayed here throughout Junior Walker's set. They said it was because it was so crowded in there, they couldn't push their way in. I knew Doreen was lying when I saw the same two blokes that had been talking to her outside the Wimpy. These were the wrong types. I took an instant dislike to them. They had badly coloured suits, the material didn't have the soft silky tone of alpaca Mohair that ours were made from; theirs looked almost like nylon! Their jacket side vents were too small, and they only had cotton handkerchiefs instead of pure silk in their top pockets. Obviously pricks. What worried me was Doreen's lack of Mod discernment.

I asked her about those guys. She looked confused; I thought she couldn't hear me over Edwin's lament about his SOS and being in so much distress. I shouted even louder into her ear. An ear that once allowed me to kiss it now recoiled from me. I had shouted, "Why are you dancing with these pricks?"

You can tell when women are lying; when they say things like;

"Those guy's? Oh, they were interested in my friends, not me. I'm not as good looking as Mary and Clare, they were interested in them. Anyway you know I'm not 'like that', like they are, and that's what those guys wanted." You have to unravel the hidden undercurrents, the real meanings.

The answer that women want from such remarks can also get you into trouble; whatever you reply will probably be wrong. They want you to believe them, and at the same time, incongruously, they want you to know that they too are just 'like that' – like the girls they are criticising. They try to keep your perception of them up as they fabricate it, and probably want you to believe they wouldn't behave in such a sexually flirty way as their friends are doing, just because you're their 'boyfriend' and you respect them!

Bollocks, you can't win. Women want to be both options simultaneously; flirty and saintly. But most of all they want attention from all sides: 360 degrees, twenty five hours a day and eight days a week. It's a battleground. They give no quarter. Not much is commonly understood between 'blokes and birds'. When they have an issue with you, you're expected to know it by some kind of sixth sense!

My thought processes continued to run along this track. Subject: women - they want to change you. There's no doubt about this, but if they loved you for what they saw in you before becoming involved with you, why change what they appreciated? What they loved? Why do they want to modify that indecipherable set of elements that attracted them to you originally? It beats me; it beats every bloke.

The answer is they were looking from outside, and things change when their view is switched to the inside of a relationship. It's a logical view to ask why they would attempt to change what was once the object of their attention and attraction – but of course, they're not logical. They're completely illogical when it comes to their emotional level. Women have strange powers; they can disconnect, and cut a man off with a type of silence that's like the atmosphere just before a major thunderstorm, and it's always your fault. Because you as a man have no sense of their condition

– you have to be a woman to know this in the first place, but as a bloke you've got no chance. In their eyes, being a bloke without the slightest chance of understanding their state is no excuse.

You can test this: when they sulk, just ask them, 'Why, what's the matter?' They won't tell you. So there's no point in asking them. They expect you to already know! They expect you to be aware of a damaging remark that they took offence to, when to yourself such small matters are passed over and forgotten as completely inconsequential. They know the time and place, and what they and you were wearing when the ugly deed was committed by you – and like elephants they never forget it. Women pull their face if you ask 'What's up?' They reply, 'Nothing', and you say, 'Must be something'. Every bloke knows this game.

Speed was not called by that term for nothing, everything was speeded up. You could dance, and you could talk, you could think at a very intense and fast pace. Simultaneously you could have parallel thoughts that stacked up around the context of your mind: conversations, answers and opinions. These understandings were available, often like disembodied voices, or tracks of thought that just died in an instant once your mind became distracted. I could think multiple streams of associated ideas in an instant. A huge nest of such ideas hovered around me, tinged with paranoia. They were waiting to seize their opportunity and snatch themselves into my conscious thought stream as my internal tirade of frustration with women petered out.

External events could change your drugged mind instantly. Thoughts that a split second ago were important could be vanquished in a moment, and consequently my thoughts about Doreen and women were soon wrested aside as Angelo started off the Conga in time with the 'The Locomotion' by Little Eva, which had just started to play.

Everyone moved their arms locked together like the side-wheel bars on an old style locomotive. All the arms connected together, the hands of the person behind grasping the elbows of the one in front, moving together, around in a clockwork unison; locomotive style. Further up in front of me, one of the guys I saw earlier with Doreen was right behind her –he had his hands on her arse, and she didn't appear to mind!

One effect of taking speed was you didn't look for or want any trouble. As a result everyone was very nice, courteous and polite when blocked. It was rare to experience anger of the type that was welling up inside me now.

Arrogance was undoubtedly a major part of being a Mod, of being a Soul music fanatic and being in with an underground 'in crowd'. It had status, so why would she lose that status for a prick like him? I was boiling over – paranoia and jealousy were building, obviously fuelled by the adrenaline overload initiated from the Amphetamines. Maybe so, but I was right. Wasn't I?

I was a Soul Mod, with a brilliant record collection. The voice inside me shouted that those 'pricks' were imitations; it was probably their first All-nighter. Why couldn't she see something as clear as day? My inner thoughts were pushing me deeper down a paranoia track as the 'train Conga' moved off and went upstairs.

The front part of the Conga jerked upstairs led by Angelo. It reached the café area, and was immediately turned around and back down again by Ivor Abadi, shaking his head with a look of resigned incredulity on his face. The effect was funny – we had about a hundred people nodding and smiling at each other as both passing parts of the train respectfully acknowledged each other. Down the stairs we went, making it back to the concrete dance floor below, now with an almost clear dance area. On it some guys who hadn't joined the Conga were using all the space to show off their steps.

The sound system had changed; a groovy 'Kansas City' was now pouring from the speakers and Wilbert Harrison was on his way to get himself one of their crazy little women. I watched in admiration as those guys moved in unison. Checking out their moves and losing sense of time in the process, I lost sight of Doreen. I guessed she was dancing in one of the other rooms. Jimmy McCracklin followed Wilbert with 'The Walk', after that

Gary U S Bonds took us to 'New Orleans', and then the DJ changed from these old R&B sounds to a chain of more modern Soul numbers, beginning with Chuck Wood's 'Seven Days Too Long'.

The Wheel's ground floor basement was a series of joined rooms with concrete floors. Cartwheels were set into alcoves in the black painted brick walls, and the same sound system played in all these rooms and the upstairs café bar area. When the live acts were on in the stage room the sound system echoed all around, except for the far DJ room where the DJ was positioned behind a wall of bicycle wheels, with cogs and spokes. This room always played records and sometimes the upstairs café area was also switched to it. Many people danced in the DJ room when the live acts were playing. Maybe they had seen them before, or they couldn't get near due to the place being packed tight, or simply wanted to keep dancing or were just so blocked they had no idea the live act was even happening! Quite often those in such a significantly 'out of it' state would say in the morning, 'Shit, how did I miss them? They were my reason for going last night!'

They would say 'time just went so fast', with a look of surprise that they'd been completely and fully blocked up with no recall of events. Some people staggered about, looking ill. These amnesia types could end up being shipped off in an ambulance. If you took a dozen pills at the last All-nighter, you would need at least a couple of extras to get to the same high state as before. Scary amounts of pills were being dropped. The inevitable consequences were that almost every other weekend, someone needed a rush visit to hospital to have their stomachs pumped out. Often such borderline cases would be outside in the morning, sitting or standing around chewing mouthfuls of stale gum, or smoking, or both, many looking like alien characters from the USA TV show 'The Twilight Zone'.

This was due to colliding with the walls, which ran with seams of condensed water: a mixture of sweat and dirt. The walls were wet and dirty due to the condensation from the heat generated by the dancers. If you touched the walls then rubbed your face and eyes, you were a mess. Sometimes guys would look as if they had more mascara on than the girls. This was a problem all the time, and you had to be wary not to lean on the walls or your suit would need cleaning. In the general crush, you had to be wary of people smoking and dancing, holding cigarettes that could easily put holes into Mohair suit jackets. I was particularly wary of this as Angelo delighted in 'fixing up', in his words, somebody's suit. A person who he may have taken exception to, maybe just too much of a show-off dancer, or some 'Flash Harry' who was dancing around impressing the girls and taking up too much floor space, which was at a premium in the club. He would dance up behind them, draw on his ciggy – making it into a bright red incendiary – and then stick it into their suit at the back before dancing in front of the victim, just smiling and looking at them with his knowing grin and gleaming mischievous eyes.

Right now I had a candidate for his talent.

'Beauty Is Only Skin Deep' by the Temptations came on, and a line of guys were doing the Temps' dance. I joined onto the end, bending down and up, with a finishing quick spin around; doing my David Ruffin impersonation. These group dance practice sessions would go on for hours. Once you got hooked into events, dancing or just talking, you could soon end up with morning approaching. It was a mental effort to fight the Amphetamine rut and go and do something else. I wanted to find Doreen. Yes. But at least she wasn't with the two pricks I saw her with earlier. They had just come into our room and began to dance nearby. One guy near me knew them and I asked the name of the one who had groped Doreen in the Conga line. I was told he was called Pete – Pete Crompton from Langley estate, a massive council housing overspill estate near Middleton.

I smirked to myself. Not about their dancing – that was crap, anyway – it was their suit material. They were underneath the blue neon strip light that brilliantly lit up any white particles on your clothes. They were lit up like Blackpool illuminations; white bits, tiny sparkling dots and white fibres all over them; hopefully some of it on their shoulder padded suits was dandruff. We all knew about this light; we either avoided it, or we made certain our suits were brushed thoroughly to remove all such crap if we were going to dance anywhere near it.

In their drug haze, they seemed oblivious to what we were now all knowingly winking to each other about, until it eventually dawned on them. They danced stupid, then looked stupid and eventually realised they *were* stupid – and off they scuttled, to my great amusement. I liked that light. It helped show those twerps up for what they were. Surely Doreen couldn't fancy any of these guys? I pointed out 'Pete' and his mate to Angelo, and he followed them. He returned later and made a big animated draw on his Benson's ciggy and exhaled with slow curling smoke. "The guy got a Catholic suit," he said. This was his code word for a 'holy jacket'.

My all time favourite Motown song came on the sound system; 'Helpless' by Kim Weston. I was lost to the music, to the dancing fever; lost once again as the intermittent periodic drug effects rippled back in from the little Green and Clear time capsules inside my stomach. I danced and danced along with all the others in the club. Track after track, 45 after 45 played. We got right down to the real Nitty Gritty, we rode our Ponies, we got our Backfield's in motion. We did the Swim and the Duck and the Harlem Shuffle. We were in the Land of a Thousand Dances.

Exhaustion set in as the last record played to mark the end of the All-nighter; it was Jimmy Radcliffe's 'Long after Tonight Is all Over'. It was often used to signal the end of the All-nighter, and strangely it immediately affected everyone, like a Pavlovian reaction. We were all knackered. My emotions stirred again; I had to find Doreen. Daylight swept in through the big back doors under the fire escape. Eyes found it difficult to accept this glaring light of Sunday morning Manchester.

I headed for the Salvation Army, as I guessed Doreen would be there.

* * *

The Manchester Wheelers

CHAPTER THREE

That Sunday Morning Feeling

'You've lost that lovin' feelin'...'
- The Righteous Brothers

I was impressed the first time I met Dave Leyton. It was at work. We were engineering apprentices at a huge factory in North Manchester. At first glance, he appeared as a dopey looking, thin and spindly spotty-faced guy with heavy black-rimmed glasses. He looked like a starving, ghostly Hank Marvin, the lead guitarist in Cliff Richard's backing group The Shadows. My first impression of Dave immediately changed when he told me he had the original 'Twist' record – of course not the one by Chubby Checker, whom everyone thought was the original Twist Man. No, Dave had it by Hank Ballard and The Midnighters and Dave informed me Chubby had nicked it from Hank!

Forget about his spindly appearance – here was a guy with prestige. He obtained his nickname 'rubber legs' from his dancing style. When he danced he was fantastic, but when he danced 'blocked' he moved up a couple of levels. It was quite amazing to watch him. It seemed like slow moving vortexes ran up and down his legs; somehow through his body he could create rippling waves. It was absolutely amazing, and he could easily dance better than any of the black or half-caste guys. He claimed to have seen Major Lance on a late night Granada TV show and got his steps from him. The rippling effect though was all his own, but probably owed something to James Brown. 'DL' was in the know about all things Soul. For example, we were going with him a few weeks back to see The Temptations. We could hardly believe they would be on at a working mens club in Salford called 'The Devonshire'. Georgie Fame was on at the Wheel All-nighter that night, and we had seen him so often we thought it would be worth missing an

The Manchester Wheelers

All-nighter to see the Temptations!

We knew these guys were not the right ones when they came onstage at around 11:30 pm. None of them looked like David Ruffin, and their covers of Temptations songs were not bad, but hardly correct. DL went up and made a request. We were all astonished when they sang his request: 'What's Wrong With Me Baby' rang out, and yes, these guys were really the Invitations!

Not many black guys went to the All-nighters. They showed off their dancing talents at other places like the Blue Note. The exception was Hovis, a Pakistani lad from Oldham. He was called Hovis because of the TV ads for Hovis bread. 'Don't say brown, say Hovis' was the catch-phrase, and it just caught on when referring to him – it wasn't malicious. There he was, Hovis, with DL by his side, now both exhausted and heading for the queue to get a drink of tea from the Salvation Army.

The second to last record that had played in the Wheel was Freddy Scott's 'Hey Girl', and it was still slowly rolling around in my mind. I was thinking on a parallel track about Doreen. Where was she? I looked for her when the dancing had stopped. People had climbed off the fire escape, gone back through the club and out the back doors that had opened, disgorging the suddenly weary all-night revellers. The doors had closed behind us all, and a large crowd had walked slowly into the dank morning light seeking drinks in the silent Sunday morning. It was too early for church bells. In front of me three girls were holding each other's arms and dancing side to side singing 'What Kind Of Fool' by the Dixie Cups.

Looking around I saw wide eyes, large dilated pupils, guys with thin lines of black and brown etching a stylised outline around their lips, and they rubbed at the blisters on their fingers from finger poppin' all night long. Old chewing gum was spat out. The girls who had previously been gorgeous Julie Driscoll look-alikes now resembled the brides of Dracula, with thick black mascara stains beneath their eyes and running down their cheeks. Others that had touched the walls and rubbed their eyes were worse. One or two looked ready to join the BBC's Black & White

Minstrel show.

Everyone headed for the toilets at Piccadilly Station, or across town to Victoria station. Many went over the road to the derelict land where the Salvation Army had their tea wagon; a white caravan with a type of barn door opening on the side used as a serving hatch. This service was set up for the homeless, the drunks and down and outs that moved around shadowy night-time Manchester at the weekend. Their new clients for tea and coffee this morning were all dressed in the latest fashion: smart Mohair suits and girls with Mod style black and white Op-art dresses and high heels, all in line at the 'Sally Army' tea wagon.

The Salvation Army were our friends. Every Sunday morning they would be there waiting for us in the crisp morning air, after the Wheel had finished around 7:30 a.m. The Salvation Army provided us with free hot tea and coffee. One time, Doreen complained that they didn't have any orange juice – saying it partially as a joke – but the next week, they had it! They never once rammed religious beliefs down our throats. They never preached. They never once condemned us. Maybe they had no idea we'd spent the night blocked and were now coming down fast. I've never forgotten their attitude and humility. I would always put something in their collection boxes when they would collect in the city centre pubs, dressed in their uniforms and selling copies of the 'War Cry'.

I took a tea in a plastic cup. DL was there raving about Junior Walker and quite rightly so. We agreed it was the best act we had ever seen. I could see Doreen wasn't there, so after arranging to meet DL and Hovis at Rowntrees later, I moved on.

What goes up must come down. 'In a right 2 & 8', that's how a cockney would describe the early morning crowd as they drifted slowly from the back door of the Wheel to distribute themselves around their favourite recuperative haunts in the city centre. Various groups were straggling along London Road, looking pale, gaunt and whitewashed. Most had large black bags under their eyes, and sore fingers with burst blisters from incessant finger clicking. One of the worst things was dry and sore lips, even after a double coating of 'Lypsyl'; it was caused because you unconsciously licked your lips all night long. Often awful stinging blisters would arrive on the end of your tongue. Sometimes you might find you had bitten through the insides of your cheeks, or your tongue, or both. If so, the mirror revealed caked black dried blood around the edges of your mouth. The bones ached in the legs, ankles, arms and feet. The feet were the worst.

Everyone had a limp or a staggered drunken gait. We were all knackered. Few people spoke, silence prevailed amongst us as distant church bells were now beginning to ring, announcing that last night was long over. It was time now to move on and refresh at the station toilets.

Breakfast – the only thing to eat was a packet of Spangles, and these were all I could face. Real food was out of the question, and the worst thing about sucking sweets was that they helped to make sores and tongue blisters far worse, adding to the morning's misery. It was the result of taking amphetamines like Benzedrine – they were certain to keep you dancing all night as they staved off sleepiness, but they're also a diet drug, an appetite suppressant, and an anti-depressant. They can have euphoric effects in larger doses. But very large doses produce hyperactivity and paranoid thinking – psychotic, and sometimes violent behaviour and intermittent spasms of sickness in the stomach. It certainly stops all thought of an early morning fry up.

At the station toilets swarms of guys would be shaving, cleaning teeth and changing into jeans; holding them up with braces, keeping on their suit jackets and neatly folding their trousers back into their airline bags. Large groups silently went through a practiced routine; washing, combing hair, squeezing spots that had miraculously grown from nowhere overnight, staring in mirrors, hoping to look cool again. Then after completing all that, they would reload their mouths with fresh gum, fix their dark glasses and behave impeccably, like gentlemen; leaving to allow a fellow Mod to take up the mirror space. Suit jackets might be changed for Denim ones, shoes were re-polished and shirts were changed, usually from a smart type to a chequered casual one, or a Ben Sherman T-Shirt.

Then you'd be out of there to locate your secret stash to get recharged – just a few more uppers for the midday and early afternoon sessions of dancing at Rowntrees (Stakis), and then on to a solid R&B and Stax Soul drive at the Blue Note Club Sunday evening bash. It was at the Blue Note that we could start to eat again, they gave away free hot buttered potatoes. NIL BY MOUTH was an in joke from hospital experiences, a sign that would hang on the bed of a patient that was soon to be operated on. Nil by mouth was also our state after the All-nighter, as the pills' side effects made you nauseous, unable to eat. Many pills like 'black-bombers' were in fact slimming pills, appetite suppressants, and they could make you feel really hideous in the morning. Some people couldn't eat for several days.

Some of my friends had old 78's of Blues guys and some jazzmen like Duke Ellington. These jazz artist's shellacs originally belonged to parents, uncles and aunts. During a night out midweek, Angelo and I had discussed these old records with some American guys we met in the Long Bar on Oxford Road. They really digged Duke Ellington, and we liked these records too, especially 'a Train', and 'Satin Doll'. Interestingly, we then found out a little more about the Duke. DL had read an article about him – he was a great snappy dresser, Mod-like. He folded his pants to keep the creases in them by rolling them up as he travelled across America between shows.

We had the same problem after All-nighters. So to keep our strides' creases sharp we did exactly what Duke Ellington did. Instead of folding them, which meant more lines and creases in the wrong places, we rolled them up and put them into our airline bags. It worked really well. We kept this a secret between those who were our close mates. Keeping smart was not just something to try to do; it was a Soul Mod's code of honour. We had our own ways of changing and looking after our clothes in a smart way. It was essential.

I had spent quite a while in the toilets in Victoria Station getting ready. After shaving in the rusty edged mirror, applying the 'Aqua di Selva', cleaning my teeth, rolling up my suit pants and putting them in my airline bag, I then changed into a Ben Sherman chequered shirt and dark blue Levi jeans, transferring my braces onto my jeans and putting my suit jacket back on. Finally, I was ready again for dancing. Well, almost – first I had to take a few more booster pills. I also needed to find out what was going on with Doreen. She was not only behaving oddly and distant, she had kept away from me all night. Had she chucked me? I drank down some more gear – five more Green and Clears I had hidden in a little bottle stashed in a crack in a wall down a back street. I'd bought a bottle of Lucozade to help swallow them; this drink caught on as the right accessory for downing multiple tablets.

I joined a silent queue. Everyone was trashed. We showed our membership cards and paid our shillings at Rowntrees in Spring Gardens, then shuffled inside. Wilson Pickett's 'Three Time Loser' was playing but nobody was dancing. Then I saw her sitting there at the side of the dance floor: I had caught up with Doreen. The two blokes from last night were still hanging around, looking gaunt and bedraggled at a table nearby. I was hoping I didn't look anything near as bad as them.

Why did she like these guys hanging around? Don't answer, I thought. I know, it's attention, any attention! Women love it. Men stare at them, at their tits, legs and arses, in a too long lingering look that they criticise with statements like: 'Who you looking at?' 'Ave yer seen enough?' They might say something as though they objected, but most often it's an outward show, a pretence, and they miss it if a bloke they like doesn't do it. They love to be gawped at. My mind was rattling away again, as it re-connected with the theme I had followed the night before.

I had stopped Doreen coming to the All-nighters with me in a stupid and futile attempt to protect her from drugs, but it set off the curiosity in her. So, she'd wanted to go more and more, and the more I told her not to, the more she thought I was hiding something. Eventually I couldn't stop her; we had arguments about it, so the inevitable happened. I gave up. She went, and as it went with the territory she also started on the gear.

Rowntrees was an entirely different club from the Wheel. It was a nightclub, a posh looking place with a long bar and a large polished dance floor, and all around it a carpeted area with lots of tables and chairs. Doreen was sitting at a table with her sister and their friend Mandy. They all had Cokes and were sleepily playing in unison with their straws; pushing down the straw again and again each time it bobbed up inside the neck of the bottle. I walked across the empty dance floor. Her face turned pink. My heart seemed to drop a couple of beats with foreboding. I sat down next to her. She recoiled from my outstretched hand; she was acting like a stranger.

She bent down and got her handbag - it acted like a barrier between us as she plonked it down on top of the table between us. She pulled the handbag that was now like a fence between us open, and started to repair her fingernails. These were stuck on nails from a packet. She probably got them cheap or free from Angelo or Brian, as they were dealing in knocked off cosmetics. They were probably from Boots originally. She took out a small bottle and opened it. The smell of acetate went up my nose bringing me more awake. It was a smell with childhood associations; Pear Drops the sweets we got from the school 'tuck shop'. She was painting her false nails pink with a small brush that was fixed to the bottle cap. She had adopted a false air of being busily absorbed. The tension between us generated a strange atmosphere. I thought of what to say but could find no words.

I just stupidly sat there. Doreen then looked intently and silently at her sister. I was certain that some subliminal messages were passing between them. Then in a quick and flustered manner, puffing and blowing Doreen took her handbag and went to the Ladies. Her sister and their friend followed. Why do women always go in there in numbers? I thought about it as I sat there, and after a while she returned from the toilets and sipped at her Coke.

I had lots of things planned in my mind ready to say to her, but I was unable to say anything. The situation overwhelmed me. I think it was a fear, a paralysis, a dread of hearing the actual words that gave finality to what I already knew. The DJ was onto a Wilson Pickett theme and following 'Three Time loser', 'Mustang Sally' got going, and then it was 'Ninety Nine and a Half'. But in spite of Wilson Pickett's efforts, a strange silence descended

The Manchester Wheelers

around us. A deep silence filled the emptiness that had come between us. All around there were people talking, a few people began dancing; the DJ was keeping those records playing. But we sat in our pool of silence.

Everyone who has endured the end or the breakdown of a love knows this special, unnerving silence. An eternity passed, but outside our small silent world the DJ had only played another three songs. The last one was 'A Little Piece of Leather' and as it faded away she got up and walked out. I doubted Donnie Elbert wrote it as an end to love, but that was what that song then became for me.

I look around. Everyone in Rowntrees was knackered. Then a false state of bravado engulfed me. I marched over to the DJ and sort of demanded he played 'Get Out of My Life Woman' by Lee Dorsey. He searched for it, and then apologised that he hadn't got it with him – but as a true Soul professional, he then found it on a 'B' side by the Mad Lads. "OK, thanks," I said, and he put it on the turntable.

I sat there thinking about when I first met her, the times she promised she would be with me forever. We'd been going with each other for over two years. On the way to the previous night's All-nighter she had danced around me and sang 'I'll always Love You'. What had changed her mind? I felt anger, then self-pity, all sorts of emotions and thoughts went through my head, ending almost in tears. I was also shocked at the quick succession of emotions that had taken control of me.

Then I jumped up out of my seat. Suddenly I remembered it was my grandma's birthday, and my dad had asked me to come to her 'do'. It was at a pub in Blackley, 'The Berkshire' on Victoria Avenue East. It was her seventy-fifth, but she always lied about her age – she was probably seventy seven.

As I got up to leave, the two blokes opposite got up too and followed me. Near the door they grabbed me and immediately hit me, shouting that my mate had ruined their suits. As I hit the deck, I almost laughed out loud but managed to stop myself. Bloody hell, Angelo had done both of them!

It was always a good move when being attacked to drop to the floor. Being a long term and devout coward, it was an effective strategy that was tried and tested – and as they began to kick me, the bouncers pounced on them and threw them out.

The bouncers dusted me off sympathetically, thinking I was the innocent party, but I knew I wasn't so innocent. I waited a while, peeping out now and again and making sure the coast was clear. Annoyingly the DJ had now put on Lou Johnson's 'A Time To Love, a Time To Cry', which stayed with me as I went over to Cannon Street and got the number 17 bus. It went to Rochdale. I decided to leave my scooter where it was and get it later at night, just in case the guys who were after me caught me crossing town.

I decked off the bus as it was slowing down to stop at Victoria Avenue gaining a few yards and walked to the pub. Most of my family were in there. My mother and father, my sister, my uncles, aunts, great aunts and many of my cousins - all from my father's side of our family. My grandmother's two sisters and all their assortment of families were there, we filled the pub with all our relations. Everyone else in the place that weren't family were friends of my grandparents. Everyone was buying, most were singing. It was 1 pm – we had an hour left to closing time. I was going to get pissed.

'She's a Lassie from Lancashire' rolled out from a host of voices with the nasal tones of Mancunians. It was followed by 'If You Knew Susie', the three seventh decade sisters taking the lead. It became a bit tearful. I knew they were remembering, whilst singing that song, their mother and my great grandmother, Susie.

It was another pub, another time, a few years back - the Clogger's arms on Oldham Road, Newton Heath. Everyone was singing this song and she had got up to dance; she was in her nineties. The song changed to 'Knees Up Mother Brown', she pulled up her skirts and began kicking her legs – but then fell backwards; she just fell down to the floor, dead.

The Manchester Wheelers

The singing stopped. My father, my uncles, and Jimmy, who was Susie's second husband, and I all carried her between our shoulders round to her small terraced house in Holyoak Street, just off Droylsden Road. We put her lying full stretch on top of the piano. My gran tied a white ribbon to hold her legs together. It was all dealt with in a 'matter of fact' way; these people had seen a lot of death in the Manchester bombings in the war. Somebody brewed up, and we sat in silence. Everyone lit up cigarettes – my dad even tried to get me to have one.

"Yes," said my aunt, "It'll do you good, David." She forced a Players Waites into my mouth and my dad lit it up for me. Then my uncle Frank who was sitting at the piano got the keyboard cover lifted and played 'If You Knew Susie', slowly at first. Soon everyone started singing with Frank at the piano, and Susie lying full length on the top looking pasty. I kept expecting her to rise up and sing along with us.

On reflection, it was a belting 'do' the day my great grandma died. The current one was equal to it, but my gran didn't get up to dance. She mostly drank a Mackeson, the black Stout from Whitbread, or a Double Diamond. At other times it was a half of Threlfalls mild. That day she had got through several of both stouts, and she wasn't opposed to a couple of Whiskey chasers that were turning up at each round.

She sat there at the small table which was over-stacked with glasses and pint pots. In the centre was a large overflowing ashtray. My gran, 'Lizzie' sat there talking without words. My Pop Danny was sitting in his spot next to Lizzie clutching his pint, as if someone was about to pinch it. My gran was forming words with her lips in an animated display sending non-verbal messages to another lady across the bar in the Snug. They had both been Mill Girls in the cotton mills of Manchester. She had told me of those days long ago; she would say 'you couldn't hear yourself think because it was so noisy with hundreds of clattering looms'. So to be able to talk you had to learn the hand sign language and the silent lip-forming that enabled conversation to take place without hearing any words. They never lost this skill. Quite often I watched her have conversations that only the recipient could decipher. God knows what gossip they silently transferred.

My father always said 'use your noodle before opening yer gob'. He called girls 'bints' - one of the Arabic words he got from serving in the war in Egypt. He called money 'akkers' (again I think, Egyptian for money) and said everything was 'all to cock' these days. He often said I was 'not to argue the toss' with him, said 'bloody' or 'blimey' at the end of every single sentence, and often said 'bloody Norah' as an exclamation mark, even though that was his wife and my mother's name. He only ever drank halves, as he joked that he had to visit the toilet twice for every one he drank.

I could drink loads of pints, but this also meant frequent visits for a piss in the gents. It meant standing there in the stones with my head down balancing against the wall. I was pissed and trying to avoid any splash back on my best suit pants, or on my polished brogue shoes. Everyone was drunk at throwing out time: two o'clock plus ten minutes drinking up time, plus another ten to leave; everyone then staggered about in the car park. Then even though it was my gran's birthday, in honour of my granddad, everyone started singing 'Danny Boy'.

Eventually after lingering goodbyes and kisses from aunts, my dad and I weaved our way home, singing, stumbling, telling stories. Most of my dad's were about Manchester United's air crash. A true supporter never forgot it, and he talked once again about David Pegg, Denis Violet, Eddie Colman, Jackie Blanchflower, Tommy Taylor and his most favourite player Duncan Edwards. My mother had heard it a dozen times at the very least. She went on past by us to light the coal fire to warm up the house, as was the way with dutiful and Catholic long-suffering wives and mothers. They had a way of exhibiting their suffering, acting in a hurried way and with a frozen expression which was parried perfectly by the Andy Cap style of my father: he just completely ignored it.

My dad went to all the United home games and he didn't even have a season ticket. The key factor was that he was a pal of our parish priest. Although not a Catholic himself, he was good

The Manchester Wheelers

company and a fanatical football fan. Manchester United, was a 'Catholic' club with Matt Busby as manager, who personally sent out two complimentary tickets to all the Catholic churches in the city. So our priest took my dad with him, as he had been quick to volunteer years before when the second in command priest had declined. This meant that he was sitting in a row of priests, and this fact led to his constant joke that when United went a goal down, all the fathers pulled out their rosary beads to pray for a counter United goal. He assured me that he had seen genuine miracles performed at Old Trafford!

When I got back to our house, a corporation ranch, I got ready to go back out again. I had to look sharp and recover from the All-nighter, from my Gran's boozy do, and from the shock of Doreen chucking me. So, I took a few more pills.

Often when my mother was washing, cooking and ironing whilst my dad and I were watching TV, she would say 'Idle hands do the Devil's work'. But I always ironed my suit pants; it had to be done in a very special way. I let her do shirts, but always took on the ironing of suits as a male preserve; soaping the insides along the sharp creases. Then ironing them with brown paper to get real heat to make stay sharp creases, but I had done this one time too many, and they split right down the edged seams – it was one of those days. I had to put back on my jeans and wear my suit jacket, but the event triggered emotions. As I thought about Doreen, tears welled up inside me and I sat sobbing for a few minutes.

I got my record collection sorted and I packed several hundred 45s into my holdall bag ready for the night. I was the DJ at the Blue Note Club. DL and I had taken the previous night off to see Junior Walker and the all Stars, giving a chance for a black pal of mine called Lincoln to DJ. However, I had to turn up this Sunday evening to keep the weekend Soul Scene on overdrive, and at least I'd have vodka to keep me going – DL had recently found the club's secret drinks hideaway.

* * *

CHAPTER FOUR

The First Time I Met the Blues

Not at the Crossroads, but down in a dark cellar in a backstreet in Manchester Town Centre – that's where I first met the Blues. I wasn't walking down through the wood; I was walking around in the underground cellar listening to Buddy Guy's 'Good Morning Mr Blues'.

The first time I went to the Twisted Wheel was a Saturday night in November 1963.

It was the beat music period. The Beatles were topping the pop charts. We had just left school, Angelo and I. Our school was the 'The Silesian's kids caning factory' as we called it. It was located in Alkrington, Middleton. What a place! We learned virtually nothing about anything, and didn't want to. As a rebellion against our teachers, we would show them that they couldn't make us learn anything. We mostly got religion – the Catholic type – drilled into us; same bollocks as any other type I suppose. Once out of there, we vowed it was the end of our church attendance for good. The only interesting things were the stories our teachers told us about their experiences in the war.

It was Saturday night, and Angelo and I had met up with another ex- school pal, John Smilley, who lived in a fantastic location behind Wilson's Brewery – a terraced house in Collyhurst where it always smelled of hops. Billowing white clouds often rolled down his street from the fermentation exhaust pipes. John lived in a street famous for producing Manchester United's hard man and toothless wonder Nobby Stiles, who would eventually help us win the World Cup in 1966.

The Manchester Wheelers

We were meeting for a Saturday night pub-crawl in Manchester town centre. John and his pal Pete both had black Beatle style polo necks and jackets without lapels. Their pants were thick black corduroy, very trendy, and they were dressed in the image of the Beatles. We couldn't match them, but at least we had Ben Sherman shirts, tight fitting iced blue jeans and black boots - Cuban heel styled Beatle boots.

We went first to the Britons Protection, around 6 pm, then into the Peveril of the Peak, Tommy Duck's, the Town Hall Tavern, and then to the Shakespeare Pub on Fountain Street opposite Lewis's. After drinking only halves at each place, we went on to Mother Mac's behind Woolworths. Then for some unconscious reason, we crossed Piccadilly and although we had only three pints inside us, we staggered about and went right down London Road, singing together as we wandered down by Piccadilly Station's building site; singing 'I Like It' by Gerry and the Pacemakers. We went on to the Gog and Magog pub; now long since gone – demolished and covered over by the Mancunian Way roundabout at the end of London Road.

We pushed our way into the crowded pub and stood at the bar, attempting to get served by the overwhelmed bar staff. This was one of the worst things in overcrowded pubs, standing at the bar trying to be seen, waving your money about, repeatedly shouting out your order to deaf ears and feeling stupid and annoyed every time you get ignored. It only got worse when somebody nearby distracted your attempts by starting up a conversation: "Bet you don't know what the name of this pub means?" said some old farty professor type to us. He was clutching his pint of Threlfalls from Manchester's Brewery with both hands, and standing next to us at the overcrowded bar: "No idea," we chorused almost at once.

"Well, it's the male and female gods of the ancient Britons of these Sceptered Isles," he said. "In fact they just found some massive earthworks near Cambridge, with a huge maze cut into the ground called Gog Magog, the same name as this pub."

"Fascinating," we said, nodding at him as we backed away as far as we could, passing our beers from the bar to each other. He carried on about the pub's link with ancient pre-history, and faded out as we moved backwards, absorbed by the crowd in our retreat from him.

The pub was heaving, packed tight. We had bought pints, not halves, of bitter this time due to the overcrowded bar and afterwards we stood outside; it was a warm evening. There was a live group on, attracting all the extra interest; it was the Swinging Blue Jeans from Liverpool. We all sang the 'Hippie Hippie Shake' with them. Angelo and I had the same ice blue jeans that the group wore. Later we went back to Piccadilly in the back streets and called into Mother Mac's again, and then got a bus to Sale. It was Pete who'd suggested Sale Locarno, a place filled with 'crumpet' he assured us.

Inside the Locarno a large ball tiled with small mirrors revolved in the ceiling reflecting light spots all around. We danced with several sets of girls who all went off and sat down at the tables surrounding the dance floor at the end of each song. Eventually we latched onto a group of girls who kept on dancing. Big Dee Erwin and Little Eva were on the DJ's turntable singing 'Swinging On A Star', then it was followed by 'Bits and Pieces' by the Dave Clark Five. Everyone jumped up and down or stamped the floor as the chorus line banged out.

"*I'm in pieces, bits and pieces,*" shouted out the group's lead singer, the group's drummer:

'I'm in pieces, bits and pieces
Since you left me and you said goodbye
I'm in pieces, bits and pieces
All I do is sit and cry
I'm in pieces, bits and pieces
You went away and left me in misery
I'm in pieces, bits and pieces
And that's the way it'll always be

I'm in pieces, bits and pieces
You said you loved me and you'd always be mine'

It got louder…. **'I'm in pieces, bits and pieces'**

The Manchester Wheelers

Not only was everyone on the dance floor shouting out the lyrics, everyone was jumping up and down to the beat. Then at the loudest part of the record, the bit that had a double drum beat, the entire dance floor began to shake. The girls' high heels were studding holes into the wooden floor as they landed after jumping up as high as possible, resulting in them crashing down to make even more noise than before. The girls in their three and four inch high heels were wrecking the dance floor by studding it with small 'D' shaped holes.

The manger went mad as he realised their stilettos were punching holes deep into the wood, and as he looked on the entire floor rattled and shook. He rushed to stop the record, grabbing it and pulling it off the turntable. Everyone booed. Then silence. We could suddenly hear each other speak instead of shouting to each other; a conversation began as the manager and the DJ argued, and then a quieter record was being selected. These girls told us about a new club in the town centre, the Twisted Wheel, so we left the Locarno, with Wink Martindale talking through his hit monologue, 'Deck Of Cards', and we went out with the girls, back to Manchester on the number 12 bus.

It must have been late when we eventually arrived at the Wheel. The girls signed us in as guests and then disappeared down the steps below. As we entered that place for the first time, it was buzzing. The DJ played the Beatles 'It Won't Be Long' from their second LP. The atmosphere was strange; the shuffling dancers, the low black painted ceiling, the damp darkness made an intoxicating mixture. Pop interspersed with the Blues. It was very different from the Locarno.

The Wheel was dark with interconnected rooms, and because we had never heard original Blues before it felt completely different. The Blues music seemed to generate a strange mysterious atmosphere. There was really no comparison to the Locarno. There was no massive dance floor here, just a series of rooms with concrete floors and brick walls. No turning glittering reflection ball hung from the roof here, and the ceiling was very low – the adornments were a bicycle or a cartwheel set in a wall or a backlit alcove. In the alcoves people were necking, and some in others were doing even better!

Proto-Mods in bell-bottom jeans with combed frayed ends were doing their dance; hunched up shoulders, both hands in their jeans pockets, moving to 'Stoned', the 'B' side of 'I Wanna Be Your Man' by the Rolling Stones, which was banned on radio stations.

We sobered up; mainly because the club had no drinks licence and we could only drink Coca Cola. We sat on the edge of the empty stage and listened in awe to the new sounds of Howlin' Wolf's 'Smokestack Lightnin'', Sonny Boy Williamson's 'Help Me', Jimmy Reed's 'Big Boss Man', Booker T. & the MGs' 'Green Onions' and its 'B' side 'Behave Yourself', Tommy Tucker's 'Hi-Heel Sneakers', 'My Babe' by Little Walter, and the fantastic Muddy Waters' 'Got My Mojo Working'. Most of these songs came from 2120 South Michigan Avenue, an address in Chicago we knew well due to Mr Nanker and Mr Phelge who put 2120, an instrumental, on their first EP. The sound of a wailing harmonica in that dark cellar had a strange and magical effect upon me.

We were soon to get into the Blues big time, the full shooting match: John the Conquer Root, Mojo Hand, the Devil at the crossroads stuff and so on. We were already primed to it by being big Stones' fans. Looking around there inside the club, it was quite a mixture of people. There were Beatniks dancing their shuffling style dance in their Duffle coats! This place had been a Beatnik location; it was previously called the Left Wing Club. The style was no style, but that would change! There were a few people in bell-bottom jeans following the shuffling dance style of the dosser types, patting their hands on their knees, winding up pretend bobbins of cotton with their hands. They were doing a strange dance, but we felt at home, Angelo and I. But John and Pete, dressed in their imitation Beatles gear, were getting funny looks, and they left us to it.

The following Tuesday we got the bus into town and applied for membership at the Twisted Wheel, paying our Ten Bob and getting our little red book in the post.

The Manchester Wheelers

We went to other clubs like Heaven and Hell, and the Cavern. The Cavern was the closest to the Wheel as they played some Blues, mixed with the pop songs in the charts. However it was only at the Wheel that we could hear much more of the Blues that we were becoming fanatical about. At Christmas we went to see The Chris Barber Jazz Band at the Lancaster Club, on Broadway off Oldham Road. In February we went to the American Folk Blues shows at Manchester's Free Trade Hall.

We became regulars at the Wheel by the summer of 1964, and by then we were already heavily into the Mod scene. Saturday nights at the Wheel meant live acts like the Four Pennies. They had a big hit with 'Juliet' in July '64, but at the Wheel they went on to play lots of covers of Leadbelly songs, setting a trend with the pop groups that appeared there who all did Blues. The Rolling Stones' records were rarely off the turntable alongside tracks like 'Wonderful Dream' by the Majors and 'The Cat' by Jimmy Smith.

Then things changed as the DJ Roger Eagle became more regular. He was the leading evangelist for American R&B, so he played virtually no pop, introduced Chuck Jackson tracks and Lou Johnson, kept up the Stones stuff and headed further down the Blues route with tracks like; 'Homework' by Otis Rush, 'C C Rider' by Chuck Willis but with lots of early Tamla Motown and Soul from various labels. He also kept the Surfing sounds and introduced 'Jamaica Ska' and 'Blue Beat'. It was eclectic. It was fantastic.

By this time Alexis Korner was almost living at the Wheel, with his black lead singer Herbie Goins. John Mayall, a local lad from Macclesfield who said he used to live in a tree house in his parents' garden, was now living in a bedsit somewhere in Salford, and regularly appearing at the club. Georgie Fame, another local from Leigh had a huge hit with 'Yeh Yeh'; it was a sort of theme tune at the Wheel and Georgie did lots of USA Soul covers. Many were heard first by Georgie, and us soon after. He listened to AFN Radio, and later we heard the original artists when Roger the DJ had ordered a copy of them, often directly from the States. One example of Roger's influence was his love of Chuck Jackson. He played 'I Keep Forgetting' most nights in those early Blues days, and John Mayall took up the song in his live performances at the club.

It seemed to us that there was little point going to other clubs, so we would just go to the Wheel every Saturday night and for several week nights too. New names of groups we had never heard of were advertised as appearing at the Twisted Wheel in the entertainments section of the Manchester evening News; names like Manfred Mann, Victor Broxx, Brian auger, The Animals and many more.

Dressed in brown overalls like storemen in a warehouse, and with lots of Newcastle Brown Ale bottles at the front of the stage, the Animals kicked off with their lead singer Eric Burdon shouting in a broad Geordie accent: "It's a number by some bloke from Detroit... Timmy Shaw – 'Gonna Send You Back to Georgia', or to 'Walker' as we do it....its a place in Newcastle..." and these animals really did it! Then they did 'I Got a Woman' by Ray Charles, then Eric their lead singer started talking slow, *'You got me runnin', You got me hidin', Run hide, Hide run, Doin what you want me to do...'* It was a great version of a Jimmy Reed tune, and he continued with raw harmonica Blues. All that great stuff given the English Blues treatment, then their brilliant version of Bob Dylan's 'House of the Rising Sun'. It was indeed 'reet magic man' as them Geordie lads would say… "Fuckin' brilliant," we said on the 121 all-night bus home, and within no time their five minute single was top of the hit parade.

I remember one Christmas, Boxing Day in 1964, when I took out a girlfriend – her name was Janice, and she was from Higher Blackley in Manchester. We went to see Sonny Boy Williamson; 'the second'. He was great. He was dressed in a bowler hat and in an amazing black and white tuxedo with tails, one side black the other white. I was praying he would play my favourite Blues number and he did; 'Help Me'.

He was backed by the Spencer Davis Group, and I remember the awe and respect he got from them, especially from Stevie Winwood. Sonny Boy played dozens of different harmonicas, some right inside his mouth and, to the disgust of my girl friend;

he even played a tiny harmonica in his nose! She became a fan later though. Unbelievably, when he finished his set I got the opportunity to buy him a coffee.

Later in the week, Sonny Boy appeared on Granada TV's 'Scene At Six Thirty', a program that had the Beatles first TV appearance doing 'Love Me Do'. This programme followed the news and they also had quite a few Soul artists – Marvin Gaye was on when the Motown Review Tour came to Manchester. They did a show in Chorlton at a railway station that for Blues shows had been renamed 'Chorltonville'. It was used first as the venue for broadcasting Folk and Blues artists that appeared at the Free Trade Hall. It was Alexis Korner (and Blues Incorporated) that led the British Blues boom which later included the R&B boom, all supported by the Mod movement in the city. Quite a few Rockers liked this music too, as rock and roll originated from the same roots, and both warring sets of teenagers liked Chuck Berry.

The Blues we heard wailing away at the Twisted Wheel generated a kind of mental feeling of weirdness. An undercurrent in Blues was about: all that Crossroads, meeting the Devil, black magic stuff. It was all related to the Blues; John the Conquer Root, black cat bones and Mojo hands etc. It was all from the Mississippi Delta, a place of swamps and strange looking trees with vines falling from them, and misty fogs around them in odd-sounding towns like Savannah and New Orleans.

One of the most atmospheric sounds in the Wheel, however, was from the Rolling Stones; a 'B' side - 'Stoned'. Soon everyone in the place would be! During the week we would go down two or three times, and sometimes the place was almost empty. We would dance with 'everyone' in the club, maybe thirty or forty people, all practicing together new dances, all singing along to the Miracles, 'A Love She Can Count On', 'Mickey's Monkey' and 'Sugar and Spice' and everything nice... '*That's what love is made of...*' Then 'I've Got To Dance To Keep From Crying'. The DJ seemed to catch the mood playing several concatenated Miracles tracks. The Miracles were singing:

"Clap your hands now everybody

We're gonna have some fun tonight
We better sing, shout, knock ourselves out
Everything's gonna be alright, alright
Now let the bass man start to playing
He's gonna ask the beat to make you pat your feet
Everything's gonna work out fine
We gotta say
I like it like that
I like it like that
I like it like that
That's where it's at and I like it like that..."

Everyone in the place was shouting along. In those early days at the Brazennose Street Wheel the Mod scene took hold like a vice. It became essential to be 'in'.

Scooters started appearing outside. Everyone watched Ready Steady Go on the TV on Friday nights before going down town. All-nighters had started, and someone at the Wheel even organised hiking trips on Sunday mornings after the All-nighter, with coaches leaving for the Peak District. By 1965 it was all Mod plus Soul, and the Blues was fading out, but some Blues tracks would always be in the DJ's itinerary – tracks like 'Scratch My Back' by Slim Harpo, 'These Kind Of Blues', by Junior Parker, 'Shame, Shame, Shame' by Jimmy Reed and Nina Simone's 'Please Don't Let Me Be Misunderstood'.

※ ※ ※

Another aspect of events in Manchester around this time was the missing and suspected murder of several children. In 1963 Pauline Reed had disappeared aged 16, then later that year a boy of 12 disappeared; John Kilbride. Then in the summer of '64, another 12 year old, Keith Bennett never came home from school. By the time we were seeing posters everywhere about ten year old Lesley Ann Downey from Ancoats going missing a dark foreboding arose in the city of Manchester. The papers were speculating that a mass murderer of children was on the loose in the city. The police announced they were going to fingerprint every male in the Manchester area. As we read the news in the Shakespeare pub, we were looking around at the faces around us; it could be anyone. The feeling was quite indescribable. We felt gloomy, and I believed that most of Manchester was experiencing a similarly connected sorrow. To cheer up our mood we decided not to go to the All-nighter – we didn't want to face the often depressing come down – so we did a pub crawl and agreed to go out on our bikes the next morning. It's strange how a mood can sometimes connect with simultaneous real events; as if at special times we can tap into the consciousness of the city: as Jackie Wilson lamented 'No Pity (In The Naked City).

After our pub night out we awoke to a dark cold Sunday morning. The Manchester Domino and the Prestwich Olympic cycling clubs met outside The Gardener's arms Pub at the top of Victoria Avenue East and headed off for Buxton. Angelo and I intermittently kept up infrequent Sunday training runs with our old cycling mates, and they were always happy for us to join them. We meandered through Hattersley and then to Glossop, then up the Snake pass on our way to our favourite cyclist's café in Buxton. At the top of the Snake, we saw lots of police in Wellingtons, and lots of men in suits with spades coming out of several police vans. Further over the moor in the distance there were other groups digging.

It turned out to be a thoroughly miserable day. It was the type of overcast day that people who live in Northern England are familiar with; a long deep lingering dampness that seeps into your body and chills you to the bone. We came home wet and tired and coughing up phlegm for hours. Later in the week it emerged that the police had been out digging on the moors for several days looking for the children's bodies. They had arrested Myra Hindley and Ian Brady at a corporation house in Hattersley. Later they would be infamously known as the Moors Murderers. We must have gone very close to them that day as we passed through Hattersley.

We decided that the next Saturday would see us back at the All-nighter.

CHAPTER FIVE

The Manchester Mods

> *Some blokes don't wear fishtail Parkas. The ones that do know they're further up the Mod hierarchy than those that have straight end Parkas – and it can be assumed that those that wear such lesser Parkas look down upon others that as yet have no Parkas at all.*

I had many disconnected memories of the Wheel, memories that often don't follow a pattern that can be ordered neatly into dates, times, or places. It's as if they're stored away and need a trigger mechanism to unlock them, a word by someone, a song playing, and a stray thought that leads to another, that then locates a forgotten event. With me it's music that can act as a trigger – I'll hear a song on the radio, then I'll drift away and enter a memory state; the inner memory opens up and it's re-lived with a vividness that I'm sure wasn't present during the original event. Often when I return from such reverie, I have little recollection of actually hearing the original song that acted as the initial catalyst that recovered the memory. It's as though once activated, the memory closes down the sense of hearing and the eyes lose focus in acquiescence to the inner eye, so that the memory can be fully replayed.

Once inside the Wheel you could wander about. Upstairs was the café area, downstairs the dance floors. Down there in the basement, there were several rooms to dance in, and in the original Wheel these were interconnected by dimly lit corridors.

Some artists seemed to be always playing there in the early days: Alexis Korner, Georgie Fame, John Mayall, then Spencer

Davis, later it was Ben E. King and Edwin Starr at the 'new' Wheel. Spencer Davis was the last act that closed at the Old Wheel on Brazennose Street – just off Albert Square, near the Town Hall – and then started as the first live act at the new one near Piccadilly Station on Whitworth Street.

Inside the Wheel everyone (well, mostly everyone) was a Mod, but it's fair to say we were always behind the times of London Mods. In mid '64 we were still sporting bell-bottom jeans and Cuban heel boots as casual wear and the vents in our suits had mere flaps in their sides.

Outside in the streets the question 'are you a Mod?' could be threatening, like 'What football team do you support?' In this city the wrong answer could mean a kicking. Inside the Wheel we were safe with our own clique, but even so, very few – if any – said they supported City!

No one claimed to be a Mod if they really were one – it would have been unacceptable. You had no need to claim what was self-evident to the ones that could determine such status. Usually those that said they were, were not. Those that knew did not need to say so. The whole Mod movement was internally understated and vigorously self-expressive to the outside world, if they could tell. We blended in as smartly dressed kids to most folks, but of course a real Mod could spot another in an instant.

Mods could be identified by the way they walked, their immaculate grooming, the way they put their hands in their pockets with their suit sides uniquely folded. There were lots and lots of subtle signals. No one was the leader. The Mod movement was self-generating and given purpose from within. Mods had ideals. Clothes were the thing, and the look of certain things provided style. It all added up to be more than superficial – it was far more than an outside-influenced fashion scene. In fact, for a time, fashion followed Mods. In general Mods liked Soul and certain pop groups like the Stones, The Who, The Small Faces, and The Yardbirds. For Manchester Soul Mods it was R&B, Motown Soul music and dancing that were paramount, with scooters the next in line. Having a smart Mod girlfriend also helped. The whole movement needed no outside endorsements. It was self-expressive. Mods cared little for what anyone else thought about them, except for other Mods that is and within this scene there was arrogance and often sniggering at lesser Mod neophytes.

The 'ins' and the 'outs' changed rapidly. It was very intense, yet subtle, and as a result it meant you had to be totally committed to be a Mod; especially in the early days of 1964. You had to be constantly planning to go to parties, but never organise one. Being evangelical about black music was a badge of office. Being a Mod could never be faked. Fashions and styles changed at a meteoric pace; fashions and styles were either out or in. You might be 'out' and think you were 'in', when most of the 'in crowd' deemed you to be 'out'! But if you had ever been 'in' you could catch up, if you'd never been 'in', you were probably always 'out'.

Mods lived breathed and slept Mod.

Work was tolerated; a way to get money to provide the means to be 'in' and to keep 'in'.

You worked for the weekend.

The weekend was the All-nighter.

We had 'Rhythm' from Major Lance and we were 'On The Right Track' due to Billy Butler.

London Mods tried to get into Ready Steady Go, to be seen dancing on TV. They went to London Soul clubs like the 100, Tiles, The Marquee, Klooks Kleek, Blaise's and the Flamingo. The best Mod clubs in London were The Scene and La Discotheque.

In Manchester some Mods went to the Oasis and others to the Jungfrau. The real R&B and Soul Mods went to the one and only venue for them: the Twisted Wheel, and the deeply arrogant 'Wheel Mods' looked down on other 'so-called Mods' that went to other clubs. At one time Wheel Mods got invited to dance at the live Top of the Pops studio in Dickenson Road Rusholme.

Mod style took over everything, the way you walked, the way you hunched your shoulders and stuck your hands in your pockets through your suit's side vents. The way in which you buttoned up your suit jacket would signal your status. The way you showed off secret inside suit pockets. The look of the girls you were seen with. The way that your thumbs stuck out if your hands were in your pockets, which they usually were. You had to be constantly chewing gum. It was a total lifestyle. Mods looked nice, smart and clean. They were an underground movement hidden in full view; Mods were in fact mysterious.

In the earlier years the police could not recognise Mods as drug users. They just couldn't reconcile a smart young man or girl as a drug abuser. More than once the police raided Victoria Station, as it had developed a reputation for amphetamine drug dealing. The police raid surrounded us all, and everyone else that was standing around on the station. Those dressed smartly in suits and with short hair were rapidly disassociated from the general rabble, and eliminated. How we laughed as we walked away, taking our stash and washing down the pills with Lucozade, heading for the Twisted Wheel. The police had rounded up the scruffy 'gits' assuming by their appearance they must be suspect.

Mods had to be seen to be dressed right. Looks were everything; being 'in' and cool was central. It was elitist. This was the very first youth culture that had invented itself. An enormous list of items became 'in', then often rapidly lost such status when too many 'divvies' took them up. The Rolling Stones were more 'in' than the Beatles.

'See-through' Plastic macs were definitely 'in' at one point in 1964, along with bell-bottom jeans, airline bags, military ties, paisley ties, driving gloves, brogue shoes, desert boots, black pointed Chelsea boots (Beatle boots), Baseball boots, Bowling shoes, Cuban heels, Tassled Loafer shoes, Button Down collar shirts, Levi & Wrangler jeans and jackets, Fred Perry Polo's, Ben Sherman button-down shirts and check shirts, striped boating blazers, and of course Fishtail USA Army Parkas.

Suits were always in for Mods; with side vents, centre vents, even centre pleats, increasing in size as time passed by. Cycle racing vests and shoes were in for a short period. Jacques Anquetil, five times winner of the Tour de France with his short hair and gaunt good looks, wore his France Ford Gitanes racing vest, smoked Gitanes and looked like a Mod. Casual clothes might mean horizontal striped T shirts and white or striped jeans, but of course Mods wore suits most of the time. Disciplined practice ensured that ties were tied correctly; Windsor knots. Shirts were neatly ironed; in fact all clothing achieved a look of perfection as if everything was brand new – polished, bristling and perfect.

Girls had their own 'in' clothing and status items, such as shoulder bags and patent leather handbags. Girls had black kohl eyes, glue on eye-lashes and finger nail extensions, white lipstick, white tights, Paisley dresses, Op art mini dresses, mini skirts, high heels and lots and lots of handbags. Many Mod girls adopted the short hair styles of the blokes. Fashion models were 'in', like Twiggy, Jean Shrimpton and Jane Asher. Singers like Marianne Faithful, Dusty Springfield, Billy Davis, Sandie Shaw and Francoise Hardy. Manchester United were 'in', so was George Best. In London, probably, Chelsea were 'in' and Charlie George in particular.

Back-combing our hair, high at the back was an 'in' style like the The Small Faces. Dobie Gray's 'The 'In' Crowd' was the Mods anthem; it set them apart from the rest. The lyrics to this song said it all for us and we were the Cool Jerks. 'I'm a King, I'm a Cool Jerk' by the Capitals was also a type of anthem for Manchester Mods. Arrogance suited us and other favoured records exhibiting such attitude were 'Good Time Charlie' by Bobby Bland, 'The Ten Commandments' by Prince Buster and later 'Mr Soul' by Bud Harper. The earliest 45 of this type was a record from Dr. Horse called 'Jack, That Cat Was Clean'. It was a monologue about how much clothes and cool style cost and it was Roger eagle, of course, that would play it now and again in the early days of Brazennose Street. Imagine the difference made in Manchester clubs by Roger when he started as the D.J.; other places would be playing 'Bad To Me' by Billy J. Kramer And The Dakotas, whilst at the Wheel you could hear Billy J. and Dr.

The Manchester Wheelers

Horse!

Mods favoured American original music but got a lot of acts at the Wheel that did copies, like Geno Washington, Jimmy Powell, and The Steam Packet with Long John Baldry singing the 'Hoochie Coochie Man', then Rod Stewart and Julie Driscoll doing duets like Chuck Jackson and Maxine Brown's 'Baby Take Me'.

We used to gather at Speakers' Corner on a Saturday. It was outside the Old Shambles pub and Sinclair's Oyster bar on Cannon Street. We would park our scooters outside and get a pint of Boddingtons. The Shambles also did great pork pies, and often we would have slices cut from a gigantic pie. Then off to the Cona Café, then to the Kardomah in St Ann's Square, then Henry's on Market Street to buy clothes, and do a little shoplifting, continuing onwards to Barnet Man and to Ivor's boutique shirt shop. Then looking for old records and bargains at Mazells, the Co-op on Deansgate, then to record shops in Tib Street and at the market stalls in Shudehill.

Moss Side, was a place we went to score weed, and to search the record shops for Blue Beat and Ska. Sometimes we would go to parties at Shebeens in Denmark Road; they often had illegally distilled booze (like Irish Poteen) as well as abundant weed and lots of cool guys in leather jackets and pork pie hats and glinting white teeth. We called them Spades of course. The lighter skinned variety were the 'half-caste boys', an altogether meaner bunch. Nothing derogatory was meant by us calling a black man a Spade. It was complimentary; a Spade was a good guy, a cool black bloke. Obviously in times gone by it may have been derogatory, but to us a Spade was a great black geezer who had his finger on the pulse of things down the Moss. He could point us to the right places, tell us about record shops and supply good shit.

Half-castes were mostly trouble. They liked the fact that we liked their gear, their style and their Ska music. They called us 'Rasclat's and we took up that phrase too. We mixed OK up to a point. They had a sort of chip on their shoulder that could easily break out into violence. It was rare that a Spade would roll you or cheat you on a deal, but entirely the opposite with the half-castes, who were often the sons of Spades.

Mods liked Soul, and of course all the UK Mod bands. The crowned kings of Mod bands were of course the mighty Who. A pal of mine called Adge was crazy about the Who. He had the RAF red, white and blue round target on the back of his white jacket. We met up and went around the corner from the Twisted Wheel one Saturday night to see the Who playing at the Oasis Club.

At the Wheel All-nighters when the DJ put on 'My Generation' everyone stuttered with Roger Daltry and sang 'Fuck Off' instead of 'Ffff...fade away'. It would be fantastic to see them do it live, so I risked it to go to a non-genuine Mod club.

The club was 'heaving', filled to over capacity but the Who made up for the crush that we were in. Keith Moon at one point threw his drumsticks into the crowd and used two Coke bottles to drum with instead. About a year after that memorable night the Who came to Manchester again, playing at the Co-Op New Century House, where there was a ground floor dance hall. I was there, again with Adge. It was even better than the first time at the Oasis, and Townsend wrecked yet another guitar. Apparently The Who were on at the Wheel on a Sunday but somehow we missed them and only heard about it later.

* * *

"Are you a Mod?"

It was a Saturday morning. I was sitting on the steps of the blackened statue of Prince Albert, in Albert Square. I was waiting for Angelo to come out of the underground toilets. 'Shit,' I thought to myself. I looked to see if he was coming back so there would at least be two cowards to scare the bastard off?

The Manchester Wheelers

The guy who asked the question looked like a Teddy Boy; long jacket with a greasy maroon velvet collar, heavy duty sideburns and well into his thirties. Tattoos; fucking hell, he had tattoos everywhere: neck, hands, arms, fingers with 'Love' and 'Hate'; he looked like one of those Rockers you got on the Waltzer at fairgrounds. He was pissed even though it was only mid-morning and he had an angry aura about him. Shit – I was alone, and there was still no sign of Angelo.

"No, no not a Mod," I replied. I was praying that the fucker would piss off. I even closed my eyes waiting for him to thump me. Instead he leaned forwards and stared right into my face, the horror of it confronting me as my eyes re-opened:

"Oh, so you're a Rocker then, eh?" His eyes narrowed as his sarcastic alternative option was presented to me. The dark pupils in his eyes moved even further together as he took a huge drag on his Woodbine.

I sat there dressed in my latest Mod stuff; grey strides with a band member's bright red stripe on the outside of each leg, an ice-blue flannel jacket, sand coloured desert boots, Ben Sherman collared sweat shirt, black leather driving gloves, sunglasses and high top back combed hair. What else could I be?

"No I'm a mocker," I replied. "You know, just like Ringo said when a newspaper bloke asked him the same question." I got up as Angelo approached, leaving the Ted bemused. We were off before he tried anything else.

We were very nervous about Rockers.

Last Tuesday at the Wheel there had been a fight. It had started when we were in the entrance queue. Two Rockers on their black and chrome Enfield 500s had pulled the clutch and revved up the noise of their bikes, as they cruised back and forth along Brazennose Street like marauding sharks, shouting abuse at us, wolf whistling and calling us girls, toilet traders, rear admirals and so on. Some of the smartest Mods in the queue ahead of us left and went across the street to the building site opposite, over to their scooters parked outside the 'hidden gem' church of St Mary's on Mulberry Street. Obviously parked there under the watchful eye of God's mum for safe keeping, they removed the long aerials from the back of their GT 200s. They placed these across the road on the ground, one guy at each side, crouching down on the pavement. When the first Rocker came around again, up went the aerial and down went the Rocker, choking and spluttering from meeting the metal tube at 25 miles per hour. His mate slightly behind swerved and came off.

Then several Mod lads finished them off by kicking the shit out of them, and for good measure fixing their bikes with a few repeated crash landings. We enjoyed the fun but without joining in. The Rockers were left sitting in the middle of the street and we all retreated into the club, the badly bent aerial went with us. I heard someone joke that they were probably fucking City supporters anyway!

A few hours later people came rushing down the stairs from the coffee bar shouting that Rockers had invaded the club. There were about ten, maybe fifteen already fighting; pushing the club owner brothers against a wall, as a large swell of dancers left the rooms below to confront them. The Rockers must have had no idea about the place, perhaps simply thinking the top coffee bar was all there was. Soon they were faced by a greater force outnumbering them, and with many more coming up the stairs. The Rockers put down the chairs they'd been using to hit people with, or threw them into the first vanguard of Mods approaching them. They fled outside, running up the street with hordes of smartly dressed lads chasing. In Albert Square about two hundred Mods surrounded the staggering Rockers, but were then attacked in the rear by a dozen or so riders on motorbikes who crashed up the pavements, circling menacingly around in front of the Town Hall, herding the Mods into a tighter bunch. Stylish Mod belts were removed with the buckle ends swinging around, whipping at the mounted riders. However before any real fighting took place, the police arrived in several Black Marias. This resulted in two streams exiting the Square at either end, the Rockers going towards the Library, and us down Corporation Street.

The Manchester Wheelers

Following these events, the next time I was at the club, there was a marked police presence outside. The police kept moving people about around Brazennose Street, stopping any gatherings apart from the queue to get into the club. Later, when the Wheel closed, they even had mounted police on horses escorting us up towards Albert Square. This was after the infamous Easter bank holiday when London Mods and Rockers had clashed in Brighton and the police had to ferry in more officers from London by air. As a result the Manchester police were following us in the belief we had rioting on our minds.

The fact was that we had no such intention. We stayed in groups for mutual protection, derived from the belief that alone we would soon be picked on and attacked by marauding Rockers with vengeance on their minds. We had to make it through dark streets to Cannon Street or Piccadilly bus station. The police soon mistook this clumping behaviour pattern as provocation and started to physically intervene and split us up. Then inevitably, like a herd of nervous animals, we panicked. This resulted in groups of forty, fifty or so lads and girls running along, across and down the streets, with the police on foot, some on horseback and others in cars and vans pursuing us. A de-facto running riot did result, but with no obvious cause other than the police's wish to stop one!

On another night after leaving the old Wheel, we again began to be harassed for no apparent reason by the police. They kept moving us on, irritating us, again seemingly for no other reason other than the fact that there was a crowd of us. Eventually lots of Mod-types, outpouring from other clubs, the Oasis, the Jungfrau and the like, were shepherded together with us. This was about the time of the Mod riots in Clacton, covered in the press. Then everyone broke out into a run, which then became a running riot, Mods racing down the centre of the street stopping traffic and running into and accidentally knocking over pedestrians.

I raced along around a branch of the clothes store C&A. All the windows were brightly lit up and there were nude female mannequins inside. Behind me a friend from work, Denis Westford, crashed straight through the window. He had skidded due to putting heel irons on his Chelsea boots. "Good job the police were following us," he remarked humorously some months later after being discharged from hospital, having nearly died from injuries to his neck when he went straight through the window. The police had stopped chasing us and saved his life.

* * *

Angelo and I had started trawling record shops for Tamla Motown tracks in early '64. We knew the Marvelettes' 'Mr Postman' had been released on the UK Fontana label, but copies were rare, as records were deleted rapidly if they did not reach the hit parade. Motown then moved to the Oriole label, and then on to Stateside, and in 1964 tracks like Marvin Gaye's 'Can I Get a Witness' were becoming more available. It was fair to say that the Beatles and the Stones had begun our interest in Motown. The Stones' LP had Marvin's track sung by Mick Jagger and once again on the LP's 'b' side, as an instrumental. I loved the Stones' version. But by this time I had to get the originals. I bought the Marvin Gaye single as he had been on the television during the week, on Granada Reports: Scene at Six Thirty. Marvin was sitting in a chair holding a large brandy glass singing 'Pretty Little Baby'.

I looked at my copy of Marvin's record on the bus going home from town. 'Can I Get a Witness' was in large silver lettering, and underneath in brackets it said: (Holland– Dozier-Holland). These were the writers, and this was when this string of names really began to mean something to me. I had of course been collecting Blues records, R&B and Soul but this was when the light really dawned on the subject of Motown. I turned the disc over; the 'b' side track was 'I'm Crazy 'Bout My Baby' and in brackets below the title it read: (Wm. Stevenson). I scrutinised the 45 all the way home: SS 234 Belinda (London Ltd), a Tamla-Motown Production, E.M.I. Records Limited. It was number 234. I thought to myself – what are the other 233 like?

Scrutinising records and learning about them, the labels, the USA originating label, the songwriters and the producers, all such information was soon to become an endeavour of learning and love.

It was a great year at the Twisted Wheel, and The Motown Review came to the UK early in 1965. A fantastic year – the Wheel was at the height of its Mod scene, with a huge movement in favour of Soul, taking the club away from Beat and Pop and even leaving most of the Blues for a solid wall-to-wall Soul playlist. Instrumentals like The Mar-Keys' 'Last Night' and Willie Mitchell's 'Secret Home' became must-play tracks at every daily session.

Of course Booker T & The MG's 'Green Onions' and its fantastic 'b' side had been on the record deck since the opening of the Wheel. Instrumentals were always a big play at the Wheel; this trend would continue.

By the end of '65, Mods as an entire youth movement may have stopped in London… but the theme continued in Manchester, ending with tailor-made suits as standard wear for the All-nighter.

* * *

CHAPTER SIX

The Boneyard, And Rubber Souled

When you looked at the Atlantic label logo swirling and whirling around on the record player it could send you into a trance, a 45 beat, musical dance.

One Sunday afternoon after an All-nighter, we decided to go to a club we'd never been to before. It was thanks to a recommendation to us by one of the top Mods at the Brazennose Street Wheel – Louie, who also happened to be 'the' main pill dealer at that time for the All-nighters.

So Angelo said, "OK, let's go to the Boneyard."

Louie was a dealer – in fact, the main dealer. He lived in Bolton and you could always get good gear from him, guaranteed. Even when all other sources dried up, Louie always came through. He was the first person I saw with a thirteen-inch pleated centre-vent in his Mohair suit. Apart from being cool, he was well organised with multiple stashes of pills hidden all over the place, even inside Victoria Station. He was like a squirrel. A verbal deal would be struck. Off he would saunter, never rushed. Shortly he would return smiling, from a different direction. "Here you are boys, twenty five lovely little yellow Dexys." This was Dexedrine. Good stuff, a quick rapid high and long lasting at an All-nighter, if you took half a dozen right away then topped up every couple of hours. We handed over £2 and a ten bob note. Outside the Station we gulped down six each. So we had a few top up spares, and a dozen to sell in the Boneyard to recoup our outlay. Louie had given us directions; the club was open Sunday afternoons and was near the traffic lights and near Bolton Station. He said it was above a piano shop.

Angelo kicked down on the starter pedal. The Cento coughed, then shuddered into life and off we went with a rush. I adopted the Mod position, leaning backwards, counter to the forward motion of the Scooter, pushing back on the high back seat fitting and bending it backwards towards the whipping aerial on the rear. This was the accepted cool take-off style of a Mod riding pillion on a scooter. Other jerks rode differently without style, with no panache. This style was the badge of recognition, to those who knew the secret signs of our undercover Mod, Mod world.

By the time we got past Farnworth and into Moses Gate on the outskirts of Bolton we were bombed; nicely bombed. We started to sing, clicking our fingers. Angelo was alternately letting go of the handlebars, clicking his fingers, then grabbing back the scooter controls and swerving, almost waltzing the machine in time with our guttural shouting of Wilson Pickett's '6345789': *Six, Three, Four, Five, Seven, Eight, Nine, Da dad da da da dad, Dadad da da da, DADAD DA DA DA.*' Strange looks came from people on the pavement as we coasted by them, slowly, very slowly. We were moving along slow, otherwise we would have crashed. This was the first time Angelo had driven his scooter totally blocked.

We glided slowly past the 'Welcome to Bolton' sign; our singing and scooter dancing by this time had changed to 'Meeting Over Yonder' by the Impressions.

We parked the machine outside the station, fastening a bicycle chain lock to the front wheel. Many guys took off their side panels and hid them somewhere; on derelict land, in a wall, all over the place. One bloke we knew hid them in a dustbin, but it was moved back into a backyard and he had to search through dozens before finding them, causing havoc up and down the back street. If you left them on your scooter some bastard would nick them, especially if they were chromed. However the Cento was not an LI 150 or a GT 200. There was no big market for Cento side panels and these were painted white, not the more fashionable chrome jobs. So it was safe to leave them on the small Lambretta.

The Manchester Wheelers

The Boneyard was not actually called the Boneyard – it was a nickname, and I never found out why. The club was near the station on the main road to Manchester. It was upstairs above a music shop that sold pianos, saxophones and sheet music. Its official name was the Caroline Lounge, presumably named after the pirate radio ship Radio Caroline on medium wave; 199 was their frequent call sign, and the club had a picture of the vessel on the wall at the top of the stairs. It was two and six to get in for the Sunday afternoon session. Unlike the Wheel or any other club, this one had large windows with sunlight pouring into the room, a dance floor that had been used for dance classes in times gone by.

As we climbed the stairs, the Astors were pounding out *'Gee Whiz have you seen my girl? Candy, Candeeee...'* We soon joined in, duetting with the track as it pounded around the room. We were blocked high on the pills, and now even higher with the addition of fabulous Soul music. The sounds changed to the Impressions – *'People get ready, for the train to Jordan...'* This was when I saw Sandra. She was dancing in a circular group of girls with their customary handbags in the centre. After we asked them to dance, they wanted to know where we were from, had we been to the Wheel All-nighter last night, and did we have any stuff? We soon sold all we had, apart from two each that we needed for top ups.

'Candy', the track we heard on the way in, was so good we asked the DJ to show it to us. It was on the Black Atlantic label, with that fantastic logo that swirled around mesmerizingly on the record deck. We held the vinyl and scrutinised it. It was from the original USA release on the Stax label and the track was written by Steve Copper. We were amazed and impressed; he was the lead guitar player in Booker T. & the MGs, and it sounded more like a Motown record.

When the Boneyard closed at 5pm, we walked the streets with the gang of girls we had met. We walked and talked incessantly. We went into the Italian ice cream shop in the town centre near the traffic lights, next to a large hotel. Some of the Passagnios, Pandolpho's, Sivoris and Roccas had gone to school with us, and we ranted on about them, about Italian ice cream, cycling, and cycling heroes like Fausto Coppi, as if these girls could care. But then the Dexys were doing their magic and the girls appeared engrossed! Ice cream was about the only thing you could eat when you were blocked up and we needed to kill two hours in the ice cream joint before the Beachcomber opened. It was another Bolton club that these girls told us about and we agreed to all go there together.

In the Beachcomber, as expected, it was dark and the walls were painted black. It was almost deserted; we could dance all around the place. Then after dancing for an hour or so and after taking my last little Yellow Devil, Sandra started to hang around my neck. We danced into a quiet corner. She started to furiously kiss me. But this was no fun. She then did what all blokes wish for; she put her hand straight down and unzipped my trousers and dropped down to suck me. What a shock to the system. What an embarrassment. She sucked and gulped all of it – balls, the lot - right into her mouth. It was so small, it had shrunk, like in the cold water football showers after a game in January snow. Despite several valiant efforts on her part to revive the little teapot with licking and sucking, nothing stirred. I pulled her up with a double swift movement that brought my strides up too. It was too late for any excuse; the truth was the only thing to tell such a great sport. She had already shot to top of my list of most admirable girls by her 'let's get straight down to it' approach. I mean with most girls it was a long process, if ever, to get to the stage she'd achieved in less time than it takes to unzip a banana.

I said to her, "Sandra, that's your name isn't it?" She nodded. "It's the pills," I explained, "They do that. Even if you want to, you can't, er, get the thing to work, it's just impossible to harden it till the pills wear off."

She reached up and kissed me in a really strange and licentious way, with a smile and a look in her eyes that burnt like a welder's torch. I pushed my head into her blouse, undoing it at the same time. I then bit her nipples, one after the other, and then sucked hard at one… just as the bouncer grabbed us and threw us both out of the club.

We walked around for several hours before finding a

bandstand in a park. It rained so bad we just stayed there, sitting in the park. We stayed all night. Sandra went to sleep on one of the benches. I tried another. All the music from the Boneyard flooded my brain, all of it in my head all night, again and again, around and around, the entire DJ's repertoire went on and on in my head till the birds in the dawn chorus took over. Even then, 'Candy' by the Astors continued in the background of my mind. I realised it was Monday morning and I should be at work. Fuck it, I thought. Maybe I could sneak in later. Often mates in the factory would 'clock in' missing pals.

Sandra woke up and we cuddled for warmth to begin with, and then she rubbed it; my dick. It responded. She pulled away my pants, rubbing at it furiously, and then with an expert gentleness she bent over it and took the top part of my dick just inside her lips. I thrashed around, it was wild, and it seemed to go on forever. It did take a long time as the thing needed to recover, get hard, and then switch into overdrive. I came like thunder, almost sequencing with the rain belting down around us, and she gobbled it all up, sucking all my semen into her mouth, even licking and hoovering up the drops that had gone onto my pants. I thrashed around shouting out 'Candy, Candy!' Then I felt embarrassed, disgusted at her and myself. It's a strange empty feeling you sometimes get after that kind of sex. Maybe it's just me? Maybe it's just my personal way of feeling guilty, that Catholic upbringing; all sex is sin. I fumbled with her tits for a bit just to show interest. Then I got dressed and we walked to the town centre through the diminishing rain. I wanted to get away.

After seeing that the Lambretta Cento had long since gone, I told her at the station whilst buying a ticket to Manchester that I would see her at the Wheel All-nighter next week.

It was one of the few I missed. I never saw Sandra again.

* * *

Saturdays: Collecting Records

We used to put a great deal of effort into obtaining records. Because we had low wages, we had to resort to shoplifting and searching out reduced-price discs. We would search through stacks of records at Mazells, and at the market stalls in Shudehill. One time we went into a betting shop. Someone had given Angelo and me a tip when we had gone for a pint in the Turks Head, and we won £2 on the horses. This enabled us to buy up the stock of Dobie Gray's 'In Crowd' (three pence each!). There were thirty or so copies on the London American label. We had already located them in the sale section at the Co-Op store on Deansgate and were going back to 'lift' them later, but our win changed our plans. We bought about fifteen and told friends about the others remaining. Later I sold mine for a good profit and just kept one, as I already had my prize import of it on the original Charger USA label, from an import postal auction.

Angelo and I then decided to go home to be ready for the All-nighter, splitting the records 50/50 and stashing then into our 'butty bags'. Then as we rode out of Manchester I got a puncture, which we repaired outside a record shop on Rochdale Road in Collyhurst.

Outside the shop upon a table, in a box of records marked 'reduced', we discovered lots of great records: 'Hi-Heel Sneakers' by Tommy Tucker, Sugar Pie Desanto's 'Soulful Dress', Howlin' Wolf's 'Smokestack Lightnin'', 'Help Me' by Sonny Boy Williamson and 'I Put a Spell On You' by Screaming Jay Hawkins. All on the yellow and red Pye International R&B label, and all for sale at three pence each.

We could easily have nicked the lot and rode off; being well into shoplifting records by this time, but something stopped us. I think we were just so impressed at finding an out of town shop that had any of the highly prized music we valued above everything in the pop charts. Plus there was the fact that all these great records were being sold for such a small amount when we would have expected to pay six and fourpence for each of them.

The shop was owned by an elderly man and his wife; Mr and Mrs Bowker. For some reason over many years Mr Bowker had bought several copies of classic Blues and Soul records. It must have been a result of the sales representative finding him an easy touch to sell to – who knows? The shop was a goldmine of Blues and deleted Soul. Rare, rare and even rarer, and all alphabetically catalogued in neat wooden pigeon holed boxes that dominated the wall behind the shop counter. I remember Mrs Bowker criticising her husband for keeping everything when he could have returned them for credits. She was doing this whilst we asked for obscurities, which he quickly retrieved to our great admiration. Did he have this, and that? – You bet he did, and several copies too!

It was the start of a long lasting relationship, as over the years we mined out the seams of rare Soul vinyl in the shop. Mrs Bowker made tea and Mr 'B' moaned on about Harold Wilson – our Prime Minister – then moved on to the Americans in Vietnam and Manchester's housing policy and their demolition plans for the area.

I told DL about the shop and soon every week on Friday pay days, we went straight there on the bus after work. We spent hours at work compiling lists; more often than not Mr Bowker had several copies so we could both feel happy. I was building up a substantial record collection. As a result I was always skint, due to spending so much on records and clothes.

※ ※ ※

Rubber Soul: Christmas 1965

Often before going to an All-nighter in late 1965, we would go to Oldham Astoria. We did so for the Saturday night dance sessions because they played quite a bit of Soul.

On one occasion, the week before Christmas – the 18th December – it was to be John Mayall playing at the Wheel All-nighter.

Brian collected us from each of our houses – Angelo, Moston Dave and me – and soon we were outside ready to go into the Astoria, but we then decided to go to a party with some girls who were obviously Mod types, and who we'd danced with at the Astoria the previous week. We bumped into them again at the front entrance – they wanted a lift to the party and were also going to the Wheel All-nighter later on. Christine was with her pals: Veronica, Suzanne and Christine's brother John, a big guy and even bigger with his Crombie overcoat – he looked the same age as us but turned out to be only fifteen. The four of them needed a lift, and the party was in Royton, on 'the tops' above Oldham.

"No problem," we said, "we can all get in Lord Snooty's car." It was our nickname for Brian – he was so named after the posh Beano comic character. So off we went, completely overloaded, and when we got up to the tops at Royton it was snowing.

At the party, the Beatles' new LP, 'Rubber Soul', was played continuously. Eventually we left for the Wheel. Just before, we took two bottles of Co-Op orange juice from the fridge in the party's kitchen and all of us took our gear, washing them down with the drink before climbing back into the car. Moston Dave put the rest of the pills in the glove compartment: a couple of hundred assorted Blueys and Dexys he'd bought from Angelo and was selling at the Wheel later. Due to the fact that there were so many Daves around, he was nicknamed Moston because he lived there in Rivington Avenue.

Outside, whilst we had been partying it had snowed even harder and the road was icy under the 'white-out' of four inches of snow. The car, overloaded and wobbling in the middle of what Brian believed was the road, skidded and went up onto the pavement. It bounced up heavily and continued slowly, eventually doing a skidding, sliding stop. We ended up with the front wheels hanging over a huge drop with the twinkling lights of Oldham below. We got out. There were eight of us out in the freezing cold, and the snow was coming in vertically like stair rods. Even though it was a gusty wind-driven blizzard we didn't feel the cold, probably due to the pills. We pushed the car backwards onto the road, but as we did so a police car pulled up alongside and two policemen got out and helped us. They looked wide-eyed at the white skid lines going to the edge that were now beginning to be covered by fresh snow. Then, as is the way of the suspicious minded Fuzz, they realised we were too many for the four-seater vehicle.

"Who's the driver?" said one of the coppers.

Lord Snooty, elegantly dressed, pulled out his licence and insurance from a posh leather wallet and handed them to the cop. The man scrutinised the documents in the gale, and then looked us all up and down.

The second policeman asked if we were all in the vehicle.

"No, they're not with us," we said. Lying to the Fuzz came easy to us. Lord Snooty went on saying that the 'others' – the excess people, as the cop had described them – were waiting for a bus, and we didn't know them, and so on. He was sounding like Billy Bunter telling lies to Mr Quelch on the BBC TV show.

We all joined in babbling and worried, in case the cops were suspicious and searched the car – but they didn't. After watching from inside their car to ensure the people who 'weren't with us' returned to stand at the bus stop, they drove off at the same time we did. It took a while before we lost them, driving slowly down the blizzard covered road. As soon as the police overtook us and disappeared into the white distance, we did a 'U' turn, headed back and re-loaded everyone back into the car.

Then we were off to the Wheel singing *'Baby you can drive my car'*, from the Beatles song we'd heard repeatedly earlier. Moston Dave was so relieved; he opened up his stash container and gave everyone three extra pills each.

* * *

To the Wheel

The unique atmosphere in the Wheel is hard to adequately describe. Like trying to explain the shades of green leaves in a tree to a blind man, it had to be experienced to 'know it'. This atmosphere wasn't created by any one element. The primary ones were the music, the crowd, the ambience in the place, and of course the 'gear' that sustained the dancers. It was not due to the DJ or the club owners – it was a community of those belonging to an underground musical scene and dress code. It was a cult but one without a leader.

Certain records seemed to generate and echo the atmosphere, like Bob and Earl's 'Harlem Shuffle', 'I Have Faith In You' by Edwin Starr, The Miracles 'Going to a Go Go', 'Baby I've Got It' by Jimmy Ruffin and lots more. Probably one of the most popular tracks at the Wheel was: *'Walk right on in, Stretch out your arms, Let the lovelight shine on my Soul baby, And let love come runnin' in'* – Darrel Banks' 'Open the Door To Your Heart', which became the opitimisation of Soul and all its associations, feelings and dance moves. That one record, if you had to choose one, was it. It summed up the feeling of the Wheel, and it was 'discovered' by Roger, the Wheel DJ who was in fact not a Mod, but dressed like a 'Dweeb'. He looked like and dressed like our collective dads!

* * *

CHAPTER SEVEN

Meeting in the Jiggy

The Jiggy used to be the Manchester Cavern Club in early 1964. Its DJ was Dave Lee Travis. Lulu and the Luvvers sang 'Shout' there. The Undertakers did 'Just A Little Bit'. Screaming Lord Sutch did 'Jack The Ripper'. Arthur Brown wore a toilet seat around his neck and set 'Fire' to his head long before it became the Jigsaw.

September 1966

The first time I met Doreen was a Thursday night, and I had gone to the Jigsaw Club with Angelo. The Jiggy, as we called it, used to be the Cavern; the Manchester Cavern. It was located in a narrow back alley off Corporation Street called Crompton Court. That night the club was almost deserted. The DJ's selection of music was crap and uselessly echoed about the empty club, so we went back to the entrance and got a pass out to get a few pints in Seftons Bar just along the alley from the club. Like most clubs, a pass out was an inked image from a rubber stamp; a black inked jigsaw outline on our inner wrists. By this time they were wise to the duplication trick – people used to go out and then push wrists together with their mates waiting outside so they could come in later for free, but these days the doorman checked for reverse transfers. In any case, no one was outside. It was a quiet night, and boring in the club. We had no plans to go back in. I could easily have missed her.

It was a strange evening, a pink sunset sky, an unusual light. I lagged behind, looking up at the sky. Angelo went in the pub to get the pints. I stood outside momentarily transfixed: first by the colour of the sky at dusk, and then by a strange chattering noise.

I wondered what it was, and then a black cloud of Starlings swooped down over Marks and Spencer's opposite the front of the pub.

Underneath the wavy rippling concrete canopy of the building, people waited to meet. It was a focal point for meeting friends and dates. The people standing waiting could not see upwards, the canopy obscured the sky dance I was looking at. Curling and twisting high overhead, a dark cloud made up from dots that were individual birds was moving and changing direction without any sign of a leader. Instantly they changed direction and swooped together up, up, rapidly around and around overhead – and then were gone. These birds often darkened the sky over the city as they came in from miles around to roost in the tops of buildings and the window ledges of the town centre at dusk. I had seen them many times before, but this was the first occasion I had really looked. I'd seen them moving instantaneously, changing directions without any leader. How could they do that?

The thought was in my mind later as I sat there drinking my pint of Boddingtons Bitter. Angelo was talking about how awful Red Barrel was. It was a new beer that came in a thing called a 'Keg', and it filled up from the side into a plastic or glass tube before it came out into a real glass pint pot. This was progress – there was no need for manual pump action. Some of this modernistic progress was shit; we stuck to pints being hand pulled and struck several progressive pubs with such equipment off our visiting list.

Angelo said that a barmaid pulling away at the bar pumps was one of the finest sights around, especially when she had a low cut frock on and a good pair of 'Fellolopers.' That was Angelo's description of a certain size and type of tits that we both favoured. He pointed out that the Seftons barmaid had a really great pair of 'Fellolopers'. Perfect they were; large but not big, they had movement up, down, left and right and were also capable of independent action - wobbling clockwise and anti-clockwise simultaneously. The movement of tits was something Angelo was acutely aware of. His favourite were a variation on his descriptive theme; 'Fellolopers walking' - a woman in high heels walking

The Manchester Wheelers

towards him in the street. The heels made them walk in a certain way that added a pulsation into the 'Fellolopers' that simply drove him wild. They had a similar hypnotic effect on me too!

For our next pints we were both at the bar peering down there, as she gazed into our rapidly filling pint glasses – she could do two at once. We stared down too, but hardly looking at the beer foaming up into the glass. It brought me back from the Starlings. This bird had it all. We sat down with our pints and decided to go on a pub crawl instead of going back into the 'Jiggy' – but when we came out of the side door, we heard an irresistible sound coming from the club.

'Break Out' by Mitch Ryder and the Detroit Wheels was banging away. We looked at each other and laughed as we hurriedly walked back into the place. We showed the inked pass out stamps on our wrists. We danced a bit with some black guys we knew and their girls, then sat down. The club was still empty. We moved through the place to the back room stage and sat on it.

We hadn't taken any gear; we very rarely did midweek as it lessened the weekend buzz. However, one black guy obviously had; he was dancing with the roof support pole that was positioned in the middle of the dance floor. It was made of fancy cast steel, like the ones you see in Victorian railway stations. He and the pole were the only ones dancing; he moved around it, his Pork Pie hat pulled down like a visor obscuring his eyes. The track playing now was Ben E. King's 'Spanish Harlem', a slow and soulful song, so everyone – and that wasn't many – had sat down.

I looked around and across the virtually empty dance floor – and there she was.

I saw her for the first time. She was sitting lost in a world of her own. She had a Mary Quant hairstyle, with one side cut short, the other much longer with a sharply pointed long curve at the front, pointing outwards just under her chin. She was intermittently sucking at this longer part of her hair, sticking it in her ear and wiggling it around slowly, very slowly, and then deliberately pulling it out, and entering it again and again into her ear. Occasionally she would remoisten the end in her mouth, and then put it back in her ear – and as a result, each time she did it her entire body was shuddering with the delight of the resulting tickling sensations. She was giggling to herself and completely oblivious of anything else. I was captivated, fascinated, hypnotised.

Her lips were white, thick with Dusty Springfield-style lipstick, black ever-so black eyes with extraordinarily long, long lashes. I was later to find out these were stuck on in a ritual with glue and swearing, followed by application of black eye makeup that took about an hour! She looked just like Julie Driscoll the singer from the Brian auger Trinity, but with a mouth and shining white teeth like Diana Ross. She had a black and white 'Op art' dress on with a hole in the middle showing her belly button. She was pure Mod. Her long, long legs were stretched out in front of her and as the moistened hair arrow entered and re-entered her ear, simultaneously her feet would turn about, the toes of her shoes touching each other, twitching, and then pulling apart, out flat. Each time she did so I could see right up her tiny short mini-dress. I was captivated, time stood still, Ben E. King had become a distant far off echo and I had a steaming hard-on.

She was giggling almost uncontrollably each time she repeated the ear tickling process. She was unconscious of anyone or anything else. She was so absorbed that I doubted she could hear Ben crooning away. She had no idea I was gawping at her. Right there and then I fell in love with her. It was instantaneous! I was actually quite shocked at the emotion she had aroused in me, so instantly. She'd got me higher than Amphetamine Sulphate!

I never usually had much courage to go and ask girls to dance – but there right then, something possessed me. I strode across the empty dance floor, past the supporting pole with its dancing attachment who was now caressing it with one hand, the other holding his spliff delicately between two fingers and drawing deeply on the last drag of it. As I passed him, the unmistakable pungent smell of Hash went up my nostrils.

And then I was there, standing in front of her.

"Will you dance?" I said.

She looked up. I held my breath. Would she? Especially now it was a slow number, and an empty dance floor?

The DJ had probably left a Ben E. King LP playing. The next track was 'Amor' sung in Spanish.

Would she?

Time was frozen.

She let the hair fall out from her ear and looked at me. I scrutinised her face. I stared at her through a strange grey mist all around the edges of my vision. I was thinking to myself on several simultaneous threads. I was very nervous, I was very aware of my physical state and – yes – I confirmed my earlier opinion; she definitely looked like a cross between Julie Driscoll and Diana Ross. She had the same smile as Diana, all big white teeth in a smiling row with the addition of Driscol bright wide eyes and large black, black lashes. She was also very thin like Twiggy, thin as a rake as my dad would say. To cap it all she had the perfect Mary Quant hairstyle. She was stunningly beautiful. Stunningly Mod.

One thing I hadn't noticed before – she was chewing gum, and as was the method in those days she wasn't just chewing a single piece. The whole packet was in her mouth, so she took her time to re-position it to be able to speak. It seemed to me like ages passing.

When she did answer, she held the gum by pushing it with her tongue against her left cheek, and looked down shyly, away from me. In an absent-minded way, she said: "OK."

I took her hand, and pulled her up off the alcove bench where she'd been sitting next to another girl, who was now looking up and studying me. The girl in my hand was tall, lanky and thin, but not as tall as me. We walked to the centre of the dance floor. Ben E. King continued awhile, then the DJ seamlessly connected to another slow number on his twin decks: 'Hey Girl' by Freddie Scott. I almost trembled as I held her close and listened to Freddie crooning and pleading with his girl not to put him down. My dance steps were fumbling, nervously motivated and made all the worse by the 'stork on' I had in my pants.

I silently pleaded with the DJ to keep slow records going. But like all D.J.'s he wanted dancers on his floor, so as soon as he noticed us, he slid the tempo up with a more up-beat 45.

The Supremes 'Come See about Me' moved the mood onwards and Angelo asked the girl that was sitting next to Doreen for a dance – she was Doreen's sister. We released each other from the slow dance embrace as the others joined in. The sisters kept giggling at each other and began intermittently whispering in each other's ears as we all danced together in a circle. They had a kind of secret language between them. Doreen's sister Jenny was called 'Jinny' and Doreen was 'Dreensy' for some inexplicable reason that wasn't forthcoming – no matter how many times we shouted the question to them both, they just giggled without replying. Our shouting to each other above the dance music was contorted, stunted, stupid – mine had additional nervousness, due to the effect she had had on me, and the fact that I had to keep surreptitiously moving my rock-hard dick around in my pants so that it neither hurt me nor embarrassed me.

We asked if they wanted to go to the pub for a drink. They said OK. We all went out together, the girls were stamped and we went back into Seftons. We had more pints of Boddingtons, they had Brandy and Babychams. We sat and talked, and I found out they lived in Gorton. We did cockroach racing by sticking the ends of our lighted cigarettes under the arses of the cockroaches on the floor under the tables – building a match stalk corral start and finish line, and betting the next pint payment on the losers. We had a great time. We had hit it off!

Then we went back in the club. We danced and shouted in each other's ears for a few more hours - just monosyllabic shouting, comments on the records, finding out that they liked, which was of course Soul and other Mod stuff. The last few records were 'smoochers' and I got to hold her close again, and immediately my brain moved into my underpants.

When the 'Jiggy' closed we took them to the bus station in Piccadilly Gardens. 'Dreensey' aka Doreen and I kissed, and then she said I could see her again. She and her sister were both going to a party tomorrow – Friday – somewhere in Dickinson Road. We arranged to meet them at 8 pm at a café on the corner of the main road coming out of Manchester city centre; Anson Parade. They were so exact in their directions; I knew for certain they would turn up. I'd arranged several dates with girls I'd danced with before —
it'd be something vague like meeting at the clock above Marks and Spencer's; and after half an hour past the agreed time, I'd be still there, humming Sandy Shaw's 'Girl Don't Come.'

I floated six inches above the pavement as I walked along to Cannon Street bus station to get the Number 17, and I could easily have ended up at the end of the line in Rochdale. My mind was that preoccupied, and completely tuned into the thoughts of that night out – meeting Doreen, and the thought of seeing her again. I had a girlfriend! I was at Blackley Tram Office, and had to run down stairs and 'deck off' as the bus pulled away from my stop. Like the song by Doris Troy, it really was amazing, it was 'Just One Look'. It had been love at first sight!

✳ ✳ ✳

The Manchester Wheelers

CHAPTER EIGHT

Going to a Go Go

'Let me tell you bout the birds and the bees and the flowers and the trees, and the moon up above and a thing called love...'
        - Jewel Akens

It was a cold Friday night. We had been to this area often. Lots of parties happened around and along Dickinson and Wilbraham Road, as most of it was flats. The area had a bit of a buzz as it was the studio location for BBC's 'Top of the Pops' in a converted church. We had gone to a flat here on one memorable occasion when Roger eagle was stoned on some very nice black afghan and told us for hours about his interests in music whilst sharing his joints. He never did pills, he would never touch them, and he said he had seen enough of it at the Wheel. He said they fucked up your mind; whereas pot let you think and helped you to appreciate music.

Marijuana makes you relax, makes you talk. Often at the time it seems important, these conversations that takes place between 'tokers', but upon reflection if you can remember anything, it's usually inconsequential, even stupid. You tend to laugh a lot, often too much at nothing at all. It makes you hungry, especially for chocolate or other sweet things; it can enhance sex, and it can promote paranoia.

THC is the chemical ingredient; tetrahydrocannabinol, which gives initial stimulation, giddiness and euphoria - the rush. Then, after that initial high follows a period of sedation and often pleasant tranquillity. A room of pot smokers can be silent, because pot can initiate vivid dreaming sleep. Mood changes and altered perceptions of time can happen. Thinking can easily become disrupted with silly, fragmented ideas and memories. Increased appetite, heightened sensory awareness and pleasure may be on the beneficial side. Negative results are mental confusion, sometimes acute panic, anxiety attacks and fear without knowing why or where it originates; a sense of helplessness and loss of self-control – a feeling of being watched by invisible eyes. But apart from that, its users speak very well of it.

In anticipation of meeting Doreen again I was wearing my new coat. It was a long length double breasted navy blue overcoat in a Napoleonic military style, with very large buttoned-down lapels and eight large dark blue regimented buttons running down along the front. Angelo had a very large oversized high-shouldered Cromby that fell straight down to his ankles; it had a three-inch broad belt and buckle.

The café was indeed on Anson Parade just as the sisters had said; it was a paved shopping area with Dickinson Road on one corner and a junction with Upper Brook Street, with areas for parking scooters off the road and off the pavement. Very clear instructions for girls!

We took up seats on the tall chromium stools at the counter that was completely constructed of glass and chrome fittings. Inside it had sandwiches and cakes on display. There at one corner was a large Lemon Meringue Pie and an arctic Roll. Although arctic Roll was regarded as the greatest invention since sliced bread or at least as amazing as a fourpenny frozen Jubbly, I hated it. I had always been suspicious of how the ice cream in the centre never seemed to ever really melt but stayed in a kind of splodge. This suggested it was not made from ice cream at all, but something akin to Angel Delight which I also hated – to me it tasted of washing up liquid, maybe because of the amount that my Mum used to clean the pots with. But I was not entirely convinced that her cleanliness regime was the answer, and remained convinced that the factory put Fairy Liquid in as an ingredient to stop it from thawing out.

This café had a coffee making machine, the same type as the

Italian coffee machines in town centre cafés and also at the Wheel and the Cona and the Mogambo. It was a highly chromed up Gaggia that was singing away whooshing and slurping and generating that unmistakable fantastic smell. We sat there. We waited. Girls were always late. I kept looking at the desserts behind the glass counter. Angelo and I were both mad about cakes. Soon we were into large slices of the pie with forks, not spoons (another Mod thing), shovelling the pie into our mouths just as the girls entered. We had worked on our image, thinking we were so cool sitting there smoking in our overcoats, but now we were somewhat embarrassed, losing our cool, and caught eating lemon meringue pies like a pair of kids.

We both had black Chelsea boots with Cuban heels, and under our overcoats we wore Ben Sherman shirts and sweaters and straight navy trousers. Both of us were reeking of Visconti di Modrone's Aqua di Selva eau de Cologne. We were smoking W H &
O Wills oval cigarettes: Passing Clouds. They had a Cavalier on the front packet. Trend setting and image was everything to Mods; it generated an air of arrogance and superiority.

It didn't seem to trouble Angelo but I was extremely image conscious on this occasion and wondered if eagerly tucking into lemon meringue pie had looked juvenile.

I had come on the pillion of Angelo's Cento Scooter, as mine - the brunt of much derision and jokes - had finally packed it in. The thing was a maroon Durkopp Diana.

I had bought it fourth or fifth hand for nineteen pounds. It was an incredibly powerful 250cc when it went, but more often it didn't. After it fucked up that night, I vowed we were parting company and it was probably heading for the 'cut' (the canal) as nobody in their right mind was going to buy it from me. The thing was German – every time I parked it at work it got a laugh and the same old shouted jokes as I chained it to a post in the work's car park: 'Who's going to steal it?', 'Did you get it from yer' dad as war reparation from the Gerry's?', or 'Where did you find that, was it shot down?', 'Is it a Junkers 88, or just junk?' and so on. I often wore a long black leather coat and ended up getting Nazi salutes from the Rocker types who parked up nearby. It was also spoiling my image with my Mod mates who all had LI 150s or GT 200s. If I went down to the Wheel on it, I had to hide it down some back street and then finish my journey on foot, whilst they all proudly pulled up directly outside the club. My closer mates called it the Dunksopp.

I put down the fork, picked up the cigarette I had parked in the thick glass ashtray and took a long pull on the oval shaped fag. I was internally, silently singing to myself a Beatles song, like a prayer as the girls approached:

'Last night is the night I will remember you by... Treat me like you did the night before...'

"Hiya," she said in a full Mancunian nasal accent. Doreen was dressed and made up just as she had been the night before. She asked if she too could have the same dessert. Relieved that my image was intact, I ordered her a slice of the lemon pie, and provided a cigarette to go with it, and then we talked.

She worked at an office on Whitworth Street near the Wheel! She lived in Gorton, along Hyde Road up past Belle Vue, near the Wellington pub. She had just bought the Otis Blue LP, and didn't go to the Wheel All-nighters but wanted to, just as soon as she could persuade her mother to let her stay out overnight. Whilst she was telling me all this I could see again that kind of misty glow surrounding her – and then the whole world had gone away, except for her. I had the same almost sinking or melting feeling from the other night. She was the fulcrum of my entire attention and I was sliding into a feeling that was becoming more intense with each moment. All of a sudden everything she said seemed to have fantastic importance – it was all of great value and interest to me. We stared into each other's eyes in a dreamlike state. Nothing else seemed to matter. I was on a Doreen high.

I was really falling in love. I felt it as a distinct new state of being. I knew it for certain. It was physical and emotional and completely engulfing. It was never like this before. I gave myself completely to this feeling. I wanted this. I wanted to listen and look at her. I only wanted to talk to her. I only wanted to talk about her. I had seen this before from others, and watched them become boring, just talking about the person they were going out with constantly. But it's a sure sign of being infatuated, of being in love. And I was falling in love!

Her interests, her hair, her mouth, the look in her eyes, the way her clothes looked on her, the scent of her perfume; I felt drunk. Time seemed as though it was standing still, there was only this moment. As I looked at her I began to notice more of that strange peripheral mist – it was around her head and I was viewing her through a tunnel of bright light. Electricity was rising from the base of my spine, tingling electricity, it was similar yet different to being blocked. It was a tight sensation in my spine, up it came and moved outwards, reaching my fingers. I moved my hand towards hers as she sat on the stool next to me. Then hers touched mine, our fingers met and melded together and the tingling intensified. My entire body jolted with it, I rose up at least an inch off my seat and a flow of something I can only describe as an exchange of static electricity flowed between us, but somehow I knew instinctively it was something different. It flowed between our fingers as we pulled them slowly apart. We both laughed and knew each other felt this same flow. Our hands played together, fingers entwined, moving exploring each other's hands as we looked in each other's eyes and knowing with an unspoken certainty we were both experiencing this delight, this magic touch, this magic moment, a strange new state which we had never known before.

Then I had the sensation of another familiar feeling; inside my trousers there was an uncoiling. I had a steaming hard on. Then I had another level of feeling. It was an awareness that I had done all this before, that as each moment unfolded I knew how it would do so and exactly as it did. Then like a whiz-bang magic trick, I was in two places at the same time. As all these internal events were unfolding, I was also somewhere else! I'd had these strange events throughout my life from being a kid. It was a déjà vu event, but this one was different from the previous type I had encountered. I could catch onto it and hold it and 'see' it in a detached way. Not only did I have the feeling that I was in two places, I was aware that there existed another me that could dispassionately observe these simultaneous events.

My body and its sensations were one thing I was acutely aware of and the other was a new clarity of thought about the physical and mental processes themselves that I was experiencing. I became extremely and acutely conscious. Then I had an incite: that there was indeed another layer to all this, there was a further observer. Was this my mind experiencing madness? Maybe? Maybe not? It was a little like the strange type of anxiety feelings that sometimes came with high grade Smack. I wasn't frightened by this discovery. I didn't believe I was losing my mind. Was this the result of too many pills and too many All-nighter sessions?

I considered what was happening. It was a feeling unlike a normal déjà vu - if there is such a thing. They were fleeting instantaneous events, impossible to latch onto; but this one was very different, this one was continuing much longer than the déjà vu experiences that so many people describe. My inner perception was expanding backwards in time like a string of pearls, each one connected, each a small déjà vu event from my past. I also understood this was not simply a connection with the past; it went the other way up too!

Then whilst continuing to touch fingers, another simultaneous event unfolded as my hands played with Doreen's. Suddenly, I was looking down from above at another person who was also me! This other 'me' was looking down through a round porthole window from a very high place through clouds to a beautiful view of the Earth moving slowly beneath, a brightly lit ocean and land, slowly creeping along at a steady incremental pace. A strange realisation hit me; I was sitting in a plane looking out of the window and I was crying. For a moment time was frozen – and it was weird, as I had never been up in a plane. It all happened in a flash, and yet was a complete and timeless experience in its own right. Then it was gone and only the face of Doreen existed.

Although I was shaken by the experience, I shrugged it off quickly. It was put away, but not forgotten. Later I began to be curious about mental states, drug-induced thinking, emotions and how they affected the brain. The mind and the emotions and 'uppers' all being entangled together at certain times could produce a weird cocktail of inner states.

We both became intrigued with the electric energies produced by touching each other, and began pointing fingers at each other, almost touching but not quite. It had the effect of a tingling electrical discharge, especially at the point between the eyes on the forehead. We played at pointing our fingers at the space on the lower forehead between our eyes. She cringed and shook and giggled. She was sensuous, full of this strange electricity. She did it to me from a distance and it still generated the same effect. It was as though all the strange emotional and sexual and electrical feelings I had been experiencing were drawn together to that point in my forehead. That place on my forehead above my nose between my eyes became intensely sensitive. It pulsated. It hurt. I now understood where her obsession with sticking her pointed hair into her ears came from!

Then we came down to earth and out of our mutual absorption to find the two people behind the counter staring in our direction. Angelo and Doreen's sister were also looking weirdly at us; now we became self conscious and slightly embarrassed.

'I Just Don't Know What to Do With Myself' by Dusty Springfield was now playing on the jukebox. Until now we had been oblivious to it and everything else around us. I asked Doreen if she liked it, and she started to rave about Dusty, saying she was her favourite singer.

I said the song was first written for Dionne Warwick, by Hal David and Burt Bacharach – and then immediately felt stupid about my display of knowledge, like I'd spurted it out to impress her. Why couldn't I just shut up? I sat there, chastising myself, feeling like an idiot.

Then Angelo came over from where he and Doreen's sister had been sitting and said, "Let's go to the party - it's just along from here."

I picked up the 'party' can of Red Barrel we had bought at an off-licence on our way here; it held seven pints, it would be our admission ticket. I kept it against my chest with my other arm around Doreen as we all left the café.

When we were in the large flat that held the party, we just talked to each other. Finding out more about each other, about what we did, what we liked. She liked George Best, the Coasters, especially their comedy track 'Shopping for Clothes' and she owned their LP. I was still impressed even after she admitted that the LP was her brother's, who had been a Rocker. She said how big a fan of the Beatles she was; Mods preferred the Stones, but what the hell, we all secretly loved the Beatles. I told her my secret Beatles admiration, that I also thought them to be just brilliant. Then we talked about Otis, we both loved Otis. We were engrossed in our conversation, once again oblivious to anyone else in the room.

She had a kind of strange capacity that was hard to describe, a type of 'allurement' something beyond beauty that captured something inside, somewhere deep. It certainly got into my heart, and I think it unconsciously affected quite a few of the men she met – but this I would learn later. She had fabulous legs and her short skirt showed them off perfectly. She sat on a very low settee. I and everyone else there could see all of her long legs, right up to her knickers. She had no stockings on, and I found out later she dyed her legs! She wore no undergarments like corsets, and hated to wear tights. As she told me about this quite a few people, especially the blokes, were staring at her. It was time to go. Doreen and her sister had to be home early, and it was a good time to leave, especially as Angelo had nicked a handful of singles. We slowly went to the bus stop to put Doreen and her sister on their bus after a bit of 'necking', and arranged to see them on Saturday afternoon at the Kardomah café in St Ann's Square in Manchester.

***

We sped through the traffic on the Cento.

Angelo was doing his favourite 'dare' - going right through red lights. Angelo had stashed the records he had 'acquired' inside a pocket sewn into the inside of his coat for such a purpose. We both had shoplifter's coats. We had done it ourselves, borrowing our mums' sewing kits. He passed the records over his shoulder to me. I sorted them out on the way home, 'Que Sera Sera' - The High Keyes, 'What Kind Of Fool' - Dixie Cups, 'I'll Always Love You' - The Isley Brothers, 'Oh Carolina' - Folks Brothers, 'Every Little Bit Hurts' - Brenda Holloway. 'Two Lovers' - Mary Wells.

"Must have been a girl's record collection," said Angelo. "Oh well. Every little bit helps." We laughed.

The last one was the Mindbenders – 'A Groovy Kind Of Love', which was a cover version of the original by Patti Labelle and the Blue Bells. I slung it under the wheels of a passing bus, and then passed the rest back to him. He stashed them away again under his coat as we headed for home.

I reflected on my second encounter with Doreen. I couldn't tell Angelo anything about my feelings. That would be soppy. Birds were for fucking – then on to the next one. Love was fucking with kisses. There was no way to tell a mate about love; I couldn't discuss the secret and strange mental events brought about by the feelings of being in love, and there was no way to talk of electrical finger touching.

* * *

The Manchester Wheelers

CHAPTER NINE

Otis Plays and Plays

'Smoking cigarettes and drinking coffee...'
- Otis Redding

I was 19 years old, she was just 17, and the way she looked was way beyond compare. Doreen lived in a distant part of Manchester on the route out to Hyde. I was singing the Beatles song as I cycled there, as the 'Dunksopp' had yet again failed to start.

I put my old orange 'Cinelli' racing bike inside the entrance hall in her house. I had brought the Otis Blue LP with me. At that time it was the pre-requisite badge of a real Mod to be seen with it, often tucked under an arm. It used to be that Mods once carried around 'The Rolling Stones' LP, followed by The Sue Story LP, but of course that time had long passed. In any case no-one could see the LPs I carried – they were stuffed inside my shirt, held against my chest. I had also brought my Elmore James, Howlin Wolf, Sonny Terry and Brownie Magee, and my prized Memphis Slim LPs from my collection. I guess I did it to show off my roots in Blues music and to impress her, but of course the 'Blues' stuff had no such effect.

I had skipped 'day release' at Moston Technical College to see her again. At the last session at college, I had been asked by the English class teacher to bring in my Blues records to play to the class. She had asked about our interests, and was setting a task for us to write about them. I had been selected because my enthusiasm for my Blues collection had made me shoot my mouth off. As a result I had been recruited to give a talk about the Blues.

However, a strange miracle intervened; just as Howlin' Wolf

was getting into 'Goin' Down Slow' on the College record player; the 'b' side of Smokestack Lightnin', a lightning bolt lit up the room. Suddenly it was chucking it down outside, and the lightning flash was just a reflection through the windows of a gigantic fork of lightning that covered the sky with a strike of zig zag lightning filaments, held frozen in time. It was quite amazing – it was a real 'smokestack lightnin', and it hit the chimney on a terraced house outside.

There was an almighty crack and a terrible smash, and bricks lay out all over the street; it would make the local builder smile. Then the sky reverted back to black, from the silver it had once instantly been. We all stopped and stared at the chimney outside where a strange event was unfolding; it was ball lightning. An intensely bright yellow globe was on the roof, it ran down the chimney, a bright ball of light, and then it stopped and just floated on top of the rainwater gliding over the blue grey roof tiles. All the class ran to the windows to watch it as it floated over the roof and slowly glided down the wall, very slow, it was 'goin' down slow' in the time and the same beat as Howlin Wolf's lament.

The fire brigade arrived and put out the fire inside the building, and then the firemen just stared dumbfounded at the wrecked chimney. Wow, I thought, that was a real demonstration of magical Blues power. A real coincidence? But who would believe it. Only I saw the relationship with Wolf's 'Smokestack Lightning', which in reality was the flame from a train chimney funnel. I never did give that talk, and I guessed they could do without me after the events of that last Stormy Monday, so I dodged college.

I had arranged this meeting with Doreen when I said goodbye to her at the bus stop after the party near Dickinson Road on Friday. I couldn't wait all week to meet her at the Kardomah. Of course, I couldn't see her at night on Saturday – that was reserved for the All-nighter at the Wheel. And Sunday, well – Sunday was reserved for more of the same, and all day coming down. So Monday it was. The only problem was ducking out of college; it was 'day release' from working in the aircraft factory as an apprentice, and if you skipped off, you got reported.

It started out badly. Of course my scooter had fucked up; 'Fucking Dunce-cop,' I cursed inwardly. The Germans were supposed to be so efficient. So it was the pedal power and a reunion with my Cinelli racing bike.

Doreen's parents were out. I told her I skipped technical college, and she said she'd dodged work telling them she was sick. She was a clerk at an office, and she told me that most workers there felt obliged to have a couple of week's worth of sick days each year! I retrieved my LPs from my shirt. They would not fit into the 'butty bag' I carried over my shoulder whilst riding, and inevitably the only one she wanted to hear was Otis. I put it on the Dansette and set the auto-changer arm so that it would play repeatedly.

As we sat listening to 'Otis Blue' on the settee, we looked at each other and held hands. We had no words; sometimes words can't say what you're feeling. A nervous tension built around us. Almost immediately I felt that same tingling up my spine, exactly as it had occurred before. As I looked at her, the same strange thing happened again; she started to have a sort of mist surrounding her as though my eyes only wanted to see her, and the rest of the room became fuzzy and misty. Her face lit up, her eyes suddenly had more brightness in them and seemed to have an energy pouring out to me. Her lipstick shone with a wet-look glow, and as I thought about all of this, as Otis was lamenting *'I don't need you old man trouble... I don't want you old man trouble...'*, I kissed her. I was compelled to kiss her. For a long, long time our tongues twined around each other's. It was dreamlike.

Otis continued on through: 'Ol' Man Trouble', 'Respect', 'A Change Is Gonna Come', 'Down In The valley', 'I've Been Loving You Too Long'. Then it repeated, because the record player arm was set to auto change. Doreen and I had no feeling of time passing. It stood still. When Otis had finished side one for the second time, I became aware of it and put the flip side on, resetting the record player on automatic. 'Shake', 'My Girl', 'Wonderful World', 'Rock Me Baby', 'Satisfaction', 'You Don't Miss Your Water', all of them passed by as a background to another endless kiss.

We kissed and each kiss seemed to last an entire track. Each time the LP finished, Otis would go again. I realised later that was probably why I got such an excited feeling every time I heard Otis. I also thought how amazing it was, and this was without any 'charge' –usually you only got these kind of 'insight' feelings if you smoked high quality dope.

We spoke about that strange tingling; we both knew it for certain and we laughed, because we knew then that this was something special. I put my finger about two inches from the centre of her forehead, and she shook as if she'd been electrocuted.

We slid to the floor. We were inside a timeless cocoon. Slowly I pulled at her clothes, got her bra off and kissed and sucked and bit at her hard, sticking-out nipples. I pulled down her white knickers; they became wrapped around her ankles. Her ankles and legs were white as a sheet, as the weekend leg dye she used had washed off. As I entered her for the first time she screamed – she said she was a virgin and had "never had it before." I wasn't so sure I believed her, but after what seemed like ages pushing with pain for both of us, I asked if she wanted me to stop, and she said, "No, no don't stop. Keep on pushing." She then cried and laughed, saying it was great pain, and I began to believe it.

We thrashed about on the front room floor to a continuing Otis soundtrack. It was probably only minutes, but it felt like time was non-existent. Then it got to be just too much with the pressure building up, too much to hold back and I pulled out quickly. It was so intense; I laughed uncontrollably, I couldn't stop. She hit me, slapping my face, and then she cried. I cried. She reached for her cigarettes. We smoked. We kissed. We laughed. It was silent; Otis had long since finished as the record player had been kicked over and stopped. We were lying there naked, and I stared at her. I had never really seen a completely naked woman lying before me, and one that didn't have pubic hairs. She was closely shaved between her lovely long legs. Then I heard something at the door. We both turned from looking at each other to see the face of her father staring in through the front bay window.

The Manchester Wheelers

I knew I was In Love. Doreen, Doreen, Doreen, I kept saying as I rode home on my push bike. I started singing loudly, lots of romantic Soul songs at the top of my voice as I cycled home to Blackley in North Manchester. I was on a love high, but came down off that cloud the following day when my father was taken into hospital.

Next time I met up with Doreen we went to her local: The Lord Nelson on Hyde Road. It was an old pub with old-fashioned oak beams overhead. I sat there with my pint. She sat opposite me and sipped her brandy and Babycham and got her cigarettes out from her patent leather handbag. Doreen smoked too much, but I could easily forgive her as every time she drew upon her Benson and Hedges it captivated me. Her lips moved forwards to meet with her hand inserting the cigarette into her lips which stuck out and pointed around the cigarette tip. Her lips became a Marilyn Monroe kiss, slowly caressing that cigarette. Vertical lines in segmented strips formed horizontally along both the top and bottom of her ruby red lips just like parallel train lines reducing at the sides of her mouth, converging where the huge dimples in her cheeks began. She sucked at the 'ciggy' and the cigarette end brightened and rapidly sped along, consuming the white cigarette paper. Her lungs inhaled the smoke and air pressure rushed to caress her deflated cheeks. I could forgive her chain smoking routine because every time she lit up a new one, it turned me on.

She said her father had not mentioned seeing us on that fantastic Monday afternoon. He had opened the front door and had quietly gone into the kitchen and stayed there whilst we dressed hurriedly, putting our clothes back on as if it were an Olympic gold medal event.

He'd had a double shock that day – Doreen revealed another story as I downed most of my pint. Her father worked at a local garage and sometimes came home at dinner time to make his own lunch before going back at 1 pm. On that day I had arranged to come at one-thirty, and she'd spent a long time in the morning getting ready. She said that as she sat in the bath after cutting her finger nails, she looked at her pubic hairs and decided to cut them all off. She did this and put them in a pile on the side of the bath, but forgot to flush them down the toilet when she got out of the water and went to her bedroom to dry her hair. No sooner had she gone into her room, her dad ran up the stairs to use the toilet. He must have sat there staring at her mound of cut pubic hairs! She told me that nothing was ever said about it. She laughed about it. I went to the bar to get more drinks.

We met again on the following Saturday at the Kardomah in St Ann's square, where we ate chocolate cake and had hot chocolate in glasses that were held inside a chrome bracket with a handle. She wanted me to take her to the Wheel All-nighter. She already knew I was planning to keep on going. It caused our first argument. She wasn't pleased and wanted to go to the All-nighters with me – but I didn't want her to start on the pills, which would be an inevitable outcome if she went. If this was love then would I rather be lonely? I didn't know. I just didn't like arguing with her.

***

CHAPTER TEN

The Blue Note and Stax

Stacks of Stax; A Stax Soul club in Manchester – and then, on the 23rd of March 1967, we went to the amazing Stax show at the Palace Theatre on Oxford Road.

It was Saturday afternoon. We had once again been in the Kardomah café restaurant drinking cappuccinos and eating chocolate cake in St Ann's Square. It was a hangout for lots of Manchester Soul Mods. Most of those hanging around were the more affluent lot; the Jewish guys and a few Jewish girls. Behind our backs they called us the Gohyem, behind theirs we called them tight-arsed bastards due to the fact that they repeatedly disappeared into the bogs in the pub when it was their round.

There was a Jewish Soul Mod 'clique' in Manchester. Some of them knew or were relations of the owners of the Wheel, the Adabi brothers; one of them even got a job as a DJ there. I had a few friends who were Jewish lads. They used to joke about Saturday, their Sabbath, which of course they didn't attend. In a similar fashion they lied to their parents, just like we did as Catholics to ours. Their story was that they were attending a special out of town synagogue, and their parents reluctantly believed them. They often sang its theme tune: '*Going to the Synago - Go...*'

It was one of these lads, Lez verner, who tried to tell us of a new club that a family friend had opened near London Road, but we didn't take much notice. We were more interested in checking out record shops. This was something you needed to periodically do, to check out refreshed deletion piles. So we went over Piccadilly Gardens to Mazell's; a large second hand record shop on London Road. After half an hour going through the rows of cheap 45's I found the Marvellows on the ABC label: 'I Do', and next to it was a Doo Wop Rock and Roll track 'Book Of Love' by the Monotones at three pence each. Then as we came back up towards Piccadilly Gardens, with our cheap deleted records, we heard in the distance that unmistakable sound. It was a Stax record, coming from an open door on Gore Street just before the Waldorf Pub, near 'Dracula's Place' as we called it, at the end on Roby Street; the 'Blood Bank'. We were just like the 'ah Bisto' kids in the adverts for gravy on the TV. We were forced to follow it to its source. I said to Doreen, "This must be the place Lez has been going on about."

As we got closer we saw what looked like a house with a big door. There were a few steps up to the half-closed door and coming out from it was that chunky Stax riff I'd know anywhere. It was Booker T. & the MGs with Sam and Dave singing 'Hold On I'm Coming'.

I went in first and Doreen followed. The music changed to Eddie Floyd's 'Knock On Wood'. I was sneaking down the stairs inquisitively to see who else knew this music. I went down the steps and around a corner, and there at the bottom was a glamorous gold-bejeweled Jewish lady sitting reading behind a small desk. I turned to go back up, but she said, "Its OK, come down."

She was called Debbie Fogel – this was her new club, and we were the exact clients she wanted to recruit. She said there would be free baked potatoes! She asked us to look around.

We did, and it was amazing; there was a bar and a small dance floor. It was to be a Soul music club, and they had a new DJ who used to work at another club. She asked if we went to the Wheel, then said that Roger the DJ there had left to work right here at the Blue Note. "Fantastic," I said, and I couldn't believe it. Roger playing his record collection in a club with a bar? Heaven on Earth!

* * *

The Manchester Wheelers

Roger Eagle

There he was, sitting on the stage area checking out his discs from his holdall bag. Inside it he had a wooden box he'd had made to ensure his 45s didn't get damaged. I said hello; I knew him from a few occasions at the Wheel when I'd made requests – also from talking to him now and again in the Wheel, in the Cona café, and on one occasion at his flat when he'd shared some smoke. He said he had some great new imports from the USA, all Stax stuff.

Roger was obviously in a good mood. On occasions he could be very prickly, especially when deejaying; if you requested something he had a low opinion of, he would give you a resigned look of frustration. It was a look that said you ought to know better. He was in a good mood and praised me for buying the Monotones 45 I had showed him. He said that Doo Wop groups were the linear originators that eventually lead to the sound of Detroit and Motown.

Roger went on to tell me that working at the Blue Note was temporary and he was getting his own club. He was going to call it Staxx with two x's, so it would not be like a rip off of the record label from East McLemore Avenue in Memphis. The club premises he had in mind was once the place that Jimmy Saville used to have on Fountain Street called The Three Coins, opposite the Royal Oak Pub.

Roger was severely pissed off with the Adabi brothers who owned the Wheel. "Tight Jewish buggers," he called them. There was no doubt he was the one who knew the right music to play and the live acts to book, and he was responsible for much of the success of the Wheel. He never claimed to have generated the scene there. The Mod thing was nothing to do with him, he could claim the surge from Blues to Soul was something he started, but it had all taken on its own momentum. Roger was forthright in his condemnation of us, "the pill heads" as he called us. He was never a part of the overall combination that made up the whole scene; he was its backdrop, mostly invisible, playing fantastic sounds. He was very bitter that the brothers wouldn't recognise his contribution, and wouldn't give him a pay rise. Roger got his pay rise from £3 to £5 at the Blue Note.

Recently at the Wheel he was often in dark sullen moods. When he looked like that, we avoided asking for any requests. He couldn't abide fools, but did recognise the spirit of those who loved his music. At the Wheel he did play requests, but mostly preferred to be left alone to play exactly what he chose to put on.

DL had plagued him with requests for Surfing music, his other love after Soul music.

'Bucket T', 'Little GTO', by Ronnie and The Daytonas, 'Out Of Limits' by the Marketts, 'Wipe Out', by the Surfaris, 'Pipeline' by the Chantays, 'Miserlou', by Dick Dale, 'Surf City' and 'Dead Man's Curve' by Jan and Dean were all OK – but when he asked Roger to play 'Surfin' Bird' by The Trashmen, a recording that was funny but could drive you crazy, Roger flipped and said he was banning all Surf music forever, with the only exception being the Beach Boys.

He was plagued with certain types of 'know-it-all' record collectors, or persons testing him to see if he had certain obscure records. This behaviour he countered in his own style, often by insults, sometimes with humour that few understood, but I guessed he did understand his own private jokes. He might say few words but when he did it was usually correct, and sometimes apocryphal. After being hounded for several hours by groups of know it alls he would quietly say some obscure thing to tantalise them.

I remember one occasion when he told a group about Lou Rawls relating a story about 'The Hawk', the name given to the biting cold wind that plagued Chicago in the winter months. He told them there was a record he played about it. They looked puzzled. He looked very pleased with himself. They had never heard it. The reason was that he cut out the intro that had Lou relating the tale about the 'Mighty Hawk' – when he had to get out of the city and away from his poverty. Lou Rawls told the story in a spoken monologue on the introduction to the song 'Dead end Street'. They knew the song, but had never heard the intro because

Roger positioned the needle on his deck to cut it out. They went away bemused, probably planning to search through all the Lou Rawls singles and LPs, to be able to know what Roger knew, looking for a track called 'The Hawk'! He was a Soul master with knowledge about black American music that no one could possibly match.

Roger often complained about the money he got at the Wheel, and was always saying he was leaving. He did a trade to supplement his DJ salary of three quid a night, apart from working by day in Trafford Park at the Kellogg's Corn Flakes factory. This trade was selling records. He was most likely the first person who could potentially hype up a Soul or R&B record to increase its sales value, as he knew they were almost impossible to obtain. But he never did so, or at least not intentionally. He charged fair amounts, especially to those he knew were music fans, and not idiot collectors, as he called them, who were drawn to the rarity thing for boosting their own status. He also sold copies of his magazine called the R&B Scene, but that was a labour of love only costing a shilling. Neil Carter was his pal and assistant on the magazine, and also a DJ at the Wheel.

Roger respected those who were really interested in the music. He liked those who knew nothing and said so. These he advised, while those that 'knew everything' were beyond his help. He liked a whole range of music and intrepidly introduced it. He imported a large amount of records, often bringing them to the Wheel at the same time they were released in the States. He told me he had a couple of mates who did this for him. He gave me an address in the USA where Soul records could be bought or bid for by mail list auction. That's how I got my copy of The Radiants' 'Ain't No Big Thing'. He got free packages of Stax records direct from Stan Axton at Stax records and was organising with Duke Records to send him DJ releases direct from the USA and hoped for a similar deal with, Motown and Atlantic who he had written to. He had a certain respect with record company's: a few had been sending him pre-release and D.J. advanced copies of Blues, Soul and R&B releases due to the magazine he had published and often sold at the Twisted Wheel: The R N' B SCENE.

Roger did not like 'pill heads' as he called everyone in the Wheel although he was spotted now and again with funny smelling roll ups, and didn't give stuff for Mod bullshit as he called it. He was a DJ without glamour. Jimmy Saville was a nice bloke, but he charged a fortune, was always announced as a star and 'worked' for about forty minutes, coming on after his warm-up side kick, Ugly Ray Terret, or Tony Prince. Although a Yorkshire man, the best thing about 'Jim' was that he was a keen cyclist and lived in a council flat in Great Clowes Street Salford.

Dave Lee Travis ponced around Manchester in a US Army Jeep; Jimmy Saville was in his 'E' Type, and Roger was on the buses. These blokes had cultivated catch phrases and looks; Jimmy Saville had dyed white hair, and was careful always to be seen with a cigar. Roger had none of these attributes, he was not a self publicist, he rarely spoke over the PA system, hardly ever introduced records, and this meant you had to ask him what it was. And he worked at it for hours at a stretch, bringing all his own records and 'all for three quid', as he would remark. He was never going to be a big star like Jimmy or the other Manchester high profile DJs, but this didn't bother him. He was a crusader for black American music and, as he said, he did get to meet and mix with many of his music heroes. He had a photograph of himself playing cards with Muddy Waters in the dressing room at the Free Trade Hall.

Roger was instrumental in starting a few dance crazes. He had obtained quite a selection of USA imported records on the Mar-V-Lus label like The Dutones and the Duettes and Alvin Cash, first with 'Twine Time' and later the 'Philly Freeze' which was a dance anthem at the Wheel in the summer of 1965. Alvin chanted: '*I like it, I like it, I like it like that... Now freeze!*' And all the dancers did as instructed, singing along with Alvin's lyrics and then standing still on the word '*freeze!*'

I remember being at Roger Eagle's flat once on Wilbraham Road, in an exotic part of town called Chorlton-cum–Hardy. It wasn't a party – it was more a meeting of people of all types who were there because of music. Roger and his friends discussed Jazz, Blues and Gospel. Roger said that Soul was the convergence and fusion of these into a new unique sound.

Soul he said was made on the roots of rock and roll, itself being a white manipulation of the real originators, the black artists, who called it 'boogie woogie'. A friend of Roger told us to seek out old shellac 78s from the market stalls in Manchester town centre – Ruth Brown, Joe Turner, La Vern Baker, The Clovers and others.

Doreen was still talking to Debbie Fogel, the club's owner, as I continued to speak to Roger. So he had finally done it – he had left the Wheel! He said he had to because the brothers were tight arses and were always making promises they never kept.

I told him a Jewish joke but it had no effect on his mood:

"God said to the Phoenicians, 'Would you like some of my commandments?'... 'What are they like?' they asked. God explained a few... 'No thanks,' they said... God went to the Egyptians and asked if they would like some of his commandments... 'Thanks a lot, but no,' was their reply... On and on God traversed the entire world until finally he came to the Jews. God asked them if they would like some of his commandments, 'How much are they?' the Jews asked. 'Why, they're free,' replied God. 'OK, we'll take ten,' said the Jews."

I left him to sort out his records, assuring him I would come, and that I was keen on hearing his latest Stax imports, as well as the latest stuff he'd told me he got from his mate at Sue Records in London.

We promised Debbie to tell our friends and come along for free on Tuesday night; she gave us lots of free tickets. There was going to be hot buttered potatoes for free too! as we climbed the stairs, Roger put one of his Stax imports onto the turntable, a track that would be played at every session that Roger did at the club for the next five months: 'Changes' by Johnnie Taylor.

* * *

The Manchester Wheelers

Tuesday

The best thing about the Blue Note was that it had a drinks licence – or at least a working one, whilst the appeal not to lose it was being fought for at a future date in court. Until then, the bar was open. The Blue Note was different to the Wheel, it was much smaller. It had no live acts; essentially the main difference was the music. The Wheel in early '67 predominated with smoother and faster paced tracks, aimed at keeping the dancing going and sticking mainly with the Motown sound, whilst the Blue Note's emphasis was definitely more Blues and R&B based, with a very strong leaning to the Stax and Sue Records sound. Of course all the best Motown was played too, but due to Roger's influence lots of new Soul record obscurities found their way onto the turntable and lots of the slower sounds of Soul. This was a tradition set by Roger that the Blue Note DJs kept up, seeking out Soul tracks that other clubs never played. It would last almost to the end of the club's existence, when it was virtually overrun with Jamaican music. The Wheel and the Blue Note in '67 were having a love affair and a dance craze with The Fascinations' 'Girls Are Out To Get You'; but it was only the Blue Note that turned it over and made a hit out of the 'B' side 'You'll Be Sorry', a slow Soul lament.

The Chief Constable of Manchester was a 'religious' bloke who vowed to clean up the pubs, bars and clubs. There's always someone out to spoil things, and this man was on a moral crusade. It's the kind of thing that goes down well with politicians who all agree with such policies. As a result, the Blue Note would eventually lose its drinking licence following a police raid, catching the place crowded full of extra late 'lock-in' drinkers after hours. It was Debbie's father's club – he gave it up to his daughter when he knew his drink licence was going to be lost, but it took a while to come into force.

The Blue Note was fortunate to be musically moulded by its first DJ, who imported lots of USA singles, especially Stax tracks. He was the first to play lots of great Stax stuff at the Blue Note: 'Grab This Thing', 'Honey Pot', 'Last Night' and 'Philly Dog'. All the Mar-Keys instrumentals, 'Marching Off To War' (the fantastic

'B' side from William Bell), 'Toe-Hold' and 'Blues In The Night' from Johnnie Taylor, together with lots of other great Stax and Atlantic songs, and lots of Soul ballads – it all made the club eclectic. The biggest Stax hit of 1966 was 'Knock On Wood' by Eddie Floyd. Roger had introduced it first at the Wheel, and then incessantly played it at the Blue Note. It was at the Blue Note that the Du-Ettes track 'every Beat of My Heart' took off on the imported Mar-V-Lus label. He continued with 'Who's Cheating Who' by Little Milton, and was able to generate strings of successive plays of standard Wheel tracks mixed with great obscure sounds, such as both sides of Jackie Edwards single on the Island label and Russell Byrd's 'Hitchhike'.

I asked Roger who Russell Byrd was and he told me that it wasn't his real name; he was a Soul record writer and producer, a white guy who wrote and produced for the Isley Brothers, Garnet Mimms, Solomon Burke and lots of others. Roger was a mine of information on a good day; moody and silent on a bad one. He also began to play more Ska, like 'King of Kings' by Jimmy Cliff, 'Humpty Dumpty' by Eric Morris, Prince Buster's 'Ten Commandments' which he played first at the Wheel. 'Al Capone' and 'Carolina' were always featured, as was Roland Alphonso's 'Phoenix City', 'The Guns Of Navarone' and 'Perhaps' by the Skatalites. He was the first to locate and play 'Train To Girls Town' by Prince Buster.

Roger's Soul collection was gigantic. For a time it was a battle as to who had the best vinyl; Roger's collection at the Blue Note or what the other DJs could muster at the Wheel. Roger's 45's and LP collection was extensive, and he personally owned all the rare stuff that the Wheel was famous for. He introduced a torrent of Stax along with his usual stuff. The new DJs at the Wheel often had to play secondary versions like 'Stay' by the Virginia Wolves and 'Sweet Thing' by Georgie Fame because Roger had the originals. This cranked up the search for deleted singles and obscurities even further.

Then Roger left. He only stayed at the Blue Note for about five or six months. He was replaced by Lesley, whose claim to fame was that he was a friend of Tony Prince (a DJ who came from

Oldham, who was also a mate of Jimmy Saville) and he modelled himself on 'Ugly Ray Terret', another of Jimmy's Manchester DJ sidekicks. It was Lesley, or as we nicknamed him 'Lez-Lee the dancing DJ' who always paraded his gorgeous girlfriend as a prize, sitting next to him on the stage. She would be our lustfully unobtainable bit of crumpet.

Unfortunately 'Lez-Lee' was a bit of a pain in the arse; he used to put on Billy Preston's Hammond Organ instrumental 'Billy's Bag' when the dance floor was empty and dance on his own. Some wondered if this was to encourage people to start dancing, or simply to show off to his girlfriend audience of one. Everyone else just thought he was a prick for doing this. Only after smirking at him once he'd returned to his DJ plinth did anyone think of dancing, otherwise you risked also having the piss taken out of you for joining him. He even thought his copy of 'Billy's Bag' was rare on the UK Sue label, so one night someone organised loads of people to bring in their copies. When he put it on and got down on the dancefloor that night, about 10 people held their copies up above their heads like judges at the Winter Olympics. Boy was he pissed off! I think he got into a fight outside – somebody kicked the door of his mini in and it developed into a street brawl outside the club.

By this time John Fogel had taken over the club from his sister Debbie, who'd disappeared; the rumour was that she ran off to Australia with the bouncer at the Blue Note.

Doreen and I became Blue Note regulars. So too did all our friends, but as Doreen was very keen on the Jiggy, and as it was the club that we'd met in, we still went there too. Quite often during the week, we would meet and go there. On one memorable night the club had booked The Move. I think it was in February 1967. Angelo was in the club and was complaining about the act that was preparing to play. "It's the fucking Move with a fucking 'Night of Fear'," he said, and it meant that for the duration of their set we would have no Soul tracks to dance to.

Soon the activity of setting up the stage equipment became frantic, eventually ending with the group apologising that due to electrical equipment failure, they could only do one number – an acoustic version of their number one hit song. There was a rumbling of cheers and applause, and soon the DJ was back delivering Soul dance numbers.

Angelo told me later that he had nicked their wa-wa-fuzz pedal box and hid it in a cavity in a wall at the back of the stage. Without it they couldn't feed their electric guitars into their amplifier, and they were scuppered!

* * *

Stax Comes To Manchester

Doreen had bought me a portable cassette player for my birthday. It was 'the latest thing'; and with its microphone attachment I was going to find Otis and record a conversation with him. Otis Redding was appearing with the 'Hit the Road Stax Soul Show' and I had booked tickets for the early show so I could find him, with time for a second chance at the second show. However, it turned out that I missed every opportunity to speak with him. First he was there in the Palace entrance, a towering figure, but by the time I had plucked up enough courage to walk up to him, he was completely surrounded by his manager and other people. I waited, and suddenly he had gone. I tried after the show but I never did get to see him again. Soon he would die in a plane crash.

Our seats were in the middle of the stalls. Hundreds upon hundreds of Mods were there, and so too was Ralph of Ralph Records fame (a Soul record shop near Victoria Station) and his wife, and Ivor from the Wheel. In fact, a large group of the Prestwich Jewish contingent was there.

Everyone in the audience was excited, shouting to each other, chatting, coughing, and then it just went quiet; the compère came out. It was the pirate radio station DJ Johnnie Walker, standing in for Al Bell. He introduced Booker T. & the MGs.

The place was in uproar as 'Green Onions' thundered out and the stage curtains opened. Steve Cropper's guitar riff was chopping through the venue, with Booker T's Hammond rhythmically pouring out in perfect accompaniment, 'Duck' Dunne adding the bass, and al Jackson Junior peering out and smiling over his drums.

I shouted into Doreen's ear, "They're bloody fantastic just like the record! This is going to be great!" and it was. Soon the Memphis Horns joined them as the Mar-Keys; they were into 'Last Night', 'Honey Pot', 'Grab This Thing' and 'Philly Dog'.

In between each song and as introductions were taking place, 'Cleo's Mood' – the instrumental track from Junior Walker – was tinkled out as background sound by Booker T. & the MGs. This continued right throughout the event.

The band members were individually introduced at one point, and when it was Steve Cropper's turn, the place erupted in shouts and thunderous applause. Steve looked stunned. I guess he thought we wouldn't know about a simple guitarist member of a 'session' band, but we did, we all did. We had read his name on songs by a whole host of Stax artists; he had written 'Candy' by the Astors, 'In The Midnight Hour' with Wilson Pickett and 'Knock On Wood' with Eddie Floyd.

Steve stepped forward and introduced Sharon Tandy, an artist that he had met on tour in South Africa – and she did a great version of Johnnie Taylors 'Toe-Hold'.

Then it was Arthur Conley who went on to rip the place up. Everyone was dancing in and on their seats, many moved out into the aisles. Ushers were rushing about trying to stop people dancing; they eventually gave up as Arthur was just encouraging everyone to dance.

Eddie Floyd obviously began with 'Knock On Wood'. It was just great, a track first launched by Roger Eagle; he had imported it before its UK release. Then Eddie got down off the stage at the side steps, as the band began the riff to 'Raise Your Hand'. Soon everyone was swaying about hands raised. He ended with a thundering rendition of 'Big Bird'. Wow.

Sam and Dave came on next. The ushers tried to get everyone back in their seats. But as soon as they began to sing, pandemonium broke out as half the audience moved down to the front. And then it was Dave Prater and Sam Moore from the stage, just encouraging everyone in the audience to get up and into the groove.

What followed was quite simply filled with the greatest soulful, gymnastic, awesome musical atmosphere I had ever encountered. Towards the end of a string of their hits they started swinging their arms around in a competitive way. Eventually they left the stage to rapturous applause. How could Otis follow that?

Dressed in a shiny tight-fitting red Mohair suit, Otis Redding walked onto the stage from the side, and soon we were mesmerised. He marched along from one side of the stage to the other, back and forward. He made us sing, he made us dance, his begging lamenting style made us cry. Here on this stage was a Soul singer who plugged into the audience's soul; he played our emotions like an instrument as our bodies moved, swayed, our hands clapped in unison and our legs danced around.

I knew it was such a great emotional experience that it would stay in my memory for a very long time.

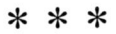

* * *

The Manchester Wheelers

CHAPTER ELEVEN

Torquay: Hi Ho Silver Lining

Holidays; two weeks away from Manchester in work's Wakes Weeks – but not in Blackpool, because it coincided with similar weeks of holidays in Glasgow. Blackpool Town would be full of Jocks, many seeking a fight. So instead, it was way out West for us.

Time had passed by: 1965, 1966 and then 1967 - years that had been fantastic for All-nighters at the Wheel. Most of our Soul dancing nights by this time were spent at the Blue Note where they had a real dance floor and space to move. Many weekends would produce house parties to go to and some areas of the city became infamous for pre-all-nighter parties like Palatine Road.

Parties were always a part of the scene; Friday nights and Saturdays. Of course, on Saturdays we could only attend the 'early session' of a party. Then it was off to the Wheel at midnight. We would rush to leave in desperation, just like Cinderella at the Ball. If there were no parties and we didn't want to go to a club, often we would go to the News Theatre on Oxford Road. It stayed open later than all the other cinemas and it was where continuous showings of newsreel films from Movietone and Pathe News and loads of Looney Tunes played. It was quite interesting watching all those cartoon characters whilst the Amphetamines were kicking in.

All through June in '67 they had totally shit acts on at the Wheel, so most of us had no interruption to the main business of records, dancing, and of course incessant talking. On these occasions we never even went near the rooms with the stage. In these low periods when proper American acts weren't booked, the

Wheel rolled out the likes of The St Louis Union and in our eyes - other unworthy 'artists'. One particularly awful group was the Richard Kent Style, and as a result the stage room was almost empty apart from two girls sitting on the floor and looking up at them in awe; obviously they were relatives, or more likely girlfriends of group members. The rest of the place was packed tight, dancing to the DJ's 45s instead. Records were not just the first reserve at the Wheel; most times they were the main act.

We found out later that the Abadi brothers had moved into group management, and had seen an opportunity to foist their acts on us instead of booking real USA originals – probably due to Roger's break with the club and the owners' attempt to fill the gap. Pretty soon, however, they realised they had to bring back the USA acts.

July was worst as far as live acts were concerned. The only highlight was Geno Washington on July 15, and then we were on annual holidays: Oldham and Manchester Wakes weeks. Geno of course was fantastic, the room with the stage was so packed it seemed as though people were hanging from the walls listening to 'Water' and 'Hi Hi Hazel'. Manchester Wakes Weeks coincided with the end of July and first week in August. I heard that the Wheel was suspending the All-nighters, so off to Torquay we went, loads of us.

The girls; Doreen, her sister Jeanette and their friends Jean and Mandy all went together on a coach, and had already booked bed and breakfast digs by post. The lads; Brian (Lord Snooty), DL, Angelo, Moston Dave and me went in two cars. DL had his dad's Ford Anglia and Brian had recently upgraded to an MG Midget and had it repainted for the trip. The real reason for the repaint was due to an event at a party in Oldham the week before, when the house had been trashed. It was nothing to do with Brian, or the rest of us, as it had happened after we had left around eleven to head for the Wheel. According to reports we heard later, the damage to the house had been blamed on 'out of towners' headlining on page two of the Oldham evening rag and associated with them was apparently a 'green MG' as it was the most easily remembered feature parked outside, so now it had become purple! Brian did a very good job of the paintwork because he was a painter by trade.

It was a fifteen hour drive in DL's dad's ice-blue Ford Anglia and we kept our spirits up by singing songs heard at the Twisted Wheel. One track especially fitted our destination in the West Country; 'West Coast' by Ketty Lester. Telegraph Hill that summer took its toll on many radiators, and we had to push the Ford Anglia along with lots of other holiday makers helping. It was reminiscent of scenes from 'Monsieur Hulot's Holiday' by Jacques Tati. Then we sat in lengthy single lane jams in the unusual sounding town of Indian Queens. In spite of these incidents, summer holidays in Cornwall were something everyone looked forward to. Last year we had been to St Ives, and with England winning the World Cup, beating Germany 4-2, it had made the summer holiday extra fantastic. Most of our times there, we were in the Yacht or the Sloop Pub drinking Courage bitter. This year we planned to go to Torquay in Devon, because in March of 1967 the crude-oil super tanker the Torrey Canyon, had ran aground and ruined the beaches in Cornwall with major oil spills.

It turned out to be a good move as we found the Compass Club. The first night we went there was a Saturday, and they had Alan Price on singing 'Simon Smith and his amazing Dancing Bear'. He also did several tracks from The Beatles' Sergeant Pepper LP, which had been released a month previously (June 67). He did a great job and miraculously got the entire place rocking; he looked very pleased with the huge audience participation. In fact he looked completely amazed. But I doubt he knew that at least three quarters of the audience, many Mod type refugees from London and our lot from Manchester, were stoked up on Amphetamines, just going wild for the sake of it, sort of taking the piss and looking forward to the Soul music coming back on at the end of his set.

After Alan left the stage, the DJ played 'The Girl's Alright with Me' by the Temptations, 'Tears, Tears, Tears', by Ben e King, 'Ain't No Mountain High enough' from Marvin and Tammi, and then 'Take Me In Your arms (Rock Me a Little While)' from Kim Weston. 'I Can't Satisfy' from The Impressions played, and we knew we were in for a great night and it proved to be so – whoever that DJ was, he was well up on Soul.

Next night we took lots of records to the club; we had them with us because we had brought along a portable record player so as to keep up the Soul music on our holiday. At the club we loaned a few of our 45's but kept an eye on them, watching them being played and collecting them immediately afterwards. We were wary, and knew they were targets for being nicked – after all, that's how we'd got many of them in the first place! We ended up going most of our holiday nights in Torquay to the Compass Club.

Angelo had dyed his hair for the holiday the previous year when we went to Cornwall; he had always been a surf music fan, so it had to be blond. He did it himself in a bucket filled with very strong bleach – he nearly choked to death on the fumes! The effect was worth it, though; he was the first bloke I ever saw with brown hair with a central white streak. He looked like a Mohican warrior from a distance! a year later, it was still growing out! It exhibited strange effects of mottled white, blond and brown. He checked himself out in mirrors, and if there wasn't one available a shop window would do. He was incessantly combing his hair like 'Kookie' in the TV series 77 Sunset Strip. However, he thought he looked more like a blonder version of Steve McQueen. The fact was he did, and this went down well with girls. The other attribute he had was a nine inch prick, which he was so proud of that he frequently flashed it around.

We had booked into digs when we arrived after coasting around looking for vacancy notices in windows, or others stuck on poles outside the rows of B&B places in the back streets. We had to split up into two separate locations; the three Dave's in one place, Brian and Angelo in another.

'Lord Snooty' didn't have a top hat like the character in the Beano comic, but amazingly he did sport a pocket monocle! He wore glasses but carried it off well; he was tall, thin and had an air of the distinguished English gentleman about him. The suits he wore were all pinstripe, he often wore a cravat and was the first to start off the dicky bow fashion at the Wheel; it was a carefully cultivated image that he had. You would never suspect that his 'lord of the manner' air disguised the fact that he was a painter and decorator during the week.

'Lord Snooty' a.k.a Brian was a big fan of Peter Cook, the tall dry-humoured comedian who partnered with Dudley Moore. Brian tended to behave rather like Cook, with an air of superiority. He had spent the afternoon driving around Torquay looking for the house Peter Cook was born in. When he finally came to the beach, of course, he was fully dressed in his immaculate three piece suit, with his driving gloves on and a scarf. The temperature was in the mid 80's, and his head was covered by his Yorkshire woollen chequered flat cap that was the custom of MG Midget drivers. It was a heatwave and we were all stripped off, wearing our bathing costumes. Brian, acting out his 'Lord Snooty' caricature, sat behind us reading the newspaper and listening to the cricket on his portable radio, now and again announcing the scores, looking up from his newspaper, impeccably dressed, suitable for dinner at the Ritz.

Pink Gin was Brian's drink. He took it with soda water, not tonic, and with lemon plus Angostura Bitters. He would sit at the bar with his little cigars and trendy drink, smoking with his driving gloves on and always with a cravat or a long university scarf. He was often a pain in the arse and often in an irritable mood. We had left him with Angelo (both of them being posers) at the posh white hotel in the town centre, whilst us, the three Daves; 'DL', Moston Dave and I, were out for pints. Did I ever mention that there were just too many Daves around?

Moston Dave was a very cool bloke; he was a hard core original Mod who was always at the Wheel. He used to go on about Mods all the time; once, a couple of years back at the height of the Mod scene in Manchester, he even suggested we declare war and physically attack all the Mod impersonators that went to the Jungfrau Club near Manchester Cathedral. He was always in demand from the best looking girls, and was often taking them for a twirl around the streets of central Manchester on his GT 200, with them clinging onto him as he rode like the wind down Market Street to scare them. He was a fashion setter, often the first to begin and end a trend. Right now he was growing long sideburns. All the girls fancied Moston Dave and he 'pulled' everywhere he went. Right now he was going out with Doreen's pal Jean. But at one time, he got very close to being unable to keep up his image due to a shortage of funds.

Dave was a cycling fan - in fact most of our mates were. Angelo and I were members of the Prestwich Olympic cycling club; although by this time we had parked up our bikes in favour of Wheel All-nighters, which didn't allow for the Sunday all-day training sessions that were required the day after. As a result, we only kept to the club meetings in the pub now and again to mix socially with our old mates. Another meeting place was at Harry Hall's bike shop at the back of Manchester Cathedral – near the Jungfrau Club. Quite often we used this as a location to meet up, because our old cycling pals worked there on Saturdays and it was good to pass the time waiting there, just staring at bright shiny Campagnolo chain sets and Derailleur gears. It was a cycling thing! However, if anyone in our bygone cycling days had asked Angelo to show his chainset, he quite often laughed and pulled his knob out!

We were there at Harry Hall's to meet Moston Dave, who was still in a North Manchester cycling club called The Manchester Domino. He used to go to their meetings at the Gardener's arms pub before going down to the Wheel during the week. They wore black and white domino style racing vests in amateur road races, similar to the Peugeot-sponsored cycling team vest that Tom Simpson wore. We used to dance wearing our racing vest tops at the Wheel in 1965 and then saw others dancing live on Ready Steady Go wearing similar kit. It was the one time when we guessed that Mod fashion in Manchester was synchronised with London Mods.

Dave told us he was seriously short of cash – he was struggling to keep up payments on his heavily accessorised chrome side-panelled GT 200 and the numerous suits he had on the drip. He had come up with a scheme to get some cash in.

His plan was to get fully dressed in his racing gear, cover it over with his parka and ride out to part of the circuit of an amateur third category race he had entered that passed through Todmorden. This town was well known to cyclists. It was a place we passed to and fro on our training runs to Hebden Bridge and 'Tod' (the town's nickname), had a convenient railway station with direct links to Manchester Victoria station. This was necessary for Dave's initial escape plan, but he changed it later. He outlined the entire thing to us and it was going to happen the next day – Sunday. We awaited news of the result all week, until we caught up with him at the next Saturday's Wheel All-nighter. So that night in the queue going into the Wheel, he told us it had gone really well and he was now waiting for a cheque in the post. What he had done was this:

Finding out that his racing bike was covered on his parents home insurance, on a policy that itemised it as a valuable item, gave him the 'idea' (it was because it was a top of the range 'Campag throughout' Gitanes machine; worthy of Jacques Anquetil), Dave was expecting about £65. He was also going to sell his Campagnolo equipment, wheels, saddle, handlebars and centre pull brakes as second hand items to Harry Hall. He expected to be raking in a further £35. He said it was too risky to sell the frame, so he'd cut it up with a hacksaw and thrown the pieces of Reynolds 531 tubing into the Rochdale Canal.

The 'event' as he called it, had gone well. Dave's cousin had driven the scooter and dropped Dave off, well behind the road race where it had passed some shops on the outskirts of Todmorden. He gave his parka to his cousin after being certain none of the race marshals or anyone else was observing them. Dave emerged in full racing kit with his bidon empty, then he ran into a nearby Newsagents shop and asked if they could fill up his water bottle.

An obliging lady went into the back and returned with it fully filled; Dave bought a Mars Bar for a tanner and ran out. He quickly returned telling the lady that his bike had been pinched!

Then with a somewhat forlorn look on his face, he told us that he soon became embroiled in an emotional scene as the shop-owning lady and her husband became very upset on Dave's behalf and insisted on phoning the police. Dave however, was hoping for a quieter, less disturbing outcome, i.e. without involving the cops directly. Mr Plod duly turned up and dutifully took down the details; after all, it was a big crime for Tod. To Dave's embarrassment, the shopkeepers by this time had almost adopted him, providing both him and Mr Plod with plenty of tea and cakes. Eventually he had extricated himself, but not without further embarrassment – Mr and Mrs Shopkeeper insisted that they give him some cash to pay for a train ticket back to Manchester. He told us it was really awful, as it generated a lot of guilt that only passed later when he thought of the cash that was coming to him. The last thing he'd seen there had been the shopkeepers standing outside their newsagents with Mr Plod, all waving him goodbye.

He legged it towards the station. Found a way over the rail lines, scrambling up hill into the woods, then down and over and along the canal to the next station, Walsden, where his cousin was waiting with his scooter and Parka for the journey back home.

It was one of those stories that got repeated time after time. One evening in Devon, Dave was going through it once more as we went on a pub-crawl, and we all took just a few Blueys to set up the night. The girls - Doreen, her sister and their pals Mandy and Jean - went to the Compass Club to dance around their handbags. We went out on the pub crawl to get rat-legged, and as we did, we spotted a poster outside the Town Hall advertising an upcoming appearance of Pink Floyd; 31st July 1967, The Town Hall, Torquay, Devon. After seeing the notice for Floyd, we went up the street singing… *"Emily tries but misunderstands…"*, then ducked into the first pub we came to. Lemon tops were the drinks we had - it was a pint of draught rough cider, with a topping of lemonade.

Later, we were playing darts in the last of a string of pubs we had visited. It was a pub on a hill up at the back of the town. When they called last orders at 11pm, we doubled up and got two pints in each, then got hassled to drink up fast – this was a big mistake! Once we were out in the cooler air we became more thoroughly pissed. God only knows how many pints we'd drunk. We laughed hilariously at one particular private joke, which would go something like: "Dave, it's your turn to get a round in," and the other Daves would reply, "Not me – it's Dave's round!"

We staggered about outside the pub. DL simply disappeared down an alley to vomit his guts up. Dave Moston and I staggered around in circles, clutching onto each other, as we waited for DL to return back up the alley. Then, in that mindless forgetful state that takes over drunks, we forgot about him and staggered off downhill as if gravity was pulling us along. We went staggering and trotting down to the harbour.

We had our arms around each other and staggered like men in a three legged race, much to the annoyance of passers by coming up the street in the opposite direction. They had to guess which way to get past us as we staggered locked together, moving in spasms, broad-siding the pavement. People went into the road, or dodged between us and the walls of buildings and houses as we struggled forwards, sometimes wobbling backwards, sometimes shifting onwards via a series of jerky, crab-like movements.

Along the way to the Harbour we lost it completely, wildly moving in jerks and pulling at each other's clothing for support. I was in that awful state where you feel like your head is coming off your shoulders. Sounds floated in and out, lights seeming to bounce around as my feet faltered, and my brain tried to make sense of what my eyes were trying to focus on.

The next thing that happened was stupid, and later on when I had recovered my senses, I tried to sort out the memory of it. I don't know exactly how it happened – but we just walked straight off the harbour side and dropped right down into the sea.

It all seemed to happen in slow motion – and then suddenly, we were under the water. I realised that the lights had changed, they were wavy and streaming and strange, as I was seeing them through the water as I submerged. I still had my arm around Dave's neck and his around mine. My mouth opened to shout. I don't know what I was attempting to shout, it wasn't help or anything like that. I was well past panic. That just never occurred to me. I just contemplated in slow motion how interesting it was that bubbles of air were coming out of my mouth and not words. If you could have read the bubbles, they would have spelt out: F U C - K I N G - H E L L.

We hit the bottom. I knew we had, as my legs bent at the knee allowing me to go on, further downwards. My eyes were open. Of course they were. I was astonished because this was something I could never do at the swimming baths. I was impressed that it was quite clear down here, then I realised I had breathed in a lung full of water. I was just standing there on the bottom locked onto Dave. We were both dazed; motionless there on the seabed about ten feet down and both of us with lungs full of water; like wet frozen rabbits caught in the headlights. I wasn't bothered if we died. It never really occurred to me. There was no panic. I was strangely paralysed, unable to make any decision or movement and due to being so drunk I simply didn't react. Dave must have been in a similar condition. We both just stood there underwater, and it seemed like ages passed. I could see rippling lights above - they looked very nice. Then my light show was disturbed and all the nice lights were washed away with a big wavy disturbance.

A pair of boots came into view, then some legs followed from above with half mast watery black pants, a belt emerged, then a military style jacket that had round silvery buttons. This apparition slid down in front of us in slow watery motion – it was a bloke.

He was facing us for what seemed like ages, his cheeks swollen and bulging with air, his thin line of a mouth shut tight like a vice. His wide-open eyes looked at us with a wild stare. It was all in slow motion; time had stopped. He looked like a policeman but wasn't. Perhaps a coastguard, a captain, or a ferry cruise officer, a postman; possibilities flashed through my brain. He grabbed us both and pushed us upwards, as he rapidly descended down in reaction to thrusting us up. We surfaced. The mysterious uniformed man pushed again, and quick as a flash we were against the harbour wall, gasping for air and coughing up a mixture of lemon-top booze and sea water.

The mystery man got out of the sea, then leaned over us and

then pulled us both out. I sat there coughing in a pool of water, looking at the harbour. It was calm, there were no waves; the sea was like a duck pond, apart from the ripples flowing outwards from the place we had just exited. We had been seconds away from drowning. My nose was full of irritating salty stinging and running snot. Our rescuer saw we were OK and just vanished. Coughing and spluttering, Dave and I continued staggering along, eventually finding our digs and collapsing onto our beds; we were completely 'cream crackered' and went off to sleep instantly.

We didn't see anything of our girlfriends that night, but in the morning they saw our state and took our bedclothes, soaked with salty seawater stains and dried vomit, to the laundrette, along with the jeans and Fred Perry shirts we'd had on the previous night.

Dave and I tried to recall the events of the previous evening, but our minds had shut out the experience. Only parts of it were there. My confused memories didn't seem to fit with his, and eventually we gave up trying to work out what had occurred. Then DL turned up from his room in our boarding house digs. He was bright as a button, telling us he'd 'honked up his load' last night but was fine this morning, and he kept on rubbing it in.

I don't think we sobered up till midday. We just sat around staring at the walls. When we did sober up a bit, we went to the harbour to The Yacht pub for a pint; a 'hair of the dog'. We sat in the pub dazed for a couple of hours with DL talking at us about record collecting. He didn't really need us to actually listen, he was just happy enough that we sat there looking like we were listening. What we were listening to was something else. Our minds couldn't concentrate on DL's barrage, and instead locked onto the music streaming endlessly out of the Juke Box. People were continuously selecting 'Hi Ho Silver Lining' by Jeff Beck on it, and as a result *You're everywhere and nowhere baby, in your hippie hat....*' had been imprinted into our minds by the time Brian and Angelo showed up.

Angelo and Brian had come up with a great scheme in Torquay; they were selling cosmetics to girls very cheap and getting a shag thrown in now and again as part of the deal. I was becoming slightly envious of them and their enterprise. I was with just one girlfriend. They had hit upon a fantastic scheme, becoming wealthier and with sex thrown in with multiple short term 'girlfriends'. Well, it was supposed to be the swinging sixties!

Angelo had put plan 'B', as he called it, into operation. Back home in Manchester, several mysterious break-ins had already occurred at Boots shops. Of course, these were an inside job. When the date and time of these break-ins was established, Sid and Terry would arrive round the back, often late on a Sunday night, and Angelo would pass out the back door several large tins containing selections of amphetamines. They paid him later after their sales were completed – everyone was very happy, no one had to pay up front.

When they had gone he would set about trashing the shop. He later told me he took a package of harder stuff. He smashed the door of a locked cupboard containing Morphine and other noxious stuff, to make it look like a planned and more serious drugs raid. These hard drugs he later threw into the Irwell. The second time such an event occurred before leaving and getting a lift from Brian, he had what he described to me as 'a fucking momentous brain wave'.

He stacked up loads of cosmetics and got Brian to load up the car with them. Then he locked and closed the door after first forcing it off its hinges. It looked like it was locked. The impression he wanted to leave was two robberies; the first was the addicts, the second an opportunist taking the cosmetics after seeing the door open. He had copied the keys a month before when he had worked at this shop; he was often moved around as a trainee. As a result, Angelo got a share from Sid's All-nighter sales, and together with Brian they now had a secondary revenue from all the cosmetic sales items.

He was well on the way to his deposit. He had planned for a GT 200, but now he was going for a Mini, maybe a Mini Cooper on HP! They'd cruise around the harbour and other main streets in the MG Midget; its boot full of girlie stuff. Of course, their spotting activities were confined to Mod-type girls. They would curb crawl alongside their selected target at walking pace. Angelo would roll down the window and shout out his fantastic sales pitch and pick up line: "hey you girls, do you want to buy some cheap make-up?" Soon they would have half a dozen inspecting the eyeliner, the lipsticks, the long false eye lashes and lots of other girlie stuff that they had displayed in the boot.

Later, they were supplementing cosmetics with dresses, Mod-style dresses they had shoplifted from boutiques in the Town. Manchester Mods were seasoned and adroit shoplifters. These places had no defence against such skilled big time operators honed on stashing away loads of 45's. Dresses were a new challenge. They even persuaded girls that had bought cosmetics to be temporary 'girlfriends' looking around shops, whilst their 'bored' counterfeit 'boyfriends' wandered about, intermittently secretly stashing away several dresses whilst the shop sales assistants were concentrating on the females.

Restaurants suffered a similar fate from all of us doing the old toilet trick, then everyone exiting without paying and doing a runner from several Indian and Chinese restaurants. It all became a challenge and a joke!

Giving out dresses became popular in the pubs at night time; polka dot dresses, op art mini skirts, Mod dresses with holes around the belly button, others with button on-shoulder straps - these were the required types and styles. Angelo was stealing to fashionable order. It wasn't long before we were all giving a helping hand. Girls began to ask for other items like swimming costumes; there was a crime wave in Torquay in 1967.

Nights were spent in the pubs, at the Compass Club, days on the beach with our portable record player pounding out Soul tracks to the annoyance of families nearby, who eventually moved away. Sometimes we would try the radio, mostly for the weather reports. We listened to Radio Caroline, and at one time a road report said that the a6 was 'blocked up' and everyone cheered! Some days we took the cars and went to other places like Perranporth beach, and on others we tried surfing – especially skim boarding. But all too soon, the holidays were over; it was back to Manchester and back to regular Wheel All-nighters.

Doreen was determined to go as well.

* * *

CHAPTER TWELVE

On The Buses And A Little Spastic Girl

> *The Leyland and Bedford Buses on the all-night routes often had guards with distinctive styles; low-slung leather bags with change on one hip, and a wind-around roller ticket machine on the other. The guard's cap was often on in two types of style – one almost falling off the back of the head, the other like a prison officer, pulled down over the eyes.*

The method of getting home after an All-nighter weekend was the late night bus on Sunday. The all-night bus service in Manchester was usually packed, you'd often have to wait for up to an hour, but even once you were safely onboard, there could be other problems to face:

"Who you looking at?"

Oh fuck, I thought.

A bloke on the bus had taken exception to my long stare.

It used to happen often, and lots of people have had these scary incidents. It used to be a nightmare daily occurrence at school. You'd inadvertently make eye-to-eye contact with some lad, and off they would go, shrieking; "Who you fuckin' looking at? You want to make something of it?" and so on. Why were they so threatened by a glance? Is it something primeval? This one was an obvious hard nut.

Such occasions could be worse now, due to another after effect of the All-nighter amphetamines. It was the unconscious lingering stare when coming down. You just looked at something, anything, and it seemed to lock into your attention; and then a de-focused state of passivity would set in. You might find that a lot of time had elapsed before shifting your gaze. Often you weren't aware your eyes had landed on something or someone. But they felt the eyes on them, even though you weren't actually conscious of it. It was something you had to learn, to be aware of, just where your eyes lingered. When an event like that occurred, you had to quickly move your eyes to an innocuous location and stare at the bus ticket, or read the signs:

'No Standing Upstairs.

41 Upstairs.

28 Down.'

Perhaps read and re-read the word 'Strike' above the match strike pad fixed to the seat in front. Fights rarely broke out on the bus, but just to be ready I began slotting pennies between my fingers, making a temporary knuckleduster fist ready for possible agro.

"Not looking at anything," I mumbled to the irritated, tough-looking thug on the opposite aisle seat. I then cast my eyes down, scrutinising my ticket intently. He was a greasy type, with black rail-line hair combed into a 'duck's arse' at the back. He had LOVE tattooed on one set of fingers, HATE on the other. I was silently hoping he would get off soon. Praying he would go before my stop. I had decided I would stay on as long as it took, even if it meant legging it back. He kept glancing back but eventually, after what seemed like ages, he got off – but not before purposefully colliding with me as he went past. I expect he gave a menacing look, but I didn't look up to find out. I had learned from similar incidents to keep low; live to fight another day; but without the fighting part.

* * *

Hey, Harmonica Man

Wailing riffs from the back seat; it was the harmonica man. He was often on the all night bus. He or one of his doppelgangers would be on this and lots of other buses. It was always Blues. Now and again he took requests, especially 'Help Me' by Sonny Boy Williamson or a Jimmy Reed tune, which in fact were mostly all the same. Sometimes he gave a discourse about getting the best out of a Blues harp, like hitting it to make it better and putting it in a bucket of water over the weekend to weather it in. Then he would relate the names of the Harmonicas, the best being Hohner, Marine Band and in F or C or whatever. Such events happened on the late bus home. However, one event was more unusual than others.

It was late one Friday night in Piccadilly bus station. No buses were moving, yet loads of buses were parked up. I think the drivers and guards were meeting, probably discussing strike action or something similar. Everyone waiting to get home was thoroughly pissed off; we had been waiting ages and the buses were just standing there. We queued up in parallel lines with rail bars between us. In these lines there were quite a few people I knew, including Barry – he was further along right near the front. Each of us was waiting for a different bus, hence the separated queues.

Barry was well drunk and off his head. He had been on Guinness and 'shit' all night. He favoured marijuana, Moroccan or Afghan Black on weekdays and on nights off from the All-nighters. He'd recently got out of Borstal at Risley, a prison detention centre near Warrington. The judge, who sentenced him to six months for a first offence, which was very harsh, had called it "a particularly heinous crime."

At the time, Barry had been under the influence of booze and roasted crumbly Afghan smack – he'd been tasting it at a wholesalers meeting in the Denmark pub in Moss Side with a load of our friends from "de Caribbean" as he would say. He'd imitate their accent – "Try before ye buy, mon" was their sales phrase, and Barry did so wholeheartedly, with pints of Guinness on the side. "It was an all black situation, mon," he related later in his imitation-Jamaican drawl.

When he got outside the pub, he walked along the shops and got talking to a lad he vaguely knew outside a butcher's shop. Having spent all his cash and needing some to get tickets and gear for the forthcoming All-nighter, as well as being in a strange mood that he was prone to, he asked the butcher's apprentice if he could lend him some dosh, as he was completely skint. The guy said he had nowt himself so couldn't give Barry a penny. Now this conversation took place with a small girl between them. This 'girl' wore a short blue dress. She had one leg in a metal calliper, her eyes looked up appealingly and she held out a collection box in her arms. She was a mass produced mannequin that adorned many city streets; a collection point for the Spastics' society.

Barry's attention turned to the girl. He said to the butcher's boy, "OK then, let me knock this off." The lad agreed, but lost his bottle when Barry ran of with the 'girl' over his shoulder, intent on smashing it open over the road with some bricks from a patch of wasteland. That's where the police found him. He was much more incensed that the butcher's boy had grassed him up, rather than his actual arrest. He had the presence of mind to lose his marijuana, kicking it under a nearby stone.

When he got the six months custodial sentence, Barry had told me that the judge said it was both heinous and despicable to steal the poor Spastics' girl who was innocently collecting for seriously ill people. "He spoke as though she was a fuckin' real person," said Barry, who had related this tale to us after his release. He was also on the prowl looking for a lad on a butcher's bike with intent to "maim the little twat." He would spend an hour or so at the scene of the crime, eyes scanning for a lad on a bike whilst kicking over bricks and stones in a fruitless exercise to locate his long lost stash.

As I was recollecting this story at the bus stop, I noticed in his eyes that strange, devil-like glint he was prone to have. The next thing I knew, he had gone. I was moving nearer to the front of the queue as other people gave up and either decided to walk it or get a taxi. Then a bus screeched to a halt next to the stop, with the drivers cab in line with the front of the queue, when normally it should have gone past to line up its rear door with the boarding point. The driver flung open the small driver's side window, and I saw it was Barry! He shouted, "Dave, mate, get on!"

"Fuck off," I shouted back and tried to shrink back into the queue of people around me. Then several policemen with a couple of bus inspectors came running along behind the bus. Barry put his foot down and sped off in his red double decker 59. However, being unused to such a huge vehicle he couldn't make the bend from Piccadilly into 'Black Shirt Lane' – or Mosley Street, to give it its correct title. Inevitably the bus mounted the pavement and hit Lewis's window, smashing it and knocking over several female mannequins in the process.

The last vision I had of Barry was him legging it round the corner into Market Street with three Coppers chasing. Then the thought occurred that I could end up involved, obviously knowing the culprit, so I disappeared into another queue and headed the long way home, using two bus routes. I thought it was odd in a funny way – both incidents with Barry had involved dummies!

* * *

The Manchester Wheelers

CHAPTER THIRTEEN

Night Train, Night Train

There is a place on the very edge of sleep. The aim of the body is to pass through it into total sleep, but a mind that is switched on to overdrive can have other plans. The repeated weekend timetable and its repetitive 'come down' experiences could have strange and weird mental effects.

Getting home after being out all night each weekend at the All-nighters – often returning around 12 midnight the following Sunday night – I would stealthily open the front door and creep in. However, I was often met by my mother shouting: "Where have you been…?" It was endless with my mother; quite often she would belt me as I passed her going through the doorway.

After a hectic and typical weekend, it would all collapse inwards in the bogs at work, where I went to attempt to recuperate after clocking in at 7:30 am on Monday morning – and so Blue Monday would begin.

It was the typical weekend series of events, and the routine of it was mixed with memories:

Friday night - cycling home from work, having a bath, ironing a suit, watching Ready Steady Go, then on the 26 bus to Manchester town centre, visiting a few pubs like Sinclair's, The Chop House, Town Hall Tavern, Tommy Ducks, the bar at the back of the Midland hotel, then the Blue Note; home on the all night bus - the 121 that terminated in Langley, with everyone pissed, decking off at Blackley tram office and legging it up

The Manchester Wheelers

Charlestown Road: Friday finished.

Saturday - the main item on the agenda for Saturday was making certain you scored your stuff, your 'gear' for the All-nighter. Visiting records shops and clothes shops like Ivor's and Barnett Man, and its owner, sometimes showed up at Manchester clubs. Then to the Kardomah in St Ann's Square, then the match, or just sitting around in pubs and calling at places like the Mogambo coffee bar, waiting for the Blue Note to open. Then dancing in there until we switched around before midnight, for the Wheel All-nighter. We would be popping loads of speed intermittently, then downing the mother load just before going into the Wheel All-nighter at Midnight and dancing all night: Saturday finished.

Sunday 8 am - to a station, either Piccadilly or Victoria, for a wash and brush up, around 9 am to Rowntrees Spring Gardens then home to get changed about 4pm and off to the Top Ten Club at Belle Vue, sometimes we even went ice skating at Sale Ice Rink were they played Dave ` Baby ` Cortez's 'Rinky Dink!

One memorable occasion I went there with Angelo to see Stevie Wonder; he was fantastic. At one point he got so excited he almost walked off the stage. He would have been safe if he had done so, because a hundred pairs of hands were upraised to catch him. After Stevie, we went outside round the back to smoke some weed. We went over to a round caged monkey enclosure. Some of the little blighters came over to us. Stupidly I put my hand through the bars and as soon as I did one of them grabbed my hand in its own and began to pull like hell with its feet pushed against the bars for extra force. The others began to circle and jump around, and then one of them looked like it was about to assist the first hand puller and join in. Angelo saved the day by putting out our spliff on the monkey's hand; off it shot howling.

Sunday night - at the Elizabethan Ballroom at Belle Vue; Jimmy Saville did the records on a revolving stage that turned around like Sunday Night at the London Palladium, to reveal the artists from the other side. Jimmy did play quite a few Soul records, but of course being the Top Ten Club, it was always predominated by the records in the pop chart. Often we would refuse to dance to them, walking off whilst others flooded onto the floor to dance to the latest hit. We would leave to go to the bar for a pint or a barley wine. The girls usually had a Brandy and Babycham. The ballroom had a wooden floor, and pockets of recognisable Soul people could be seen dancing on its surface in ways they couldn't achieve in the Twisted Wheel. They were interspersed by the majority, who looked and behaved quite differently. By midnight we were wasted. At each interval in the day, we topped up with even more pills. Then it was off home to lie awake in bed waiting for the birds' dawn chorus, which might – or might not – signal an end to the night long replay of all the Soul tracks playing out and repeating the weekend in our minds.

Monday - that Monday morning feeling was always a strange brew. Coming down after being awake, dancing all Saturday night and being unable to sleep the following Sunday night, spending a second night wide awake. James Brown with full orchestral accompaniment would be going full tilt to Miami, Florida on the: *'Night train, night train...'* – all night long, with my overactive mind reliving the All-nighter and replaying all the sounds heard over the weekend, relentlessly keeping me awake. I'd try and get it to shut up, but it was like my mind wouldn't listen, and immediately the music would start up again. Chunky staccato rhythms would begin, and then inevitably James Brown would kick back in again with *'Night Train, night train...'*

Eventually the endless chain of repeating music would diminish. One strange thing that repeatedly happened during these nights of attempting to sleep was that I would always open my eyes just as the Orion stars were crossing my window – didn't sailors call these the dog days? The next event to follow would be the birds and their early morning chorus. Then as I relaxed, another curious event would always happen. Sharp points like needles, but not quite as unpleasant, would seem to prick me all over my body. If I scratched the place, another location would instantly react. Scratching that point would trigger the next at an entirely different location and so on, and it could go on and on and on. It was like automated acupuncture, and it ended with the alarm clock ringing out, or the whistle of the kettle singing downstairs as it boiled on the stove, placed there by my mother who would soon be shouting up the stairs for me to get up.

In that alarm clock moment I must have fallen asleep – and as I fully awoke with a start, for an instant I was not 'me'. I couldn't remember 'myself'. The alarm faded, and I pulled on my work clothes like a brainwashed robot. The mouthful of coffee was enough to get me on my bike; I had to clock on, visit my work bench, and then retreat and 'come down' in the bogs. Soon I would be sitting there in the bogs, staring at the light bulb above me, trying to get my eyes right and to reduce the gigantic size of my deep black pupils. First I had to get there. Quite often it was terrifying. On some occasions I would see things, due to lack of sleep, residual amphetamines and paranoia. The worst time was when I looked at the shadows and darker corners of the room and saw black shapes that slithered. On another occasion, I was convinced I saw a troop of ancient Roman soldiers walk straight through the bedroom wall!

7:30 Monday morning at work; and the only thing on my mind was to get into the toilets as soon as possible. I grabbed my backrest and slid it down the front of my jeans and put my overalls back on to hide it. I had made this device some time ago; the idea occurred to me after I had built something similar for my scooter. This was a pillion passenger seat backrest, and at that time it was the 'in thing' accessory for scooters; two long chromium plated tubes with a cross member at the top fitted with a leather covered foam sponge, all 'procured' in the large engineering factory I worked in.

On that occasion, I'd taken it to the chromium bath in the Anodising and Plating department, and I'd asked a bloke there to chromium plate it. It turned out to be the foreman – normally I wouldn't have asked him, but he'd taken off his distinctive white overall with its bright blue collar denoting his status. I mistook him for an ordinary skiver.

"Could you plate this for me?" I had asked.

"Fuck off," he said very loudly, then continued... "We're fucking pow'd out here with rush jobs... Leave it over there on that trestle table, and put your docket under it or tie it on... Come back in a week or so..." He spoke in a clipped tone and his general attitude was just like Peter Sellers in the film 'I'm All Right Jack'.

I said: "Sorry, I've got no docket. It's for my scooter... Forget it, it's ok, don't other," I stuttered and began to get out of there.

Then he called me back. "Sorry lad. You should have said it was a 'foreigner'. We can always do that – now what do you want exactly?"

"Just chromium plating on this tubular bracket," I said.

"OK, I'll get it done and properly. We'll undercoat it first with a fixative pre-coat. It'll ensure that chrome won't rust for fifty years." He laughed, then said: "Come back tomorrow morning. It'll be ready by 11 a.m."

That was the first time I learned how things 'really' worked here; anything required for personal use took precedence over the official daily grind. That could always wait; after all we were only refurbishing the RAF's nuclear deterrent Vulcan Squadron – what was the rush? It was now outdated and soon to be replaced by Polaris, for the Navy - bought from the Yanks.

To ensure comfort for come-downs in the bogs, I made a second one of these backrests. It was made flatter and it had no need for chromium plating. I made it out of lightweight aluminium, and it was for an entirely different back-resting purpose.

The factory management had tried to make the bogs skiver-proof. The toilet seat was two strips of wood with two large rounded brass pointed protuberances sticking out on top. These would dig into your legs, and the only thing to lean back against was a cold steel pipe. It soon became agony if you sat there longer than ten minutes. But the needs of a 'coming down' all-night all-weekend reveller who required rest forced imaginative solutions to the problem.

Once I was in the toilet, out it came from down my pants: my foldaway contraption – it fitted neatly over the outcropping bolts on the wooden 'seat' and folded back against the pipe, all surfaces having foam rubber encased in leather. It was perfect to sit and sleep on for a couple of hours.

Over time my idea caught on. I should have patented it. The toilets in this factory were quite numerous. There were thousands of workers on this site. The toilets were in rows of about thirty 'trap' doors facing each other over a row of fifty wash basins. They were called the 'traps' due to the event that happened once a day. The only period they were deserted was dinner time. As the siren sounded, all the doors would open and the occupants rushed off to get their dinner, just like opening the traps at the Manchester White City greyhound dog races.

Often you couldn't get in and had to queue up. Only emergency cases were deferred to, and only maybe, as lots of blokes were seated comfortably on modified scooter backrests reading the morning papers; at least, those not on piece work, or those on less demanding jobs like non-punch card operations. It got so packed at certain times that those in real need of a toilet visit had to shout out, pleading to those known to be only resting to give up a place to a genuine deserving cause!

Typical shouts heard would be:

"Come on lads, I had a curry last night!", or, "For Christ sake have pity lads, or I'll have to drop my load right here!"

I was an apprentice, so free to disappear for hours on end without anyone caring. So I collected my special seat, a newspaper or a book, and then went to join the queue for a seat in the 'rest rooms'. When I couldn't get in the bogs, if the queue was too long, I sometimes hid inside a fuselage under the floors of the aircraft being built. There was always a sheet of foam rubber around as workers needed this for long stints of riveting on their knees. Now and again I slept so long they would have moved the entire fuselage into the paint shop. I had to climb out down steps past men in breathing masks spraying green protective rubberised mothball coatings over the completed aircraft fuselage for onward shipping to the airfield. The entire hangar was a mist of green fog; it was a surreal sight to wake up to.

Once seated on my 'chair', I could try and relax. Quite often I was totally exhausted. Some of the All-nighter crowd just kept on taking a few pills each day to avoid the 'come down' effects. I knew that was a bad idea – it would catch up with you eventually and be worse, so I used my Monday morning visits to the bogs as my come down location each week. My eyes were already wide with a fixated stare; open, dilated, staring wild black pupils longing for rest. Staring up at the light bulb reduced the eye pupil size, but left an intriguing after image that put a vision of a multi-coloured ghostly light bulb everywhere else that I looked. It was there even when I closed my eyes. After staring up at the light bulb in the works toilet or reading for a while, I would eventually begin to feel sleepy; a precious half hour would usually be enough. Sometimes it could be an hour but on many occasions I awoke to find that everyone had disappeared and the bogs were deserted – it was lunch break and no one was in there in their own time!

The toilets had row after row of doors with a very large gap at the bottom, making them quite draughty in the winter. There was more than one set of toilets of course; multiple bogs were located around the factory. This was a huge engineering works, and the staff office areas had slightly better ones. Accommodating Monday morning toilet requirements must have been awful for the teams of bog cleaners. They trudged around polishing the taps and rows of large white basins in the centre of the twin rows of the 'trap' doors facing each other. The bog man would be oblivious to the taunts, wisecracks and shouts of the queue such as the odd Major Bloodnock whine from the Goon Show of "No more curry for me, lad!" Bog loitering or skiving off the job was an art form here, and getting in usually took around fifteen minutes.

Sometimes favourites got in immediately like union shop

stewards. The bog man kept a few reserve doors closed and escorted the union guys to their reserved seats – not that these places had real seats, of course. On one occasion, when I reached the head of the queue, my relief was short-lived. A bloke rushed past me to the attendant and shouted out at the entire seated company that he had had a bad curry last night and was an urgent, desperate and 'genuine' case. He emphasised 'genuine' slowly and very deliberately, as everyone knew the game in the bogs; most were skivers reading the morning papers. A few sympathisers emerged, and I was also able to race away to claim a cubicle.

There were no locks on the doors, just a large hole where the locking bolt and mechanism used to be. The first job was fixing the self assembly locking device. This was essential, as the bog-man would patrol along the doors from time to time pushing at the doors looking for vacancies. Then, the next step was retrieving from down the front of the pants the mechanical over-seat fixing; my device designed for turning the bog into a place of comfort.

Finally, I began to recline on my over-seat, but as I closed my eyes I was not greeted with blackness; a colourful panorama was there awaiting me. It was a mental mosaic that I could view from afar and then zoom into. Here I could experience again a flood of thoughts and reflections. My inner conscious mind was affected by the physical strain, and the drugs; and this mixture initiated a new inner mental state.

A strange curious state of dreaming would begin; it was a state between sleep and wakefulness. It was also my exhausted body requesting rest, but with my mind still on 'go fast' mode. I was knackered. I was at the very edge of sleep. I would drift and float with it. Peacefully recapitulating random events with amazing inner clarity, I would view them in full colour, sound and vision, yet I also knew I was half asleep, 'seeing it all' like a cinemascope film. Each subject had a key, or a starting element that only required a slight recognition from me to expand it and enable it to be replayed. I could choose to just watch it, or to step into it and become engrossed, reliving the event, or allow it to pass as the next montage fused into my consciousness to replace it. This was a strange state. I could tell my body was totally knackered and probably asleep, yet my mind was independently aware.

The irritating artificial insomnia induced by all the weekend's pep pills faded. I was hanging at the threshold of sleep. But the first barrier to obtaining unconscious sleep was the constant repeats of the music and continuous dialogue inside my mind. Once this was passed through or became diminished, it was replaced by other images; reminiscences began to replace the musical replays. My surroundings began to fade as a fitful waking sleep replaced the external world, and a lucid waking dream state came over me. I often tried, but I could never knowingly capture the actual transition point. It was a seamless border zone, and once on either side, the other became somewhat distant and unreal. Dimly at first, then flooding back, re-living the past events, it was much more real than a movie on a screen. I felt like I had dual consciousness, like I could step out of my mind and then, like a magician's flash bang effect, I was back there. I had entered the re-run zone.

* * *

Remembrances – *and an encounter with schizophrenic paranoia?*

It was mid week in Manchester. I went with Angelo to the American Folk Blues show at the Free Trade Hall in 1964. The effort of attempting to remember the date as events unfolded as a replay was too much to hold onto, as I began to see again the artists re-perform their acts from the past; Buffy Saint Marie, July Felix and several Blues artists. The immersion was almost complete. The memory rolled out, but with me as a viewer and not as a real participant.

After the concert, Angelo and I headed for the nearby Waldorf Hotel on Fountain Street. Whilst we were standing at the bar with a pint of Boddingtons, in hopped Rambling Jack Elliot; the funniest act from the show we had just seen. He got a pint and stood right next to us. We said we'd just seen his act and we asked him more about the 'rambling' tales he had told the audience, and about breaking his leg. He had broken it, he told us, in the USA, practising the new craze over there called skateboarding. He said he was best at falling off it.

His show was rambling just like his nickname, and he was rambling now, about all sorts of stuff. Like how he knew Woody Guthrie and that Bob Dylan stole his style of playing and singing but he didn't mind really, as 'Bob' was a great talent and imitation is the best sort of flattery. He said he was a cowboy and did the Rodeo. He certainly had the right kind of Stetson cowboy hat. He was interested in what we did and wanted to know about the music we liked. We liked Blues of course, and Soul. He was very enthusiastic when we said how much we liked Jesse Fuller, the one-man band: 'The San Francisco Bay Blues' man, as we had called him. Amazingly, he told us that he had personally introduced Jesse to Bob Dylan!

We couldn't tell if it was true or all bravado, as his style of talking was with an Americanised, boastful tone. He was like a person with a head even bigger than his ten-gallon hat. He respected our views, as we had very opinionated ones about Blues, R&B and Soul. Our opinion was that only black people could sing the Blues correctly. He didn't take it as an insult; anyway he was a Folk singer. He said he had a deep respect for the Blues, he loved Howlin' Wolf, adored Muddy Waters, and so he quickly won our admiration.

We told him about All-nighters and he asked if he could get some Purple Hearts, so we took him to the Twisted Wheel. He was a great hit there dancing with a pot on his leg. I lost contact with him during the night and I think he went off with a girl. I wondered for years whatever happened to him, and whether the stories he told us that night were true.

As this questioning part of my mind surfaced, his smiling face with the big Stetson hat on his head moved away from me. I felt like I was flying slowly away from him, backwards and up. I viewed the scene from above. Down there below me, Jack was looking up waving his hat at me. I was floating above him. He began to fade. He saw I was leaving and he shouted up at me: about Woodie, about Jesse Fuller and Bob, about banjo-playing

'Mr Nice Guy' Pete Seeger; shouting about his pal called Dave van Ronk, about 'The House of the Rising Sun'. As he saw me going away he shouted, "You've gotta believe me kid, my real name is Elliott Adnopoz. Just listen to my 'Ain't A-Gonna Grieve No More'. You'll see, you'll see. These are facts, man. That's where Bob got it all from, man."

I was waking up; I had pins and needles in my left leg. I left the memory of the cowboy in the Wheel and I came back awake in the bogs. I automatically massaged my leg, sleepily shifted position and then drifted away again.

Ain't it funny how the mind operates? I was then humming 'Shimmy Shimmy Walk' by The Megatons, and that brought in a memory of a guy called Eric – his scooter popped into my mind, and I could see him clear as day. He was famous on the Manchester Mod scene, one of the coolest Mods, and he had an amazing scooter with a sidecar! The scooter, an LI 150, had purple side panels. The sidecar was matching purple too – how amazing is that?

Eric had a friend called Eddie who had something to do with 'Barnet Man' - a clothes shop on Corporation Street. He was a bit of a show off, and he was in with the Jewish clique from Prestwich. We knew them because our cycling club Prestwich Olympic was based in a pub on the main road in Prestwich. They hung out in the Woodthorpe Hotel on Sheepfoot Lane, where quite often the car park was full of Mods revving up scooters.

As I regurgitated these memories, a more forceful one entered my mind and 'Boogie Chillun' began to play in my head. The lyrics from the John Lee Hooker song paralleled the problems that we encountered from our parents, and it was slowly building up in my mind. 'Boogie Chillun' was a constant player at the first Twisted Wheel. The DJ Roger Eagle was a great big fan of John Lee. The song might have described the feelings of club attendees at the Saturday All-nighters. John Lee's mother *'don't allow him to stay out all night long, But John Lee don't care what momma don't allow, He's gonna' stay out anyhow...'* – just like us!

The Manchester Wheelers

John Lee toured the UK in 1962, returning in 1964 after his hit with 'Dimples'. He played at the Wheel several times before he teamed up and met his backing band The Groundhogs for the first time. Watching them that night, you could see they idolised John Lee and after a very short rehearsal, they gave one of the best Blues performances I ever heard. He appeared there at the Wheel quite a few times. On that occasion, Roger the DJ made sure he did a live version of the song he had on the turntables at most club sessions throughout 1964-5. And when I heard him, I swear he put the 'Twisted Wheel' in the lyrics:

'Boogie Chillun'
Well my mother (won't) allow me (she said)
To stay out all night long (Oh Lord)
Well my mother (won't) allow me (she said)
To stay out all night long
I don't care what she allow
I would boogie anyhow
Well, I put into town people
I was walking down Hastings Street
*Everybody was talking about ....**the Twisted Wheel***
I decided I'd drop in there that night
I say yeah people
They was really having a ball - yes I know

Boogie Chillun
One night I was laying down
I heard mama and papa talking
I heard papa tell mama '
Let that boy boogie-woogie
It's in him, an' it's got to get out'
And I felt so good
Well I would boogie just the same'

So his Ma and Pa were arguing about letting him stay out all night doin' the boogie-woogie, and his dad was telling his mamma to let him stay out all night. It reminded me of my own mother. She was from brainwashed Irish Catholic stock and constantly went berserk with me about disappearing and staying out all night at weekends. She said I was up to no good. Sometimes when I returned, she would even thump me as I came in the front door.

What she was really annoyed about was that her son was not in the ranks of other mothers' sons at Sunday mass. As soon as this thought-link was activated, my dream state picked up on one particular memory and re-enacted the entire scene.

Early one Sunday morning after the All-nighter, I came home with Angelo. My mother was ranting on about the Whit Walks. As a kid I was brought up a Catholic, but by this time I was free of their conditioning. A Catholic upbringing in the 1950's was based on certain Jesuit principles. Mine was worse; our school and church were run by the Salesians - not the Germans, but an Italian group of Jesuit related fanatics initiated by Don Bosco in Italy to save 'lost boys'. Although begun in the 1880's, these methods had probably not changed much since the middle ages. Catechism was drummed in by the bare knuckles of our spinster headmistress. Whacks were given on our foreheads if we recited it wrong.

"Who made me?"

Answer: "God made me." We would all chant it mindlessly, by rote.

"Why did God make me?" our school leader would say, as she strutted about like an SS Major up and down the rows of small desks, past all of the 52 kids in our class. She accompanied this strutting style by now and again banging down her knuckles on a desk or a head.

"To know Him, to love Him and to serve Him," was our collective, droned answer.

Years later, the next school for over-elevens was a Secondary Modern. Inevitably our overcrowded class mostly failed the eleven plus exams that might have provided a Grammar School route to freedom from thought control. I, along with many others, was straight-jacketed into another Salesian-run school. The best thing was that it had lots of Italians; many were football and cycling fans. It was at this school that I met Angelo.

The Manchester Wheelers

Whit Walks were a big family and religious tradition in Manchester. The 'Prodidogs', as we called the Protestants, walked through Ancoats one week, and then we did it the next. They called us the 'left footers' and both had really good pipe bands. It was our local church that was having a local parish procession that day and my mother wanted me to walk with them. We had returned from the Wheel on the number 88 bus back to Blackley. It was still quite early Sunday morning and my Mom had already been and come back from early mass at the local church. On this special day, the church's annual Sunday procession was beginning after 11:30 mass.

She would rant and rave that I was committing a 'mortal sin' by missing mass. On several occasions during the week she would leave the house, then after a while there would be a knock on the door and hey presto, standing there was the parish priest, asking why he hadn't seen me at mass for a long time? I told him I went to St Mary's, the 'Hidden Gem' church on Mullbery Street in Manchester town centre; it was near the Wheel. This held them both off for a while, but on later visits he found me out by asking me what colour the vestments were. Priests changed the colours of their tunics depending upon the celebrations of the saints and other festivals throughout the year. I said green, when it was the purple season. The game was up, and I was reported to my mum who sulked all night. It was every Irish Catholic mother's aim to have a son join the priesthood. Mine had long since given up on that and just wanted to keep me going to church. She was well intentioned – it was all to save my soul, but I had already taken care of all that and had a great Soul collection already.

She informed us it was St Don Bosco's walks today, a procession round the streets of our council estate. She sarcastically said: "I bet you two won't be going."

We looked at each other, laughed and said" "OK, we will."

We were still blocked, and had returned home to get recharged from a tin full of yellow Dexys we had hidden in a Cadbury's Cocoa tin underground near a large tree in the back garden. We needed a top up and were going back downtown for the afternoon session at Rowntrees. We had time to kill. We were in high spirits, so we laughed at each other and said: "What the fuck?" Mum was delighted, ignoring our swearing, and said that she would immediately cook us a great big breakfast. She didn't know we couldn't have attempted to eat anything; the thought of fried eggs, sausage and bacon was just too much to contemplate. Almost in unison we said, lying: "No thanks – we had that already in Manchester, at the Favourite Snack Bar in Albert Square."

She was bristling with pride as we escorted her to the church where the procession was gathering. We said we would just fit in with the men's section of the parade, with some of our old school friends we had seen gathering. There was a big crowd of people forming into ranks; the Boy Scouts, the Girl Guides, the brass band, the priest in black and white, and a dozen white clad altar boys all in filigree white cassocks. School kids in their school blazers and caps, tiny kids in their best clothes, mums bustling about, and the Knights of St Colombo in their best war demob suits. Of course we were by far the smartest dressed. We had grey Tonic Mohair suits with 13 inch side vents, highly polished black boots, colourful military ties, and white Ben Sherman shirts with button-down collars, gold cuff-links, and top pockets filled with correctly folded silk handkerchiefs.

We saw some of the Knights of St Colombo blokes struggling with the statue of 'Our Lady' the Madonna, or JC's Mom as we called her. They had the metal lapel badges of the Columbus Knights on their jackets, but we had real hand-stitched button holes in our lapels, so we outranked them. We grabbed the statue before they lost control and dropped it, just as the procession kicked off. We kept the authorised carriers of the statue at bay and marched off carrying it at the front with two other blokes assisting at the rear; we were right behind the priest at the front of the parade with the band just behind.

My mother looked on with amazed pride, the two official statue handlers just gave up and followed along behind. After all we looked better in the role than they did. We put on our shades and then pulled out our lightweight driving gloves to get a firmer grip. As a result we got a small cheer from onlookers as we grappled to pull on the gloves whilst keeping JC's Mom aloft. This audience participation and the 'couldn't give a shit about anything' attitude that we had, it was all due to the second stage of Amphetamines beginning to take effect, making us begin to show off even more. We marched down the centre of the road with all the traffic held up by the police, including our return number 88 bus, and began to dance. The band was playing 'Faith of Our Fathers', the crowd was singing: *'Faith of our fathers, Holy faith, we will be true to thee till death...'* but we were singing *'Going to a Go Go.... You'll see some people from your block and don't be shy... We're goin' to a Go Go...'*

Then the scene faded and the 'Going to a Go Go' lyrics I was internally singing fused and changed into 'Going to the Limit'. I moved position in the toilet cubicle due to leg cramps and made a re-entry into the dream, which had now changed to a new memory.

The Limit Club was at the bottom of Wood Street in Middleton on the outskirts of Manchester and had opened when Angelo and I were in our last year at school. The school was really quite notorious with a reputation for 'yobbos'. Funny thing was that it was named after the Catholic Italian saint who started a school for yobbos; it was called St Dominic Savio's and he was a special pupil of the Don.

The teachers frequently beat up some of the kids, and gangs of kids retaliated if they caught such a teacher out of school grounds. It was a harsh place. Only the strong survived. All the kids in the school knew about the Limit; one of the very first groups appearing were Red Hoffman and The Measles and they were from the nearby Langley overspill estate - a tough place. Another group from yet another overspill council estate, Wythenshawe, was Herman's Hermits, who played at the Limit. If you went to school in Middleton in 1963, the Limit was the place to be seen to go to, mainly because school kids were officially too young to get in!

The club was upstairs over some shops, just a crummy room really, all painted black - a square room with 'Boys and Girls' toilets and a stage. No alcohol was allowed; they had no licence.

The members - you had to be one with a little membership card shown at the door - were mainly 14 to 16 year olds. Strictly speaking anyone under sixteen was not allowed. It was a challenge for school kids to get in, like going to an 'X' at the pictures, but really the management and the door bouncers knew that without under-agers they'd have no one in the place. Our cycling mates never came to the Limit, they went to Brown's. It was a school of dancing near the Ben Brierly Pub in Moston.

The Limit was the first club Angelo and I went to. The music was all pop charts, mostly the Mersey Beat sound. The first time we went, the DJ played the entire 'With the Beatles' LP.

Funny thing memory; as I was reminiscing in my mind's eye about the Limit, I simultaneously remembered then that I was told about the opening of a new dance club in Manchester town centre on Saturday 27th January 1963 with Karl Denver. He was a Scotsman who lived in Polefield Road in Blackley. He had a big hit with 'Wimoweh' after the Tokens did it in the USA in fact most of the pop music in those pre-Beatles days were rip off British copies of USA chart hits. Karl was a Catholic and went to our church, and it was my mother that told me he was on in Manchester as he had been mentioned in the priest's sermon, as a good local successful catholic role model. She read it out from the Manchester Evening News, "opening a new club called 'The Twisted Wheel". It was like predicting the future! But at that time we were loyal to the Limit, and to cycle training. Another predictive item was that the Limit not only played the Rolling Stones records but somehow they had a copy of 'Fanny Mae' by Buster Brown, a track I would hear again at the Wheel. As I shifted position, once again on the toilet over-seat, Buster's wailing became my new soundtrack as my thoughts, a mixture of reminiscences, flooded into me again and I dozed in a semi-conscious dream.

I often tried to analyse my state; what I felt like in my 'come-down' mood. Often these current thoughts melded with other past memories like waking dreams of past events. Usually they had a connection, maybe an insight. Being in a residual drugged mental state and passing eventually into a calmer one made me think about the nature of consciousness. Where did ideas come from? How did thoughts operate? When I caught myself in this frame of mind I tried to establish and observe where these thoughts and memories popped up from. I felt as though I was split into two. As soon as this theme came to mind, I had the ability to enter it, concentrate on it and analyse it. The state of mind I had reached was, I imagined, similar to some of the strange ESP related stories in some of the books I had read. I tried to be positive and not consider the paranoid possibility of emerging schizophrenia. As soon as these thoughts arrived, a description of my state came to me, a definition; 'separateness and absorption'. When my conscious 'I' was observing, I became disconnected and separate from the observed re-play event. I was distinctly separated, becoming 'the watcher' as dream events unfolded. When my separated consciousness wavered and I became absorbed within the 'events', of the regurgitated dreams, then the 'me' or the 'I' that was once the independent observer disappeared!

Taking drugs was proclaimed by some artists, poets and songwriters as inspirational. Had I reached into such states? I reasoned I might have done so; certainly interesting thoughts ideas and possibilities resided here. However, I guessed that most artists settled for a little inspiration. I was determined to find out what was the reason and the truth behind such a mental cornucopia.

Science fiction was a passion of mine, and within some of these stories I read were concepts and ideas that were new and exciting. When I was younger at school, I was told off by teachers for reading such 'rubbish' as Isaac Asimov's 'Foundation and Empire', 'Childhood's End' by Arthur C Clarke, 'Slan' By A. E. Van Vogt, and 'A Canticle for Leibowitz' by Walter M. Miller.

Once again the intermittent absorption took over as I recalled a science fiction related event. It was simple to make assertions about these states of mind, far harder to carry out and to be in control. The thinking itself triggered memories, and as they re-played the analytical mind disappeared. On one occasion I was with my mother in the doctor's surgery; she had taken me there as I had severe tonsillitis. I was reading 'The Corridors of Time' by Poul Anderson, when a man sitting on the opposite chair pulled the book out of my hands and angrily said to my mother that kids should not be reading such utter rubbish. People in those days were very opinionated, and this man was passionately against anything that was not classed as literature. This attitude spurred me on to read even more Sci-Fi. I reasoned that idiots were not going to stop me, and that man's attitude in fact had the opposite effect of what he wanted to achieve. The best and easiest way to spot Sci-Fi books was looking for GOLLANCZ SF titles, because these were bright yellow books. There was no section for this category in the local library; books were only sorted by author alphabetically and not by any genre related to Science Fiction.

I returned to my contemplative state, like re-surfacing slightly up from the sub-absorption recall level. This analysing state I had achieved enabled me to choose to think, to simply view events in the past, or consider deeply things that aroused curiosity in my mind. My thinking continued whilst my body was in a comatose sleep. I wondered whether writers who used their imaginations for Sci-Fi were tapping into a vast pool of consciousness, or unconsciousness. Who knew for sure?

As my own thought stream progressed, my slumbering analysis continued. Maybe Science Fiction authors weren't restricted by the common thought patterns of standard literature, and so break out of the boundaries? Then, when they tap these 'idea places', they home in, retrieve and bring about entirely new concepts. What I thought about there in the toilet, is that many of these concepts can or may become true. Small segments of books describing certain things, like the litany against fear in 'Dune' - *'I will face my fear... fear is the mind killer'* – have some value within themselves. Ideas like satellites, moon landings, or telepathy; they were in my own imagination, and I had read them being described as a portion of some future reality within a story. This also contributed to my interest in the vitality of these books. Who else was writing about frontiers in the 1950's and 60's? No one. I had recently read 'Dune' by Frank Herbert, a book that resonated with many strange yet believable parallels.

In my opinion, these authors were enabled with new ideas because they had dispensed with the common enclosure barriers of generalised literature and had crossed some threshold. In doing so, they'd reached what Carl Jung meant about the pool of the unconscious. I recalled this from a BBC TV programme about him, narrated by Laurens van der Post. Artists, poets, musicians and painters reached in here. Was I now in that same place?

My mind was displaced. I was able to think my thoughts, yet also observe the thinker of these thoughts. It was also a little frightening, like looking into a mirror inside a mirror, with reflections going onwards forever. Which of all these images was the real me? I began to panic…

…and then slowly, I became aware that 'I' was 'really' here in this toilet, thinking this stream of ideas, but observing it from a distance. I mean REALLY HERE and really AWARE of myself: I was really 'coming down', but then for a flash of a second I was above myself, yet floating downwards and looking at myself thinking my own thoughts.

Was all of this real? Was I going schizophrenic? Had my mind split into two? Was all of this flowing stream of consciousness gabble only a result of the drugs? And was I somehow just more susceptible to it?

My thoughts raced onwards, streaming though from subject to subject. Once I landed on one single thought, it would expand and become fuller and 'real'. But I noticed I couldn't hold two or more together concurrently, like considering a subject, and then holding another one with the same clarity and force of mind. Holding both simultaneously was impossible. One would override the other. I wasn't able to think in parallel, and yet I could almost 'see' the stack of thought items held in some strange separate location in my mind. But as they entered the focus of my attention, each single subject faded out and began to erase the previous dominant one. Usually the next in line forced the others aside into oblivion, like dream landscapes that fade upon waking, and my insights into Science Fiction had now vanished in this way.

Probably due to exhaustion, a time came when all thought

about the process of thought as well as the entire associated background soundtrack stopped.

I was able to hold the concept that there existed several mental states with defined boundaries inside my mind, and the one I had reached was on the borderland of total silence. It was easy from there to eventually fall off to complete blank sleep. What intrigued me was the fact that there was a 'me' that looked on at all this and was separate from it. Often this 'me' or 'I' became submerged and totally lost, indulging in and becoming fully identified and absorbed with each thought. Yet in this state, this other newly found 'me' was passively there watching. It was there in a peaceful state of non-committal awareness; this 'I' called separateness.

At first, I was certain that these strange concepts were entirely due to my indulgence in weekend drugs, and also that I must be more susceptible to the effects than others. But I still remained convinced that there was something important and truthful there, a new perception of knowledge. It was a place where thoughts were not processed linearly, but instead in a sort of positive passivity, untarnished by descriptions. But then, just as soon as this perspective was made, an attack of negativity, anxiety and panic was generated as I recalled an event described in a book by Damon Knight called 'Beyond The Barrier'; a story where a scientist splits into several time travelling 'personalities'. One of these alien personalities is a thing that grows in consciousness – an alien reptilian creature called a Zug – and eventually it displaces the original personality and mind and emerges from the body of the professor, like a cuckoo in a host's nest; his own mind is pushed out and his body gives birth to the alien thing! This hideous paranoid thought was given life and entered my terrified brain. I suffered more panic, but then I understood once again that it was only a part of my mind playing tricks on me. Then I felt that the understanding of this game and the overcoming of it was important.

This fleeting glimpse was of something important. I understood it was important, and it reminded me strongly of the message in 'Dune' that 'the sleeper must awaken!' Then, I guessed that the message was not about ordinary, everyday consciousness. The thought occurred to me as a question: where is memory stored? What is this place where all thoughts can be held together all at once, when in ordinary mechanical thinking, one thought has to follow on from another, often triggered by an association to the previous one?

This semi awake perception continued. What is consciousness? A part of my mind was asking the question. Why did it seem that one part of me was disassociated from an apparent stream of others? Was this 'me' the left brain hemisphere talking to the multiple me's in the right hemisphere? Was it interplay between my conscious and subconscious mind? Is my mind located within my brain? Was the brain simply a conduit, a machine played through by the mind, which existed in a higher dimension? Surely, I thought, even within a two-hemisphere brain, this 'mindplace' that I was observing was so vast and beyond any definition that I thought then and there that it was impossible to simply fit within the brain.

One fact I had learned for certain was that when that endless stream of repeated music played, 'I' was separate from it. I wanted it to stop, and that act proved I was not 'lost' in it – but when I was hearing it live, I was absorbed into it, almost joining and becoming the music at the All-nighters. On these occasions the 'I' that could step aside was absorbed, and as a result I *was* the music.

I began to think about dope smoking sessions, when conversations took place in which people often said similar things; things they deemed important but just couldn't grasp enough to describe to the others. I had 'willed' myself to try and understand, to bring positive observations back from these places or states that the drugs could launch me into.

Like a trigger, these thoughts projected me to a state in which I knew I could interrogate my thoughts. I was dimly aware of a mechanism; it began to emerge as a mental card index with a question mark bubble floating in front. The question mark seemed to trigger a continuation of my previous question:

The Manchester Wheelers

How does our consciousness operate?

The card index produced both a written image and an answer. It was not a voice – it was more like a simultaneous feeling, 'spoken yet unspoken'. It said: 'Do you really want to know the truth?'

'YES,' was my reply thought.

The card index's combination of voice and image stated that to understand consciousness it was necessary to begin long ago in biology, with single cell 'beings'. It said that all life is derived from a single starting 'template' and every form of life is connected at the cell level. These 'beings' have a small consciousness that assists them in their life, it explained, and most of their consciousness comes from the organising template that exists in their surface connection with their external environment, and also with a parallel dimension. Then it stated that a power is available which spins around all things from micro to macro as the heavens turn so does everything else including cells, and this is the life force.

I started thinking of Science Fiction again and the weirdness of what I was experiencing. As I did so, the question mark card index began to fade from view. I had the presence of mind to try not to analyse what I was being told. Something from somewhere advised me to shut up. I did. The card index continued its strange method of printing internal words and speaking directly to me:

'Living matter is first organised in another dimension which assists life to form and grow and evolve in the physical dimension. Primitive single cells have information from their environment and a primitive brain that organises their existence. At the beginning of life everything is built up from single forms that first split and then group together. Often the drive to group is initiated as a signal to reproduce and they turn about each other. This is a strong signal, and this signal is harmonised from the external dimension. Cells clump together. They combine their intelligence into a collective. They begin to form organisations that begin to share and evolve as interdependent symbiotic communities; amoeba, cilia and so on. These 'beings' have many cells performing actions of benefit to the whole entity. These 'beings' operate together as a community and feel a strong connection with the harmonising directive from the parallel dimension within, which is the full realisation of the intent of the 'organising template.' From this point you may see the ladder of progression to the animal and then a greater step to the human 'being'.

I made no response.

'The human 'being' is in fact made up from a large scale integration of cells that have formed in time to become components; heart, liver, kidneys, lungs, eyes, etc. Each of them a conglomerate 'being' made from lesser 'beings' in turn formed from cells as first explained, although apparently species independent organs such as eyes, once generated are shared and so all subsequent life may have a form adapted to there need from the 'eye' template. The brain is also made in a similar fashion, but it is the membranes encapsulating the cells that are the real brain – it is the surfaces that communicate. The human 'beings brain' has far greater capacity to know and feel its environment than a cell, yet the cell links almost directly with its corresponding template and organising associate. The human 'being' has lost this capacity in its movement towards independence and potential 'evolution'. In other words, the human 'being' is cut off from the originating template in exchange for independence even if it is limited. If the human was fully cut off, it would die. Your subconscious mind evolved without you. It is faster than you, and it has to be so to protect you.

'This is the reason why you are confused with multiple inner voices and separate selves. The template is there and the body brain parts can act out what you call subconscious thought, but connecting to them at a deep level is unavailable to you at this time. That is why your struggle with the belief of separate 'you's' is troublesome to you. If you cannot learn to integrate into one positive self, then connection with and limited 'control' of these biological and 'mentalised' formations will conversely control you at times, and on certain occasions it is imperative they do so. Also in your current state of embryonic intelligence your perception cannot re-connect with the originating template; this is the important quest of the evolving human to become a 'realised being'. The first step is understanding that your higher conscious mind must learn to communicate and harmonise with the subconscious mind without a struggle'.

'Your conscious mental struggle to know what is happening in the controlling elements in you're 'being' have been triggered by the drugs that affect your brain, and its parallel dimension template. Be warned: drugs are not the path to this knowledge. They are only brief triggers, and continued drug ingestion will result in positive thought burnout, replaced with addiction, a false belief in reliance upon the need for drugs. What will follow is a negative downward spiral into repetitive drug dependence. It will be total dislocation without any chance of conscious connectivity and harmonisation with your subconscious, and it will also mean further dislocation from your 'template'; to which re-connection to, is the evolutionary aim and purpose of your species.'

Christ, this was weird stuff. It had a shock effect upon me and I switched out from it, with the residual feeling that the words 'beings' and 'templates' were only descriptions of a possible reality well beyond my understanding. It was beginning to sound barmy.

I thought again about how I couldn't stop the tunes from repeating endlessly inside my mind.

As soon as I had the thought, the card index voice said: 'Perception of these inner mental events is a good starting point. At last you have become aware of this. What was observed by you was a learned and conditioned 'reflex' action. Because you have been in a certain state of mind, the music has gone 'deep' and replays automatically by a trigger response. And yes, instinctively you want to stop it at your command because the action is in fact taking up the energy needed for different subconscious duties – but because it was not initiated by deliberate intention, it runs its 'own' course, and shows you that 'mind' can operate without 'you' and at levels you have little or no control over.'

The Manchester Wheelers

I thought then about how I could gain control and stop something that was not only annoying but wouldn't let me rest. Surely I had free will to control my own mind?'

The answer came as a puzzle: 'That's a different matter. It requires stillness and a passive control of the mind. To reach it and to do this requires relinquishing most of the behaviour you have been conditioned to adopt. Simply believing you can do something does not make it so, if the facts are something else. Force has no effect.'

I reflected that even when I was 'within' such important thinking, I could easily be diverted and drift away from it. Or was I moved on by an external force? Was this again paranoia? With just that thought occupying my mind, my attention moved away from observing my own inner processes. There again was the flow of thoughts and another 'me' slowly breathing, chest expanding up and down with each breath, silently watching distant floating thoughts. And again, the absorption took over:

A new heading popped up. It was quite automatic: 'Pulled by the Fuzz'.

The replay began. It was Angelo riding the Cento Lambretta Scooter with me as the pillion passenger, and of course no 'L' plates. The Cento was a small 125cc scooter, and although we initially tried to outrun the police car that was sounding its siren behind us, we soon had to give up the chase. By this time the cops were randomly stopping Mod types on scooters wearing Parkas as we were. The copper asked for Angelo's licence and insurance certificate. Soon it dawned on him that the licence was provisional. Angelo had not even applied to take a test for a full licence yet. He spurted out that I had a full licence, as it was ok for a full licensed pillion passenger, but no other passenger type was allowed. Obviously, I also only had a provisional licence.

"What's your name?" the cop said to me. Before I could open my mouth, like something from a TV farce, Angelo answered and shouted out: "He's Dave Moston... Dave – sorry that's his nickname – he's Dave Bramwell."

The cop looked at me, "OK then, Mr Dave Bramwell. Have you got a licence?"

I felt cornered. "Yes," I said, "but I don't carry it with me."

The cop took on that forlorn hapless look they do so well, and got out his pad. "Right. Name... Address..." Slowly he filled in the particulars as falsely as I could dictate them. Then the same with Angelo. He issued us both a receipt; we had to report to a police station with all our correct documents to avert a crime. Later, Angelo spent quite a while in the Ben Brierly pub trying to persuade Moston Dave to take his full licence down to the cop shop, but he refused. Of course we didn't show up, but eventually the police did. A knock at Angelo's door some months later after tracing the Cento's registration plates and road tax licences. Then the search for Dave Bramwell began, but they never did catch up with me. Angelo got a fine at his court appearance. I waited outside, avoiding being seen by any of the police. Later we went to the Wheel. They were having a lunch time dance session for city centre office workers.

The memory bubble then floated away. Another was approaching and, as is the way with memories, it had a connection with the last one, the trigger being the police.

The next heading in my memory stack came into focus: its keyword or title was 'Moroccan Kif and Bowling Shoes'.

It was Saturday afternoon, and Angelo suggested we should all go bowling: DL, Brian, Moston Dave, Jimmy Riddle from Stockport and a guy called 'Motown' Dave from Bolton. It was a nickname he'd picked up due to the fact that he was a member of the fraternity of Soul Mods who were buying every Motown record – from all the Stateside releases and on the UK Tamla Motown label, all in strict numerical order.

We met Len, who was a milkman. He had just scored some

terrific Moroccan Kif and he too was up for a bowling session. We ended up smoking plenty of his stuff, which he amicably shared with everyone. He even offered a draw to the bloke who was exchanging our shoes for the special red ones you had to wear on the bowling alley.

We played one game, and then booked another. In between games, what with the Kif kicking in and the Boddingtons Bitter, we all got that strange ravenous hunger that came with good shit. So we ordered meals from downstairs. The bowling alley at Belle Vue was upstairs.

By the time the meals were on their way up the stairs, we had gone into that type of barmy, fooling-around overdrive that seems to take over inebriated groups of men. We had taken out lots of balls from all the racks and started throwing them around. By this time the last family of other bowlers had hurriedly departed and the entire set of lanes was all ours. We started bowling at all of them, and soon we were bowling at each other and hopping over the approaching balls. And then as the waitresses ascended the stairs, Angelo let off two large balls towards the top of the stairs, rapidly copied by Brian.

The balls moved across the carpet towards the stairs like slow torpedoes. Once launched there was no return, no way back from the act that had released them. It dawned on all of us just how stupid it was. However there was nothing we could to change events. In slow motion the balls moved in concert to the top of the stairs, then the four bowling balls - two in the advanced column, with two more arching slowly around to follow, began to bounce down the stairs. They disappeared from our view, but we could hear and imagine the result as the balls met the girls with our meals coming up in the other direction. The plates were dropped. The girls ran down. There were shouts of panic and a thunderous clatter and several thudding sounds. Well, four continuous thudding and thumping sounds, followed by a sharper impact as the heavy balls hit the stone ground floor.

Nobody was killed.

The Manchester Wheelers

Silence.

Then there was a shout from downstairs: "I've called the police. They are on their way." We guessed it was the manager shouting up at us.

We looked for another exit but there wasn't one – so we rushed all together in a mob down the stairs. Speeding past the mess of dropped meals, we ran out the front doors, passing the manager who was shaking his head and holding one of the loose bowling balls he'd just retrieved.

"Shit," shouted Moston Dave, "the Rossers."

A Ford Zodiac Panda car was outside and two policemen were getting out. Fortunately they were engaged in putting on their helmets as we rushed past. Instinctively knowing how to avoid being nabbed, we all split up, heading in different directions. I ran straight across Hyde Road and all the way up past the swimming baths before turning to look around.

No one was after me. We had all escaped.

I slowed down and headed across the road again to get a bus into town. I was exuberant and singing to myself: *'We're off, we're off, and fifty Rossers are after us and we don't know where we are'*. The fact is that the cops only give chase if they really have to. It's rare for them to expend too much effort as they are all, or mostly all, lazy bastards. They join the police force for an easy life where they can throw their weight around but without any exertion, basically in cars or at walking pace. They aren't creatures that are prone to speeding up, either physically or mentally.

We reassembled later in Manchester City centre at the Station on London Road – a known gathering point for All-nighter goers. Two Mars bars had taken care of my hunger craving, bought from the shop at the station, where I was aimlessly wandering about in expectation of everyone arriving. The station had a bar and a newsagent that sold sweets, drinks and the Manchester Evening

News. It even had a barbers shop downstairs in the gents' bogs. It had a vibration machine – sixpence in the slot and you stood on a flat surface that hummed as it vibrated. I had a go. Dropped my 'tanner' into the slot and the bowling shoes became assimilated as one humming appendage to my legs melding with the vibrating platform below. In our rush to escape the manager and the fuzz, we had all shot out the bowling alley in bowling shoes. No-one was going back to retrieve their original shoes, mostly brogues. However, that night at the Wheel we set a bit of a trend, all dancing together kicking about, all in the same red bowling shoes. The Temptations had nothing on us!

Pins and needles in both legs brought me back to the real world and I knew it was time to leave the toilets. I knew that if I stared at the light bulb overhead in the toilet cubicle for long enough, it reduced the dilation of my eye pupils, but it made me stagger about like a drunk for a while after emerging from the traps. I worried sometimes that someone would look into my eyes and know the signs; therefore this light bulb stare was often my last act before going back to do some work.

On this occasion I came out of my sleepy, dreamy state fully awake and refreshed. I was ready to leave the bogs and do some work. As I began to think about leaving, I noticed a spider running across the floor. It immediately stopped, frozen, motionless. There I was looking at the spider. Then I knew something, and instantly at the same time I knew something else: it knows I'm watching it. The certainty of this knowledge came from elsewhere; I had not reasoned it out, it was instant certainty and it was implanted into my mind. It was 'knowledge without learning', without thinking. And now I had two puzzles. One was: how come the spider knows? The other: how come all of a sudden I know that the spider knows? Was there a dialogue at a level in the mind that we don't often have switched on? Was this dialogue between part of my mind and the spiders? Or was it coming from some place that has all this kind of knowledge in some kind of storage; like the previous encounter with card index file I had connected with?

Returning to the spider, my reason kicked in, whilst still holding onto the strange link I had re-established to the imaginary card index system. My reasoning continued: obviously the spider stopped because a moving spider is easier to be seen by a predator than a stationary one. But how was I a threat?

Then the card index in my mind flipped to a new statement: MY SHOE CAN CRUSH IT, was printed boldly in black capitals on the white card surface on my inner vision, yet the accompanying voice I experienced before was missing.

Why would my foot do this without 'me' giving my foot the go ahead?

The index flipped again:

BECAUSE IT'S AT AN INSTINCTIVE LEVEL TO AUTOMATICALLY STAMP ON A CRAWLY CREATURE. IT NEEDS NO ACTIVE THINKING – JUST MECHANICAL UNCONSCIOUS ACTION.

But I knew I had a choice. I decided not to stamp on the spider.

And no sooner had I made this decision, the spider ran off.

Did it know it was safe?

The index system flipped and gave me the answer:

IF YOU ARE CONSCIOUS, 'YOU' CAN CHOOSE INSTEAD OF USING INSTINCTIVE ACTIONS.

I pondered this. But then how did the spider know that the possible threat had been removed?

The card index rolled again, and this time the voice was there as well: 'at the level of consciousness which you had established, you become linked to all things at a level to which spiders and all creatures instinctively are also connected. It is interspecies telepathy, and the spider received a transmission from you about your decision not to harm it.' Having stated this, the card index slowly faded away.

Or, of course, I told myself: it was the after-effects of sleep deprivation and residual Amphetamine poisoning as I returned to my daily ordinary consciousness. But it was something I could test. I resolved to try it when I next saw a running spider near my foot. It was a future experiment that required exactly the right set of circumstances, and of course I forgot all about it.

I returned to the real world to do some work. However, in these periods I began to notice this odd kind of thinking happening at work. After recuperating on Mondays and into Tuesday, I would be back to normal – but my internal thinking was changed, I had 'panic' attacks and quite often my concentration would noticeably wander. For example, I might have to go to a different part of the factory to collect something. It was a huge place. On my journey I would drift into daydreams, becoming lost in automatic thinking. It would happen by itself, like the function of the automatic record player in my head. I didn't have to be present. I noticed that 'I' had not been 'there' after long periods of this automation. I was like a robot and operated without being conscious, like walking past the place I was supposed to be going to, passing my objective, then waking up with a start and having to retrace my steps. Was this a new experience, or one that I and everyone else had, and which I was just now beginning to notice? Again I had to ask myself whether I was more susceptible to the effects of these drugs than others?

Sometimes I got a sense of paranoia, a terrifying feeling when alternating between states of mind in which one moment I was there, the next lost. When 'I' tried to catch the crossover point, I could feel great fear and panic inside me. As the 'me' that was passed to the 'I' that I then became, the 'me' that was conscious faced a sort of anguish, a type of death.

Astonished, I understood that there are lots of 'me's' inside my mind and they live and die in a constant stream of awakenings and terminations. When I am immersed within them, there is no conscious 'self'. Without that 'I' which is the one I call 'The Observer', the rest of the 'me's' can just move me from one unconscious state to another. The day would pass, and apart from a few pivotal events forcing conscious effort to the surface and providing awareness, the day would not even be remembered. Then it dawned upon me that I effectively spend most of my time in a state of wakeful day dreaming sleep.

Was everyone in a similar state?

I became convinced of it.

When these thoughts came to me, I often experienced panic, because I always ended up feeling like my thoughts were controlled by someone else, like we have no free will and we are all at the mercy of a puppet master. Yet in spite of the panic from time to time after getting over the weekend's effects, I found myself pondering such ideas. I feared I was becoming psychotic or paranoid. Yet on another level, I had a belief that I had discovered something. 'The sleeper must awaken' – the line from 'Dune', which I had read in the summer of 1965 – seemed to echo inside my mind. I began to ponder and turn over and over again in my mind and seeing that my experiences of these episodes were very weird. I never spoke of it to anyone, as I decided to put it down to a residual drug effect. However I did learn the prayer against fear from Dune, and used it periodically as it intrigued me – it described that when fear had passed through 'me' only 'I' remained. I wondered what the author was getting at. Had he experienced multiple 'I's' or 'selves' inside his head? And was the real one left when purged by passing through a state of fear?

The fear I had was of the onset of mental illness. For my own peace of mind, I decided to put the series of dualities inside my head down as just a residual drug effect.

* * *

The Manchester Wheelers

CHAPTER FOURTEEN

The Lost Stash

'Don't think of it as lost. It's just temporarily out of reach. We can get it anytime we want. All we have to do is demolish half of the house.'

"That's five hundred Blueys and two hundred and fifty Green and Clears, and over two hundred little yellow Dexys – top stuff, so look after it." Angelo's words were echoing in my mind as the aluminium container slid from my hands and fell into the cavity wall. "Fucking shit," I shouted, nearly falling off the rim of the bath I was balancing on.

My mother shouted upstairs, "Are you alright David?"

"Yes, yes Mum, I'm ok. I'm just in the toilet and the seat fell down," I shouted back to her.

I had hidden the stash – enough stuff to cover our All-nighter needs for several months at the very least – in a place I thought was safe.

I silently cursed myself. What a stupid cunt I was. I'd put the pill container in the air vent built into the wall in the bathroom of our council ranch. Manchester, like many English cities, had massive council owned housing estates where all the houses looked alike, with bay windows and tiny rooms. The only differential factor was the colour of your door and matching gate – ours was purple. The bathroom had an air vent; a brick inlet that I had put the large Boots aluminium screw-cap container into. I hadn't realised it was perched so precariously on a ledge. As I reached in to retrieve it, I had pushed it inadvertently. It was only very slight touch, but it was enough to knock it over. It fell, down into the cavity brick wall beneath.

After surveying inside and out, I it dawned on me that it was impossible to reach it without demolishing the wall. When I told Angelo about my accident, he said: "No problem. Let's take out the bricks."

It was Saturday morning and we were only thirteen hours from the All-nighter. It was approaching noon. My mother had sent my sister to the chippy to get our dinner whilst she was putting her face on, getting ready to go to my gran's. After the chips, off went Mum, leaving us to begin at hammering out the bricks along the wall underneath the air vent that was upstairs in the bathroom.

We hacked away at the red bricks, hitting them with a large jemmy of steel we had obtained from our coal shed, and periodically bashing the wall with a spade. It was dangerous work, as it had to be synchronised without losing my fingers; me placing the jemmy, then Angelo whacking it with the garden spade. Each whack was followed by me twisting the steel crowbar in the wall, and so on, loosening the bricks and then removing them. After an hour's work we had demolished about a third of the house wall above the foundations, and my sister was shouting saying she was going to tell Mum. But the worst of it was that we couldn't find the tin!

We had to abandon the idea, and put the bricks back but without any mortar – we simply poked the chunks of it back into the gaps around the re-fitted bricks. I guessed the tin had lodged itself onto a narrow part of the cavity wall higher up than we had excavated. I was also relieved that Angelo had accepted the loss of all his stuff as a shared problem, and had refrained from bashing me with the spade.

We had a plan to do it all again, but never had the opportunity for long enough to be successful. We would need to rebuild and cement it all back again after the more ambitious demolition and it would take a day. This event put the kibosh on our back-up safety stash, and probably made Angelo more determined to make his plan happen regarding disappearances of stock from Boots happen. That tin is still there to this day.

After giving up, we got the bus to Piccadilly to meet our pals and get some 'stuff' from the street pushers before going on to the All-nighter. The usual meeting place to obtain 'gear' before the All-nighter was outside the Wimpy and along York Street at the back of the Piccadilly Hotel. There was a shortage and everyone had sold out, so we could only get Black Bombers and some Black and White Minstrels that were two bob each due to the fact that they were double strength. Black Bombers were pharmaceutically called Durophet.

They were the pills of last resort; most of the real head bangers favoured them. They must have had some extra ingredient alongside a double dose of amphetamine, because ordinary Bennies felt different - these things made you feel oppressive. Black and White Minstrels sounded joyful due to our nickname for them, but were just the same thing from a different company. We had heard that a company in Liverpool called DISTA made them, and some blokes from the Wheel All-nighter were planning a factory break-in there. Angelo was used as a consultant to tell these guys the locations of drug manufacturing companies; some at Ciba Giegy were close in Trafford Park, another was in Wythenshawe. Raids were planned, but we never heard of any realistic results.

Of course Angelo knew about drugs, being a trainee pharmacist shop manager. He was really an upgraded shop assistant helping out the pharmacist; you had to go to university to be a real pharmacist, but Angelo had gone to the same secondary modern that I went to. We were both turned out without any certificates, as we were in a class so lowly thought of that our teachers never even pestered us with the option of exams.

Angelo was self-educated in pharmacology by assisting the chemist in the shop. He could tell you the funny Latin type names for all the pills we had nicknames for. He knew all the correct terms – Methylphenidate, Ritalin, Diethylpropion, Tenuate, Durophet, Amphetamine, Benzedrine, Dexedrine, Methedrine, and lovely Drinamyl - our favourites. Purple and blue hearts were so popular and 'abused' more than all the others, that the manufacturers changed the shape periodically – possibly to confuse those without an officially prescribed batch? Durophet was prescribed as a slimming drug. In the quantities we needed them they stopped your appetite for around three days and made you feel constantly sick in the stomach.

The very best stuff, but rare, was a white powder: Amphetamine Sulphate. Now and again it was available. You snorted it up your beak, and it didn't half clear your nose! That's how we found out about nasal decongestant inhalers. They were sniffed at, because the cotton wool inside these plastic things had Amphetamine Sulphate in it. We used to suck it. Little grannies swore by its ability to clear the Lancashire ailments like a blocked up nose and aching limbs. Gee's Linctus was a cough medicine easily bought at the chemist's. It was ok if you drank a couple of bottles down in one, but it wouldn't keep you going for an All-nighter. Angelo said it had codeine, kaolin and morphine in it.

Then there were the Morning Glory seeds. By the time we had found out about them, they had been removed from display due to the publicity they had received. The papers were claiming that fashionable Sloane Square and Kings Road Mods were snorting the seeds to get high, but it turned out later to be a hoax, similar to the one Donovan the Folk singer started off about 'Mellow Yellow' leading to people smoking banana skins!

Large amounts of amphetamine generated all sorts of physical and mental states. It felt as though adrenaline was being pumped at a greatly increased rate. More often than not it was a sex suppressant, but if you got past that initial droopy phase they made you shag for hours, although it was difficult to cum.

At the All-nighters lots of people took so many pills they were always close to an overdose situation. Maybe the dancing exercise burned off bad effects? Overdose symptoms were known: they included extreme over-stimulation like a racing pulse, palpitations, sometimes severe chest pains, difficulty breathing, shaking, sweating, muscle spasms and a slow engulfing stiffness.

The mental problems were acute paranoia, and a weird feeling that the room was closing in on you, with you becoming small and wanting to withdraw inside. There were quite a few alternative mental activities that I came across; the strange contemplative states experienced in my come down analysis, which some others experienced, but most never mentioned. A large dose of these pills sometimes generated a weird paranoia the day after; like the fear of losing control whilst your mind just rushed away. Our music was from the United States, and our minds were often in states of anxiety for several days after the weekend.

Sedatives like sleeping pills could bring you down fast.

I only took sleeping tablets once, and never again. I hated the 'come down' experience, everyone did. But it was far better for me to face that without any extra pharmacological assistance, than ever having to face again anything like what happened to me on that occasion. What happened was this:

Sunday night I took two sleeping tablets, the recommended dose to help the 'come down' go OK. I was trying to sleep; it was early Monday morning after a weekend of pill shifting. After about three quarters of an hour the internal chattering and the endless music playing in my head faded. I was on the edge of sleep, yet feeling very irritable. Then my entire body became stiff, paralysed. I couldn't move. Part of me just knew that my body was in fact asleep, but another 'me' was wide awake. 'I' knew of this state, but this was different. I became extremely distressed and panicked as my thoughts raced: 'I' was aware, asleep and awake - both states at once. I couldn't move. I was there watching all this, and it was very disturbing, I felt split into several 'me's'. Panic set in – I couldn't move a muscle. Then it got worse.

I must have gone to sleep for a few minutes, and then when I came to, I became terrified. There was a man underneath me and his erect dick was sticking into my arse!

I couldn't move. I couldn't open my eyes.

The bloke underneath me was breathing heavily. As he was breathing in and out, I was bobbing up and down to the rhythm; at first this made my panic increase further.

Then I had the realisation that this bloke beneath me was me! It was my sleeping body.

It was so strange, because I was above it exactly matching it in a body that was just positioned slightly above the other one below. The worst thing was the fear. There was nothing I could do. I couldn't move. I had no physical controls. I was paralysed. My mind began to go to pieces. How was I ever going to get out of this situation? Was I dying? Was I dead? Had I died due to an overdose?

No, I was breathing at least. The 'me' below was too, but I had been expelled from my body. Was this a coma? The panic went on and on and on.

This panic was so acute that it engulfed me. I screamed a huge scream that raced silently away into the distance; it was a mental, internal scream without any audible sound from the mouth below. I was in a place where there was complete silence, and my screams of panic inside a body that was welded into an immobile, rigid state went unheard.

Eventually, after what seemed like days, not hours – there was no comprehension in this state of any movement of time – I gained some sort of composure. I felt like I had entered a world from a Sci-Fi book I had yet to read, as this story had never been told. This could be the fourth dimension, a place without time. Finally I found some mental rationality; I willed myself to calm down.

As I did so, my arms – the arms in the body I was inside that were floating above the physical ones beneath – began to drop. My right arm went down into the arm of the body beneath, but it did not stop! It went into it, then passed though my physical arm and came out the other side underneath it. I could sense it passing down, was it elongating? It went on, right through the bed mattress, then it passed through the floorboards and stopped.

I tried to move my phantom arm, or at least the fingers. They closed around a hard triangular-shaped object, so I found that I could control something. At least that was a start, and this rationality began to calm me. Then I woke up. It was instantaneous. What I remembered was the way I awoke.

I felt as if I had fallen down a long way, hearing a loud bang as I hit my body. It was all very rapid, instant. My body jerked awake with the shock of it. I had a feeling that I had dropped from a great height. My eyes opened. I was still alive. It was 6.50 a.m. and my alarm was ringing. Worse still, it was Monday morning and time for work.

The strangest thing of all was when I came back after work around 4:45 p.m. I went upstairs to my bedroom. I had been haunted all day with the memory of it all; it just wouldn't go away.

I looked at the bed, then the floor. I went downstairs and found a hammer and a pair of pliers. I removed the floorboards exactly where I remembered the position that my phantom arm had been. Underneath, in the exact position, I found a triangular shaped piece of wood, obviously left by the house builders. It shocked me to the core, so much so that I vowed never again to mix Amphetamines and sleeping tablets. I didn't ever want to go back there again!

* * *

The Manchester Wheelers

CHAPTER FIFTEEN

Another Monday

Another Monday morning in the bogs: part 2 and 3 'if we have time'. Memories re-encountered in the 'come down' state that wrapped past events into envelopes of dreams within other dreams, and yet each dream was an actual past event, vividly re-lived.

Another Monday morning, another 'come down' session in the bogs. I was re-living All-nighter events again. They were clumped together in no particular or sequential order or timescale; each episode had some random quality, often from events not related to the weekend's activities. For example, my inner mind mostly re-played Soul tracks, but right now Procul Harum's 'Whiter Shade of Pale' was drifting along inside my head.

As I floated there on the edge of sleep, coming towards me was the stream of sounds and the vivid pictures of events remembered. We collided together, the Procul Harum song was displaced, and I was once again inside that bright and lucid zone packed with endless streams of memories.

I was again in the Wheel All-nighter where I had tried to dance, but it was hopeless. Quite often the club was so packed that dancing was impossible. All you could achieve was shuffling about on the same spot. It was reminiscent of the early dancing at the Old Wheel in Brazennose Street, when frayed cut-off ends on bell-bottom jeans were fashionable. Even with space to dance, the 'in' dance then was just to shuffle about. Finding that real dancing was impossible I went to the bogs, but as I went to push the door it opened, and Angelo waded out with his pants hitched up.

"It's a fucking flood in here. My feet are soaked. I'm going for a piss on the fire escape," he said.

I could see inside and the place was full of wading Soul fans. I decided to join him and keep my brogues smart. These floods happened frequently. In the morning, your shoes would have acquired at least one white line all around them; it was the residue from water, toilet cleaning chemicals and Amphetemised piss.

It was a warm night. We pissed simultaneously over the rail, watching the streams of glinting liquid flowing in an arc, and ending in splashes down far below. After staring down for a few seconds, we lit up our Benson and Hedges cigarettes.

"Do you remember that night we went to see The Stones in Rochdale?" said Angelo. His words were punctuated with exhaust smoke exiting his mouth in a controlled, intermittent flow.

I did. Angelo had prompted my memory of an event that ended in a riot. These types of random event memories were a side effect of being blocked, as if their stored energy was not released in physical activity like dancing. It found another activity path of release resulting in the vivid recall of past events. As he said it, I entered yet another sub level of my dreaming state. It all came back in sharp detail. I was remembering a past event, one wrapped inside a memory of a discussion of a memory.

"The Kubix Club in Rochdale has got the Fucking Rolling Stones on TONIGHT!" shouted Angelo, decking off the 121 bus as it turned the corner into Cannon Street.

He shouted to me, "Quick, jump on that 17 and let's go!"

We ran for it as it was pulling away, jumped on, and ran upstairs. After we had paid the guard, Angelo told me he had heard some old people complaining that 'they were awful, filthy, long haired, scruffy and that they were appearing at a place called the Kubix Club in Rochdale' – The Rolling Stones! He recounted the conversation he had heard on the bus to town, from two old fogies sitting in front of him.

"So that's why I wanted to get there fast, 'cause it's bound to be packed," said Angelo.

We had arranged this meeting in Manchester to go to the Cavern Club. On previous Saturday nights we had seen Lulu and the Luvvers, The Big Three, Arthur Brown, and Screaming Lord Sutch, but the thought of seeing the Stones was far better.

When we got to the end of the journey near the Town Hall in Rochdale, loads of people were crowding about in anticipation; hundreds of Mod looking types. We found the place down a back street just as the police arrived with dogs. One broke lose from a copper who was threatening us with it. We jumped over a wall to avoid the vicious snarling beast and went straight down a ten foot drop into the foaming, stinking, river Irk below. Soaked, we climbed out downstream at a bridge, got a bus and then went home.

"I doubt they were even on," said Angelo as he got off the bus in Middleton, leaving me for another dozen stops to Victoria Avenue.

I came up back to the level where Angelo had asked the question. I remembered the Kubix Club and Rolling Stones fiasco, which had instantly re-played in my mind's eye, triggered by his question.

"Yes," I said, "Well, my feet were a lot wetter that night, and I'm sure it was just a rumour. I bet they weren't on."

"That was a laugh that night. My socks were more than soaked then," he said, taking his shoes off to dry his socks, as more people joined us on the fire escape platform at the back of the club.

Soon quite a crowd had gathered on the fire escape. We were joking about being in the final scene in the Stanley Kramer film 'It's a Mad Mad Mad Mad World', and then Angelo jumped up and down to get the entire contraption shaking.

"Stop fucking about, you'll get us all killed," shouted a tall bloke who was talking to three others at the sloping-end edge of the ladders. We moved down a bit to hear him.

"You see, all Soul music originated from Gospel. All of it, well almost all..." This was Len from Salford: Len the milkman and constant spliff smoker. What he didn't know about the background and history of Soul music, you could write on a postage stamp.

Len lived in Broughton Salford, but as a kid he'd lived in Warrington near the 'Nut House' - Winwick Hospital. His mother worked in the American version of the NAAFI at Burtonwood, the American army air force base. They had a jukebox there. They also had American artists appearing for their R & R, and many black guys stationed there were into Blues, Doo-Wop harmony groups and Gospel. Len used to hang around in there while his mother was working and he heard all sorts of great R&B tunes on the Wurlitzer Juke Box. He listened to AFN, the American Forces Network, and that's also where Georgie Fame heard the R&B songs he would make his versions from. Consequently Len learned a lot about Black American music, and while there, he became a 'Stogie-smoking' aficionado. Len informed us that a 'Stogie' was what the Negro GIs called marijuana reefers - we called them spliffs.

He was into Blues before anyone, and used to lend records to Roger Eagle back in the days at the Old Wheel when Blues was king. He soon followed on with Soul. It was Len that let us know when Alvin Cash and the Registers were appearing at Burtonwood. On that occasion we missed them, but a few days later they were on at Warrington Co-Op after appearing once again at the Airbase. That time we didn't miss them.

It was a great show, the Cash brothers: the younger ones did gymnastic displays, whilst their elder brother Alvin did the singing. They did sequenced acrobatics, slow cartwheels, splits and other dance routines to the sounds of 'Twine Time', 'Alvin's

Boogaloo', and of course 'The Philly Freeze'. Alvin Cash was recorded on MAR - V- LUS records, distributed in the UK by President Records.

I think he was impressed with the audience who were all dancing, and instantly froze when he sung '*Freeze*'. It was from months of practice at the Wheel All-nighter. Alvin told the audience at the end of the show he was off to play for the GIs in Vietnam. As he did so, Sid was pinching several leather overcoats from those piled up in a heap at the edge of the Co-Op hall ballroom. 'Twine Time' was the first recording by Alvin Cash to be heard at the Wheel, followed by 'The Philly Freeze'. Both soon caught on as a dance craze, with dancers holding still when Alvin said '*Freeze*'. Alvin was from St Louis, Missouri, and he and his brothers Robert and George started out as dance entertainers. The Crawlers were his backing band and initially were called the Registers.

Len was there of course. He had orchestrated the train journey from Manchester. There was a large group; we all had platform tickets and it was Len who warned us of the approaching guard inspecting tickets. As the train slowed to enter Warrington station, the doors flew open and we all jumped out and rushed for the exit before the guard caught up with us. Nobody had a legitimate train ticket. On the platform DL jumped over a wall to avoid capture as the train guard shouted to his colleagues at the station. They chased him, enabling us to escape through the normal exit. We caught up with DL outside. He had seriously sprained his ankle, but this didn't stop him dancing. He took a stack of pills and felt no pain, but we had to carry him home later.

My attention re-focused upon Len's lecture.

He gulped a large breath of air, and then continued with a theme he was expounding to a small group now half in the club, half out on the fire escape ladder.

"Virtually all these Soul singers were brought up in the Church – the Pentecostal Church," said Len, rolling a joint with one hand. He had acquired this remarkable technique due to his job as a milkman with associated Dairies. He drove his battery-powered machine along at about 5 miles per hour, often seen with one hand rolling or caressing his smack whilst keeping the other on the wheel. He always had a large gang of kids following him on the corporation estates on his rounds. These kids liked to help him and delivered the milk for him, running to and fro from doorstep to doorstep, then back to re-load from Len's truck. He gave instructions as he went down the streets: "Number fourteen," he would say to a kid, "that's Mrs Gresty, that's two pints of cream top and one bottle of orange juice." Then to another kid, "Number 12 - that's Mrs Thompson, one pint," and so on. The kids scurried about doing all his delivery work for free.

Of course on weekdays when the kids – at least, most of them – were in school, he had to get off his electric wagon and stick the bottles on the doorsteps himself. He didn't like that part. He wanted his job finished as soon as possible to get on with his real life, selling afghan Black to bus guards. He had the corner on this lucrative market. His other interests were of course scoring dope for the next Saturday All-nighter, a little shoplifting, and collecting records.

He lit up the joint he had been toying with, and after a big drag, he came back to his subject. "Aretha Franklin's dad, C.L. Franklin–" he stopped dead mid-sentence, as people do after swallowing and holding down the smoke. He looked down at his left hand; it was all yellow with nicotine stains from his habit of only smoking with one hand, as the other was usually holding the wheel. He shrugged, slowly exhaled, and then slightly gasped. Coughing lightly, he continued, choking slightly: "Yeah... the Reverend C.L...Franklin... I got an LP of his from a mate of mine who stole it from a bloke in Warrington. He had got it from a black guy who was at the US Base there, or somewhere near. It might have been in the brewery there..."

He paused for quite a while, then he came back to his subject, "...anyway, the guy was a Preacher or a Chaplin. I heard it and got it right away, considering I was charged up on some fabulous Tunisian weed at the time. Man, I got it all in a blinding flash of faith so to speak... Gospel singing from the African slaves, all that cotton picking and singing in the fields and always suffering. The cotton husks have like fucking vicious spikes on them. They're probably a bit like them wild blackberry creeper things, really vicious. So you see they were slaves, and even their work was torture. So they sang, they danced for cakes, sang their songs on Sunday and called their dance the cake-walk. The best dancers got a cake off the gaffer. Singing, dancing, it was their heritage man, from Africa."

"Then the suffering, that's what brought about the Blues. The singing was allowed in the church, but the suffering comes through, and it comes out as well in Soul music. It's got the right fucking name man, Soul music - it comes from history, it comes from suffering. It's deep; it's got deep roots man. Soul is in the heart." It was rambling but informative and Len's delivery had a certain humorous authority, so nobody interrupted.

"Anyway," Len continued, "all the Soul singers grew up with this background. Most of them were connected to Gospel church music. They sang for God and that was allowed. Originally 'allowed' in church by the white man, but then carried on by the black preachers. But the black preachers really hated it when Sam Cooke left the secular for the popular. To them he had gone over to the Devil. He was one, if not the first, to lead the trend towards popular Soul Music rising out from Gospel. Sam Cooke invented Soul Music; some say it was Ray Charles, but in fact there's a long heritage, going way back to the Forties, of Rhythm & Blues from black artists. But what I also got in that flash of understanding, listening to old Reverend C.L. on that LP, was his voice. He was like – no, he was better than any Soul singer I had heard. Maybe Otis Redding is an exception…"

He took another drag and passed on the remainder of his joint: "…anyway… the Reverend C.L. was just a Soul shouter; he was doing a performance that was all Soul. And then I saw it. That church gospel religion thing is all emotion. Just pure emotion rhythmically delivered. It was Soul. But it wasn't religion. I knew right then that they, the preachers, man, they were the false ones. They were whipping up emotion, and they claimed it was for God, but it's pure voodoo man. Does God need this emotion?"

The Manchester Wheelers

Len posed the question to his captive audience. No one responded and as Len didn't expect them to, he continued, answering himself, "Nah. So I hear it in the Gospel singers who became our Soul singers and they're more pure. They do whip up that emotion and sing deep from their souls, but they never claimed it to be religious. And that for me was more pure, man. It was right. Listen to the undercurrent of emotion in the Radiants track 'Ain't No Big Thing'. They're singing about losing a lover, and they can accept that it really 'ain't no big thing' compared to real Negro suffering, man. It's there and it comes from a wellspring of past suffering… Anyway… Those church guys frowned on popularising their church tunes… some even said Sam Cooke was cursed 'cause he moved from secular music to pop… and got his reward, when he was murdered in a brothel. Does God fix things up that way? I doubt it. The real God is all forgiveness. That's true religion."

Len could go on and on like this when he was really charged up with his staccato stop… start… and non-stop delivery, often continuing all night. If he did dance it was slow like his milk van. Much of what he said was probably factual, some of it made sense. He always had a point to make. I wanted to hear this C.L. Franklin for myself, as he was the father of three Soul singer daughters: Aretha, Irma, and Carolyne.

Len went incessantly on. We moved to the other end of the fire escape, back near the opening back inside the club where more chatter was taking place.

We joined on the periphery of another conversation:

"Dean Parrish, he's a white bloke."

"Bollocks," someone said.

"He did 'Determination'. Not the one by the Contours. They're both great, but his 'Determination' is completely different. Its brilliant," said the bloke who'd started off explaining that Dean was not a black Soul singer.

The Manchester Wheelers

"Yeah, that's correct," agreed a few people.

This group of people were discussing and arguing. I knew Dean Parrish's 'Determination' was a huge hit with us at the All-nighter. The 'B' side, 'Turn On Your Lovelight', was equally good, and so to a lesser extent was another song from him called 'Skate'.

I agreed, "Yeah, he's a white bloke – 'Tell Him' was his first record, originally by the Exiters. It was covered here by Billy Davis."

Someone else said, "There are loads of singers that sound black, but are white."

"Who?" said a group member.

"Charlie Rich," was the reply.

"What, the one that does 'Mohair Sam'?" someone said with a snigger of disbelief.

"Another one is the cover of Major Lance's 'Ain't No Soul in These Old Shoes'. He's a white bloke - even worse he's a country and western singer…" said the bloke who had started this whole thing off. "He's called Ronnie Milsap."

"Fuck me," one of the bystanders said.

"It's a pretty good version though," said someone else.

"Well, that's what happens when that smart arse DJ keeps on playing the wrong track because he hasn't got a copy of Major Lance's," said another.

"Roger took all his stuff when he left," said the first guy, and then he went on: "'Love Is After Me' by Charlie Rich is pretty good."

Another voice at the back threw in that "the white bloke's version of 'Aint No Soul' was better than Major Lance's."

Someone said, "It's not just blokes. What about white women singers?"

"Who?" said another.

"Chris Clarke... Timi Yuro... Dusty Springfield... We know she's white, 'cause we see her on the TV. None of the American Soul singers get on the TV."

"Not even on the fucking radio," someone else said.

"Yes, but if you close your eyes and listen to Dusty she easily becomes black. And Billie Davis, she's white and English. She did 'Tell Him', a cover of the exciters'," said the person next to the one who'd raised this point.

"And Tami Lynn's 'I'm Gonna Run away From You', that was done by Kiki Dee - that bird from Bradford," someone else said, "She did a good record called 'On A Magic Carpet Ride'."

"'My Boyfriend's Back', the original, is by the angels. They're white. Most DJs now play the Shirelles' version, but Roger used to play it at the Old Wheel years ago by the Angels."

Everyone in this group of Wheelers started to join in at once, and it became impossible to keep track of who said what.

"Bob Kuban – he's white," someone said.

"...Anyway, I'm stunned Dean Parish is white. Never in a million years would I have thought that."

The person who tried earlier said, "Bob Kuban - you know the one who did 'The Cheater'? He's white. Lonnie Mack too."

"Mitch Ryder," shouted someone at the back.

"Travis Wammack, 'The Scratchy Guy'."

We were all getting going on this subject.

"Cannibal and the Headhunters... twats they are. They're a white group and they're crap, just copying the original 'Land of a Thousand Dances', by Chris Kenner."

"Yeah, that's right and what about the Blendells'? It's good, but still a copy of a Stevie Wonder's 'B' side, you know?" said one of the guys who joined in from the back.

"Yep, *'La la la la la'*," sung someone else.

'The Blendells are OK. They're sort of black, 'cause they're Spanish Americans with a sun tan," said some bright spark.

"'Stay' by The Virginia Wolves, another heap of shite copying a great original by Maurice Williams & The Zodiacs - even The Hollies' version is better!"

"'Nobody But Me' by The Isley Brothers has been ripped off by some white dopes."

"And what about this DJ playing that crap version of 'Under My Thumb'? The Rolling Stones original is just brilliant. Why can't he play that? Doesn't he know that the Stones were a real influence on this place?"

"'You Can't Sit Down' by The Dovells gets played now, because he hasn't got the original by Phil Upchurch. The Dovells turned it into a vocal and it's no way as good as the original instrumental."

"What about good guys like John Schroeder, 'agent Double-O-Soul'?"

"Dusty did 'I Just Don't Know What To Do With Myself', that was Tommy Hunt's originally."

"'A Touch of Velvet - A Sting of Brass' by The Mood Mosaic."

"'Sweet Thing' by Georgie Fame gets played because the original by the Detroit Spinners went with Roger. You can only hear it at the Blue Note now!"

Quite a large group of people were now engaged in this discussion. It started close to the fire escape where it was possible to hear without shouting, but as it spread those further away had to shout really loud to be heard.

The Manchester Soul crowd at the Wheel really hated imitations, and worse so if they were white. Only originators were accepted fully. It came out from the intolerant Mod attitudes of being elitist and knowingly the best. Equality for blacks was something we were all for; most of us were up to date on politics in the USA, as it dominated our TV news. We all wanted the USA apartheid to end, as well as a pull-out from Vietnam. All the Mods at the Wheel supported the USA civil rights movement and knew about Martin Luther King. The only great achievement our Prime Minister Harold Wilson did for us was that he kept us out of that Asian war; for fuck's sake, we all could have been there. If it was left up to L.B.J. and those fucking Yank warmongers, we could be on a battlefield instead of a dance floor. Even the Aussies had been called up! These political issues made it into much of the pill-fired talking in the Wheel. Political matters were sometimes under discussion when we were blocked; we weren't just idiotic pill heads like Roger the DJ had christened us.

The discussion about white Soul singers continued and someone was shouting, "Chris Clarke – if you listen to her singing slow songs, you appreciate what the Motown sound is all about. It's not just a loud thumping beat with tambourines, it's got essential and lasting quality," said a guy in a fantastic green Mohair suit. "She's a white bird, yeah, and what does she sound like with the Motown sound around her? Yeah… a fucking black chick, man… that's fucking magic that is…"

The Manchester Wheelers

DL joined us, his knowledge repeating much of the previous conversation, and as usual he filled in all the blanks. He started by saying, "Yes, poxy imitators like The Human Beinz! Copying The Isley Bothers 'Nobody But Me', who did it in 1962. The Virginia Wolves! 'Stay'; some people think they did the original! They never heard the original; they think these jerks are the originals. They won't know that Hank Ballard did 'The Twist' before Chubby Checker. And that 'Supergirl' shit he's playing now… Oh, well, at least that Wayne Gibson's song is original…but this DJ is still a wanker."

"Yeah," someone else said, "he is a right wanker. He played 'Run Baby Run' by the Newbeats. Rubbish!!! 'He Likes Bread and Butter' - awful!!! And they're white!!! He must have found an old 45 and thinks it's a discovery; what a twat!! That 'Run Baby Run' was played at the last All-nighter, and everyone in the DJ room booed until he took it off."

"I don't know what he is called it's not Bobby Derbyshire he was brilliant but looks like he has disappeared?"

"Well what about 'Run around Sue' by Dion? It was Rock and Roll, but it's frequently played now at the All-nighter. Anyway, there aren't any Rockers left; that war's long over."

"The fuckin' Virginia Wolves – they're a pile of white shite, they copied 'Stay'!" said someone who'd joined the debate late, but everyone just shouted at him to shut up.

DL attempted to switch to songwriters, saying that Carole King was fantastic and wrote loads of Soul hits, but then the sound of 'The Ten Commandments' started coming through from the DJ room. As the Prince was making his introductory statement, the conversation switched: "Prince Buster was escorted by loads of London Mods when his coach was taking him from place to place with his band, not just as fans, but to make sure they got protected from racists!" said the Soul Mod in the Green Mohair. "I read it in the Evening Standard last time I was down there in the Kings Road, getting some new clobber."

This was typical of the Speed-assisted conversations in the Wheel. Information sharing about music was a major subject in conversations there; in the coffee bar, the toilets, near the cloakroom, on the fire escape. These were quieter locations – in the rest of the club it was so loud you had to shout into people's ears to be heard and conversations there were pointless.

"Edwin Starr was first on the Polydor label with SOS, and on the 45 it said Golden World. That was the original USA recording company." This was a lecture given by Karl, a guy who looked so emaciated he seemed to be fading away. He looked like a figure in one of those kid's pop up books, almost as though you could reach behind him and find that he was just a flat outline. His eyes shone bright with his subject. "Edwin, everyone loved Edwin at the Wheel," he said, licking all around his lips between sentences. "Edwin's been here more often than the fucking drug squad! And the best thing that happened to me was meeting him last time in the coffee bar at dinner time. He was really friendly and sat down and talked to a few of us. He said he was amazed when he first came to England and to the Wheel, to find so many 'white kids' loved his music."

Karl continued, "We asked Edwin questions and he told us he recorded 'SOS' at a little recording studio in Detroit, with some guys from Motown. When it became a hit the chiefs at Motown were pissed - he meant annoyed not drunk, and they bought the entire studio, Golden World, to get at Edwin's recordings. He said it was a great deal for him as he always wanted to be signed to Motown, but not so good for the other acts there."

Karl had a craving to join the army. People used to avoid him, as he was blocked up all week avoiding a come down break and always parroting on and on about the army. He never came down like most people. He topped up every day. We tried to advise him to give it up during the week. But he just kept on about joining the army and cursed Harold Wilson for not getting us involved in Vietnam! He wanted to go to British Honduras – what's now called Belize – where there was a war on for the British army. A few months later we heard the news. Karl wasn't selected for the army after failing the medical; his physical condition was pretty bad. Shortly after that he took an overdose of his mother's sleeping tablets, and that was lights out for Karl. He had a death wish. It was there hovering about him. I only understood this later when reflecting upon his absence. Strange how you can miss someone that previously you avoided on sight. Guilt, I suppose?

A distant noise. A siren entered my mind and faded away; my internal re-run system carried on, and for no reason whatsoever it latched onto Television adverts: 'Drinka Pinta Milka Day', which joined on to 'Go To Work On An Egg', which joined on to 'Coughs and Sneezes Spread Diseases; Trap Your Germs In A Handkerchief', and then it tuned me into Tony Hancock shouting it at a poster in his 'Blood Donor' sketch. This was the image and repetitive monologue I had in mind as I emerged from memory land.

I had surfaced from the All-nighter reminiscences. Strange how they joined up with the adverts, but I had no time to ponder, as I heard the factory siren for dinner time was sounding. It had roused me from my drifting state. Outside my stall, all the doors were banging as a host of bog skivers rushed out of the toilets. 'Fuck me,' I thought, 'I've been in here for four hours!'

* * *

The Manchester Wheelers

CHAPTER SIXTEEN

Blackpool

Along the Golden Mile at various places coaches were lined up with blackboards leaning back against their radiator grills, announcing local trips. The joke was that the 'Mystery Tour' went back to Manchester!

Doreen pestered me almost continuously about going to the All-nighter. She complained about how I virtually disappeared on Saturday nights, to re-emerge on Sunday mornings at Rowntrees where she said she sometimes had to nurse me due to the state I was often in, and listen to my ceaseless idiotic chatter.

Ivor, the co-owner of the Manchester Wheel, gave us some free tickets to go to the opening of The Twisted Wheel Blackpool, which was owned by his cousin. A coach trip was organised, and lots of Mods went over there on scooters. So it was off to Blackpool for the weekend.

Travelling to Blackpool on that coach reminded me of previous visits to the seaside town. As a child we went often on a Duple coach – rather fitting, as they were manufactured in Blackpool. In those days everyone on the coach looked out for the Tower, and then the windmill, and shouted to be the first to see them. Later as a teenager I went with my sister, and on that occasion we discovered that the Beatles, plus other 'Merseybeat' groups, were on at one of the theatres. I spent all my pocket money on the Beatles 'Twist and Shout' E.P. and my parents paid for us to go to see them live, they even came along. We sat right on the back row, and I became very embarrassed as one group after another spent half their set telling dirty jokes – The Swinging Blue Jeans, The

Big Three and The Fourmost.

At the interval we had ice cream in little paper tubs, with wooden sticks to eat with. I was hoping the Beatles wouldn't be telling jokes or swearing like the others, as that had made my dad furious. Eventually the fire curtain went up and the Beatles were standing there: John Lennon with his guitar high on his chest, Paul and George a few feet away with a tall microphone, Ringo sat at the back with his drum kit and upon the biggest drum was that fantastic Beatles logo. They took off with 'I Saw Her Standing There'. The entire theatre rocked with shouts and screams. Showers of Jelly Babies hit a laughing George as he swerved from side to side to avoid being hit in the face. They were great, and did so many songs there was no opportunity for blue jokes.

* * *

Blackpool Rock Fight

Within eighteen months I was back in Blackpool again on a Saturday coach trip, this time without my parents and heading for a Blackpool booze-up. There were quite a lot of Mods in Blackpool on this occasion, which was soon after the riots at Clacton and Margate. Probably inspired by the antics in the South we were out looking for a similar experience, but hardly any Rockers or motorbike 'greasers' were about. So eventually we gave up looking.

However, not long after splitting up from the main group we did encounter a gang of Rockers – they just lunged into us without warning, catching us completely off guard. One of our pals – Johnny Hart – went down with a broken nose after a crashing blow from a guy with 'Triumph' painted on the back of his leather jacket. Johnny was out of it, and we only saw him again later the next day on the coach back. His nose was black and blue and disjointed to the left, and his nostrils were filled with black caked blood. He had just wandered around dazed. He never went to the hospital, and consequently the bone re-set at an angle. It was a noticeable feature, and due to it he was a star for a period at subsequent All-nighters with his visible fight trophy.

The fight continued but as Johnny hit the deck we scattered and ran at a rock stall. These wooden market stalls were all along the 'Golden Mile'. It dawned on us that we were in a dead end of rock stalls. No back way out. We exchanged startled expressions, and then all at once everyone rifled the stalls, arming ourselves with the biggest bars of red Blackpool rock. Waving it about to the horror of the stallholders, we then charged as if with sabres at the Rockers. The useless rock shattered on the Rockers' heads without harm and they managed to lamp us one without any return action from us. We all took a beating and ran off in all directions, leaving the Rockers and the stall holders staring down at a huge pile of shattered pieces of rock with 'Blackpool' written throughout.

That was an old memory; this time we got off the coach and went into the seafront pub called The Manchester, and after a quick pint we all headed for another at Diamond Lil's bar at the Pleasure Beach, and then got a tram and ended up in a bar at the end of the North Pier. It was here that we teamed up with the guys who had come on scooters; they rode right up along the pier, all the wooden boards making a tuneful cackling noise as the scooters rattled over them. They rode right down to the end and parked outside the bar. The juke box was playing 'Yeh Yeh' by Georgie Fame, a firm Mod favourite as a herd of Parka clad Mods came in and joined us. They looked fabulous – they all had Eaton school style swirling ring schoolboy caps on their heads, looking as cool as cool gets.

We had free tickets for the opening of the Blackpool Wheel which was to be the next day, on Sunday afternoon. Another two coach parties were to arrive Sunday morning after the Manchester All-nighter. To avoid facing the inevitable need for gear, I had suggested going with Doreen and spending Saturday night in Blackpool. We had no plan to stay in a B&B overnight, so after the pubs shut everyone split up to seek out free lodgings. It was like the old days when we dossed down anywhere; at parties, in All-nighter clubs, under the beach harbour tunnel at St Ives. But with a girl in tow it would have to be a bit smarter, so we went over the railway walls at the back of the town. Blackpool was a popular place for rail travel and had large sheds and shunting yards stretching for miles. We soon found several parked up carriages and located a nice coach, the type with the very long seats at each side. It had everything we needed, comfortable seats and toilets just along the corridor.

Early next morning we were disturbed by the banging of a rail worker. He was going along the coaches banging the wheels. We hurriedly left, climbing back over the wall to emerge in the town, and then seeking out a café for tea and a bacon butty.

It was still early and after we had long overstayed our welcome in the café, smoking cigarette after cigarette, the owner was visibly relieved when we finally left. We wandered back down to the end of the North Pier; it was a nice day with clear blue skies, and the anti-rust red painted Tower was shining in the sunlight. Then a sound came drifting by. Doreen and I sat on one of those elaborate long Victorian cast iron benches that ran all along the sides of the Pier and listened to an organist playing Debussy's 'Clair de Lune' to himself as he practiced on the organ inside the theatre at the end of the Pier. The magic of those few minutes was exhilarating; we were lost in time, in our own world and in that enchanting music. There was no need for words, no need to talk. We just looked at each other in dreamlike love; just being in her presence was fulfilment enough. We touched and our fingers tingled and our bodies vibrated with love and desire for each other.

It didn't last – such things can't. We lit up cigarettes and made our way hand in hand to the pier's front entrance, and found again the scooter Mods from last night.

Soon there was a major gathering, with the two coach loads joining from Manchester. Scooters were revving up and gliding around and around clockwise and anti-clockwise on the pavement outside the front entrance of the North Pier. The crowd was getting bigger and bigger. Scooters played and toyed around the trams that were trying to pass through the crowds that spilled onto and over their tracks.

The Manchester Wheelers

Angelo was there, with DL on the pillion. Angelo was enjoying himself tormenting the trams into a game of chicken as they attempted to go past. As soon as a tram got near, Angelo's eyes gleamed and he confronted it like a crazed matador. DL looked pasty, and staggered off the back of the scooter the next time Angelo did a dead stop in front of a green double decker tram. The driver opened his little window and bellowed at him. Angelo just stuck up a two-fingered Churchill salute at the bloke in response, and shouted at him to fuck off.

Inevitably, it wasn't too long before the police arrived. Everyone scattered. Two LI 150's stopped and gave Doreen and me a lift. Soon we were heading in a battalion charge down the centre of the road heading for the South Shore, with the oncoming traffic swerving to avoid us. "Chickens," shouted our scooter chauffeurs at the rapidly diverting drivers.

When we reached the Pleasure Beach, a black Mariah and a police Ford Anglia shot out of a side road with their sirens going. The plan was to meet here, but with a new set of Rossers after us we all carried on going further down the road to St. Ann's. Our cavalcade raced on with the cops at the rear, going past the holiday camp on one side and the sand dunes on the other. Some scooters headed off over the pavement into the dunes, others continued into the centre of St. Ann's.

Eventually about half of the original group of around thirty machines ended up racing around on the sand flats. One scooter got stuck right at the sea shore. Everyone else parked up well away from the sea and ran to help the sinking Mods. Two guys staggered away from the group trying to release the sinking scooter from the quicksand. They struggled towards us. From their appearance they had been knee-deep in sinking sand – their best suit trousers were soaking and coated in dirty wet sand. Doreen and I were just onlookers as the spectacle unfolded at the silver glinting edge of sand and sea.

Several volunteers made numerous attempts to get the scooter out of there, but the tide was coming in fast. Eventually they gave up. We all gathered to watch as the sea covered the scooter in low but forceful encroaching waves.

"Fuck it," shouted its owner after a huge and thoughtful drag on his cigarette, "Let's go to the Wheel."

The Blackpool Wheel was not a cellar club; it was upstairs over some shops on Coronation Street. On street level was a café that served full English Breakfasts in the morning and plates of steaming Lancashire Hot Pot at dinner time.

We trooped upstairs after being in a queue for a while. The DJ had started to play Arthur Conley's 'Sweet Soul Music' for the second time as we got onto the small dance floor; he would go on to play it another half a dozen times as it was hugely popular at that period.

After we had a few dances, Doreen spotted DL slumped at a table in a corner. We went over thinking he had overdosed, but as soon as we arrived he perked up. Off he went for a furious dance to Chuck Wood's 'Seven Days Too Long' but he came back totally knackered. DL had recently signed up for a course of dancing lessons, including tap and ballroom. He told us his latest dance was modelled on the Nicholas brothers; two black tap dancers that had danced with Gene Kelly. He told us he saw them on TV recently in an old film called 'The Pirate'. Then he started rabbiting on and on about gibberish and nonsense. Doreen said he reminded her of me the way I was on many Sunday mornings. Her statement made me think seriously about my own condition and what I must be like after the effects of several uninterrupted strings of All-nighters. It made me think about it. Was it possible to go on week after week, year on year, like this?

Apart from being on the beautiful side of pretty, Doreen was also a bubbly kind of girl. To her, everything was fab or fabulous, or brilliant. This was no put-on act; it seemed like every new thing she encountered would light up her enthusiasm. Of course, this was a very attractive element in her personality; she was instantly likeable because she instantly liked everyone she met. Blokes locked onto this right away, and consequently I had lots of rivals.

The Manchester Wheelers

She encouraged it, too; she would flirt, but told me frequently and often that she was my girl. I began to think seriously that leaving her on successive Saturday nights could be a risky strategy. So the next time she pushed to go to the All-nighters, which she did even though she was critical of the state we all ended up in afterwards, I knew I would give in. Soon we'd be making plans to go together. I thought at least I might be able to keep an eye on her. Inevitably it meant she would be taking the gear – and in fact, as it turned out she took to it quite well – but this all started at a time that coincided with my own second thoughts about it.

I found myself pondering things. The DJ was playing 'Since I Found You' by Maxine Brown. At Christmas I had bought Doreen an eternity ring – but would it last forever?

* * *

One cycling footnote to the year was the Death of 'Mr Tom'. In our cycling days we went in the same café in Hebden Bridge. I read the full report in my cycling magazine. It was drugs related news:

Tom Simpson took amphetamines whilst racing in the Tour de France. He died on the 13th of July 1967 on a climbing stage on Mount Ventoux. It was a very hot day, and he was riding in the National British Team - Harry Hall from Manchester was his team coach. Tom was helicoptered to hospital, but never came out of a coma. The last words he spoke, before being airlifted were: "Put me back on my bike…"

More bad news came along in December:

Otis died in a plane crash on the Tenth of December 1967. It seemed to me that Stax died that day too. Soon that great blue label with the overflowing singles would change to a finger popping hand.

* * *

The Manchester Wheelers

CHAPTER SEVENTEEN

Tales from the Wheelers

Sitting talking over many years, during Sunday morning 'come downs' at various locations; cafés, station waiting rooms, clubs and a few Wheel and Mod related events. Also: an encounter with **Mandy**.

'I dope because everyone else dopes.'
- Jacques Anquetil, five times winner of the Tour de France

The Twisted Wheel was not just about All-nighters on a Saturday. It opened most nights of the week including Sunday evenings, and many of the top All-nighter acts did a show at the early session on Saturday nights.

A Mod with high back-combed hair said to his mate, "Do you remember seeing The Small Faces? They were pretty good... and small. It looked like the audience below the stage were as tall as them on the stage! We all put one finger in our ears when Stevie Marriot did, and all shouted and sang along with him '*What yer gonna do about it.... What yer gonna do...*' it was one of the best nights at the Wheel, that Autumn of 1965".

* * *

We sat down next to the tall, lanky black singer who had just finished, and asked him, "Who was it you said did that song you did last?"

"Charles Brown, man. 'Drifting Blues'."

"Don't you mean James Brown?"

"No Charles. He's my main man," replied Herbie Goins.

He was the singer with Alexis Korner. They had just finished and Herbie was drinking a Coke next to us, sitting on the edge of the stage. There was only about fifty or sixty people in the place. It was Tuesday night and Alexis's Group played at the Brazennose St. Wheel three nights at least, every week.

Herbie went on about how great Charles Brown was, "Yes, James is fantastic, but Charles's style of the more Bluesy stuff is my real bag," he said, whilst I was feeling like a complete pillock for not knowing who Charles Brown was.

* * *

Mohair Soul Mods:

"Do you know where Mohair comes from?" asked the guy in the tailor's shop. We had asked for Mohair in Frank's Tailors on Conran Street in Moston.

"No, no idea," we said. Frank climbed up on a chair and pulled down some shiny rolls of cloth. Winded slightly and out of breath as he climbed down, he said, "South America – from the Andes, from Llamas in the high mountains in Ecuador and Peru. This lot comes from there but is made up here. Woven in Bradford at Salt's Mill. It's alpaca, better than Mohair."

We looked at each other, and then touched the material; it was smooth, silky, shining. This was the business. We could be real 'Mohair Sam's in this stuff.

"Centre Vents? You must be mad – no way. I'll do you side vents, though," Frank instructed. It was all arguments with him.

"Not sold much of this material since the Italian styles of the late Fifties. So, how come you boys come in here and ask for

Mohair?"

We didn't answer him and gave him more instructions instead: button hole instructions and seventeen inch vent commands.

"Button holes in both lapels. Hey, I'm beginning to like you boys. It'll cost seventeen pounds, but with the waistcoat too. Is that OK?"

"Yes. Can we do it on the drip? Three and six a week for the next hundred years!"

Walking along Conran Street outside the Tailors, we were singing 'Shoppin' For Clothes' by the Coasters.

* * *

I Do Love You – I do, do, do:

"I got groped by Billy Stewart... the fat bastard," said Carolyne.

"Did he have a stutter, did he ask you for a ssshhhh... aaa... aaaaaaa... aaaaa... ggggggggggg... aaGGG?" Angelo's question was put with a near perfect copy in tune with Billy's intro for 'Summertime'.

"Look, fuck off Angelo, you smart bastard," Carolyne said as she got her ciggies out of her handbag. After lighting up, she told us the story.

The Billy Stewart All-nighter was packed like a tin of sardines. Everyone wanted to see this Soul master live.

But Carolyne's story put things in another light.

"We got right to the front. I just love his song: 'Sitting in the Park', even the version by Georgie Fame. It's a great song, and

The Manchester Wheelers

so's that stuttering 'Summertime'," she said, glancing knowingly at Angelo. "But the best, the very best is that fantastic 'I Do Love You' – it's so romantic. So I wanted to be at the front. Christine was with me. All the time he kept looking at us, he sang 'I Do Love You' directly to us on his knees and held both our hands. When he finished he asked us to come around the back to his dressing room. We sat there talking to him, and then he stuck his hand straight up my skirt. Then he grabbed Christine's tits as we tried to go. He said we should come back to his hotel, the Piccadilly Plaza. He said he would give us lots of money."

"So why didn't you go?" asked Angelo, pushing his luck.

"She wants to do that with Dave," said Christine.

"Shut it," said Carolyne, annoyed.

"No point," said Angelo. "He's so blocked he wont get a hard on till next Thursday."

Angelo was frequently heard singing '*Summertime, and the Shagging ain't easy...*' He even stopped singing 'Oh Carolina' when ever he met Carolyne, replacing it with his new annoyance technique... He never did like her.

* * *

The girls like the Drifters:

"Yes, I like the girl groups like The Shirelles – especially their song 'Soldier Boy' and The Chiffons' 'Sweet Talking Guy' – but my most favourite of all are The Dixie Cups. Their song 'What Kind Of Fool' is just great. I've heard it a thousand times and I'm never tired of it."

"What about the Drifters, I thought you girls liked them the most?" asked Angelo.

"Yeah, we all do," answered a group of girls he was talking to

The Manchester Wheelers

in the café on Victoria station, the morning after the All-nighter. I think he was surprised by the knowledge that the leader of this group of girls had, when she said: "Did you know the Drifters go back to the very early fifties? Their original lead singer was Clyde McPhatter. Later, Johnny Moore did the lead, but they had an argument with their manager and he just went out and got a completely new group. That's what started out several Drifters groups doing live tours in the USA, and two going round England."

She continued: "On my LP it's got the names as Ben E. King, Charlie Thomas, Dock Green, Elsbeary Hobbs and Reggie Kimber. And not one of those guys here the other week looked anything like their photograph on my LP cover. Ben E. King wasn't one of them, he went solo years ago." She paused, reached into her handbag and put more Wrigley's Gum into her mouth. After chewing for a bit, she said: "When Ben E. King left, the lead singer was Rudy Lewis and he died soon after. That's when Johnny Moore became the lead singer."

"How do you know all this stuff?" asked Angelo, sort of amazed. Usually it was blokes that could spout such details, which were often designed to impress other Soul obsessives.

"Oh, your friend Roland gave me and Pat two tickets. He had loads of tickets, he'd printed them. They were forgeries, but we got in no problem. After the Drifters had finished, we went into the room at the back to talk to them. We got in because their manager was a nice lady called Fay. We spoke to the oldest guy, Johnny."

"We told them all their records are just fantastic, and it was him who told us the recent Drifters story. He said he'd been in the group twice and he was really annoyed that there were loads of Drifters fakes. He said guys are just going around pretending to be the real ones, like Bill Pinkney's Original Drifters, who've only got one of the early Fifties members. He told us he was the only real one left – the only lead singer that is. He thought it was only happening over in the States, but he said he was pissed about the number of them operating in England. It was funny – I didn't think he was pissed, he didn't look drunk... did he Pat?" She was looking at Pat, who looked over with glazed eyes and didn't respond. Then she laughed and explained: "We thought he meant he was drunk, but in America pissed means angry. He told us he was pals with the Dells, and they had even more imitators in the USA than the Drifters!"

More chewing intervened, and she made a final statement: "Well, he was a very nice man, Johnny Moore was."

"Especially so, as you got in free as well!" said Angelo. "Maybe they were the other ones with this guy, just pretending to be one of the blokes on the records." He told her about DL asking one of the Drifters tribes to sing a request, and they turned out to be the Invitations!

* * *

No room to dance:

Dancing in the Wheel – both Wheels, Brazennose Street and Whitworth Street – was only expressive during the week or at quieter All-nighters, even after the place was expanded. Mostly at the All-nighters it was packed tight. Dancing on the spot or in a small space was all you could do; circles with turns in the middle allowed the 'insider' to move.

* * *

Gene Chandler's sister?

"Have you heard of Lorraine Chandler?" asked Johnny from Blackpool. "She's, er, I think she's Gene Chandler's sister. I have an import I got from an auction list. I got it just because I guessed the name could be Gene Chandler's sister…"

"Could have been his mum," someone said.

"It's pretty good. I'll see if the DJ will play it. It's called 'What Can I Do'. It's on RCA Victor."

***

In the beginning:

"Do you know how the All-nighter started?"

It was a rhetorical question, and the question poser continued without a pause, "Maybe London was first, but the Wheel was one of the first, along with other Manchester clubs like The Cavern, Heaven and Hell, The Back Door Club and others.

"It was because the drinking laws were very strict in Manchester. Yes, there were late night 'cabaret' type places, where you could get a drink after 11 pm on a Saturday night as long as you had a meal too. But clubs like the Wheel weren't licensed – they were just coffee bars with dancing. They could have extended opening times, completely unrestricted. So these club owners thought, 'where do people go once they've got tanked up and been thrown out of the pubs on a Saturday night?' The answer was obvious: simply open the coffee bar with music till the early morning. That's how it started."

***

Unsatisfied 'B' side:

'A Time To Love - A Time To Cry' by Lou Johnson was turned over by the Wheel DJ and the 'B' side 'Unsatisfied' became massive. Hundreds of people in Manchester bought it, but the record company must have thought it was the 'A' side that was selling. Lou soon appeared on Ready Steady Go and sung both sides.

***

Who is on tonight?

"Tonight we should dance all the time and not talk all night... like last fucking week. We spent all night on the fire escape, rabbiting on about everything under the sun and missed Ben E. King. I heard later that his backing band the Senate from Glasgow were pretty good too. Who the fuck's on tonight?"

Reply: "I never know. I just come here every fucking week and miss everyone."

* * *

Thick as a Coppers helmet:

"The police are thick," said a Mod girl to her mate. They were standing in line waiting to get two hot chocolate drinks in the Kardomah in St Ann's Square. Without waiting, nor expecting a reply, the Mod girl said, "I got my handbag searched on Piccadilly Station by a police woman and two plain clothes detectives from the drug squad. They insisted on getting my name and address, so I told them my name was 'Ann Coates'. Do you get it?

Living at 23 Spring Gardens Manchester. Silly buggers. 23 Spring Gardens is the main Post Office." Her mate laughed and asked if they wrote it down. "Yeah, they got the police woman to put it in her notebook. They said they'd be calling round to speak to my parents about the danger to young girls with drugs and going to all-night clubs."

* * *

Gunshots:

A gun fires with a ricochet – it's Roy C's 'Shotgun Wedding'. Someone shouts, "aagghh, that reminds me – I've gotta ask the DJ to Play 'Mr Bang Bang Man' by Little Hank."

Someone else says, "What about Lee Dorsey's 'Ride Your

The Manchester Wheelers

Pony'? That's got guns in it too!" This starts off a sort of quiz conversation, with everyone remembering songs with guns or gunfire in them: 'Shotgun and the Duck' by Jackie Lee, 'Shotgun' by Junior Walker, 'Western Movies' by The Olympics, 'Shoot Your Shot' by Junior Walker, 'Al Capone' from Buster's all Stars.

* * *

Screamin' Jay:

Roger the Wheel DJ played piles of original Blues and R&B records. A couple that were often on his playlist were 'I Put a Spell On You' and 'I Hear Voices' by Screamin' Jay Hawkins.

Fred, one of our mates at that time in early '65', said he talked to Screaming Jay upstairs in the coffee bar. He had removed the bone in his nose, and no longer had 'Henry' – his 'Skull on a stick'. He had given it to John Mayall, who had come along to watch. Fred said he had left his kids in Cleveland USA and was living in Hawaii where he had more kids! And he said that Nina Simone's version of his 'I Put a Spell On You' was really a great version. He said he'd met her in Paris and liked her; he said he was going to live there someday. Fred asked what he thought about Manchester and England; Screamin' Jay said it was full of gangsters that were after him?

> 'How many drips in a tap, how many croaks in a frog... How many barks in a dog...'
> - Screamin' Jay Hawkins.

* * *

Boney Moronie:

Larry Williams was another hero of the Wheel DJ. A huge poster of the New Orleans R&B man hung on the wall in the Wheel over the stairs leading down to the dancing cellar in Brazennose Street. Larry appeared live at the club in spring of 65. His great track 'Boney Moronie' was a big favourite at the club:

'I've gotta girl named Boney Moronie, She's as skinny as a stick of macaroni...'

Larry followed it up with 'Short Fat Fanny'!

* * *

Searchin' gotta find her:

"Did you see the police last night going around again with photos of a missing girl?"

"Yeah," replied another girl. "They weren't out to bust anyone. They had a photo and showed it around asking 'Have you seen this girl?' It was a police woman and the others were the girl's mum and dad. They were all in there looking for their daughter."

* * *

Closing the Wheel:

"Tell me it's just a rumour! The Wheel can't be closing down?"

Tony was asking this of Bob, and Bob replied: "It's true – next Saturday its closing. Spencer Davis and John Mayall are on for the last All-nighter… but it's going to open up again somewhere near Piccadilly Station."

"Fuck me," said Tony.

"No thanks," replied Bob.

* * *

Stolen from Ivor's:

Saturday afternoon, many Mods would be at the Kardomah

café in St Ann's Square having cappuccinos and chocolate cake. Others were on the town shoplifting records and clothes. 'Stolen from Ivor's' was written on the bags given out with purchases from one of Manchester's top men's clothes boutiques, the joke going round though was that much of it was!

* * *

On My Radio:

Most of the blokes that went to the Wheel would listen to the Pirate radio shows and to Radio Luxembourg DJs; ones like Mike Raven, who played Soul, R&B and Blues. He would introduce new songs and artists for us to follow up on. It became a kind of method of enhancing your esteem with other Soul Mods to know about obscurities and new artists. It tended to be a male only pursuit. Mike Raven introduced his show with a theme tune, a re-recording of King Curtis and the Kingpins' 'Soul Serenade' by The Mike Cotton Sound. The Wheel DJ made 'A Touch of Velvet- A Sting of Brass' by The Mood Mosaic a very popular Mod track, and another Manchester DJ Dave Lee Travis took it as his theme tune.

* * *

Lunch hour Wheel:

The Wheel opened its street level café at lunchtimes and served cheese on toast known as Welsh Rarebit. On one occasion we were in there and The Radiants' 'Voice Your Choice' was playing. Then after finishing that track, it changed to 'Girl Don't Let Me Wait Too Long' by The Time Box, or the shitty Time Box as Angelo called them. The original was by Bunny Sigler and had been in the USA R&B charts. We often checked out the billboard listings in the New Musical express, to keep up with Soul releases and then import them from advertisers, or wait for postal deletion auctions. This song was one we had obtained as an import, and here we were sitting in the Wheel with imitation Soul rattling out!

It pissed us both off, that so-called Mod groups just snatched Soul tracks from the USA before they got any recognition here. "Fuck it," said Angelo. "Fuck it, playing that version here at the Wheel and they also did a crap ruinous version of Cal Tjader's Soul Sauce." I told him it was the girl serving in the cafe that was putting on the records. He resisted the urge to thump her when our toast arrived.

He went on to say that so many Soul records had been copied by UK groups, and that the Stones and the Beatles had at least made a fair job of it. We discussed this theme further, remembering that the Hollies did 'Just One Look' by Doris Troy, 'Searchin'' from the Coasters and 'Can't Let Go' by Evie Sands. The Moody Blues did Bessie Banks' 'Go Now' and there were hundreds more.

* * *

Some D.J.'s:

There were two Rogers at the Brazennose Street Twisted Wheel; Roger Eagle and his friend Roger Fairhurst. Between them they had a record collection of amazing breadth and R&B depth. When Roger left the Wheel the records went with him, because the best were all his own collection and he also had access to his pals who had stopped DeeJaying. The Wheel's owners, the Adabi Brothers, did start buying in house records to compensate for the vacuum left by Roger, who took himself and his records to the Blue Note, giving that club instant Soul cachet. Ralph's Records - a record shop near Victoria station - was called in to assist, but failed as ninety percent of popular Wheel tracks were long since deleted. The remedy was to bring in a family friend, who rounded up loans of appropriate singles from friends to get a passable playlist. They were eventually saved by appointing Paul Davis as main DJ. Paul was a Soul fan who already possessed a huge Soul collection. In the period between '67 and '70, there were lots of DJs bringing their own record collections, notably: Bobby Derbyshire, Phil Sax, Brian Rae and Brian Phillips. DJs didn't become part of the 'scene' and never took pills. During '69 and around '1970, the Wheel's own record collection disappeared.

The Blue Note was the only place to hear tracks that Roger had introduced. Multiples of these eventually became huge underground sought after tracks, while quite a few like Eddie Floyd's 'Knock on Wood', first played by Roger, went on to be major hits. Roger left The Blue Note, and also left behind hundreds of Soul fans owing him a huge debt for turning them on to fantastic music for the first time; and in '67, Soul emerged from the underground scene to make an impact on the pop charts. Artists like Otis Redding, Sam & Dave and many more were all played first and enthused about before the rest of the pop brigade picked up on them.

Roger was the first to play loads of original Blues artists and then moved on to Soul, introducing Alvin Cash, Jerry Butler, Major Lance, The Drifters, The Impressions, Booker T. & the MGs, and literally hundreds more. He was also the first to play Wilson Pickett's 'In the Midnight Hour' which was probably the major identifiable Soul track that kicked off the Wheel's move from Blues domination to Soul in early 1965. Previously it had been a mix of Blues, R&B, Pop and Soul music covers by UK artists, alongside the original releases like The Drifters, Sam Cooke... The list was almost endless.

In Manchester clubs Roger eagle worked at the Wheel, then the Blue Note, then the Jigsaw, then Stax Club - he managed or owned it. Then back at The Jigsaw when it later became a 'hippy place' called the Magic Village or something like that.

* * *

Sunday places:

The All-nighter was the focal point of the week, but the Soul Mods that lived in the city could attend the Wheel four or five nights a week. There were lots of other clubs that had All-nighters but only the Wheel lasted. It was the best by far.

The scene connected with the Wheel was much more than one night, though. It was the night and the following day. In the morning you had a choice to go home, as many of the 'out-of-towners' did. For the rest, we would be topping up our pills and heading for Sunday lunchtime sessions at the Boneyard in Bolton and the Catacombs, but more often staying in Manchester town centre to go to Rowntrees. The Stax club, owned by Roger Eagle, opened at 11 am. Even the Plaza and the Mecca dance hall on the other end of Whitworth Street opened their doors to dancers on Sunday and at lunch times during the week. These places ended around four or five, then it was another wait till the evening clubs started around 7 pm: the Blue Note, Jigsaw, Sounds and others. This meant a further top up. All of which added up to more and more pills to keep going. It also meant around a two day fade out at work before recovering around Tuesday evening, and then off to mid-week sessions. The Wheel and other clubs were open most week days.

It began to take its toll on quite a few people. Often at Rowntrees you would see people coming down, or suffering from the 'come down', and now and again there were uncontrollable overdose cases. Apathy ruled; the music played, but groups of Mods just sat around talking, many staring blankly in silence, a few dancing. People in states of depression, some girl crying whilst others were so far up they spoke complete gibberish, or just danced to oblivion. Often people would see things and become scared and paranoid, others relentlessly chain-smoked. Then a record, like 'Helpless' or 'Stop Her On Sight', or 'I'm Gonna Run Away From You', would come on and everyone got up. They just couldn't help themselves and had to dance. Some were even dragged out of their state to move again, which always seemed to help their condition.

* * *

In October 1966, we were in the Paper

"We made it into the evening News on Monday," said a Mod with a 'deck chair' style striped jacket. He returned to the table next to ours with two coffees. We were once again in Victoria Station's buffet cafeteria.

The 'deck chair' Mod related the story, pulling out the newspaper cutting from his pocket and quoting from it: "Says 'ere, the headline: 'Sunday Scandal on a Station of Teenage Shame', then it says that we are 'ill-dressed and slovenly' – the cheeky fuckers!"

"It says we are 'affected by drugs and drink, and are like lost children monopolising the buffet and the wash and brush up rooms'. It says we are 'from all-night clubs'. The next bit reads '...bona fide rail passengers have no chance of getting a coffee or tea, because 300 good-time teenagers are queuing'. It gets better – listen to this: 'they have fixed staring eyes, and the girls hide their signs of drugs and lack of sleep with heavy make-up.'"

"Stupid fuckers," said a girl listening on the next table. "Thick eye make up is fashion."

"Listen to this bit," said Deck Chair, "... some are well dressed and obviously come from good homes'. That must be us then..." He continued reading it out loud: "'a waitress in the buffet said they should be charged for all the sugar lumps they put in their coffee! And they are putting powder drugs in their coffees too'. Says - the only way to stop them is to close the clubs."

"I don't like that last bit," said Deck Chair's mate, a scooter Mod in a Parka with a large Union Jack sewn on the back.

* * *

No Originals:

November 1966 and the Coasters were on at the Wheel All-nighter – except they were impostors. We looked, we listened, but we couldn't find 'Speedoo' or 'Mr Earl' anywhere. Their 'Charlie Brown', and 'Yakkety Yak' sounded very pedestrian, and when we shouted for 'Little Egypt' and 'Shopping for Clothes' they ignored us.

* * *

Keep On Pushin' in:

On one occasion in the queue outside the Wheel, I was standing behind two guys from Cheadle when a bloke pushed in the queue further up.

"Cheeky cunt," I said, under my breath. The two guys in front turned around and one was laughing with an obviously blocked up type of laugh that was tinged with another factor, a bit wild like Cesar Romero's Joker in the TV series 'Batman'.

He had long sideburns, turn-ups on his suit trousers, and very wide braces holding them up. He was standing in that cool way with his hands shoved in his pockets, his suit jacket pushed around his back, exposing his blue button down shirt with a red military stripe tie dangling down. He looked up from glancing at his feet, which were enclosed in brown brogue shoes.

"Yeah he's a cunt, and he'll get it… no doubt," he said with a menacing look.

"Get what?" I asked.

"Oh, he'll get fucked now for pushing in. Oh yes."

"Who by? Are you going to roll him? Is Ivan on the door going to send him to the back?"

"No, no, no," said the Mod bloke, "it's all part of the English thing we all do," he said, and without pausing he went on:

"No one will say anything to him, right?" I nodded. "We all do it, this type of thing. It's our English way. Now most people think it's being polite or having no nerve to bash the fucker, but it's none of these. We know something secret about these types of events, we the English. Lots don't get it, that's why they act like twats – like he does. And those of us that don't, we subliminally know how it's going to come out in the wash."

"We do?" I muttered.

"Yes, of course we do," he said and carried on his explanation, "we know he'll get his. Maybe not today, but he will eventually, and we know it. It's the fact that you, me and loads of others cursed the bastard under our breaths silently, right? You don't think that has no effect, do you?" The Joker's laugh kicked in again.

I gave a blank look in response.

"No way, he's certainly going to get it. Today, tomorrow, sometime, he'll trip up, bang his head, lose something, or miss his bus, whatever. The punishment fits the crime, but the only unfortunate thing is we probably won't be there to see it. If we could all see the results of this stuff we would all *have* to behave. The rest of the world don't get it. Most of us English subconsciously know it, and that's why we behave in the right manner, that polite manner we all do. It's nowt to do with breeding or manners. It's retribution, it's fucking invisible retribution, man."

"Well, you might have a point," I said, bemused. And I thought about it until I got into the Wheel. Maybe he was right?

However, his mate who had stood by listening just gave me a wink.

* * *

Len on Rock & Roll:

Len was in the Mogambo coffee bar. It was full, all the tables taken; it was another Sunday morning after the All-nighter, and we had just seen Ben E. King. I bought him another frothy cappuccino and sat there sliding sugar into mine carefully, so as not to destroy the topping. Ben had sung 'Amor, Amor', a song in Spanish, and we were talking about 'Spanish Harlem'. Len said it was a sector in New York near the Harlem district. What he'd been talking about to another friend of his sitting at the next table was Rock & Roll.

Len continued, and I listened:

"I got to talk to a lot of black GIs at Burtonwood and they told me that in the USA they had their own radio stations. The guy who told me most about it was called Lincoln and he was from Baltimore. The whites didn't listen to black radio, but the white artists like Elvis stole quite a few of the songs. Lincoln said Rock & Roll was stolen from black artists and was really Rhythm & Blues; 'Rock & Roll' was actually their slang for fucking! But the whites didn't know it. Lincoln said that for a long period after the Second World War up to the Sixties, black radio in Baltimore featured great black artists that had their tunes copied by the whites calling it Rock & Roll. He said no one seemed to know about it here in England, even us that like Soul and Blues. According to him, we have no idea about how big a rip-off took place."

"He said many of these records were still available, but mostly on 78's, like Ruth Brown, Ray Charles, Joe Turner, Big Maybelle, Little Willie John, Lavern Baker, The Cadillac's, Chuck Willis, The Dominos and Charles Brown. He said a few made it big with the whites like Ray Charles, Frankie Lymon and The Teenagers. He said Chuck Berry and Bo Diddley constantly complained about being ripped off by acceptable white artists, even Buddy Holly blatantly copying Bo's stuff."

Len's pal on the next table said, "The trouble is that all those old records are sort of tarnished by us as belonging to the Rockers, when really we should be digging out these originals."

* * *

Gangster tales:

In 1966 gangster styles, along with the hats, took off at the Wheel. Braces and sideburns caught on too. Len told us that Chicago in the Twenties was Al Capone's city and that he liked music. Opera was his favourite, but he liked black music too. He had Fats Waller kidnapped on one occasion to play privately for him, and afterwards arranged his delivery back to New York City with his pockets stuffed with thousands of dollars!

The local gangster in Manchester was a Roman Catholic who went to St Clare's church in Blackley and he had something to do with 'Mr Smiths' a late night club. His name was Dougie Flood and on one occasion he threw several of us out of the club because he caught us drinking our own booze – er well actually it was the Blue Note's. We hid bottles of spirits in our girl friends handbags so we didn't have to pay his excessive bar charges.

* * *

The Entertainer intro:

Overheard conversation in the bogs:

"You know that record by Tony Clarke 'The entertainer'? It's been on my mind for years, the introduction bit. It's driven me mad trying to think what it was, what it's from."

"Well, what's it from then?" said the other guy, as they waited for a space at the stones to piss in.

"It's from the opera by George Gershwin: Porgy and Bess - the song called 'I Got Plenty Of Nothing'."

"Wow," said the second guy, humming it. "Your bloody right it is!"

* * *

No Hendrix:

In January '67, a rumour went around that Jimi Hendrix was at the Wheel, the same night when The Spellbinders were on at the club. I wasn't there that night and never heard about it at the time. If he was, with the hair style that he had, lots of people would have known about it, so it's just an urban myth. Unlike the story about the Rolling Stones at the Brazennose Street Wheel – that's true, and it's also true that Roger the DJ began playing the original R&B and Blues tracks that they had popularised!

A week after the Hendrix rumour, one of the best remembered acts was there gyrating on the small stage in the Wheel; it was Alvin Cash and his brothers, playing as The Crawlers.

* * *

Queue's:

Queues: you often had to queue three times at the Wheel All-nighter; first to get in, then to put your coat in the cloakroom, then in the morning to get it out again. If you were a girl, there was an extra queue to get into the toilets.

* * *

Booker T's Face:

Booker T. Washington was the original civil rights crusader, and Booker T. Jones was named after him. Martin Luther King's speeches were inspirational, and he was the current figurehead of the civil rights movement in the USA. Many of our Soul singer heroes supported Dr King and so too did almost every Soul fan you met in Manchester. On one occasion I took Booker T.'s Soul Dressing LP with me to work so I could loan it to a pal, but I was totally unprepared for the reaction it received from my workmates. As I walked through the factory with the LP tucked under my sleeve, but still showing Booker T's black face and wide eyes, people shouted abuse at me. When I got to my work bench I proudly displayed the LP prominently on top of my tool box, but it was soon snatched and waved about with shouts of 'What a hideous picture' and that I was a 'Nigger lover'.

I was shocked. Until that time I thought everyone in England would be supportive of the black man's plight in the USA, and indeed in South Africa. How wrong I was. I had to put the Soul Dressing LP into a brown paper bag to cover it up and stop anymore ridicule from passing workers!

I soon found myself singing whilst filing away at the metal on my bench's vice, working off my anger with the words of Sam Cooke: *'It's been a long time coming but I know a change is gonna com., Oh, Yes it will...'*

More, More, More of your pills:

If you went regularly to the Wheel, you were soon into rapid acceleration and quantitive increases of pill swallowing. It was accepted as 'normal' that break-ins at chemist's were ok, in fact necessary. Shoplifting was required due to the need to be smart and 'in'; most people didn't have the cash for everything, so low level crime became acceptable to people who under different circumstances would never have opted for such actions.

Everything was openly discussed within 'our' fraternity of Wheel goers – this was mostly everyone that attended the All-nighters – but never with outsiders. The secrets were kept because virtually everyone was taking Amphetamines, and those that didn't weren't regarded as 'in'.

On one occasion we drove into the car park behind the Whitworth Street Wheel – four of us in two Mini Coopers. We parked and got out, only to be surrounded by the police. They searched us, finding nothing, because by this time we never carried any gear. We asked what it was all for, and they told us that the club over there was a notorious drug taking location.

We gave them puzzled looks and said we were just parking and off to a town centre pub. They then apologised for bothering us, and said that the kids that go in there are usually on the bus or scooters anyway, not cars!

The Manchester Wheelers

* * *

She wouldn't, couldn't tell... could she?

The All-nighter wasn't the only event in the week. We went to the Wheel, to the Blue Note, the Jigsaw and other places; this added up to a lot of music and dancing. Quite often people we met at the All-nighter would invite us and loads of others to parties, often on a Friday night to start off the weekend bender. On one such occasion, we were invited to Stafford for one of these parties, and gathered at London Road station. No one got a train ticket; it was a game to show off your 'bottle'. A platform ticket was all we paid for. However, a very diligent guard caught us all as the train approached Stafford Station and got us to produce some identity: library tickets, driving licences, etc. Before he let us off, he wrote down our real addresses and took so long that the train was delayed. "Fuck it," said Angelo, "at least we delayed the train." It was a 'fuck them up' consolation for us.

We brought along our girlfriends – Doreen and her sister, and their pal Mandy, or 'Randy Mandy' as we called her. We had known her for years as she lived in Moston near to Dave's house. The girls had all bought real tickets.

We met up in the Royal Oak pub, meeting our contact who'd been putting it about at the previous All-nighter about the party: 'Andy 'T' from Stafford' was his official title. We got a bit high on some shit that Len the milkman had – in fact, he always had the latest and greatest stuff. He'd slowly drawl that it was "Great hash, afghan black," and then pause, followed by the obligatory end of sentence "man," obviously indicating another somewhat comical meaning.

A crowd gathered in the pub, then it was off to the party, which was in an old Tudor style farmhouse. The parents were away and the two sisters who lived there were giving the party. After a few hours the place was becoming trashed, and then the home owners returned.

The Manchester Wheelers

We understood this was because of the neighbours hearing the racket and phoning the police. We were all evicted and returned to Manchester very late, splitting up onto our respective all-night buses.

Mandy got on mine, as it passed near her house. She started playing around; we were on the back seat. Inevitably it ended up with me getting off at her stop and going into her house. Her parents were asleep upstairs. It was just one of those wild things that happened. I regretted it afterwards, and Mandy said she did too. Doreen was, after all, a friend of us both. She wouldn't mention it would she? No. No, certainly not.

* * *

The Manchester Wheelers

The Manchester Wheelers

CHAPTER EIGHTEEN

English Bands at the Club

When Doreen began to go to the All-nighters, it was unfortunate that most acts were from England and not America. However, the news came that soon Junior Walker would be appearing. It was to be a very special occasion.

It was Doreen's first All-nighter and it was the end of August after our return from holiday in Torquay. By this time her Mary Quant hairstyle had changed to a very short Mod crop, it was shorter than my hair and it accentuated her beautiful facial features. We were on the lookout for Angelo or Lord Snooty to give us some gear, but when we couldn't find them we decided to head for the Dive Bar to see if Louie was around, as the pub was his hangout. Louie always had stuff to sell, but on this night we couldn't find him either. So we scurried off to Chorlton Street bus station where we met a group from Oldham, but they had nothing spare. We were getting a little desperate when we bumped into Sid and Terry outside the Rembrandt Pub. They weren't associated with it, as it was becoming as notorious as the Union on Canal Street for harbouring 'pooftas'. They had emerged from under the canal bridge next to the pub. In a wall cavity below was their hidden stash.

I bought thirty. Then Sid gave Doreen six Blueys for free! It wasn't in his nature to give things away for nothing and it made me wonder as we walked through the back streets.

The Allan Bown Set was the group appearing at the All-nighter. They were quite good and next morning we were singing their single 'Emergency 999' repeatedly as we visited the usual early morning haunts, before pressing on to the usual Sunday afternoon and evening meeting places.

The next month we went to almost every All-nighter: Chris Farlowe and The Thunderbirds, Georgie Fame and Graham Bond were the ones that stood out. The English groups who appeared at the club were all doing R&B, Blues and Soul copies of the USA originals; it was painful to here bad versions of songs we idolized like a UK version of Jamo Thomas's 'I Spy For The F.B.I. The ones that had been appearing the most over the years were John Mayall and The Spencer Davis Group of course they were top quality and well loved by the Manchester Wheelers.

Someone who knew John Mayall when he lived in Macclesfield had told me that he used to live in a tree house in his parents' garden. John was a huge fan of Elmore James – he'd written a great song about the loss of 'Mr James', after hearing that Elmore was dead, and he put it on the 'B' side of his single '(Life Is Just a Slow Train) Crawling Up a Hill'. 'I'm Your Witch Doctor' was another great song from John, and sure enough he put all three in his repertoire.

Spencer Davis included two brothers in the group, Stevie and 'Muff' Windwood from Birmingham. Stevie had an amazing voice and the group did covers of lots of American artists who we adored. However, we could easily forgive this misdemeanour due to Stevie's superb voice; it sounded so much like a black artist. The group's big hits were 'Keep On Running' and 'Gimme Some Loving'. Both were dance anthems at the Wheel and stood up alongside all the original Soul tracks that were played at the club.

This month however, neither Spencer Davis nor John Mayall were appearing. To kick off September's All-nighters it was Chris Farlowe, whose hit single 'Out Of Time' was written for him by the Stones – Keith Richards and Mick Jagger, credited as 'Nanker and Phelge'. Chris Farlowe did a really great show and also included an amazing sounding 'Stormy Monday Blues'. This got a really enthusiastic response from the crowd at the Wheel, who remembered the old Blues days at Brazennose Street. After that, Chris said his version had been released on the Sue label as Little

Joe Cook, and it might be still obtainable. We were quite astounded as we already had it, and had believed it to be by a black bloke from the Mississippi Delta!

The week after Chris Farlowe, it was Georgie Fame; we skipped it to see the imitation Temptations in Salford, who turned out to be the Invitations.

We had seen Georgie Fame probably every time he had appeared at the Wheel. He was without doubt one of our favourite UK artists. Georgie had the honour of being the warm-up act for the Motown Review when it hit the UK. He made many fine copies of American artists' songs: 'The Dog', 'Green Onions', 'Do Re Mi', 'Sitting In The Park', 'Barefootin', 'Sweet Thing', 'Sunny', and he had his own major hit with 'Yeh Yeh'. He did many live shows covering large amounts of R&B classics and some jazz numbers. Big favourites at the old Wheel by him were 'In The Meantime', 'Pink Champagne', 'Getaway', 'Point Of No Return', 'Let The Sun Shine In', 'I Love The Life I Live', and 'Get On The Right Track Baby'.

The next two All-nighters had insignificant bands on, or we were so far out of it we couldn't remember who they were.

But the last All-nighter of the month was fine; it was Graham Bond and he always managed to keep things moving. I was also a big fan of anyone who played the Hammond organ. Of course, Graham did several Jimmy Smith numbers, and then introduced his single, 'Big Time Operator', which went down so well he did it again, and again.

Over the years, many notable UK groups had appeared at the club. Some played there repeatedly like Victor Brox and his Blues Train, who entertained us with trumpet solos, Alexis Korner who had educated us in the Blues, The Steam Packet with Rod Stewart and Long John Baldry, Zoot Money and his Big Roll Band, and The Brian Auger Trinity with Julie Driscoll. Then there was Jimmy Powell and his Dimensions who did serial copies of Soul songs, The Mike Cotton Sound with their version of 'Soul

Serenade', Wynder K. Frog doing his 'Green Door' on the Hammond organ, and Geno Washington, who was originally from Washington USA, but had been adopted by UK Mods as a home grown Soul outfit.

October's first Saturday. It was 'The Ferris Wheel' but no one knew who they were. We got reports from someone who ventured into the room where they were playing, and informed us that not only was it was empty, but they sounded like a Folk group! We decided not to find out and danced all night in the DJ room instead. It was the records that were played at the Wheel that were the real stars. I danced with Doreen, going around and around her in circles, singing along with the Temptations' 'You're Not An Ordinary Girl.'

At one point around 6am, a group of blokes gathered around Doreen. It got me thinking jealous thoughts again. The main problem with having a very beautiful and sexy girlfriend is that they know it and want the attention of everyone. The other problem is that they get it, and then you're constantly thinking that you've got lots and lots of rivals. I was so besotted with her; I was seriously thinking about asking her if she would get engaged.

The thought I was experiencing was answered internally with a song from the early sixties hit parade by Jimmy Soul, *'If you want to be happy for the rest of your life, Never make a pretty woman your wife...'* In England it had been covered by some comedian.

In the morning we spoke with the same group of guys who were now being very enthusiastic about next week's All-nighter, and of course it was one not to miss; Junior Walker. They were suggesting that as many people that could dig out their scooters should come down to Whitworth Street for a mass drive-by, like we used to do.

Doreen was enthusiastic about going, but suggested that I didn't dig up my old scooter, despite how determined I was to do so. She said she wouldn't ride on the back; she was acting very funny. I found out later that people thought she'd been out with someone else, but I didn't know that then. I was looking forward to seeing Junior, and she was thinking how she was going to finish with me.

* * *

The Manchester Wheelers

CHAPTER NINETEEN

Sid Nicks the Records

It was 27th April 1968. Ike and Tina were appearing at the Wheel All-nighter. It was a while now since Doreen split with DJ Dave who was playing Soul at the Blue Note, just a few streets from the Wheel.

The Blue Note Club didn't do many successful All-nighters, and it was DL that would DJ at them, not me. So now and again, I went to the Wheel – whenever they had special acts on that I really wanted to see – and this intermittent attendance weaned me off taking drugs. Of course I had to do a few on these occasions, but nothing like the '65 to '67 period. If I'd continued doing that, I probably would have ended up a hospital case. Also, the original crowd began to move on and only a hard core of the more determined types were left as regulars.

"It's Ike and Tina Turner tonight at the Wheel," shouted DL to a friend of his as a group of people emerged from the Waldorf Hotel; it was almost next to the Blue Note. We arranged with our pal Lincoln to DJ for the Blue Note's All-nighter that night, so both of us could see the show.

I think DL wanted to get me going out again on the hunt for 'crumpet', now he knew I was no longer going with Doreen. It was his enthusiasm to see Ike and Tina that encouraged me to go to another All-nighter.

Ike and Tina plus their Ikettes – one with a broken arm – were truly fantastic. How they all got to fit on that small stage was nothing short of a miracle, and after watching them we settled down to full scale dancing in the DJ room, where the DJ began a series of tribute plays of the night's act's recordings. It kicked off with 'It's Gonna Work Out Fine', a song that echoed memories of the 'Old Wheel' as it had been heavily featured there by Roger.

DL and I were dancing with some girls when Sid and Terry joined us. There's always someone or something to bugger up your day (or early morning, in this case). Sid appeared to be in a particularly belligerent mood and shouted to me: "'Ain't That Peculiar' and especially 'Take This Heart Of Mine' by Marvin Gaye had better get played tonight, or else that fucking DJ mate of yours will get his head kicked in." In fact he played three Marvin Gaye tracks; the ones Sid wanted and then 'Little Darlin', to the great satisfaction of Sid. It probably saved the Wheel DJ from having his records stolen, a fate that would within an hour be that of the Twisted Wheel's own collection. Terry was messing around dancing in front of the DJ bank of wheels, playing on the spokes with his fingers, tapping in time with the beat.

As a long tribute to Ike and Tina, Paul the DJ had been playing more of their 45s. He put on the turntable 'Anything You Wasn't Born With' and then he made a fatal mistake. He shouted to Terry through the mesh of spokes, and asked him to mind the shop while he went for a 'quick piss'.

"No problem," said Terry.

But there soon would be!

Terry squeezed past Paul and took a few records from out of his hand. Paul had got them from his record box, and shouted into Terry's ear: "These and all those in that box are mine – stick the ones I've given you on, and keep it going if I get held up on the way back."

I heard a year or so later that Sid and Terry repeated the following event to a far greater extent, and caused a huge crisis at the club when it was discovered that almost all the club's collection had vanished. I knew it was them, because they came into the Blue Note to try and sell some to me. I didn't want to get involved and told them that in any case I already had my own copies.

Tonight was to be a full dress rehearsal for the later event.

As soon as Paul had gone upstairs, Terry went into the cupboard beneath the twin Garrard record player decks and snatched handfuls of the Wheel's records, passing them out through the wheel spokes to Sid, who simply handed them out to everyone dancing around.

Most Wheelers were adept at knocking off a record or three, quickly shoving the free 45s down the front of their trousers and carrying on dancing with a widening grin on their faces. The girls that got a few just disappeared from the room, stuffing the 45s into their handbags.

DL attempted to make a few requests to Terry, but only ended up with 'earthquake' by al 'TNT' Braggs, which he already had. He was seen later, arguing with Terry upstairs in the bogs and trying to swap it for a Soul City record: 'Don't You Worry' by Don Gardner and Dee Dee Ford. Terry wouldn't exchange, though, despite not knowing anything about either record – he was just enjoying teasing DL. It reminded me about DL's 'Boogaloo Party' which I still had in my possession. I thought guiltily that I should give it back to him, but I didn't.

* * *

The Manchester Wheelers

CHAPTER TWENTY

Last Night

On the way up you can't see the way down, but inevitably all things end – and the seeds of the beginning of the end were established in our constant risky behaviour.

It was a completely random event that led to Angelo's downfall, but even then he was lucky he only lost his job. It happened like this: from the proceeds of his activities with Lord Snooty, Angelo had paid his deposit on a brand new ice-blue Mini Cooper. He had parked it at Piccadilly station car park and walked over to the Queens Hotel, looking for anyone going to the Wheel. It was another Saturday night, and that meant meeting up with any of our mates in town before the All-nighter. This hotel on the corner of London Road and Piccadilly was a favourite of Lord Snooty's. On Saturdays he was usually at the bar sipping his Pink Gin or some other posh cocktail before closing time, ready to head down the road to the Wheel.

This time, there was nobody that Angelo recognised as a 'Wheeler' in the Queens, so he continued over to the Dive Bar, a pub situated on the corner of York Street at the back of the Piccadilly Hotel that dominated Piccadilly Gardens in the heart of Manchester. The pub was at the other end of York Street from the Wimpy. It had two levels; ground level and a cellar bar downstairs, and it was heaving. The cellar bar was full of mixed groups of all ages: grandmas, aunties, uncles, shop workers, Mods, drunks and football team visitors to Manchester. He had just got a pint before last orders when the fire alarm started and the pub was evacuated. Outside, the Fire Brigade were putting out a fire inside a large metallic rubbish bin. A crowd including everyone from the pub stood around watching. Angelo was feeling OK: he was 'coming up'.

Then he saw a commotion at the back of the bins. A couple of firemen had spotted a guy at the back of the remaining bins that hadn't been on fire, and were shouting to him to come out. It was Louie. He was reclaiming his hidden stash before it could be found or watered down by the firemen. They shouted to him to come out again, but he continued attempting to locate the stuff he'd stashed in one of the bins. He was confused due to the firemen moving them around – eventually he located the right one and put his stash inside his shirt, just as two firemen arrived to remove him from the scene. Unfortunately, he hit one of them.

Angelo looked at the commotion in the dark smoky distance and saw a fireman nutting a bloke who was arguing with him amongst the bins. He didn't know it then, but this was Louie. Outraged that a fireman with a helmet on would use it to nut a defenceless bloke, Angelo stupidly went to Louie's rescue, just as the police arrived!

Louie was a pill dealer and this back street along from the Wimpy was his patch. He had argued with the brigade and they thought he had started the fire; of course he hadn't. He just wanted to retrieve his amphetamine collection. He knew a lot of All-nighter goers were depending on him.

Seeing Louie being picked on by several firemen, Angelo went to his aid, but this was a big mistake. The firemen turned on Angelo and a short battle ensued. It was really bad timing –the police arrived at the same time that he hit a fireman with a dustbin lid. As he was doing so the police grabbed him from behind as their first priority, and slapped him handcuffed into the back of their Ford Anglia police car.

Assault on a fireman whilst he was trying to attend to a fire was a charge that wasn't going to look good to the presiding 'Beak'. We saw the commotion up the street from the 'Wheelers' hangout outside the Wimpy, and became onlookers as the second culprit was arrested. It was Louie, handcuffed and thrown in the police car alongside Angelo. Off they went. Everyone was booing or cheering as these events took place, before the crowd returned downstairs back into the boozer, as the street theatre ended.

I had been on the lookout for Angelo or Lord Snooty to cadge some gear and had gone to the Wimpy, our usual meeting place. When I couldn't find them, I had already decided to head for the Dive Bar to see if Louie was around, as the pub was his hangout. That's when I saw him with Angelo - both nicked by the police. So I hopped it quick.

I headed on down the road to Whitworth Street to see Edwin Starr. I was only going now and again to see important live acts. I had managed to buy some gear from a girl I knew who lived on the Langley estate near Middleton. I was aware that Angelo was in the police station just over the road. Late in the morning, they moved him to Bootle Street cop shop. The police associated the two together, and at the station Louie was searched to reveal a few hundred pills in his shirt. After checking up, they learned that Angelo worked for Boots. Bingo!

They then took them both to Court on Monday morning. The charge of wholesale supply was eventually dropped, but it resulted in a notification letter to Boots and the sack for Angelo. We never saw Louie again. He was remanded to Risley and never returned to the All-nighter scene afterwards.

Angelo met me the next Friday in the Blue Note, where he recounted the events of the previous Saturday and about being 'bound over to keep the peace' – a suspended sentence and a fine of £25. He said he'd given up All-nighters and pills and was only going to the Blue Note from now on. He'd obtained a job as a waiter on the Intercity with British Rail, and would be paid more.

He reiterated that it could have been far worse. The police had recovered Louie's stash of two hundred Dexys and Black Bombers. The charge of fire raising was dropped in favour of drug dealing. Dealing was a first degree offence. The drug squad interviewing them said 'Strangeways was beckoning'. Then they found out where Angelo worked. He said that the cops had tried to frighten him.

Then he told me about his very last caper, and he began to go over the very last fun he had enjoyed at Salford; It was at the Regent Road corner with Ordsall Lane, a 'Boots the Chemist shop' and this Boots was the last to be subjected to a mysterious break-in. When giving a hand loading up with Brian – aka Lord Snooty – he would sing 'Break Out' by Mitch Ryder, but changing the words to suit the occasion singing *'Break – in!'*

Thousands of footie supporters used to pass by on alternate Saturday afternoons on their way to Old Trafford, legging it from Manchester city centre going past the shop. It had been difficult to get Snooty's' car past them as they streamed along passing by. Eventually Angelo had loaded up the MG with assorted Dexys, Black Bombers, Green and Clears, plus the bulky stuff; cosmetics and additions to their range that now consisted of women's toiletry products. It was an inspired addition after Angelo's aunty had said how nice the bath salts were that he had appropriated for her birthday.

They had enough goods to coast along for a while, and Angelo said if they had known it was their last operation, they'd have robbed everything and then fire bombed the place! I guessed it was his anger speaking, and knew he and Brian were now both resigned to more legitimate pursuits.

It was almost miraculous that no connection was made by Mr Plod with the Boots break-ins. They never connected it with an in-house job. Angelo got sacked for frequenting with Louie, who was sent down to Risley as it was his second offence.

It all added up to the end of our secret 'insider industry'; supply and easy access to pills. From now on, all our gang of pals would have to barter for gear from the open market. This really was the beginning of the end of our All-nighter activity. Most of my friends became regulars at the Blue Note, probably going most nights that it was open during the week and Saturdays. After this, just a few would still be going on to the Wheel All-nighters.

∗ ∗ ∗

The Manchester Wheelers

CHAPTER TWENTY ONE

A Time to Love, a Time to Cry

A DJ's life is not a happy one – 'cause now that you've left me I really know the Blues and the Soul has left my shoes, and you sure miss your water when your well runs dry.

It was a while now after Doreen had walked away from me the morning after the Junior Walker All-nighter. No words had been said, but she was finished with me. Chucking me was the correct Mancunian term for it. I consoled myself at the Blue Note, playing all the great Soul tracks, but like the lyrics in the song by the Four Tops, they all seem to have a different meaning *'since she's been gone'*. Every now and again I had bouts of depression. I was really missing her.

All that time, for months after she had gone, lyrics would come into my head, tormenting me. I saw her everywhere. *'Nadine is that you?'* sounded in my head – with the name changed to hers in the version that went round and round in my mind. When eventually Chuck Berry's song left me alone, the Beatles immediately replaced Chuck's song and they haunted me with 'No Reply' – *'I saw you walk hand in hand with another man... I nearly died...'*

I had always wanted to be a Soul DJ and when Lez Lee had left - he had been recruited after Roger eagle had gone - I got my opportunity. After Lez Lee had given it up it was John Fogel the club's owner playing the music at the Blue Note. John was getting complaints about the club's playlist sliding towards only popular Soul tracks, but these were all he had. He soon realised there was more to it and recognised the need for someone with a large Soul music collection to be doing the job. I immediately volunteered. I learned later that Doreen had suggested ages ago to John that I would be a good candidate, owning lots of the best Soul records. Even so I had to sharpen up my music supply. I did it on my own for several months, then got DL to help out. Bringing along his collection, added to mine, and made the club formidable in comparison to the Wheel on non-All-nighter days. Even so, we still had to scour round our contacts to obtain missing tracks that Roger had popularised, like 'Changes' by Johnnie Taylor. DL and I agreed that the direction of the club would follow what Roger had started, like being heavily Stax oriented. Soon we were introducing new Soul sounds and tracks tinged with Blues. Albert King's 'A' and 'B' sides became requested items as a result. Unlike the Wheel, the club attracted music enthusiasts who would sit and listen, as well as wanting to dance.

John Fogel introduced me to Ralph at his record shop and set up an account there on behalf of the club, so I could purchase new releases. Obtaining singles was a passion with DL and I, but it was inevitable that some 'must have' items would be missing. For instance, one great Motown track that was copied by Georgie Fame was 'Sweet Thing' on the Tamla Motown label by the Motown Spinners, not the Detroit Spinners – and by the time I found out about the name change, it had been deleted. Records were often deleted and returned for a credit from shops to distributors if they didn't sell in the first few weeks after release. This was one that got away. There were many more, so we had to borrow them from friends to give them a play at the club.

The Blue Note was very different from the Twisted Wheel, especially the Saturday All-nighter Wheel. During the week both clubs played more variable playlists. However, it was mainly the Blue Note that played Blues-y Soul and slow stuff like the Facinations' 'You'll Be Sorry' or Mavis Staples' version of Dionne Warwick's 'A House Is Not a Home'. Others were Bertha Tilman's 'Oh My angel', 'Just Say Goodbye' and 'And I Love Him' by Esther Phillips. Oddities like 'Burning Spear' by the Soulful Strings were typical of the varied repertoire that was covered at the club.

The Manchester Wheelers

When Fleetwood Mac released 'Need Your Love So Bad' we had been playing the version by Little Willie John for ages. The Blue Note was the first club to play many Soul tracks that caught on big, like 'Going To a Happening' by Tommy Neal, 'Wang Dang Doodle' from Koko Taylor and 'Abel Mable' by Mable John; Little Willie's sister. It continued the tradition set originally by Roger, to play a more diverse and predominantly black American R&B and Soul music repertoire. It also included Blue Beat and Ska, but that eventually led to the club's downfall. The playlist featured lots of slow Soul so couples could slow dance to smoochy numbers, and this was always a feature in the closing forty five minutes or so.

To keep up with new sounds and to find old ones, DL and I were always on the record trail.

Shirley Brickley was the fantastic lead voice of the Orlons on 'Heartbreak Hotel', 'Crossfire', 'Don't Hang Up', 'South Street' and their first hit 'The Wah Watusi'. I'd bought the lot on Cameo Parkway for a threepenny bit each, from Mazell's on London Road. I'd gone in there just for a look around and struck gold. It was a necessity to periodically check all such places, as new stock came in and flew out quite quickly. The Orlons' records on Cameo Parkway were all brand new, but deleted 45's were a great addition to my growing record collection. Many became hits at the Blue Note.

We went round market stalls, second hand shops and to Mr and Mrs Bowker's shop, who by now were our long-time friends. But mostly we bought anything associated with Soul from auction mailing lists. Most of what we got we knew about, but we would often put in low bids for ones we hadn't heard of. Many times this would produce hidden gems on USA labels – mostly deleted items with punched holes in them. When we found a good song we would play it over and over, until we got asked about it and it then became requested, but we only hyped up good tracks, like 'Ain't No Sun' by The Dynamics, 'Love Time' from the Kelly Brothers, 'Love Sickness' by Sir Mack Rice and 'Love Explosions' by Troy Keyes.

The Manchester Wheelers

We subscribed to mailing lists in the USA and studied the USA R&B chart listings in Melody Maker and the New Musical Express. Ninety percent of the records played at Soul clubs in Manchester were the popular Stax, Motown, and Stateside tracks. We covered most of these, plus a lot more obscure and rarer sounds, as well as a tinge of Blues. We played loads of Stax tracks; Booker T. & the MGs' 'Slim Jenkin's Place', Dee Dee Warwick's 'We're Doing Fine' and 'When Love Slips Away', Mabel John's fantastic 'Your Good Thing (Is about To end)' and the great version of 'C C Rider' from Joe Tex. Later, I was at last able to push songs by Johnnie Taylor; 'Toe Hold', the fantastic 'Blues In The Night' and 'Testify (I Wanna)', a modernised version of the fabulous original track from the Parliaments.

I got two records on the USA Sims label just by chance from a random buy on an auction list. I played both at the Blue Note. I liked 'You're That Great Big Feelin', which was one of those copy songs inspired by Tommy Tucker's 'Hi-Heel Sneakers'. The other was 'Love Time', and it was this that eventually took off at the Blue Note as a sure fire way to get everyone up dancing.

Other notables were 'Looking For a Love' by The Valentinos on an import 45, and DL's choice of Dean Parrish's 'I'm On My Way', which was played at the Blue Note. 'Determination' by Dean Parrish on the UK Stateside label was a big dance floor filling track at both the Wheel and the Blue Note – even the 'B' side was popular, and 'I'm On My Way' was also absolutely brilliant. Released in 1967, DL got it direct from New York as a deletion from an auction list. They had a copy at the Wheel, but DL reckoned his was the only other copy in Manchester! One or two great tracks didn't make it though; like 'Tainted Love' from Gloria Jones, who was the girlfriend of Marc Bolan. Whenever DL played it, the dance floor immediately emptied, and I'd have to put on Roy Docker's 'Mellow Moonlight' to get everyone back on the floor.

I had completely forgotten again about DL's 45 that went missing that night ages ago, and I finally gave him back his 'Boogaloo Party'. Angelo had given it to me a few days after 'nicking' it, but I had hung on to it.

The Manchester Wheelers

Some nights DL and I worked together. 'The Horse' by Cliff Nobles was an instrumental with vocals on the 'B' side. It was so good that we bought two copies each, so we could use the twin decks to seamlessly play one and run it into the other.

DL was a dragster race enthusiast. He went to Santa Pod drag racing with his younger brother and their dad. This made him a dragster and Surf music fan. The Beach Boys did 'Stick Shift'; Ronnie and the Daytonas did 'Little GTO' and 'Bucket T'; Jan and Dean did 'Dead Man's Curve' and 'Surf City'. He'd often requested Roger at the 'Old' Wheel to play them until their bust-up over 'Surfin' Bird' by the Trashmen. Then after Roger left, he got the new DJ to start playing them again by getting loads of people to periodically ask for them. However, Surf music faded out at the Whitworth Street Wheel, as Soul took a firmer grip on the place. When I asked DL to assist me at the Blue Note he inevitably stuck in a few of his Surf favourites.

Being a DJ at The Blue Note effectively stopped me from continuous All-nighters at the Wheel. I still made it to see artists that I just had to see, but I soon became weaned off pills. I had to give up – each weekend was taking its toll with larger and larger amounts of pills, smoking, drinking, and the process of coming up and coming down. Also I'd caught a severe dose of Bronchitis that was followed by Tonsillitis. It was so bad that my tonsils turned septic and I had to go into Ancoats Hospital to have them removed.

I was in a bad physical state - then it got even worse. I had given up pills, but got a dose of the other. In the words of Albert Kings 'Born Under A Bad Sign'; 'if it wasn't for bad luck, I'd have no luck at all.'

After Doreen had split up with me, I wore my heart on my sleeve and sunk into a depression. I suspected she'd dumped me for another bloke, but surely not for that twat with a holey suit? I couldn't get her out of my mind, or the thought of who she had packed me in for, and why. Was it for the manager of the group that used to practice at the Blue Note late at night after it closed? Was it someone in the Wheel? I had no idea. She'd kept it a secret, and I never saw her again. Could it have been my own fault? I did stray once with her friend Mandy, but surely Mandy would never have told her – would she?

A friend of mine did tell me she'd been cheating on me anyway by going out with Angelo, and had shown up kissing him on my nights off at The Blue Note. Somehow I couldn't accept this news – but it soon faded from my inner struggle with 'why had it happened' when I learned, a while later, she'd skipped off with Sid and they'd gone to Torquay. It had a compelling ring of truth to it. I saw again in my mind's eye that night when Sid had given her a handful of pills for free. Funny – as much as I tried to hate her, I couldn't feel anything like anger, just anguish and self pity.

I kept getting that song by Chuck Berry in my head, inserting Doreen's name instead of Nadine. I saw her everywhere, but just like the song by the Zombies – 'She's Not There'.

The problem is that when you're really in love, it torments the mind. Just because the other person has gone, it doesn't mean it's over for you. Love isn't like a tap you can turn off. It's all the harder to take if the one you love goes off with another. If she'd died in a car crash or something then the pain would be easier to take, because the memory would be untarnished. My playlist at the club reflected my passing remorseful mood stages:

'I had A Dream' - Johnnie Taylor
'Helpless' - Kim Weston
'A Time To Love, a Time To Cry' - Lou Johnson
'Goin' Out Of My Head' Little Anthony and The Imperials
'Ain't Nothing You Can Do' - Bobby Bland
'I Need You' - The Impressions
'Tell Me It's Just a Rumour, Baby' - The Isley Brothers
'Oh Baby (Things Ain't What They Used To Be)' - Ike and Tina Turner
'Since You've Been Gone' - The Four Tops
'You've Lost That Lovin' Feelin' - The Righteous Brothers
'Love Sickness' - Sir Mack Rice
'Where Did Our Love Go' - The Supremes
'Searching For My Love' - Bobby Moore and The Rhythm

Aces
'I Got To Dance To Keep From Crying' - The Miracles
'Just Say Goodbye' - Esther Phillips
'Get Out Of My Heart' - Moses and Joshua (Dillard)
'Untie Me' - The Tams
'The Tracks Of My Tears' - The Miracles
'You're Good Thing (Is About To end)' - Mable John
'Any Day Now' - Chuck Jackson
'Ain't That Peculiar' - Marvin Gaye
'I'm Your Puppet' - James and Bobby Purify
'When I'm Gone' - Brenda Holloway
'(I Know) I'm Losing You' - The Temptations
'So I Can Love You' - The Emotions
'I'm Gonna Miss You' - The Artistics
'When Love Slips Away' - Dee Dee Warwick
'Lay This Burden Down' - Mary Love
'Ain't No Sun' - The Dynamics
'What Becomes Of The Broken Hearted' - Jimmy Ruffin
'Tears, Tears, Tears' - Ben E King
'Mr Pitiful' - Otis Redding
'Hey Girl' - Freddie Scott
'Stay With Me' - Lorraine Ellison
'There Goes My Baby' - The Drifters
'I Could Never Love another after Loving You' - The Temptations
'Have Fun' - Ann Cole
'Now I Know What Love Is' - Al Wilson
'I Got To Love Somebody's Baby' - Johnnie Taylor
'Standing In The Need Of Love' - Dee Dee Sharp
'Tired Of Being Lonely' - The Sharpees
'Ain't No Big Thing' - The Radiants
'The Entertainer' - Tony Clarke

All these sounds just wouldn't leave me alone. I had to play them and lots of others almost every night of the week. It got to me. It ate away at me inside. I would go and get a pint from the pub next door, The Waldorf Hotel, come back and shut the DJ booth doors. I couldn't talk or take requests when I was listening to the music of my love-sick soul. I began to play 'Night Life' by Marvin Gaye as my final track of the night. It was on an LP I'd bought by Marvin, 'The Moods of Marvin Gaye' and it just summed up my mood at that time.

Gin, gin and more gin; it makes you maudlin, it can make you tearful for no reason and I had bottles of it. I was sinking, but externally no one knew that I was suffering. Like Tony Clarke's 'The entertainer', the show had to go on.

DL found a secret cupboard at the back of our DJ room. It held all the drinks and spirits, all stored there from when the Blue Note had a drinks licence. John, the club's owner, was always optimistic of the licence's return, but if it did he would have to buy more stock, because DL and I were going though it 'like a dose of salts'. We were draining the bottles of Scotch and re-filling the empties with tea, substituting it for whiskey and brandy, and putting back tap water into the empty gin and vodka bottles we had guzzled. I got into such a state that I dug out a few old Doo Wop records and started to play 'Maybe' by the Shantells, a big USA hit in 1958. I got it from a second hand shop, and the song was like a prayer: 'Ma- ay- be... if I pray every night, you'll come back to me...'

I went off the rails. First I was very upset, and then this all-consuming emotion was replaced by another: anger. Then I wanted to screw all the girls I could. Funny, and strange as this turned out to be fairly easy. I found out that girls like guys who have some kind of status, and being a club DJ was good enough! It was a surprise how easily girls would just 'drop 'em' in the club after closing, even in doorways on the way to the bus station. This went on for a couple of months. Then, after noticing a couple of times that I had strange sensations from my bladder – like two sensitive lines going up to my lower stomach region and left and right to my kidneys – one morning I felt something much more disturbing. Yelling in pain, I jumped out of bed and inspected my dick. It was OK. But then right beneath the back of it, between it and my backside, I felt an awful stiff pulsating sensation. Suddenly the region at the base of my spine right between my legs felt as if it had been kicked by a horse, and I had a horrible stinging feeling all the way up inside my dick.

I went for a piss, and the pain was staggering. I felt as though I was peeing out broken pieces of glass. I knew I had to go to the 'clap clinic'. Then it seemed to be OK for a while, so I talked myself out of it – but then later that morning I needed another piss, and it was the same again, only worse. I got the bus and ended up at St Luke's, the Manchester 'clap clinic'. On the journey there I had Booker T. & the MGs' 'Soul Clap 69' running through my head's private record player, later replaced by Little Willie John's 'Fever'.

On that bus I couldn't stop the thought going over and over in my mind: who had it been? Then I started thinking about how the clap clinic treats a new client, and I was terrified. I'd heard blokes at work telling all sorts of wild stories – like the one they often repeated, about a needle they put straight down your dick. They'd press a button, and then the end of the needle would open up into a small umbrella of metal, and they'd drag it out!

I told myself that these were just wild, unsubstantiated tales designed to scare – but when I got into the treatment room, I found out they had told the truth!

I could just about stand it. In any case, I had to – there was no choice offered.

The umbrella was a very small end part of the proboscis needle that the nurse used. I recalled the foolish thoughts I'd been having about getting an embarrassing hard-on if the nurse touched my dick. No way could that have happened. The thing wanted to emigrate as soon as the needle was approaching.

That nurse was very nice, very 'matter of fact', and afterwards she showed me the gooey puss on the end of the needle. She spread it onto a pink jelly in a Petri dish and stuck it in an oven. We waited. She was the first woman that had ever held my dick without it responding. I wondered if it would ever work again. The time passed slowly. Embarrassingly slowly. Then she opened the oven door after her wind-up timer had sounded. She showed me the results; almost the entire pink area had a white fungus growing all over it.

"Right," she said, "please wait over there on the seats to see the doctor."

I sat there for what seemed like centuries, before the anonymous number I'd been given was called out.

"Gonorrhoea," said the doctor. He prescribed very large pills and told me no alcohol whatsoever.

It did the trick. And my dick did recover. But I chucked away the contact notes they said I should give to everyone I had had sex with recently. That was just too embarrassing to go through with.

I became a celibate DJ monk. And my circumstances did not improve.

The popularity of Blue Beat and Ska increased at the club, and it became more and more a mixed colour club; the only place like it in Manchester. DL would wind it up with 'Dr Kitch' by Lord Kitchener, an old Brazennose Wheel track that Georgie Fame did, along with some new stuff. There were some risky sounds like 'Bang Bang Lulu', one from Lloyd Charmers and another from Lloyd Terrel: *'Bang Bang Lulu, Lulu had a boyfriend, his name was Tommy Tucker, He took her down the alley, to see if he could f... her... Who you gonna bang, bang now Lulu's gone away...'* It all led to a deterioration as far as I was concerned, detracting from the Soul music ideal of the club.

I was more interested in classy records like Curtis Mayfield with the Impressions singing 'Fool For You', 'Choice Of Colours', 'This Is My Country' and 'Stay Close To Me' by the Five Stairsteps, or Donny Hathaway and June Conquest with 'I Thank You' and William Bell with 'Happy'. Then one night, just as I was getting going with the night's chosen Soul list, a girl requested 'Oh Carolina' by the Folk Brothers. "Fuck off," I said, "I've already played it twice tonight."

Later that night after closing, I left the club and went the back way to Piccadilly to get an all-night bus. I was heading past the

Blood Bank in Roby Street, when out from a doorway jumped two half-castes, shouting at me that I'd refused to play 'Oh Carolina'!!!

I was chased around the dark back streets by these two Jamaican-descent half-castes, and eventually I lost them. However, just when I felt it was safe to emerge from a doorway I had slipped into, a gang came around a corner. I immediately thought this was more trouble coming my way, as they were chanting football songs and had light blue scarves. It was the Kippax lads! I got ready for trouble, but I wasn't willing to use my holdall with all my precious records as a swinging weapon. I was thinking about Kung Fu kick-dancing as I walked towards them in the middle of the street.

After my escape from the 'Oh Carolina' half-castes, I'd been heading to the bus station after finishing at The Blue Note. It would be the usual after midnight madness in Piccadilly bus station, this time enhanced by gangs of Manchester City supporters on the rampage. They were a drunken mob, having been in the city centre pubs since the match finished. I'd read the match report earlier, in the 'Pink Final' by Peter Gardner; they were on a winning streak of one win, but even so they were still in a mean mood.

My mind was racing as I walked closer, leaping from one subject to the next. My granddad had played once for Manchester City, before the First World War, and he'd been a big fan of the club. My father, on the other hand, was a massive United fan. He went every week to home games, sometimes with our Roman Catholic priest. Although my dad was no Catholic, they had a common passion for football. When I was a kid, I went with my grandfather to many City home games at Maine Road. Then on the other alternate weekends I'd go with my dad to Old Trafford. My granddad's hero was Bert Trautmann, although he usually hated the Germans – he'd survived both Ypres and the Somme. My granddad told me he thought City's prior goalkeeper, Frank Swift, was fantastic, but eventually he had conceded that Bert was even better – especially after his heroic effort of staying in goal for the last fifteen minutes in the 1956 FA Cup final with a broken neck. On that memorable occasion, Man City beat Birmingham City 3-1.

The Manchester Wheelers

Bert had been a German prisoner of war at a POW Camp in Ashton in Makerfield and he had played for St Helens before signing for Manchester City in 1949. He had been sent back to his home in Bremen, but soon returned to Manchester. German prisoners of war had been kept back from repatriation after the war, working for war retribution. In 1947 and '48 they'd been requisitioned to assemble thousands of USA supplied prefabricated homes in Wythenshawe and Blackley in Manchester, replacing homes destroyed in the war by the Luftwaffe.

The Kippax lads were now in front of me – they surrounded me and began to pull at my bag containing my records. First I panicked; I needed to find a way to break out of this situation. Then suddenly I knew what to do. I shouted out at the top of my voice "Bert Trautmann built my house!!" and prayed silently that these hooligans had some knowledge of their own team's history. Bert had retired long ago – would they even know who Trautmann was?

What I'd said was true, or at least possible; as one of the Luftwaffe prisoners he could have worked on our house. We lived in a single storey prefab in Fairmead Close, off Victoria Avenue on the opposite side from North Manchester Golf Club; there was a massive estate of them, and the German prisoners had built them after the war. My father used to come in for lots of jokes about our house from his workmates who knew of his fanatical adoration for Manchester United – everyone would wind him up about the idea that our house had been Gerry-built by the rival Manchester team's goalkeeper!

My shout echoed in the air, and the shitty supporters almost froze! Miraculously they let go of my bag. My claim probably saved my record collection. I uncomfortably went on to explain I was a life long supporter of Bert, that I had attended his 'testimonial match' (which I had with my granddad) and told them the history about our house. A few began to cry, probably due to drink; they even asked for my autograph! We walked together into the bus station. They left me alone, and then in a subdued mob they quietly left the station. Ain't that peculiar!

The Manchester Wheelers

I reflected on the number 88 bus home about football and how pissed off and deeply disgruntled Manchester City supporters must be. It was 1968, and ten years after the Munich disaster had decimated the original Busby Babes, Manchester United had had a great season – they were Champions of Europe, after already becoming the Football League Champions. So, to some extent Matt Busby had achieved what was taken from him at Munich, and all of Manchester had gone Red Devil crazy. Amazingly, that final was at Wembley against the unstoppable Benfica, and they had the mighty, mighty Eusebio. We'd beaten them before – or as my dad said, 'it was George Best who beat them on his own', disassembling them with a couple of goals in their own Stadium of Lights in Lisbon. He'd said "we 'ad now't t' fear," and he was proved right.

Benfica were afraid of George and had assigned two players for close marking him, which of course let Bobby Charlton loose with Nobby Stiles marking eusebio, tailing him with not too many fouls. We got our chance in the second half; Bobby got an accurate cross from Sadler and Bobby 'Bobbed' it into the net. But with a few minutes to go, Torres headed the ball down to the feet of Graca who scored. Extra time. Two minutes into it and George scored, beating Henrique the Goalie by sauntering around him. Then within another minute Brian Kidd headed in another. In the second fifteen minutes of extra time Bobby knocked in his second: 4 – 1 and it was goodnight for the Dagos.

* * *

That same week I bumped into Len. He was coming out of an Indian restaurant called the Everest on Whitworth Street. He was wearing a Kaftan, he had long hair, dark glasses and was of course smoking a huge joint.

"What the fuck do you look like?" I said.

"What the fuck do you think, man?" he retorted back at me.

"You've become a Hippy!" I said in astonishment.

"Well, man, it's the times, you know?" and without pausing, he went on:

"Hey man, you know Roger the DJ? He's gone Hippy, man, and he's playing groovy tracks at the old Jiggy place. It's now called the 'Magic...' something or other." Len was now sounding like a West Coast American.

Len always had been a deep thinker and very intellectually verbal when smoking dope. I knew I was in for a lecture.

He told me his 'head' was at some new place these days, and that the entire Mod scene and whatever had passed – but then strangely, he emphasised that it would never be forgotten, that it would last forever. "Well, the music that is," he added dramatically.

He said he'd had a few enlightening trips on LSD, and as a result was reading all the books by black magician Aleister Crowley. He said that he was generally getting his shit together' and punctuating the end of his sentences with 'man'.

I asked him if he was still doing the milk rounds, and he told me "No, man." He'd decided to go to Afghanistan on a field trip. Then he told me this:

He said that all that Mod stuff was a gathering of like-minded souls. The drugs we took, the amphetamines, they combined us all into a tribe with a common interest and a purpose. He said Crowley foresaw this kind of thing; it was the age of Horus, the time of the youth, and the younger people were going to become the most influential in society. He said the age of the old farts dominating and controlling everything was beginning to come to an end. It wasn't going to happen next week, or next year, but the seeds had been sown in several effective places in the world.

Again I could see the old Mod Len in there somewhere, inside the glasses and all that hair. Warming to his subject, he continued: "Like the aborigines with their songs – they used to put remembrances and power into deeds and actions. It was associated with the power drawn from or into a place." He said the Manchester Twisted Wheel was one such place and another was located in California, where the hippy movement had started – it was in Los Angeles, a place called 'Ashbury' something or other, but he couldn't recall the exact name. It was typical of conversations with marijuana inhalers.

Len went on, saying: "all that dancing and all that secretive 'in' movement stuff made a tight collective group like a tribe or a cult. The dancing was like a ritual, and the purpose was focused without anyone really knowing it was to bring about the new age; the age of Horus or the age of Aquarius." He said it was "deep, heavy shit man."

I was a bit lost for words, and Len, abhorring a conversation vacuum, said: "It was about the music. Yeah, man; that Soul music will go on forever, because of the energies associated with it in all those all-night bacchanalian rituals!"

He asked if I was still dejaying at the Blue Note and said he'd heard the half-castes had taken over the place.

"Don't remind me," I said and told him of my recent escape.

We then went our separate ways, Len in his Kaftan and with beads around his neck, me in a brown Mohair suit, both going in separate directions along Whitworth Street. There goes another loony discussion, I thought, a result of too many times with weed and pills and now LSD. Who knows, though? Maybe he was right? Would Soul music last longer than the end of the decade? Would pop music? Rock & Roll was still around from the fifties. Elvis was still going strong! You couldn't just ignore what Len had to say.

* * *

The Manchester Wheelers

'68 drifted into '69, and Soul music had become mainstream. Deejaying at the Blue Note had an endless quality to it, but things were changing. It was happening in my favourite sport too; in the summer, a new name was leading the Peloton. Jacques Anquetil had won the Tour de France five times, an unparalleled string of events. Now, for the first time in over 30 years, a Belgian had won the tour – a new guy riding for Team Faema called Eddy Merckx.

My physical condition had improved when I gave up All-nighters. I'd been suffering from bronchitis and tonsillitis, plus the inner landscapes of paranoia from the repeated on and off, start-stop, up-down drug events. The physical and mental stress had made me ill physically and it appeared to have been affecting me mentally too.

I had to stop. But to stop would mean being 'out' with the 'in' crowd and all my friends were in that crowd.

However, breaking free of it had become easier when I became a DJ, and my passion for music was actually increased. I never thought I was addicted to the pills – they were just a requirement to be able to keep going all night and over the weekend. The aim was dancing to, and listening to, the music. The Soul music was the main item. I still had the music – I realised I could do without the All-nighters, along with their social scene, and still survive.

Breaking the habit of taking 'pep pills' was quite possible, because the habit was broken repeatedly each week with the come down. Any habit becomes enmeshed into the mind; it's almost a bodily need that you can set your watch by as it makes demands for the habit to be continued. Inner cravings are like sub-verbal inner voices making repeated insistent requests. Smoking is a good example, with a bodily demand for nicotine. I began to believe that addictions can be dealt with by the power of the will, if that will is reinforced. The action of making a positive decision can be called into mind each time the addictive thought request comes along, so as to coincide with it, so that the counter-thought can become a habit too. I reasoned that alternate and better habits could be set up knowing this; the trick was to kick in the will not to succumb, and to make this link – calling in the counter measure each time the habitual thought was triggered.

Of course, it's not as easy as it might sound. Every time the thought came to go to the weekend All-nighter I attempted to answer it with an alternative option, like a night at Time and Place or the Phonograph. But then the little niggling voices would begin: 'You'll miss new sounds', 'You won't meet friends', 'You won't get that 'need to dance' feeling', 'You won't hear new Soul records' and so on.

The entire thing was the habit; the scene, being in with a clique. The core value was the music, and I would always have that. Knowing that it was the music that was the important fact, I was able to see my habit and break it. After all, each week after an All-nighter I faced the symptoms of 'withdrawal'. I knew it could be stopped. By this time I'd had put aside the stranger events I'd experienced whilst under the drug 'come down' influences, but it was a subject I would come back to in the future.

* * *

One Friday night, DL and I had arranged for two of our friends to take over for us at the Blue Note Club as stand in DJs, so we could go and see Prince Buster at a club in Stockport. It was absolutely fabulous. The Prince was wearing a white flowing Arab gown and had a red 'Tommy Cooper' fez on his head. Everyone in his large band was dressed the same, and they looked great.

The Prince was doing his thing: *'Take it easy, Take it easy... Choo choo choo chuki chuk chukkkka chukkkkkka, Take it easy... cho cho cho...'* The incredible guttural sounds that man could produce – it was truly amazing.

Of course, enjoying that brilliant concert was another contributing factor for playing Buster's records, and we both dug out our full Blue Beat collections. Inevitably, lots more half-caste lads began coming to the Blue Note. They came to hear the Jamaican sounds, to mix and to pick up white girls; they all seemed to have white girlfriends.

The Manchester Wheelers

A telephone rings: *'Hello an emergency case for Dr Ring Ding,'* said the female voice on the record's introduction, and everyone got up onto the dance floor. I watched the 45 spinning around; it had a nice colourful label. The yellow and green Dr Bird disc spun around and around on the Garrard deck; 'Phoenix City' by Roland Alphonso. I loaded the one next to it with a Stax record. It was on the newer Stax label, the yellow one with clicking fingers. It was William Bell singing 'Happy'.

Immediately the dance floor cleared – everyone walked off.

"The fuckers," I shouted out inside the DJ booth, whilst outside several people were shouting out that it was crap. There was nothing for it but to follow it with 'Oh Carolina' to get them back up and keep them dancing. I kept muttering "The fuckers…" to myself, as I dug out a few old standbys and put them onto the twin Garrard decks:

'This Train' by Joyce Bond, 'Dance Cleopatra' and 'Do The Teasy' by Prince Buster, 'Humpty Dumpty' by Eric Morris, 'Jamaica Ska' by The Ska Kings. Then 'King Of Kings' by Jimmy Cliff, '007' by Desmond Dekker, 'Train Tour To Rainbow City' by The Pyramids, 'Rough Rider' and 'Al Capone' by Prince Buster. After that, then The Skatalites with 'The Guns Of Navarone', followed by 'Perhaps' and continuing with 'a Message To You Rudy' by Dandy Livingstone, and 'Its Mek' from Desmond Dekker. I guessed that lot would keep them happy for a while.

For me this was the beginning of the end. The dance floor that used to fill with fairly obscure Soul tracks and all things Stax only fully moved now to Jamaican music. Of course, it was Roger Eagle who'd started the appreciation for Ska and Blue Beat in Manchester with white club goers. These days, with DL's liking for licentious songs from Trojan records and with his particular favourite 'Bang Bang Lulu' closely followed by 'Dr Kitch', he was pandering to the trend far more than I agreed with. At least the Twisted Wheel was still going strong with Soul. I went occasionally on nights off to early sessions, to catch any new sounds Paul Davis – the long standing Wheel DJ – and his new sidekick Bobby Dee might have that we'd missed at the Blue Note.

By the end of '69, I had completely given up All-nighters, and pills had long since been kicked. I'd begun a different social scene: going to Bredbury Hall, even entering the dreaded old Jungfrau now known as T&P – Time and Place. Sundays once spent in a series of Manchester town centre dance clubs were substituted for the Boat House pub in Chester, and a few weekends at Abersoch in North Wales.

I always had a leaning towards the less 'trendy' places, and had also kept up going to the Domino nightclub on Grey Mare Lane and a few other places. In fact a large group of pals often went to these clubs, because many touring Soul artists appeared. These types of clubs had great comedians on, including Mr Manning's Embassy Club, where you tried to keep your head down when Bernard was on stage. I was convinced he got his cutting, almost vicious style from being a Man City supporter and having to cope with being second best in his home town. If you had to go to the toilets and you were sitting near the stage, you tried not to let him see you. If he did, he would always make a comment.

I remember on one occasion he tapped the microphone – it was one of his foibles – as he spotted someone standing up. "Are you going for a piss again?" he said, smiling, with that special glint in his eye. It was best to just shut up, or you could run into a lengthy bout of banter from him.

The standing bloke responded: "I need to go, because you're watering down the fucking beer in here."

Bernard retorted with: "We have to for you, as you end up falling down after three pints, saying yer drunk and then you can't fucking drive home like everyone else does."

He then got into his stride, saying: "anyway, don't you live in Moston?" and didn't wait for an answer. "That plane's engine that fell off coming into land at Ringway last month, hit your row of

The Manchester Wheelers

fuckin' houses and caused fifty quid's worth of damage."

Stupidly, the bloke heckled back with something, and then Bernard shouted: "Sorry, yes it missed your house, so you're right, it only did forty five quid's worth."

The bloke got frustrated but before retreating through the door of the bogs he yelled back: "Why are you such a big fat pig?"

Bernard, sharp as a razor and again tapping the microphone first, said: "Because every time I fuck your wife when you're out, she makes me eat your tea afterwards."

* * *

CHAPTER TWENTY TWO

Last Fight at the Blue Note

Oh Carolina you get on my nerves, I've heard you so often more than your Blue Beat deserves. Oh Carolina I guess you had the right curves to charm the Prince and the Brothers. But I am not one of your lovers, so leave me alone and someday you'll be on my turntable to play. Oh Carolina from Jamaica, I've got to make things right, it's just because you were the cause of the fight last night.

Finally it became the end of the decade and the numbers on the calendar had shifted to a strange-looking combination: 1970. I walked from Blackley, through the darkness of the Boggart Hole Clough woodland park, and headed to Moston. I was calling at a friend's house, going out with him and meeting up with a few mates in town. Richard was a member of 'our gang' that had all been regulars at the Wheel. Although by this time I had given up – along with Angelo, DL, Brian and Moston Dave, Frank and many more – Richard still attended, although not weekly like we used to. He was now semi-retired and went once a month.

He had a reputation for being a tight arsed bastard, and it ran in the family. A long time ago, I'd learned not to offer my cigs around in his company, and especially so at his home. Most of my packet would disappear as soon as the offer was made; family members from other rooms in the house would appear as if by some strange intuition and grab at my Benson and Hedges.

Richards's mother would be smoking Number 6; and, as mysteriously as the events happening to the similarly named character in the TV programme 'The Prisoner', the more expensive Player's Navy Cut Number 6 packet would disappear. It would then be replaced as a return offer of a cigarette to me from a Number Ten packet, but these were inferior in many ways – cheaper and smaller.

The family's house was a 'corporation ranch' in Moston. Near the front door in the hallway was a wooden, wall-mounted cigarette machine that a bloke came along on a weekly basis to empty the cash from, and re-load with fags. They were all known locally for being 'tight as a duck's arse' and in years gone by had 'done' their own gas meter to get coins to buy fags from the cigarette machine.

I was calling for Richard; it was Saturday night. We were meeting Angelo, DL, and our other mates for a night at the Phonograph club round the back of Kendals, and later at Time and Place, or 'T&P' as we always called it – the old location of the Jungfrau, at the back of Manchester Cathedral.

I'd just had another argument with my mother before going out. My father had been sent home a few weeks previously from hospital, and was lying on a bed in our front room. He'd lost consciousness while I was getting ready to go out. The doctor had just left, and gave us both a grim look. I only realised later why my mother was so annoyed at me going out: the doctor had given my dad something to ease things – a special injection – and she wanted me to stay in.

As I left, she ranted on at me, shouting that she hoped I wasn't starting up all of that all-night, all-weekend staying out caper all over again. We had a terrific row. Whilst in the front room, my dad's breathing changed to a strange snorting sound. She went to sit next to him, and I angrily slammed the door behind me as I left.

I was pissed off with her, because tonight was important. The previous weekend, after a small street riot outside the Blue Note, I had told John at the club that I was giving up dejaying. It had annoyed me all week, but I knew I had to do it. I had to start up a new social life, and tonight was going to be the beginning.

* * *

The last straw had been the previous Saturday. I'd been happily playing all the songs I wanted to play, and I had just put 'Crossfire' by the Orlons on when I was interrupted. It was a girl. She had banged on the closed doors that separated the club from the DJ booth. It was like a horse stable with two closable barn style doors, and I leaned out like Mr Ed the talking horse on the TV show. She asked me to play 'Oh Carolina'. I told her to fuck off and then shut the doors tight.

Next thing, the knocking on the doors got louder, and then even louder. Then the doors burst open. A dark face poked through and a knife was thrust towards me. It was the same threatening half-caste guy from my tribulations some time back. Turns out it was his girlfriend. He looked like he wanted to kill me, but he wasn't really trying to stab me; it was just a show of force, and he couldn't reach in far enough to really hurt me. He shouted: "Play the fucking record or I'll cut your head off." I slammed the doors on him, trapping his hand momentarily, but he quickly pulled his hand out of the way.

The Orlons continued: '...*Keep your eye on your guy, or kiss your baby goodbye... I looked for my baby... He was doin' the Crossfire...*'

The doors were closed tight, and I wedged them shut. The Orlons finished and had lost their 'baby', but worse things were about to happen in the club. I had to put on the next record onto the deck – 'Never Could You Be' from the Impressions – and as I did so, a great deal of banging and clattering was going on outside.

The Impressions reached the halfway point of their song. It's a quiet track, so I strained to listen, and I couldn't hear any more extraneous noises from the club. So, as Curtis Mayfield and the

Impressions sang so soulfully, '*Never could you be, happy as me... Never could you be... Never could you be... There ain't no secrets about the way I feel, It's just I'm in love and it's so very real... I don't plan to change....*'

I opened the doors, and the place looked deserted!

I crept upstairs and even Joanna and Margie the cloakroom girls had disappeared. John the club's owner was coming downstairs – he told me he'd locked everyone outside, and that just as he'd opened the letter box just to peek out, someone had shoved a breadknife through it. He was OK, just shocked, so I continued up and opened the front door that led out onto the street.

Outside it was a mini riot, with one shifting battle mob outside the pub next door and another group skirmishing right in front of me. In the middle of it was Mike, our Irish bouncer, enjoying giving a right pasting to a half-caste guy who was covering his head, doubled up on the deck, cowering from Mike's targeted kicks.

The full extent of the situation became apparent, this was now very bad. The club was beating up its own clients. It had escalated to a point were 'they' were bound to get me one night. I'd already experienced several weeks of dodging around dark streets, avoiding groups of lads on street corners, thinking these are the ones after me – and now they really would be. I decided I had to give up the DJ lark.

And as I went back down into the club –

– I felt strangely that I had done this before. I really mean, I had done this exact same walk back down these steps back into this empty club before. The Impressions record was endlessly rolling around and around each time, with a loud scratch echoing over the speakers as the needle slipped over and over onto an endless groove.

This had all happened before. It was one of those déjà vu

episodes that had come to me and it was about a deserted nightclub with a record spinning endlessly making a crackling noise. This time it was different; I became acutely conscious within this déjà-vu event and began to think along a parallel track; could I change this event? Could I turn around and go in the opposite direction, up the stairs instead of down? I tried but was compelled by a force beyond my control. I had to take the downwards option. It made me think once again about free will – and my inner voice answered, asking me like in a questioning tone: 'maybe I could end up stabbed if I took the other option?'

The mini-riot resulted in apartheid conditions for a while at the club, with no entry for half-castes! But full blacks and whites were OK. It did nothing to alter my decision, though. I quit and took up a new social life.

***

After a great night in the Phonograph, where George Best and his pissed drinking partner Mike Summerbee were hogging the barstools and making it difficult to get a drink, we moved on to T&P, danced, then queued up to get 'free' steak, chips and egg. I had a great night. I came home around 2:30 am. The lights in our house were still on. I opened the door. My mother was sitting over my father. She was tying a white strip of cloth under his chin, around his head and fastening it into a bow on top.

My father was dead.

She said it had just happened, and I had missed him going. She was crying as she told me that she was tying up his jaw because dead people's bodies relaxed before rigor mortis froze them into a death posture. After that it couldn't be changed, and to stop his mouth from yawning open she had to do this for him. Then she asked me for two pennies.

"What for?" I said.

"To put on his eyes. We need to close down his eyelids,

otherwise they'll open really wide, and he'll stare out at us like a dead fish." She used this metaphor because she used to work part-time in a fishmonger's. "The pennies are to stop that." She said it all in a matter-of-fact way, as though she was a narrator in a play.

I gave her two half-crowns; I thought my dad was worth more than pennies.

I couldn't cry. I sat there in silence; all I could think about was when he had sat up all night with me last July to watch the TV coverage of Neil Armstrong, the first man on the moon. That's when he told me he was giving up smoking, because he had to go into hospital with a bad chest. He'd been with me on that All-nighter, but on his last All-nighter I had gone missing and I still couldn't cry.

Next morning the Co-Op funeral blokes came around after I had telephoned them. They were efficient, sombre and dressed smartly all in black. They put my dad in a temporary coffin, put it into a black van and drove off. I still couldn't cry.

I went back in the house, got my bike out and rode through Manchester, outwards through Stockport and past the McVitie's biscuit factory, with its fantastic smell of roasting digestives. I rode onwards out to Hazel Grove.

The long slow drag of High Lane soon took its toll on my leg muscles and I slowed down, changing through my gears and wobbling, seeking an easier rhythm, whilst inner voices put forward suggestions to turn and go back. Just then, a white Vulcan bomber glided past overhead having taken off from Woodford, with the unmistakable sounds of its Rolls Royce Avon engine. I looked up at it as it banked away with a short shuddering, followed by a bursting plume of black smoke that coughed out of both engines. I pedalled on, watching until the aircraft faded to a distant dot, and as I watched, an associated memory locked into place.

When I was an apprentice almost out of my time, after nearly five years in the aircraft factory, I had been given a job to cut out a new baggage door on a Vulcan fuselage tail section. At that time, the fleet was being refurbished in ones and twos. The Vulcan was the UK's frontline offensive attack bomber, and carried two atomic bombs under a code name of 'Shevelin'. The fleet was to make a single attack on Moscow; all of the squadron, all the aircraft in a 'secret' co-ordinated strike. All converging upon the same target and letting the Russians know this 'secret' in advance in the understanding that no matter what they did to shoot down our planes, they wouldn't get them all. The secret was kept from the British public not from the potential enemy. The idea was echoed in the film Dr Strangelove, and I was responsible for one of them becoming unable to rejoin the fleet.

I had been given a blueprint drawing with instructions to 'router cut' the outer skin in the shape of the required door to be situated near the tail section on the starboard underbelly of the aircraft. Now, since birth I've had a dysfunction that I put down to dyslexia. I have to think, consciously, which is left and right – and on this occasion, I cut the door shape into the port side.

I was still an apprentice. Had I been a fully time-served and qualified airframe fitter, I would have been sacked on the spot. The union took up my case and I was moved to another department. However, my fame had spread throughout the factory and the next morning in my new department when I pulled on my blue overalls, someone had painted in large white letters along the arms; PORT on the left arm and STARBOARD on the other. Or was it the other way around? For a long time 'Port and Starboard' was my identifying nickname. That fuselage stayed on the ground for months whilst a team of inspectors with slide rules worked out the stress ratios. Eventually repairs were made and to my great relief the aircraft flew again.

The plane completely disappeared from view and my memory ended, releasing my mind from re-running the events. I realised I had gone a fair way up the hill in a semi unconscious state without feeling any effects or much apparent effort. My body had just got on with it, whilst my mind was fully occupied in reliving that memory.

This observation put me into a thoughtful mood, but soon the nagging voices returned, telling me to turn around and go back. My body ached, thoughts of my dad returned and I was soon embroiled in an unrelenting storm of emotions. Protesting voices in my head were telling me to stop. I stood up on the pedals, restlessly alternating from sitting with my hands pulling on the handlebars, using force from this position down into my legs, and then I was up off the saddle, bobbing up and down, looking at the horizon, looking for the top of the climb, and despising the voices in my mind. With all that noise in my head, it was hard to imagine room for anything else – but for some reason music also began to run on another simultaneous mental track: the Poindexter Brothers began to sing 'Backfield In Motion.'

By the time I'd reached the top and was beginning the low level slide down into Disley, I was joining in with Mel and Tim, and shouting out loud the lyrics to the moves in American Football related to a cheating girlfriend.

Soon I was past New Mills and Furness Vale, through Whalley Bridge, then, Chapel-en-le-Frith, then up Mam Tor Hill, onwards and heading for Castleton, then aiming for Buxton. It was here I inevitably hit the 'wall' again. I slowed on the incline, gasping and wobbling about. Under normal circumstances, minor irritations would be dismissed, but they were intensified when physical exertion was to be done. Added to my emotional state, it caused an intense wave of pain, irritation, anger; a mix of thoughts, emotions and suggestions to stop and go home.

Earlier on High Lane I had controlled things by settling down to a correct position and a controlled riding style that eased my pain, so I now dropped down through the gears, soon reaching the lowest. Twiddling my legs around, I pedalled fast for a while but it had little effect. Then, finding it altogether too uncomfortable, I was out of the saddle again, bobbing up and down once more, changing up a few rungs on the back rings and switching over my front chain ring. It was no good. I was twiddling the pedals again and became even more uncomfortable, so I switched back to higher ratio, more momentum; new levels of agony.

The Manchester Wheelers

As I rode along, my mind was once again in turmoil, but now it was far worse. Mel and Tim Poindexter carried on regardless without me. This had happened before on the last hill; all the little internal nagging voices about everything going on in my life returned, plus the agony of cycling again. The inner voices were shouting at me to stop and get off, and all the extra emotions were mixed together, rising up to a deafening internal crescendo. I commanded all this to cease, but just like the times in the toilets at work after the All-nighter, it was useless. There was no way to command, no way to stop it by force of will.

I saw a sign for the Blue John Mine. In the far distance was Peveril Peak and Castle; this was Derbyshire. My mind flashed through more chunks of nonsense and connected the hill with the pub in Manchester, Peveril of the Peak. Where did all this come from? I was talking to myself silently, verbalising the words, and I caught it. I could observe it as it flowed along; one thought after another, one talking internal 'self' discussing things with another, with the real 'me' consigned to a sideline observer. Was I going off my rocker?

I kept on moving, cycling through intermittent physical waves of agony. Breathing became laboured, the internal stuff got worse. I pedalled and pedalled and rose up higher and higher on the hill. I looked around at the views of the hills; this was called the 'shivering mountain'. It caused lots of local subsidence, because the entire hill was sliding into the valley. I looked at the horizon, then down at my arms, my hands gripping the thick red tape wound around the handlebars over and around the brake levers. I switched my hold to grip on to both of the brakes, pushing back against my Brookes professional saddle, and found I could change up a gear, going into a higher ratio and adopting a better rhythm. I began to sail along. Mel and Tim were still at it, along with the inner nagging voices going on and on. I was talking to myself whilst staring down at my front wheel and the endless tarmac passing by below.

Then suddenly, it all stopped. The internal cacophony ended. Silence came upon me; the effort had made all the inner stuff go away. It just shut down. I was exhausted, but somehow able to glide along, with the suffering centred somewhere else! I entered that state I had experienced before; it was a calm kind of detachment, and while there I was able to analyse things.

The death of my father had loomed in and out between all these rapid thoughts and nagging voices, along with the music I'd been experiencing. Such a state would probably be described by most people as a stream of consciousness, but to me it was more like an ocean of unconsciousness. And like a cork on that ocean, I had no control over the direction in which I was taken. At the same time, my body had its instructions and carried on steering and pedalling, without any conscious involvement from me. The 'me' or the 'I' that I had become was completely removed and separate from the ones that seemed to chain in and out, without 'me' or 'I' being able to stop them. Again thoughts I'd had previously came over me: What is the real me? Where am 'I'? Was this schizophrenia?

But this was different. At other times when experiencing these things I was coming down from drugs, but this time I was without any. Therefore, I reasoned that these newly acquired self-awareness experiences were independently real. My new mind state was able to analyse the situation free of the panic that had been associated with these events previously.

On this occasion, I became convinced it was no longer an issue I could dismiss and put down to drugs. I was also certain that I wasn't losing my mind. However, it wasn't a topic that came up in everyday conversation. Plato had wrestled with such things describing consciousness and awareness, likening it to the reflections coming from the mouth of a cave and casting flickering shadows onto a candlelit wall. I was determined and resolved to go outside the cave mouth and have a look at reality. Others must have had similar inward thoughts and wondered about it, about where our consciousness resides. Are we something more, beyond the 'puppet master'? Do we have free will? I resolved that after this journey I would go to the library and seek out authors who had come across these issues – maybe Sigmund Freud?

I recalled the similar mental struggles I'd had in the past with thoughts that plagued me; after-effects of too many nights without sleep and maybe residual amphetamine poison in my body. These were things I'd normally have put down to the results of the drugs, but here and now I was experiencing the same thing without the use of gear. I obtained certain insights from this line of thought: do we all have fragmented separate personality states? Is it everyone, and not just me and my drug after-effects? I was convinced we were all in the same state and nobody discussed it – or worse, few even recognised it and hardly ever become consciously aware of these shifting internal mental states.

I continued analysing myself through a new lens that was positioned above the surface that 'I' was usually submerged into, where inner noise kept 'me' occupied and busy. Where waking daydreams floated 'me' from memory to memory, from emotion to emotion, back and forth and to a place where 'I' was lost, submerged and consumed within that ocean below. I realised that I talk to myself all the time. I would try to think words without sounding them in my head, and I couldn't do it.

I was convinced that we all have internal conversations with ourselves intertwined with emotions; a mixture that keeps us conversing with no-one other than ourselves. It revolves around and around. Some of it is positive and analytical; like going over an issue, a worry, a problem and then finding a solution. But it never stops, even after a bout of positive thinking and a solution to the original problem issue. It is as though the mind continues to run on and on, freewheeling on its own groove.

Most of it is negative and self-critical. Why can't I be cleverer? Why did I say that stupid thing? Why can't I get enough money? Am I too fat, too thin? and if it's not ourselves it's assessments of others, their opinions, judging people on an internal sliding scale of biases; and running alongside all of these are physical needs to eat, to urinate, interspersed with sexual arousals as a girl goes by. On it goes between bouts of envy and disdain, giving out and receiving status, by noticing and commenting about others, and being praised or annoyed by their return assessment of us. Obtaining and giving offence, saying the wrong thing at the wrong time and going over and over the resulting consequences.

Daydreaming, weaving internal fantasies of power, wealth and employment status, the judgment on first sight of people, their appearance, their speech. It's unrelenting, on and on in a constant bubbling turmoil, comparing myself to them; and it's all habitual and automatic. We're unable in most cases to control it, and the worst of it is we hardly ever notice it's going on because we're lost inside it all. At some deep level our minds are freewheeling, operating automatically, responding to external influences from life rather than making conscious decisions. I understood that, myself included, the entire human race were simply robots most of the time.

'Baby You're a Rich Man' was being played on the radio inside a parked-up Volkswagen camper van as I went past it – and just to prove a point about having little or no control over our thoughts, mine were whipped from me. The consciousness of my previous chain of thoughts vanished, as I joined Paul and John, singing along with their song.

After a while I came out of my singalong with the Beatles. I came down a hill, and having reached the flat it was easier now. There again was that stillness in my mind that was like fresh air on a new, sparkling summer morning. I was very aware of myself – it was like a real 'me', a quiet yet forceful consciousness, and all the chattering and analysing had completely gone. There was silence – a silence of the mind that had a strange quality of assurance. It was a silence I had never experienced before.

It felt strangely enriching, and held an indescribable inner stillness and power. All around, I felt that the hills, the trees and the birds were all connected by this silence. The silence was inside my head, but there was noise around me; the birds were singing, distant car engines sounded, wind rustled in the trees. And yet, it didn't disturb the silent watchful awareness that had come over me. I got a deep inner understanding that I didn't need to punish myself anymore and so I gave up the goal of reaching Buxton. Alongside Mam Tor Hill I looked down towards Castleton and turning around I headed slowly back towards Manchester. It was a decision made from a new location in my mind. I resolved to investigate what it meant: somehow, sometime, someday.

The Manchester Wheelers

But of course, life intervenes and takes you away from the things you plan to do. After my father's funeral I was back out with my pals at weekends in pubs, clubs like T&P, Bredbury Hall, trips to pubs in Chester and weekends in Abersoch. I did keep my resolve about finishing with the All-nighter scene, but once again my aim to study my internal mental conditions submerged back into my everyday concerns – except for one occasion:

After a heavy bought of drinking, I was lying in the backseat of Frank's new car; a newer Austin Wolsey than the one he'd had a few years back, the one he used to park at Piccadilly Station before going to the All-nighter. Frank was quite annoyed with me as I had just puked up inside it before I could make it to the rear window. Frank, an old pal from the Wheel days, was now ferrying me and Richard back from a late night pub crawl in Chester.

As I sat in the back of the car feeling ill, my mind switched into memory mode and re-examined events related to Doreen. It was Frank who told me Doreen had been seen by him in the Blue Note kissing Angelo. Then the penny dropped. That night when I had got off the bus with Doreen's pal. Yes that penny had finally dropped as I realized that Mandy must have said something – that's the reason Doreen had met Angelo and that's why she finished with me. She probably didn't confront me with the real reason because she most likely got the news from Mandy somehow 'in confidence'. It all seemed to add up in my head. The analytical part of my mind felt quite pleased with its summary and immediately disappeared, leaving me with the blame.

※ ※ ※

Richard still went now and again to the All-nighters, and it must have been the last Saturday in the New Year – January 1971 – when he said it was to be the last ever All-nighter. He said the place was finally closing; the council were shutting down the Wheel due to its reputation for drugs. Over the years there had been many rumours, many false alarms and lots of warnings from the club owners to 'behave' or the place would be forced to close.

The Manchester Wheelers

This time it was the end, Richard said.

After last orders in the Sawyers arms on Deansgate, all my mates were going on to Slack Alice's, a posh club owned by George Best on Market Street. Richard said Edwin Starr would be on at the Wheel's last All-nighter. Everyone said they'd seen Edwin loads of times and wanted to go to 'Besty's' club, because the crumpet in there was a different class to the usual talent. I decided to go with Richard, and joined him in the attempt to get our old crew together. I tried persuading Angelo, Moston Dave and Brian, and tried even harder with DL, but to no avail. Off they went to the upmarket club whilst Richard and I headed for Whitworth Street.

Richard got some stuff from a guy he knew on Piccadilly Station. The Gents' underground toilets were now the focal point of pill sales. I declined.

Entering the Wheel again after around 18 months absence was odd. The vast majority of the people were no longer the crowd I knew. They were all casually dressed, wearing hipster pants and skinny ribbed pullovers or T shirts. A lot of girls were in jeans. Worst of all was the lack of style, with some blokes wearing Manchester City scarves, often tied around their middles. I didn't get that old feeling of belonging, maybe because I was sober and drug free. For a moment, I thought maybe they were drug free, too? But studying their faces, their large dilated eyes and their wild chattering, I knew they were blocked up.

I felt out of place and the music had changed quite a bit. Many records played that were great, but which I had never heard before – like 'Time Will Pass You By' by Tobi Legend. Edwin was the same as ever though, and he did a terrific performance. He had an astounding voice and could easily dispense with the microphone. I left and went home around 3.30am after Edwin finished, and unlike on any of my previous All-nighters, I went soundly to sleep as soon as my head hit the pillow. I slept till late morning.

I got up at noon and had my mom's Sunday roast dinner. I

The Manchester Wheelers

listened to 'Round The Horne' and 'The Navy Lark' on the radio, and in the evening I set off for a night in the pubs in town. I went with Angelo to the 'Cellar vie', a wine bar on Bootle Street. It was a new type of 'in' place where they only served wine. After a couple of glasses in there, we moved on to the Thomson Arms near Chorlton Street Bus Station. I told him about how good Edwin had been and I was still humming 'I Have Faith In You' as I approached the bar.

Standing there serving was an ex top-notch Mod girl who used to go to the Wheel. We recognised each other instantly as part of the old crowd. She'd once helped me obtain some gear one night when it was scarce.

"Two pints of Watney's please." I gave her a fiver; she filled the pints from the Red Barrel automatic pump and then gave me change from a Tenner and a wink. I could see at once that I was going to like her. She even asked if I had the single 'angel Baby' by Darrel Banks – it was her favourite song from the Wheel. She too had given up going to All-nighters, but missed the music.

Somewhere off in the distance, spin dryers, shag pile carpets, a detached house with a garage, a kitchen diner with Formica tops, tall kitchen stools, a fitted cooker and a mortgage were beckoning.

THE END

∗ ∗ ∗

CHARGER
RECORDS
CRG-105
American Music
(BMI)
Time 2:35
(CR-1012)
THE "IN" CROWD
(Billy Page)
DOBIE GRAY
A DIVISION OF CRUSADER RECORDS INC.

AUTHOR'S NOTE

The places remain the same, but the events and the real names have been changed. Many of the events portrayed connected with The Twisted Wheel are accurate events, but not essentially as they happened to any single individual. The 'story' is made up, but reflects the real undercurrents of that time in the Sixties, when Soul music generated a underground social movement whose ripples still reverberate outwards today in the form of Northern Soul. The attitudes and the drugs were part of that scene in the 'Swinging Sixties' and this has never been accurately described before for a host of reasons. But whatever the mixture which drove the initial Soul music and Mod scene in Manchester, it was not centrally about drugs, it was about the music: Soul Music

The sub culture should be separated from the music. The drugs were part of the sub culture. It still goes on, even along the same street years later, in the Hacienda club. However 'our music' had little to do in reality with the drug scene in the more 'mainstream' subculture of the Sixties.

For example, compare our music with the House music at the Hacienda, and the Trance music of 1990's Ibiza; those were genres in synch with the effects of ecstasy, where all the revellers needed was a beat. It goes some way to show that our music had no automatic link with Amphetamines. They simply enabled us to dance to it all night.

No one from the era described in The Manchester Wheelers, as parents and grandparents today, would recommend or encourage any type of drug abuse.

Soul music in the mainstream continues, with new artists emerging and new music. Northern Soul has its roots embedded in the Sixties, and beginning at The Twisted Wheel with its great DJ, Roger Eagle. The phenomena of Northern Soul is alive and well all these many years later, providing a powerhouse of great Soul music.

It will be interesting to see if House and Trance Music last as long.

We were not a gang; perhaps more like a secretive cult within an outwardly smart, clean and conformist group identity, hidden in full view. The Soul Mod subculture in Manchester had its own internal spontaneity. There were no leaders like in a gang, but there was a group identity of style, a collective of common conforming concepts. The code to be 'in' and its unwritten style manual was known to those who knew the lists of items, styles and behaviour that made a person 'in' or 'out'. Soul Mods evolved from the original Mod scene, and kept some of these elitist attributes, linking them to what you knew as an individual, and what records you had in your collection. A type of elitist snobbery of record collecting emerged, and continues to this day.

Those in the All-nighter crowd kept the secret of drug use.

Drugs were not taken for the same reasons as other dilettantes; they were a tool that assisted stamina for dancing to the music. The music was the main thing. Hippies had replaced Mods by late 67 as the 'in' subculture, but if one had ever come to the Wheel, they would have been laughed off the premises. Hippies were in fact a much more mainstream youth culture than Mods, and one of their drugs was mind altering LSD. Soul Mods used the Amphetamines to assist dance ability, agility and stamina. Not for aimless tripping.

For more about The Twisted Wheel see: CENtral 1179 by Keith Rylatt and Phil Scott

A comprehensive playlist of records from The Twisted Wheel and The Blue Note Clubs can be found on the Manchester Soul website, see 'Soulbot': http://www.manchestersoul.com/

The Manchester Wheelers